The Crusader

Michael Eisner

W F HOWES LTD

This large print edition published in 2002 by
W F Howes Ltd
Units 6/7, Victoria Mills, Fowke Street
Rothley, Leicester LE7 7PJ

1 3 5 7 9 10 8 6 4 2

First published in 2002 by Transworld Publishers

A CIP catalogue record for this book is available
from the British Library

ISBN 1 84197 567 2

Typeset by Palimpsest Book Production Limited,
Polmont, Stirlingshire
Printed and bound in Great Britain
by Antony Rowe Ltd, Chippenham, Wilts.

TO MY MOTHER AND FATHER

The Crusader

ACKNOWLEDGMENTS

Many of my friends and family read drafts of the manuscript and provided invaluable editing, sage advice, and enthusiastic encouragement. I am grateful to all of them: Laurie Abraham, Stuart Benjamin, John Doyle, Doug Eisner, Hallie Eisner, Joe Eisner, John and Susie Eley, the Franks (Ali and David), Lauren Gorman, Tamar Kotz, Kate Lauer, Lucy Lean, Tim Macht, Arti Rai, Lucille and Leonard Russack.

I would also like to thank Kendra Harpster, at Doubleday, who facilitated the editorial process at every stage.

A handful of people helped shape the final novel. Darren Bayne provided thorough and meticulous historical research. Wesley Gibson taught me the basics, helped me find the direction of the story, and provided inspiration as a model of commitment to the craft.

Luke Janklow, my agent, successfully conveyed his inflated opinion of the novel to others, including me. Margot Tenenbaum reminds me periodically that I'm not as important as I think I am, but makes me feel pretty important just the same. Bill Thomas, my editor at Doubleday, offered generous support and insightful editing, significantly improving the novel.

Finally, my mother suggested I write a novel in the first place. My dad pushed books on me since I can remember. And both my parents weighed nuances of phrasing so minute that only a mother or father would tolerate.

CONTENTS

The following pages contain the confessions of a knight in Christ's army, Francisco de Montcada, with commentary by God's humble servant Brother Lucas of Santes Creus, confessor of Francisco and transcriber of his words.

ANNO DOMINI 1275

CHAPTER 1

A MAN OF SORROWS

The rain had let up. I leaned forward and glanced out the front of the wagon. The pink stones of the monastery glowed against the night. A gray mist rose from the frozen earth. It was past midnight.

I had been waiting several hours for our reunion. In truth, I had been waiting several years – six years – only I had imagined it under different circumstances.

The porter came out to meet the carriage. He had been recently admitted to the clerical state, tonsured with a smooth razor so that his baldpate gleamed against the moonlight.

'Welcome to Poblet,' he said.

'What is your name, Brother?' I asked.

'Silva,' he responded, 'Brother Silva from Cerdanya.'

I introduced myself and told him to take me to the cell of Francisco de Montcada. He looked down without responding.

1

It had been a long journey, and I was irritable and impatient. 'Do you understand, Brother Silva?'

'Yes, Brother Lucas,' he said, 'but Father Adelmo has decreed that no visitors shall enter the crusader's cell.'

'I have in my hand a letter with the seal of Archbishop Sancho of Tarragona,' I said. 'It gives me custody of Francisco and charge of his exorcism.'

'Perhaps I can fetch Father Adelmo,' Brother Silva said, 'you can discuss the matter with him.'

'No, Brother Silva,' I said, 'I will see Francisco now.'

Reluctantly, Brother Silva escorted me into the church. I could smell the familiar incense of matins, the first prayer of morning. I took a deep breath – the pungent aroma awakened my senses. For me, it is the smell of God, the smell of home, the only home I have ever known. The monks had already assembled, waiting for the Abbot to begin their chanting. Several yawned, the younger boys rubbing their eyes to shake the sleep from them. As I made my way down the center aisle, every monk in the chapel turned to stare at me. One of the older monks tried to draw the attention of the others by beginning part of the liturgy, but the congregants ignored him.

When I reached the stone Cross at the foot of the dais, I knelt to say a silent prayer – *Holy Mary, bless me and keep me from evil. Please give me strength to perform my mission.* I crossed myself, stood, and

2

proceeded with Brother Silva to a corner door, where we exited the church into the cloister. We walked around the square, passing several writing stations between columns. The monks had moved their manuscripts to the stone bench under the walkway to protect the parchment from rain. I took notice of the calligraphy, the bold strokes, the confident curves.

At the corner of the courtyard, we passed into the tower. Brother Silva lit a torch and ascended the spiral staircase. I followed, trying to keep pace, but the boy soon disappeared and the bright light faded, leaving behind straggling flickers, and then darkness.

I felt my way gently up the winding steps. My sandals slid on the cool stone, and I tried to steady myself on the narrow banister. One step, then another, and another, until I had established a rhythm, and the pounding in my chest subsided. I reached the top of the staircase, where Brother Silva was waiting. I had intended to chastise the boy for his haste, but my attention was diverted to the latched door just a few feet away.

'Are you ready, Brother Lucas?' he asked.

The flame illuminated one side of his face – beardless, anxious, uncertain. I hesitated for an instant before nodding my head.

The room was bare, except for a wooden Cross hanging on the far wall. Starlight fell through a small window and cast a strange, unearthly

3

glimmer in the cell. A piece of stale bread covered with cockroaches interrupted the play of light on the stone floor. In the shadows, a human figure stirred. He was sitting slumped on a pile of straw. As I entered the cell, a foul stench of excrement and sweat assaulted me. I withdrew a cloth from my cassock and held it over my nose and mouth. Then I approached the person to get a better look. He was chained by the wrist to an iron ring embedded in the wall and wore a tattered robe that barely covered his emaciated frame. His brown hair had grown long and unruly, his beard chaotic. His blue eyes looked out vacantly. His outer appearance had altered much, but I still recognized him.

'He has not talked since his arrival here,' Brother Silva said. 'Sometimes in his sleep he will mutter words, but they are always unintelligible. Many of the monks believe he speaks a secret dialect of the devil. They fear the evil spell.'

I too was afraid, afraid of the demons that had taken hold of Francisco, afraid of the awesome power of the devil that he could so humble such a man as Francisco. I had an impulse to flee. I clutched the Cross hanging from my neck, and tried to stifle the dread rising from my stomach.

Remember who you are. Remember your mission. Remember your station.

Two steps into the darkness, and I reached out to this apparition. I placed my hand on his temple and moved it slowly across his cheek and down to his chin. When I pulled my hand

4

away, my fingers were covered with phlegm and grime.

A gust of cold wind blew through the small window and stung my face. I took a step back, and I felt Brother Silva's hand on my shoulder.

'He is one of the lost cases,' Brother Silva said. 'Father Adelmo has tried for many weeks to exorcise the demons. He has bled him, burned him, punctured him, even baptized him again. To no avail.'

I reached for the chain that bound Francisco. My eyes scanned the links down to his wrist, which was caked with dry blood.

Brother Silva seemed uncomfortable with my silence and probably felt some uneasiness with the conditions in which Francisco was held.

'Father Adelmo ordered that he be chained to the wall. It is for his own protection, Brother Lucas.'

I said nothing. My mind was whirling with images from our life together at Santes Creus – the rusted iron gate of the monastery, the purple flowers surrounding the cistern, the oak table where we took our meals in perfect silence.

I dropped the chain and brushed aside Francisco's hair in order to see his face more clearly. He seemed much older than his twenty-seven years. His blue eyes, translucent, reflected nothing. Creases fanned out from the corner of his eyes, dark ridges carving a desolate path that faded into his temples. His lips, gray and thin, parted slightly, as if he were whispering some grievous secret from his sojourns. His cheeks had grown gaunt, the skin above his beard pale and bloodless. His sideburns extended out wildly, encroaching down his face, where they met his hard jaw, protruding from his beard like a worn stone, unflinching amidst the tempest.

'Francisco, it's me, Lucas.' I repeated his name several times. He did not respond.

'Brother Lucas, the smell is unavoidable,' Brother Silva said. 'Father Adelmo forbids the monks to enter without his permission. We have done our best to . . .'

I raised my hand, and Brother Silva stopped speaking. I was not here to judge the boy or the other monks. His chatter was breaking my concentration as I scrutinized Francisco's face, searching for some sign of life, something recognizable from our past.

I found nothing.

Brother Silva sneezed. I offered him my cloth. When I looked back at Francisco, he was gazing at me. Our eyes met for several seconds before he glanced away.

'Did you know him well, Brother Lucas?'

'He was my friend,' I said.

I took several deep breaths. The stale and putrid air in the cell provided no relief. Indeed, my legs weakened. I was choking. I turned and stepped out into the corridor. Brother Silva followed, closing the door behind us.

'Are you well, Brother Lucas?' he asked.

I leaned over, placing my hands on my thighs for support.

'The world has turned upside down, Brother Silva.'

CHAPTER 2

SANTES CREUS

I met Francisco eleven years ago. He arrived at the monastery in Santes Creus at the end of summer, the Year of Our Lord 1265. He was sixteen, one year older than I. Abbot Pedro had told us of his coming, the son of a great baron, a Montcada by blood and name.

The nobility sometimes send their firstborn sons to the monasteries for a prescribed period – usually three years – to gain an education before assuming the family mantle. Cistercian monasteries generally prohibit the presence of such temporary visitors, called oblates. The path of perfection – the path of Our Savior – requires an all-consuming commitment, an infinite devotion. Abbots can make exceptions, though. And Francisco was an exceptional case.

With bloodied fingers and unwavering faith, the first Cistercian brothers in Iberia carved God's sanctuary at Santes Creus out of the wilderness over one hundred years ago. But faith is seldom sufficient. The construction and maintenance of temples dedicated to promoting and reflecting the spiritual glory of Christ's Kingdom requires a more temporal funding. And the Montcada family provided the financing from the beginning. Through this sacrifice, many members of the family have assured their place in paradise and have earned an eternal resting place in the monastery.

Lest anyone forget our patrons, the monks pass the Montcada crypt seven times a day. Hewn into the stone wall just to the right of the door leading to the church, the crypt holds the remains of Garsenda de Provence and Guillem de Montcada, great-grandparents of Francisco. During his lifetime, Guillem was the most powerful of the Crown's vassals. He led the force that captured the island of Majorca from the infidels in the Year of Our Lord 1229.

The details of Guillem's martyrdom are well known to all in the Kingdom of Aragón. The family commissioned a song to commemorate Guillem's achievements. I learned the ballad during my first year as a novice. I can still recite the verses. One of the Saracens drove a stake into Guillem's side. His entrails hanging from his stomach, Guillem continued to direct the Christian forces from his mount. He fell dead just outside the gates of the City of La Palma.

Guillem must have seen the ghost of the White Knight Saint George and felt the impending victory before letting his soul ascend to heaven. The White Knight rode horseback over the enemy defenses, striking terror in the hearts of the infidels and causing a diversion that enabled our soldiers to breach the city's walls. Once inside, Christ's soldiers unleashed a divine retribution on the city's inhabitants. They say that most of the Muslims, men, women, and children, were killed within two hours of the breach. It was a scene of such savage butchery that, but for its divine inspiration, some might well mistake its noble purpose for the devil's work.

Needless to say, Abbot Pedro and every other member of the monastery eagerly anticipated the arrival of the Montcada heir. The Abbot sent for painters from the Barcelona guild to refinish the facade of the church and several areas in the main cloister, including the Montcada crypt with the family's coat of arms, a red shield with seven bezants, gold coins from Byzantium.

I was praying silently, walking around the cloister, when I came upon one of the craftsmen retouching the gold leaf on the crypt.

'Why are there seven gold pieces on the Montcada shield?' I asked the guildsman. I had always admired the design, but wondered about the significance of the seven coins.

'The Montcadas are rich,' he answered, without looking up from his work.

'Yes, I know,' I said, 'but why not three bezants to signify the Holy Trinity?'

'They're very rich,' he said.

Indeed, Francisco was an exceptional case.

When the young heir finally arrived, I was in the Abbot's quarters entering figures in the monastery's financial ledgers. Perhaps I should explain. Every two years, Abbot Pedro chose one monk with unusual promise to act as his personal assistant. It was a great honor to hold such a position of responsibility, which I assumed in my thirteenth year. In this position, I spent the early afternoon – between the offices of sext and nones – in the Abbot's quarters. I drafted his correspondence. I kept minutes of important meetings. I reminded the Abbot of feast days according to the liturgical calendar. I counted and sorted the coins in the treasury – like cool spring water sifting through my fingers. My reappointment for another two-year term when I was fifteen reflected Abbot Pedro's recognition of my devotion and discretion. Abbot Pedro frequently confided in me his intimate thoughts concerning other members of the monastery.

As instructed, the porter escorted Francisco to the Abbot's quarters.

'Come in, son,' Abbot Pedro said to Francisco, who seemed reluctant to advance beyond the doorway. 'Welcome to Santes Creus.'

It was a scene we had replayed many times. Greeting the new arrivals. Some tall, some short, some fat, some thin. But always the same expression – a smug complacency, a keen awareness of the prerogatives of their birthright as sons of the high nobility. And perhaps a slight sneer to reflect the bitter injustice of their situation if they were second – or third-born sons compelled to take the cloth. Noble families gave these sons to the Church to avoid a division of the patrimony. In the Church, these sons would inherit no land and yet lead lives worthy of nobility that would redound to the spiritual benefit of their parents.

I rose as Francisco approached. I could see immediately that he was different. Francisco was smiling absently. Actually, it was half a smile. The left side of his mouth raised, the left eye crinkled tenderly. The other half of Francisco's face somber, the right eye focused inward as if on some private sorrow. This disjunction gave Francisco's countenance a brooding, ironic impression, as if he were amused by his own suffering.

Abbot Pedro seemed momentarily confounded by Francisco's demeanor. The Abbot examined Francisco for a full minute before speaking.

'I am grateful,' the Abbot finally said, 'that the Lord has seen fit to place you under my care.' The heavy weight of Francisco's vision seemed directed toward the window. The Abbot moved to the left in an effort to intercept Francisco's stare.

'As you well know, Francisco,' the Abbot continued, 'the monastery owes its existence to the largesse of your family. The Montcadas have always recognized the sacred work performed by the Cistercian Order.

'Our Benedictine brothers and sisters,' Abbot Pedro began his standard speech to new arrivals, 'have developed a predilection for gold and silver. And yet Christ was a man of stone and wood, Francisco. The Cistercians seek to restore the purity of Saint Benedict's original vision. Our Benedictine brothers wear black habits. We wear unbleached white – a symbol of the pristine nature of Christ's word and our mission. Our buildings are austere and simple. No superfluous decoration mars the walls and creates distraction from our lives of prayer and contemplation. We shun the new fashion of installing colored windows in our churches. If God's light is perfect, why distort the sublime rays?'

Abbot Pedro looked hopefully to the new arrival, but Francisco had no intention of responding. It was not clear Francisco was listening to the Abbot's speech. Francisco's gaze seemed to reach just beyond Abbot Pedro. The Abbot glanced behind himself, evidently searching for the source of Francisco's interest.

'Our Benedictine brothers,' the Abbot raised his voice, trying to draw Francisco's attention, 'own serfs to work the fields. The brothers of Santes Creus till the land ourselves. We use our hands as Christ the carpenter did in Galilee. We have not come to replace the Rule of Saint Benedict, which remains our guide, our path to the Almighty. We seek merely to reform some of the excesses of the old Order. With stone and wood, we expand Christ's dominion into the darkest plains of Iberia.

'Francisco,' Abbot Pedro was shouting, 'in recognition of the unusual and temporary nature of your stay here, I have prepared a private cell for your habitation. You will also be exempt from fieldwork on alternate days. And I have reserved a place for you on my right in the refectory where the food is served first. On feast days, you will be able to pick from the most succulent pieces of fish.'

'Sir,' Francisco said his first words, 'did Christ receive exemptions?'

'Excuse me, Francisco?' Abbot Pedro said.

'Did Christ receive special treatment on the Cross?' Francisco asked.

'No,' the Abbot said. 'Our Lord suffered most grievously.'

'Then I do not think,' Francisco said, 'that a Montcada merits special treatment. I appreciate your consideration, Abbot Pedro, but I would prefer to take my natural place amongst the others in the dormitory and to perform the tasks expected of any member of the monastery.'

Abbot Pedro was smiling thinly. At least, he knew Francisco had been listening.

'Would you be so kind,' Francisco asked, glancing in my direction, 'as to escort me to the dormitory?'

Despite the initial commotion concerning Francisco's arrival, he soon settled into life at Santes Creus. Francisco seemed quite suited for the rhythms of monastic life. He prayed with a marked devotion during each of the eight offices

14

of daily prayer – the Opus Dei. While some of the monks would mumble the words, particularly during matins at two in the morning, Francisco always chanted the psalms with a peculiar intensity. Abbot Pedro once commented that Francisco's prayer had a desperate quality, as if the boy were making a solemn plea to the Lord or seeking some critical information.

When the sun rose, Francisco took his place in the fields beside the other monks – four hours a day wielding spade and hoe. Sowing seeds that, like good deeds, would reap reward one hundredfold. While others might tarry in the shade, Francisco was loath to break even for water, and he worked with an uncommon vigor. Sometimes, on hot days, he pulled his white robe off. The sweat would glisten off his bare back, the smooth muscles twisting against the yellow wheat.

The others watched Francisco with curiosity. Who was this most noble of nobles who worked like a peasant and seemed to enjoy his labor? Several boys whispered disagreeable comments. I overheard Felipe González question the noble origins of Francisco.

'Perhaps,' Felipe said, 'his father was a field hand who wandered into the Baroness' chambers while her husband was away.'

In time, though, Francisco's energy seemed to infect the other brothers. Eventually, we all followed his example. After Francisco's first summer, the monastery registered a record crop of barley and wheat.

Unlike most of our new arrivals, Francisco was literate when he came to Santes Creus. He was able to take advantage of the monastery's fine collection of books. During the two hours in the library after Mass, Francisco would bury his head in the manuscript of some obscure Christian saint. His thumb was stained permanently with black ink from turning the pages. Such was his concentration that Francisco seemed not to hear the bells for sext, so that the librarian would have to tap him on the shoulder after most of the boys had already departed for the noon service.

During the day, the brothers observe the Order's prohibition on frivolous conversation. As it is written, *in a flood of words you will not avoid sin.* For a quarter of an hour each day that prohibition is lifted. The monks and lay brothers gather in the parlor to discuss whatever they wish. Invariably, the same small groups congregate. A hierarchy seems to pervade these gatherings. The monks are mindful of the social standing of each member's family, so that the highest nobility associate only with each other. Felipe González surrounded himself with an entourage of four other monks, sons of the richest and most powerful families in Barcelona. They called themselves the young lions. Felipe's father was the treasurer of the kingdom. Alfredo Martí led a rival but equally prestigious faction, whose members hailed from the northern

16

territories. The other brothers formed similar, if less exalted, groups.

Given the distinguished status of his family, Francisco's arrival threatened to disrupt the balance of factions. We were all anxious to see whether he would join Felipe's or Alfredo's group. In light of the proximity of Montcada to Barcelona, most of the brothers opined that Francisco would favor Felipe's group.

Felipe approached Francisco two weeks after his arrival.

'Francisco de Montcada,' Felipe said, 'we invite you to join the young lions.'

Francisco looked up. He smiled at Felipe, that same ironic expression from his interview with Abbot Pedro. The parlor became silent as every brother strained to hear Francisco's response.

'Thank you, Felipe,' Francisco answered, 'you honor me with this invitation. But I prefer the breeze on this side of the parlor.'

Felipe's face drained of color, slack-jawed, as if he had just learned that his family descended from serfs. It was something of a humiliation for Felipe, who seemed to have instantaneously acquired a limp as he shuffled back to the other end of the parlor.

Francisco became the subject of much conversation in the parlor, not all of it flattering. There were some that felt Francisco's rebuff to Felipe reflected a deep arrogance.

'Perhaps,' I heard one of the young lions say,

'young Montcada thinks he is above us. We shall see how he fares on his own.'

In fact, Francisco fared quite well. In time, most of the boys developed a grudging respect, even an admiration, for Francisco and his independence. It was more than his family name, although some undoubtedly were unable to see beyond that. In his quiet smile, in the tilt of his head, in the slight inflection of his voice, Francisco bore a striking dignity, a regal quality that set him apart from his colleagues – indeed, even from our superiors. Everyone seemed to understand tacitly that Francisco was different, that his destiny would take him far above the intrigues of the parlor and the petty controversies amongst our Catalán nobility. Francisco made no effort to curry favor with the Abbot or to engage in the machinations that forged powerful alliances between families long after boys had left the monastery to become prelates or barons. He seemed indifferent to the solicitude of the Abbot and immune to the flattering of the sycophants amongst the monks who sought the favor of a Montcada. He resisted the comfortable future in which all seemed to conspire to place him. He was, in short, marked for greater things. That, or simply greater suffering.

My friendship with Francisco began in the parlor. Not every brother fit within one of the cliques that formed. Because of jealousy concerning my position as the Abbot's assistant or because of the unusual circumstances of my birth, the other brothers excluded me from their circles of conversation.

Perhaps another note of explanation would be helpful. Before becoming a novice, I was a servant in the monastery. You see, several local habitants live among us. The more industrious have acquired the status of lay brothers. It is a mark of Cistercian humility that the monks consider as brothers these unlearned, unsophisticated peasants. While the lay brothers are not permitted to partake in the eight offices, the work of God, Abbot Pedro does allow them to celebrate Mass with the monks. Those ill-suited for the more spiritual endeavors, including women, become servants, who perform the bulk of menial tasks at the monastery.

My mother had been a servant in the monastery. She was thirteen and unmarried at the time of my arrival. Evidently she concealed the pregnancy underneath her wool smock. Upon giving birth, she abandoned the infant in the stable before fleeing. No one in the monastery ever heard from her again.

It was generally assumed that my father was Lucas Sierra de Manresa, a young monk who had abruptly and unexpectedly deserted the monastery several weeks before the birth. Based on this assumption, I was christened Lucas de Santes Creus. But I have always suspected that Brother Sierra provided a convenient scapegoat and that my true father was a man of much less humble origins, perhaps a visiting dignitary or even a bishop.

How else to explain my precocious development and the patronage of Abbot Pedro?

Indeed, I believe that Abbot Pedro knows the true identity of my father. He once told me I had the same black eyes as my father.

'Lucas Sierra had black eyes?' I asked.

'Lucas who?' he said.

Given the unfortunate situation surrounding my birth, I was forced to live with the other servants until the age of nine. It is, I believe, interesting to note that I never felt at home amongst the servants, and I do not believe they themselves viewed me as one of their own. Even the older servants seemed to treat me with a distance befitting the treatment that should, in those circumstances, be accorded one born to a higher station. For instance, while the servants slept huddled together in a ragged mass on the stone floor of the kitchen, they always reserved for me a separate space, underneath the chopping table.

There were some cold nights in the kitchen. I can still remember waking in the pitch dark in the dead of winter with no blanket. Waiting for the sun to bring some warmth. Trying to breathe some life into my frozen fingers. Anticipating the scraps of bread, leftovers from the monks' table, which would soothe only partially the ache in my belly.

Until one day, a miracle occurred. On my ninth birthday, Abbot Pedro called me forth as a novice, the first and only of the local inhabitants to become a full member of the monastery. Abbot Pedro introduced me to the other monks during our meeting in the chapter house. I was kneeling next to the same boys to whom I had served supper the previous day. The brown wool of my new habit felt like silk against my skin. The robe had been used briefly, worn by a monk who had passed from illness the previous month. But he had been with us for such a short time that the garment was practically new. As the former owner was substantially older than I, the habit was on the larger side. I rolled up the sleeves carefully so as to avoid the unsightly wrinkles that I had often seen in the habits of the other monks.

After the daily reading of a chapter from the Rule of Saint Benedict, the Abbot introduced me to my colleagues.

'We welcome Lucas,' he said, 'as a father would welcome a wayward son back into the fold.'

The Abbot described my admission as an act of expiation for the sins of the past and a symbol of the spirit of forgiveness that pervaded the monastery. I was grateful for the opportunity to take what I knew to be my rightful place in the constellation of God's universe, and I was determined to prove the wisdom of the Abbot's decision.

But I have strayed from my purpose. This manuscript will provide a map of Francisco's soul, a description of his spiritual struggles, not an account of the achievements of one of God's humble servants, that is, me. My friendship with Francisco began in the parlor. I believe Francisco recognized an innate nobility about my character and appreciated my skills as a shrewd conversationalist. Indeed, it was he who initiated our discussions. I remember his first remark – 'I think, Brother Lucas, your habit is a bit large for you.' Then he smiled.

Soon, the long and painful minutes in the parlor became something quite different – a period to which I looked forward – a chance to talk to my friend, in truth, my only friend. Except for Abbot Pedro, my benefactor. During Francisco's first year at the monastery, our relationship evolved toward a deep mutual respect and spiritual bond. The only impediment was the propensity of other members to intrude upon our private conversations. Sometimes Francisco unwittingly invited the participation of other brothers not affiliated with a specific faction. Francisco could be rather naive at times. He would direct an offhand, stray comment in the direction of one of these stragglers, who seized upon the remark as an invitation to enter our circle. Our little parlor group must have seemed a motley crew.

By coincidence, Francisco's sleeping mat was next to mine in the dormitory. In our proximity, Francisco and I became accustomed to each other's presence. When Francisco left the first year to spend Easter with his family, I was surprised to feel his absence. Waking for matins, I would glimpse the cold, flat outline of his wool blanket and feel just for a moment a sense of aloneness in the vast monastery.

Most of his days at the monastery, Francisco carried the ineffable spirit that made him a leader amongst our peers. There were also dark periods, though, in which he never smiled and seemed lost in another world. During these periods, his eyes seemed to look inward, focused on what manner of demons I know not. All the boys felt his absence during these episodes. For me, it was as if the sun had stopped rising.

I do not know if Francisco preferred isolation during these periods or if he simply had no choice. I would try unsuccessfully to engage him in conversation in the parlor or to exchange a glance in the cloister. When he did not ignore me, he would be cold and distant. Just when Francisco was most in need of my friendship, he remained trapped in his own solitude.

At first, I took his behavior personally. I felt hurt by his aloofness. In time, I realized that his morose demeanor had nothing to do with me – that a greater force had taken hold of him.

What was this greater force? Who can see into the soul of a person to make such a judgment but the Lord Himself? With this qualification, I will state humbly that I believe Francisco was struggling to emerge from the darkness that had enveloped his soul the day his brother died. It was a fierce struggle, and, at times, he seemed to be losing.

23

I was deeply troubled by Francisco's episodes, which could last a week, sometimes several weeks. He seemed to suffer unnecessarily. During one of his longer spells, I raised the matter with Brother Juan in the chapel. After the Abbot, Brother Juan was the most senior monk at the monastery. He had been in that position for over twenty years, but he would never rise above it. He was extremely dark, and most harbored suspicions that his family had been Muslim converts when Toledo was conquered from the infidels.

Brother Juan seemed to have a special, almost paternal relationship with Francisco. Francisco chose Brother Juan as his confessor and always spoke of him with profound respect. In Francisco's darkest periods, Brother Juan would often sit side by side with him during our silent hours in the cloister. 'A communion of unspoken sorrow' – that's how Abbot Pedro referred to their association.

'Lucas,' Brother Juan said, responding to my concerns, 'do not worry for Francisco. As the winter turns to spring, so shall the demons leave Francisco.'

I felt greatly relieved and thanked Brother Juan for his insight. As I was turning away, he spoke softly.

'Lucas, have you noticed Abbot Pedro spending more time with the servants of late? Perhaps with the servant girls?'

I hesitated, baffled by Brother Juan's question.

He looked down before I had a chance to answer.

Brother Juan was right about Francisco's demons. The darkness would burn itself out. The cloud of melancholy would always lift, and he would return to me. That is, he would resume his proper place in the monastery.

During our meals, we followed the Rule – which is to say we ate without speaking, focusing on our food, God's bounty, and His Word, read by one of the brothers. Each of the fifty monks at Santes Creus would read for one full week during the year. I would always feel somewhat anxious in the few days before I delivered the reading. Quite embarrassing to make a mistake in the oratory – an error of diction or pronunciation in front of the Abbot and the other brothers. More than one mistake and the errant brother would feel the sharp stroke of the rod against his bare back that evening.

Francisco ascended the marble staircase to the pulpit on the first Sunday of Advent. He said the customary grace. Before reading the assigned passage of Latin Scripture, Francisco added a special message in Catalan.

'I want to express thanks to Abbot Pedro,' Francisco said, 'for his solicitude for all of his charges, in particular the servant girls.'

Several monks exchanged furtive glances. I looked up at the Abbot as Francisco commenced reading the Scriptures. He was staring at Francisco with an expression of bewilderment and compassion.

Rumors circulated concerning Abbot Pedro's fraternization with the female servants. In truth, Abbot Pedro considered the girls to be members of his flock, entitled to his ministry. As the Order prohibited women from entering most parts of the monastery, the Abbot had no choice but to make special arrangements for the provision of spiritual guidance.

Several weeks after Francisco made his unfortunate remark, I saw him carving a triangular wedge during the evenings.

'Why do you carve the wedge?' I asked Francisco in the parlor.

'It is a gift for the Abbot,' he said.

I was surprised at the time, as Francisco seemed to lack the proper regard that one should feel toward a man of Abbot Pedro's station. Perhaps, I thought, Francisco had recognized the error of his ways. Perhaps his prayer in the refectory had not contained the sinister insinuation that some of my colleagues ascribed to it.

Just before supper on a Sunday evening, Francisco used the wedge to block the door of the pantry, placing the item just under the door hinge. He fetched me from my cell, where I was praying, and told me that the Abbot was locked in the pantry and that I should bring Brother Juan immediately. I went to Brother Juan's cell and hurriedly explained what I thought to be the situation.

When Brother Juan and I reached the room, Francisco and several of the other boys were already using a thin metal rod to pry the door open. I remember Francisco calling out to the Abbot several times.

'Can you hear us, Abbot Pedro?' Francisco asked. 'Are you all right? Do not be afraid, Abbot Pedro. Have faith, Abbot Pedro. We will have you out in minutes.'

The Abbot never responded. When the door was finally flung open, our victory celebration was short-lived. I saw Francisco's wooden wedge fall to the ground and quickly realized the reason for the door's malfunction. Before I had a chance to question Francisco, I looked up to see Abbot Pedro standing in the entryway, rigid, stone-faced. The Abbot stated that he had been advising one of the servant girls, Noelle, on a difficult family matter. Then he proceeded to his quarters.

We were all quite perplexed by the Abbot's behavior, a mystery that was compounded when Brother Juan walked into the pantry and picked up Noelle. She was sobbing softly, kneeling on the wet stone behind two barrels of fresh rainwater. All of us followed Brother Juan as he carried her as if she were an infant, a silent procession into the courtyard. He sat her on a stone bench and told Francisco to fetch a wet cloth for her forehead. Francisco ripped a strip from his own robe and dipped it in the cistern. Then he sat on the bench beside Noelle and held the cloth firmly to her forehead. She fell back against his shoulder. Francisco put his other arm around her waist and rocked her gently, as Brother Juan mumbled a prayer.

Noelle was the daughter of Álvaro, a peasant who rented land on the estate. Álvaro's growing debt to the monastery was a source of jokes amongst the monks. Every month he would arrive, hat in hand, to explain to the Abbot his failure to provide the amounts of grain owed to the monastery according to custom. As the Abbot's assistant, I was often present during these episodes. Lack of rain, wilted crop, a hunting party trampling the grain, demons emerging from underground to steal the harvest – Álvaro's excuses became more and more fantastic. We all knew the real reason for his failure – he was an incorrigible drunk and hopelessly unskilled in the science of agriculture.

When we opened the pantry, both the Abbot and Noelle had been fully dressed. But doubts and speculation were inevitable, especially in light of Álvaro's vulnerable financial position and the unusual location of the counseling session. Regardless of malicious talk amongst some of my brothers, I have faith that the Abbot, my mentor and patron, had merely been counseling Noelle and that he was true to his vows as a man of God. Indeed, I am quite certain.

And yet, neither my opinion nor that of any member of the monastery is of consequence. The Abbot speaks for Christ, and no man sits in judgment of Christ. As Saint Benedict wrote, the first step of humility is unhesitating obedience. The faithful must endure everything, even contradiction, even injustice, for the Lord's sake.

Several days following this incident, Abbot Pedro informed me that Francisco was in 'spiritual rebellion.'

I was rubbing the lint off the Abbot's vestments at the time.

'Abbot Pedro,' I asked, 'does Francisco rebel against the Lord or against you?'

I believe Abbot Pedro interpreted my question as a challenge to his diagnosis rather than what it was – an effort to understand his opinion. The Abbot's cheeks, scarred with the pockmarked ravages of adolescent affliction, seemed to fill with blood. He put his arm around me roughly and pinched my neck in a most uncomfortable manner.

'Lucas,' he said, 'sometimes you try my patience. The rock upon which Saint Peter built the Church represents Christ on earth. I am merely Peter's servant. He who rebels against me rebels against the Lord. It would be best if Francisco would return to Montcada and not further disrupt the serenity of the monastery.'

'But Abbot Pedro,' I said, 'many boys look up to Francisco. I could speak to him. He is my friend.'

'Friend?' Abbot Pedro laughed. 'He feels sorry for you, Lucas. Do you think that the heir to the Montcada fortune would be friends with you?'

As learned as he was, Abbot Pedro did not understand certain issues.

Correspondence with the Montcada estate followed. By letter, Abbot Pedro explained that Francisco was experiencing 'certain difficulties' at Santes Creus that might be more effectively addressed at home. The seneschal of the Montcada family responded, conveying the reluctance of the parents to cut short their son's commitment to the Lord.

'After all,' the seneschal wrote, 'Francisco has already served two-thirds of his three-year term.'

The seneschal did suggest an ameliorative measure. He proposed sending Francisco's first cousin, Andrés Correa de Girona, to the monastery.

'Andrés,' the seneschal wrote, 'has a benign influence on his cousin. He is sure to alleviate Francisco's difficulties.'

These were the circumstances in which Abbot Pedro admitted Andrés Correa to Santes Creus as an oblate. Andrés was eighteen, the same age as Francisco. The barber sheared his long blond hair before he entered the sanctuary, the yellow locks cut, strewn, scattered in the dusty courtyard just outside the church. Andrés was enormous, broad-shouldered, almost a head taller than the other monks. He stood bolt upright, not even having the good sense to stoop, if just a little, so as to draw attention away from his unseemly stature. He reminded one of the blocks of stone that compose the foundation of a monastery. In short, Andrés took up entirely too much space.

Moreover, a thick jaw and eyebrows knit together just above his nose gave Andrés a less than scholarly appearance. Many of the boys referred to him as the 'soldier,' a nickname that derived not only from his appearance but also from his violent nature, a characteristic that became apparent not one week after his arrival.

We had just gone to bed after compline. Felipe González's voice pierced the silence of the corridor.

'Did they ever find your brother's body, Francisco?'

Felipe and several of the young lions giggled. Francisco was staring straight up at the wooden planks as if he had not heard the question.

I suppose Felipe had never forgiven Francisco for that rejection in the parlor. Would that he had. Andrés stood up and walked right past me, matter-of-factly, as if he were going to answer nature's call. As he approached Felipe, the laughter ceased. He bent down and picked up Felipe like a sack of barley, one hand on his belt cord, the other holding his robe. Then he tossed Felipe out the second-story window before walking slowly back to his bed mat.

Incredibly, Felipe landed in a cart of manure and did not sustain any serious injuries – a few cuts and bruises. It goes without saying that Andrés' action, his behavior, was incompatible with the principles of monastic life. Abbot Pedro took decisive action against the perpetrator, announcing in the chapter house the next morning Andrés' sentence – twenty-five lashes and one week in the monastery prison. It was a severe punishment, but Abbot Pedro acted out of compassion for the culprit. As Saint Benedict wrote, *such a man is handed over for the destruction of his flesh, that his spirit may be saved on the day of the Lord.*

That same day after sext, I went to Abbot Pedro's quarters as I always do to fulfill my functions as his assistant. The Abbot was perusing a recently acquired manuscript as I shaved his baldpate. Francisco spoke from the shadows in the corner of the room.

'You mentioned the largesse of my family when I first arrived at the monastery.' I was so startled by Francisco's presence that my hand jerked the razor, cutting Abbot Pedro's forehead. The Abbot slapped me hard against the face. I had to lean back to stem the flow of blood from my nostrils.

'One day,' Francisco continued, 'I will become Baron Montcada, with the responsibility of making decisions concerning the family's donations.' Francisco walked in front of Abbot Pedro's desk. He picked up a gold coin, tossed it in the air, and caught it in his open palm. 'My cousin Andrés is dear to me. If he suffers, my opinion of the Cistercian way is bound to change.'

The next day at our chapter meeting, Abbot Pedro announced that Andrés had expressed sincere repentance for his act, and that, accordingly, corporeal punishment would prove unnecessary. Furthermore, Andrés' prison sentence would be reduced to three days. The young lions let out gasps of disapproval. Felipe, in particular, was terribly upset that his assailant should get off so easily.

The episode disturbed me as well, but for another reason. Francisco had never before mentioned the wealth of his family. He had never relied on his name to exact an advantage or a favor. Andrés had caused this change. Contrary to the representations of the Montcada seneschal, Andrés was not a benign but a corrupting influence on Francisco. Indeed, it was difficult to understand the basis of their close friendship beyond their familial relation. In my estimation, Andrés lacked spiritual depth and the powers of the intellect that would make him a worthwhile companion. He was barely literate. And yet, particularly in the parlor, Francisco would sometimes focus his attentions on his cousin and neglect his true friends.

I used to wonder whether Francisco would have done the same for me – whether he would have acted contrary to his own nature in order to save me from the lash. Sometimes I still wonder.

One of the lay brothers coming back from the fields found Noelle. Her body had been placed in the cistern. It was a grizzly sight, her naked corpse covered with bruises, still bleeding from her sex, her brown eyes staring plaintively straight ahead.

That afternoon in the parlor, no one spoke. Not one word was said. Not one.

In our daily meeting in the chapter house, Abbot Pedro broke down sobbing while reading from the Rule.

'Look upon the devil's work,' he said. 'Look what he has done to my children.'

Brother Juan was mumbling to himself as the Abbot spoke.

'Brother Juan, if you have words of consolation,' the Abbot said, 'please share them.'

'You . . . you . . .' Brother Juan stuttered.

'Speak more clearly, Brother Juan,' the Abbot said, 'no one can understand your gibberish.'

'I could have done something,' Brother Juan managed to say. 'I could have prevented this.'

Three days after Noelle's body was found, Brother Juan hanged himself in the refectory. Abbot Pedro said that Brother Juan, as a suicide, would spend eternity in the inferno. Accordingly, he could not be buried in the monastery's funeral plot with the other monks just outside the infirmary. Abbot Pedro gave me several coins to give to one of the peasants to cart the body away.

Before dinner that evening, Abbot Pedro said that Brother Juan's act was tantamount to a confession of murder. That Brother Juan had come close to confessing in the chapter meeting following Noelle's murder, but had held his tongue at the last moment.

'Such is the wages of sin,' the Abbot said, with

his arms outstretched, his black eyes aflame. 'Such is the justice of Our Savior. Such is the fate of the damned.'

It was a dreadful time in Santes Creus. Even the bread tasted of blood.

Only the Abbot seemed unaffected by the horrid events. Indeed, he seemed reinvigorated by the tragedies. He prayed with an unrelenting fervor and spoke his sermons with passionate conviction. I was kept busy transcribing numerous missives to members of the Crown and clergy. The Abbot was requesting funds to build a second story of monastic cells around the cloister. Such an addition, the Abbot said, would demonstrate to his flock that not even the devil's mischief could dampen the ardor of the faithful.

On the fourth day of Lent, I was sharpening the razor, preparing for Abbot Pedro's weekly shave. The blade stroked gently against the coarse leather strap. There was a knock. I approached the door. It opened before I reached the passageway. Francisco and Andrés stepped into the room.

'Francisco and Andrés,' Abbot Pedro said, 'you should be in chapel. I suggest you move along quickly. Lucas, you fool, start grooming me. I have a busy schedule today.'

I stepped behind the Abbot's chair and placed a cotton cloth around his neck to keep clean his vestments. The Abbot closed his eyes, and I began shaving gently the tiny hairs on his baldpate. Francisco and Andrés remained. They stood in the center of the room, their cool gazes resting on the Abbot.

'I have heard no footsteps leaving my chamber,' the Abbot said, without opening his eyes. 'Andrés, you escaped the lash one time – just barely. I would not again test the quality of my mercy.'

'We have come,' Francisco said, 'to discuss the death of the servant girl Noelle.'

'The matter is settled,' the Abbot said. 'Brother Juan admitted his guilt. Do you have some new information to shed light on Brother Juan's dealings with the dark one? Or perhaps the name of an accomplice?'

'Yes, Abbot Pedro,' Francisco said, 'I have vital information. I am certain that Brother Juan never harmed the girl.'

'Are you now?' Abbot Pedro said, sitting up. 'Pray, tell me, how do you know this?'

'Because,' Francisco said, 'I knew Brother Juan.'

'If I were you, Francisco,' the Abbot responded, 'that is a fact I would soon forget lest the finger of suspicion be pointed in your direction. After all, I suspect that Brother Juan had conspirators. Under the right circumstances, when his friends become his accusers, even a Montcada can burn at the stake. Or perhaps just his cousin.'

'Brother Juan,' Francisco said, 'did not kill the girl.'

'Interesting,' Abbot Pedro said, 'that you should possess intimate knowledge of this affair.'

'Abbot Pedro,' Andrés said, 'Francisco told me

36

of the incident with the servant girl Noelle. The door of the pantry jammed.'

'Perhaps, Abbot Pedro,' Francisco said, 'you could explain yourself.'

The Abbot stood up slowly. The blood rising on his neck, the red sheen coagulating in the crevices of his cheeks. He pulled off the cotton cloth and threw it to the ground. He shook his fist.

'For two years, I've had to put up with your arrogance, Francisco. You think I haven't dealt with insolent boys like you before? I put them in their place. Hard too. With the stroke of a metal rod. I don't care what your family name is.'

'We only seek the truth,' Francisco said.

'The truth?' the Abbot said. 'The truth is that the girl you speak of was a whore. I knew from the first time I saw her. She cast her spell. The carnal yearnings returned – lust. Black, infernal lust. I will not tolerate those demons in this sanctuary. Do you hear me? I will crush the devil in whatever form he takes.'

I daresay Abbot Pedro was trembling with anger. He wiped his spittle-flecked lips and placed his hand on the edge of the desk to balance himself.

'Now,' he said, 'get out of here.'

Francisco and Andrés did not move, though. I was still standing behind the Abbot's chair, breathless, holding the razor. Francisco glanced at me, his eyes tender. His gaze followed my arm down to my hand. Then to the razor. It was the manner in which he focused on the glint of the metal blade. I let out a gasp and dropped the razor, which clattered on the stone floor.

'Lucas,' Andrés said, 'could you leave us. My cousin and I have private business with the Abbot.'

I looked to Francisco. He smiled somberly and nodded, and I made my way toward the passageway.

'Lucas,' Abbot Pedro said, 'stay where you are and finish shaving me. Lucas, get back here.'

Andrés closed the door behind me. I walked to the chapel. Actually, I do not remember how I got there. I was sweating, shivering. I must have said one hundred Ave Marias before I heard the scream of one of the servants, who discovered the Abbot's body. He had bled to death.

They said that Abbot Pedro castrated himself rather than give in to the temptations of the flesh. The Archbishop of Tarragona deemed the Abbot's death not a suicide but an act of 'self-martyrdom.' Abbot Pedro, according to the official report, used the razor not against himself but against the devil's agents.

The Archbishop has filed a petition with the Pope to have the Abbot canonized. Four months ago, legates from Rome came to Santes Creus to interview me concerning other miracles that the Abbot performed. They said they would come again. I never told them about Francisco and Andrés' presence that afternoon. I never told anyone. Never.

And if thy hand offend thee, cut it off. Those are

the exact words on Abbot Pedro's crypt, the words of Our Savior. The tomb lies at the doorstep to the refectory. As the new Abbot, Alfonso de Barbera, explained to the monks, Abbot Pedro's great humility during his lifetime repeats itself in death. The monks walk over his tomb several times a day on their way to their meals.

The Abbot's portrait is sculpted ivory inlaid into the stone floor. Dressed in his finest vestments, Abbot Pedro carries the scepter to indicate his position as head of the monastery. His face is turning away and appears to be wincing. His hands are crossed strategically just in front of his genitals as if in homage to that sacred act or perhaps simply to protect himself from the footsteps of overeager novices.

CHAPTER 3

BROTHER VIAL

For seven years, I did not see him. I remained at Santes Creus and rose from monk to prior of the monastery, second only to the Abbot. I am the youngest prior ever appointed at Santes Creus. I have the potential to rise even higher. Abbot Alfonso often refers to me as his successor.

I heard news of Francisco from time to time. The Church keeps track of its patrons and their heirs. I knew that he had gone on the King's crusade six years ago. After the Spanish kings evicted the infidels from almost the entire Iberian Peninsula, King Jaime decided to focus his military prowess on the Holy Land. He intended to sail the Mediterranean to the Levant and to chase the infidels from Jerusalem. Knights of the Hospital, Knights of the Temple, and Knights of Calatrava – Francisco's Order – all joined the Christian armada. Sometimes I weep when I think of the brave knights who take the Cross, who sacrifice everything to put an end to the desecration – the devil's children trodding on, sullying the sacred ground where Christ carried His Cross.

After the departure of King Jaime's forces, I prayed every day for Francisco's safety. Every day until Abbot Alfonso's announcement in the chapter house.

'I have received news that your former brothers Francisco de Montcada and Andrés de Girona were killed during the Muslim siege of the Krak des Chevaliers. They died in the service of Our Lord Jesus Christ. Hallelujah. Please keep them in your prayers. We have a few administrative matters to address before reading from the Rule. Brother Lucas, would you explain the new policy with respect to receiving visitors?'

He said it just like that, as if he were announcing the crop yield for the month. The news struck like a mallet. I could not speak. The air drained from my body. Indeed, the chapter meeting was delayed for several minutes until I could catch my breath.

One year ago, the Abbot received word that Francisco was alive.

'Francisco was not killed,' Abbot Alfonso said, 'but captured alive and imprisoned for two years by the infidels. He arrived by ship several months ago. Regrettably, the Montcada family does not rejoice. Francisco is possessed by demons. Do I not warn you daily? No one is safe, no one immune from temptation. The dark one plots, schemes, bargains for each one of your souls. The Montcada family has sent Francisco to the monastery at Poblet,

41

where Father Adelmo, the renowned priest from Italy, shall perform the exorcism. We take our reading today from chapter sixty-eight of the Rule of Saint Benedict.'

Abbot Alfonso, who spent fifteen years at Poblet, described Father Adelmo as a man who is not afraid to employ the same brutal measures as his adversary in the struggle for a soul.

'Father Adelmo understands,' Abbot Alfonso said, 'that one must sometimes speak to the devil in his own language.'

Father Adelmo is said to have exorcised one thousand persons, most of whom did not survive, but who found salvation during their last breaths. He once exorcised twenty-five men in nearby Sabadell, fed to the Lord's flames in the town square.

With due respect, even reverence, for Father Adelmo and his accomplishments, I believed strongly that a different, perhaps softer approach would be more befitting Francisco. In the last two years, I have learned much concerning techniques of exorcism. My teacher, Brother Vial, is not an ordinary monk. He spent eight years on the crusade battling the infidels. He returned to his estate in the northern provinces of Aragón, but after a year, he took the cloth and gave all his property and wealth to the Church. Because of his reputation as one of God's most ferocious soldiers, he was offered by Archbishop Sancho of Tarragona, a cousin and personal friend of Brother Vial, a position as the

Bishop of San Victorián. Brother Vial declined. The Archbishop then offered Brother Vial the position of Abbot in the monastery at Montserrat. He again declined. He wanted nothing more than the habit of a monk, to live out his years in the poverty and humility that were Christ's lot.

He came to Santes Creus two years ago. Shortly after Brother Vial's arrival, one of the peasant girls cast a spell on her pregnant neighbor, causing a miscarriage. Members of the victim's family testified before the Abbot's tribunal that they had seen the accused place her hand on the swollen womb just hours before the tragic event. Abbot Alfonso determined that the girl was Satan's emissary and was responsible for the recent spate of infant deaths amongst the villagers. As no monk at Santes Creus was practiced in exorcism, Abbot Alfonso decided to send the girl to Father Adelmo at Poblet.

The girl was kneeling inside a mule cart, bound to the front boards, pelted by rocks and sticks from her former neighbors, when Brother Vial emerged from the church. He walked resolutely toward the cart and called for the peasants to stop throwing stones. Brother Vial spoke as a man accustomed to giving orders and having them obeyed. Indeed, several peasants already had rocks in their hands, but they did not throw them. The cart stopped moving. The driver and the other villagers looked curiously at this new monk, a grizzled, bald, and burly man.

Brother Vial climbed up on the cart and waded

through the hay. He untied the girl and wiped her bloodied face with his smock. Then he picked her up and carried her into the church.

I watched Brother Vial from the church steps. He walked right past me as he entered the church, the girl burying her head in the thick folds of his habit. The sight of a female polluting the holy sanctuary prodded me after Brother Vial.

'Excuse me, Brother,' I called. We had been introduced once, but I forgot his name in the confusion. 'Girls need special permission from the Abbot in order to enter the church. Brother, please, you do not know what you do.'

Indeed, Brother Vial knew exactly what he was doing. If he heard my words of caution, he did not care. He continued into the courtyard, around the cloister, then up the stairs to the vacant annex on the second floor (the completion of the second story has been temporarily stalled for lack of funds). Brother Vial carried the girl into one of the empty cells, then set her down. She sat still in the corner, holding her hands up as if to ward off a stone.

'Brother Lucas,' Brother Vial said, between heavy breaths, 'bring me a stool, a copy of the Scriptures, twenty blank sheets of parchment, a quill, six loaves of fresh bread, and two jugs of wine.'

As the prior of the monastery, I outranked Brother Vial. But it never occurred to me to question him. I retrieved the requested items and returned.

The stool Brother Vial sat on. The bread he gave to the girl. The wine he kept for himself. The Scriptures he began to read.

He read and read until the girl had calmed down. She ate two of the loaves and took a sip of wine from Brother Vial's own proffered cup. As evening approached, she fell asleep.

I had not left the cell except to perform Brother Vial's errands. When he stood up to exit, I began to question him concerning his intentions. But Brother Vial raised his fingers to his lips and pointed to the sleeping girl, and I ceased speaking. I followed him out of the cell. I followed him down the stairs, across the courtyard.

A cluster of monks had assembled in the cloister. They whispered to each other, no doubt discussing Brother Vial's scandalous behavior. They fell silent as we approached, staring intently at Brother Vial.

When we entered the Abbot's chambers, he was pacing. He stopped abruptly, looking up at Brother Vial, then at me. I shrugged my shoulders uncertainly.

'Brother Vial,' Abbot Alfonso said, 'I know that you have many important friends in the kingdom and the clergy. I know that you have fought many battles in Jesus' name. But I fear you do not fully understand our way at Santes Creus. The Abbot is the shepherd, the father of all members of the monastery. He leads them to the Lord. No monk, no matter how distinguished, can disobey his orders. I decided to send the girl to Poblet for the sake of her immortal soul and for the preservation of my flock. She is possessed. Rest assured, Father Adelmo knows how to deal with such cases. The Italian priest has been exorcising demons for thirty years in these parts.'

'Abbot Alfonso,' Brother Vial responded, 'I know Father Adelmo, and I witnessed one of his exorcisms when I was a young man on my father's estate. Purification by fire – a sobering spectacle even for this battle-weary soldier. I too have experienced close combat with the devil. I know his wiles and his disguises. I ask for one week, Abbot Alfonso. One week to cure the girl. If she has not been exorcised, we will send her to Father Adelmo at Poblet.'

Brother Vial would need only four days. As instructed by Abbot Alfonso, I never left Brother Vial alone with the girl, except to fetch food and drink when Brother Vial made requests. He seemed quite fond of the grapes in the monastery's vineyard.

'Battling the devil,' Brother Vial said, 'can be rather dull, Lucas.'

Indeed, Brother Vial spent most of the period reading Scripture out loud and napping.

'Never underestimate,' he said, 'the importance of a good nap in the afternoon heat, Brother Lucas.'

46

When he was not reading or sleeping, Brother Vial conversed with the girl – about her work, her family, her neighbors. It seems the girl's father had a longstanding dispute over ownership of a field with their neighbors, the very same family of the victim.

On the fourth day, Brother Vial summoned the fathers of the accused and of the victim. We met in an antechamber reserved for receiving nonclerical visitors. After introducing himself, Brother Vial told the two men that they would split evenly the land in dispute.

'If there is any confusion or disagreement concerning the division,' Brother Vial said, 'the monastery will confiscate the property. Do you have any questions?'

Brother Vial returned to the cell where the girl was sleeping. He woke her and asked if she renounced Satan and embraced Our Lord Jesus Christ. She seemed frightened by Brother Vial's grave tone and did not answer.

'Lucas,' Brother Vial said, 'do you renounce Satan and embrace Our Lord Jesus Christ?'

'Yes,' I stated emphatically.

He repeated the question to the girl, who answered affirmatively.

That evening I spoke with Abbot Alfonso concerning the exorcism. Perhaps I left out a few peripheral details, including the meeting of the fathers in the antechamber, but I confirmed Brother Vial's claim that the girl was free of demons. Indeed, she has cast no spells since Brother Vial's exorcism.

There were others. Brother Vial quickly developed a reputation as a formidable adversary of the devil, perhaps even as a rival to the Italian priest, Father Adelmo of Poblet. Brother Vial's techniques of exorcism have the advantage of a low mortality rate, in fact, no mortality rate, a circumstance that concerns Abbot Alfonso.

'I worry, Brother Lucas,' Abbot Alfonso said, 'whether Tarragona will disapprove of Brother Vial's unorthodox measures. The Church must be feared by its subjects. It would seem that during the intense spiritual struggle some of the possessed would die or suffer lasting injury. Perhaps you could speak to Brother Vial.'

But I never raised the issue with Brother Vial, and the Abbot's worries seemed to fade after the monastery received a chest of coins from Archbishop Sancho to construct a new dormitory to accommodate the influx of pilgrims visiting Santes Creus to receive the blessings of Brother Vial.

Nevertheless, the Abbot remains a bit suspicious of Brother Vial and asked me to become his supervisor. Although I have never spoken a word of instruction to my charge, I attend all his exorcisms, missing many of the daily offices in order to give Abbot Alfonso a full report of Brother Vial's activities. In truth, Brother Vial provides me the instruction, showing the different techniques to exorcise demons, some more resistant than others.

'The Word,' he says frequently, 'is our greatest weapon against the devil.'

Brother Vial spends several hours each day reading the Scriptures aloud to his subjects. He also converses with them on a wide range of topics. Sometimes he speaks of the weather. Sometimes he receives the subject's confession. At other times, he adopts a more confrontational approach, asking his subject how and why he came to the devil. For the stubborn cases, Brother Vial always takes copious notes, often sending me for more parchment when his supply runs low.

'What are you writing?' I asked one evening, when Brother Vial finished a grueling session with a woman who had suffocated two of her children and remained unrepentant.

'I transcribe her confession,' he said. 'When I read my notes, I search for the map of the soul.'

'A map of the soul, Brother Vial?' I asked.

'We need a guide, Brother Lucas,' he said, 'a map to help navigate through the dark forest of human frailty – vanity, greed, pride, and prejudice.'

'Will the map help reveal the source of the subject's possession?' I asked.

'Yes, Brother Lucas, and light the path toward salvation.'

'Have you found this path with the murderess?' I asked.

'In this particular case, Lucas, I fear we are too late. I believe our subject has wedded the devil. In such cases, there is no chance of dissolution.'

One week later, Brother Vial gave instructions to transfer the woman to Poblet to the care of Father Adelmo.

'My methods,' Brother Vial explained, 'are sometimes ineffective, Lucas. One must recognize his own limitations and take appropriate measures.'

The aforementioned case is exceptional. Brother Vial has developed an impressive record battling Satan. Of thirty-seven cases, Brother Vial has managed a full exorcism in thirty-two instances. He has transferred two persons to Poblet. Three other cases have yet to be resolved. The subjects refuse to renounce Satan, but Brother Vial has not given up hope. These persons live on the second floor of the cloister in separate cells. Brother Vial has thus far resisted sending them to Father Adelmo, although he has mentioned the possibility to two of the three persons. Brother Vial described in detail the process of purification by fire to one of the possessed persons – the strident sound of the victim's screams, the smell of burning flesh, the cries of the crowd. After we left the cell, Brother Vial predicted that the man would soon return to the Lord. We shall see.

In short, I work closely with Brother Vial and have learned much concerning the art of exorcism. I consider Brother Vial a friend and mentor. I suspect Brother Vial has grown quite fond of me. He often addresses me informally and, despite the prohibition on frivolous expressions of emotion, he frequently smiles at me when we pass in the cloister.

The news that Father Adelmo of Poblet would exorcise Francisco disturbed me. As Brother Vial says, each case of possession is unique and must be addressed on its own terms. I believed that Brother Vial's methods would be more suited to Francisco's sensitive constitution. I mentioned my concerns forthwith to Brother Vial, who seemed intrigued by my recollections of Francisco. We talked for some time.

'Brother Lucas,' Brother Vial said, 'Archbishop Sancho of Tarragona has jurisdiction over Francisco. Only he can transfer Francisco to Santes Creus, and he will only do so if Abbot Alfonso makes a formal request. Go to Abbot Alfonso. Tell him of your friend. Then ask him if the transfer of Francisco to Santes Creus might affect the distribution of funds amongst the sister Cistercian monasteries.'

Brother Vial made me repeat the question before I set off for the Abbot's chambers. I did exactly as Brother Vial suggested, reciting the question verbatim. Abbot Alfonso listened, rubbing his chin pensively.

'I would love to see that little bastard's face,' Abbot Alfonso said, 'when the Montcada heir is snatched from under his nose.'

'Whose face?' I asked.

Abbot Alfonso did not respond, but I believe he

was referring to Abbot Rodrigo of Poblet. The two men see each other once a year at the conference of Cistercian abbots. They maintain a close bond of friendship, exchanging written salutation on every major feast day.

Abbot Alfonso immediately set about dictating a letter to Archbishop Sancho requesting Francisco's transfer. He pointed out that before his journey to the Levant, Francisco had spent three years at Santes Creus.

'No doubt,' the letter stated, 'Francisco would feel more comfortable in familiar surroundings, in a location where Francisco spent what were probably the happiest and most peaceful years of his life.'

In the following weeks, I found myself climbing the bell tower several times a day to search the horizon for a messenger from Tarragona. As the weeks passed without a response, the darkness seemed to draw out longer every night.

After nine weeks, two soldiers from the Archbishop's personal guard arrived at Santes Creus. They carried a short message, two sentences:

To the esteemed Abbot Alfonso,
On the subject of your recent letter, you and Brother Vial will come to Tarragona immediately. I have provided a covered wagon for your transportation and two soldiers for your protection.
The Archbishop Sancho of Tarragona,
the twelfth day of June, the Year of Our Lord 1275.

As I read the letter to the Abbot, a wave of bliss swept over me. Soon I would see Francisco's face. Soon I would hear his voice. Abbot Alfonso, smiling broadly, seemed quite pleased as well. He told me to convey the news to Brother Vial and inform him that they would leave for Tarragona the next day.

I found Brother Vial in the cloister. I told him the contents of the letter. To my surprise, he became rather solemn. He put his hand on my shoulder.

'You shall travel to Tarragona in my stead, Lucas,' he said.

'I do not know what you mean.'

'You shall perform the exorcism.'

'But I have no experience.'

'Have you not seen me perform more than thirty exorcisms?'

'Yes,' I responded, 'but Francisco's case will be most difficult. Besides, he is a Montcada. Abbot Alfonso and Archbishop Sancho would never allow me to perform the exorcism.'

'I will speak to Abbot Alfonso,' Brother Vial said, 'and I will provide a letter of introduction to Archbishop Sancho.'

'I am afraid, Brother Vial, that your letter will not prepare me for such a formidable task.'

'You are already prepared, Brother Lucas. You spent three years with Francisco at Santes Creus.'

'I do not understand, Brother Vial.'

'Many years ago,' Brother Vial said, 'on the campaign in Syria, my deputy Simon disappeared from camp during a stormy night. Two hundred soldiers under my command, and not one of them had seen Simon leave. I sent out a search party during the morning, but they came back after a couple of hours with no sign of Simon.

'That afternoon, an old man in Arab headdress entered our camp,' Brother Vial continued. 'He asked to speak with the commander about a mutual friend. My soldiers led him to me. I was sitting beside my tent when he approached. He set forth a ball of white silk on the ground. I picked it up and unwrapped the cloth. A finger was nestled in the silk folds, freshly cut, still pulsing. At first, I thought that the old man was a merchant, selling the relic of some living saint. But then he said it was Simon's finger. The next parcel, he said, would contain Simon's head unless we delivered fifty gold dinars to a nearby cave. He gave us three days. After consulting with my lieutenants, I dispatched a company to Acre to collect the coins.

'After three days, my men had not returned. I sent one of my soldiers to the cave of which the old man had spoken. He was to request another day, to guarantee delivery of the treasure within twenty-four hours on condition that no more harm came to Simon.

'At the cave, twelve infidels met my messenger. The old man who had earlier visited our camp translated the request to the others. As my messenger waited, they talked and argued amongst themselves. Finally, the translator said that they would spare Simon for one more day.

'Dawn came with no word from Acre. I improvised a plan to try to save Simon's life. I thought the twelve Muslims who greeted my messenger were probably the entire enemy force – a small band of thieves and murderers roaming the countryside. We would try to use our superior numbers to crush them, first luring them out of hiding, then rescuing Simon by force. With this purpose in mind, I sent a messenger to tell the infidels we had gathered the ransom and to arrange for the exchange on the open plain not half a mile from our camp. I made clear that we would hand over the gold only at the same time the infidels delivered Simon.

'The Muslims agreed to my conditions, but added three of their own – we could bring only five men, and we would have to come to the rendezvous on foot and unarmed. Their conditions foiled my original plan. I had no choice but to consent, though.

'A most dangerous mission, Lucas. When the infidels realized we had not brought the treasure, they would try to kill Simon and us. And there were twelve of them against five of us. Bad odds, particularly considering the other conditions.

'I revised my plan. We would no longer rely on superior numbers but instead on stealth and surprise. I instructed the carpenters to build two wooden chests. In each chest, we loaded six crossbows. I had my engineers lock an arrow in the chamber of each bow. They would be ready to fire when the time came. Twelve arrows for twelve infidels.

'Then I chose four men to accompany me – four men to stand side by side with me on the field of battle. Four men who would not waver or fall back even in the face of such a perilous mission. Do you know whom I chose?'

'Your most able marksmen?' I responded.

'No, Brother Lucas. Nor did I choose my bravest knights. I chose Simon's closest friends – those who had journeyed with him from the province of Conflent, in northwest Catalonia. These men shared a bond with Simon that had developed over several years of training and fighting together. They would not abandon their friend to the infidels even in the face of overwhelming odds.

'We arrived at the meeting place with our enemies. The sun was behind us, in the eyes of our adversaries. We would need every advantage we could gain.

'The old man arrived first. He inspected each one of us to make sure we were unarmed. Then he asked me to open the chests and show him the treasure. I told him he could see the treasure when we saw Simon. He raised his fist in the air, and his renegade band approached on horseback. Simon, blindfolded, walked amongst them. When they stood across from us, I signaled my men to open the chests. Under the watchful eyes of the infidels, two of my comrades began to lift the lids, watching each other's progress. They had to act simultaneously. As soon as the infidels saw our weapons, they would kill Simon, then loose their arrows on us. My comrades did not wait for my order to attack. I was reaching into the chest for two crossbows when I heard the swoosh of arrows flying through the air and the screams of pain from our enemies. I grabbed two bows, one in each arm, and fired at the two Muslims across from me. I hit both.'

'Simon must have been grateful, Brother Vial,' I said. 'Surprised and grateful.'

'No, Brother Lucas,' he said.

'Then he expected your rescue?' I asked.

'Simon was dead, Brother Lucas.'

'Your deputy was dead, Brother Vial?'

'In the confusion, it was difficult to distinguish friend from foe. One of Simon's own comrades from the province of Conflent shot him in the chest. The crossbow is a powerful weapon, Brother Lucas. You could see the metal blade protruding from Simon's back.'

Brother Vial sighed and shook his head. Then he got up to leave. I followed quickly after him and grabbed his arm.

'So they failed, Brother Vial,' I said. 'These men whom you picked did not save Simon.'

'No, Brother Lucas, they did not.'

'But their qualifications?' I said. 'I thought the point of your story . . .'

'The future is uncertain, Brother Lucas.' Brother

Vial spoke sharply. 'The Lord's purpose is inscrutable.'

'Brother Vial, I'm not sure how your story relates to Francisco's exorcism.'

'Do you not love Francisco, Brother Lucas?' he asked.

'I love all my brothers at Santes Creus, Brother Vial.'

'I am not talking of Santes Creus, Brother Lucas.'

'I have not seen Francisco for six years, Brother Vial.'

'Love knows nothing of time, Brother Lucas. You spoke to me of Francisco as if you had seen him only yesterday.'

'I still remember his crooked smile, Brother Vial.'

'Would you risk your life for Francisco?' Brother Vial asked.

'I must say, Brother Vial, I am quite confused. I cannot see the relevance of your questions. I am simply not qualified to conduct Francisco's exorcism.'

'Brother Lucas, you are more qualified than any man in the world to exorcise Francisco's demons.'

More qualified than any man in the world to exorcise Francisco's demons. Those were his exact words.

Brother Vial closed his eyes and bowed his head. He held both my arms tightly.

'Lord,' he said, 'give your servant Lucas the

58

courage to perform his mission. Lord, give him the wisdom to see your path even in the darkest forest. Lord, give him the courage to resist the devil's temptation.'

Brother Vial looked up, but he was still clutching my arm. Indeed, his nails were digging into my skin.

'The devil's temptation, Lucas,' he said.

'Yes, Brother Vial, I understand.'

Brother Vial spoke to Abbot Alfonso that evening. I do not know what he said. The next morning, the Abbot observed me suspiciously when I entered the wagon with my cassock. But he said nothing. Indeed, for the most part, he ignored me during the two days of our journey to Tarragona.

This was the first time I had ever left the grounds of Santes Creus. As the wagon forged over muddied, rugged roads, I looked out the back, searching for the devil's temptation that Brother Vial had mentioned. But I did not see it. I saw the brown earth. I saw the emerald forest. I saw peasants who stared warily at the Archbishop's wagon. I saw a field of sunflowers that had turned to face the wagon as a congregation faces its priest. I saw an ancient Roman aqueduct – a silly contraption built by pagans. As Abbot Pedro said, if God wanted rivers to run on aqueducts, why wouldn't he just have created them?

Abbot Alfonso instructed me to close the curtains as we approached Tarragona. He pretended to be asleep, but I could tell he was a bit frightened by the noise and bustle of the streets. We must have passed one thousand people.

We arrived at the church just in time for vespers. I had never seen such a sacred space – cavernous, chaste. I could feel God's presence in every crevice, his fingerprints on the angelic sculptures that peered down tenderly from their perches, his warm breath in the chanted psalms that filtered through the monastery.

We spent that evening in the guest dormitory with pilgrims and other visiting monks. In the morning, just after matins, Abbot Alfonso went to the Archbishop's chambers. I remained in the cloister. After several hours, a monk approached.

'Brother Lucas?'

'Yes, I am he,' I said.

'The Archbishop will see you now.'

I followed him through the treasury and up the stairs. As we ascended, I could hear my heart beating. I was afraid my escort could hear it too. I had never been in the presence of an archbishop, or a bishop for that matter. We entered an antechamber, then passed into the Archbishop's private office.

What exquisite beauty. Yellow and blue tiles covered the floor. A large oak desk strewn with manuscripts stood in the center of the room, each document held fast by a silver buckle. A golden chalice filled to the brim with wine was poised atop a pile of loose papers. Sculpted serpents snaked up the stem of the chalice, so that the shiny heads of those creatures perched over the cup and appeared to be sipping the sweet liquid. I saw more gold and silver in that room than I had seen in my entire life.

Archbishop Sancho was reading Brother Vial's letter. His nose was long, angular, noble. His skin was sallow, with a few red splotches. He was dressed in a white robe and wore an oval hat. A silver chain with a rubied Cross dangled on his chest.

As I stood in that chamber, I felt a warmth flow into my body and a tingling in my fingers and toes. I felt at home, as if I belonged in that room, in those chambers, among those holy, sublime articles. Faith, Lucas, I told myself, one day the Lord will reward your devotion. One day, the Lord will set everything right.

The Archbishop glanced at me periodically, then back down at the letter. When he was finished, he motioned for me to take a seat across from him.

'My cousin, Brother Vial,' he said, 'informs me that you were a friend of Francisco.'

'Yes, your eminence, I was at Santes Creus during his three years at the monastery.'

The Archbishop seemed to study me for some time. I felt slightly uncomfortable and had to remind myself not to crack my knuckles, an unfortunate habit I acquired during my days as Abbot Pedro's assistant.

'Your eminence,' I said, 'may I ask where is Abbot Alfonso?'

'I sent him to the church so that I could meet you privately. You are not afraid of me, are you, Brother Lucas?'

'Certainly not, your eminence,' I said. 'It's just that I feel unworthy to merit a private audience with such a distinguished and holy man as yourself.'

'My cousin also writes,' the Archbishop continued, 'that you are more qualified than any other man in the kingdom to exorcise Francisco's demons. Do you think that's true?'

'Your eminence,' I responded, 'I am not so blind or arrogant as to support such a statement. And yet, I would be loath to contradict Brother Vial.'

A faint smile crossed the Archbishop's lips.

'Father Adelmo,' the Archbishop continued, 'seems to have reached an impasse in his efforts with Francisco. As a last resort, he has proposed cutting open Francisco's head from ear to ear to provide a passage for the demons to depart. What do you think of such a course, Brother Lucas?'

'Perhaps,' I said, 'other means could be tried before relying on such a drastic and undoubtedly fatal measure.'

'Yes, Brother Lucas,' the Archbishop said, 'I tend to agree. Our legal experts have pointed out that an exorcism resulting in the death of Francisco might not satisfy the terms of Baron Montcada's donation. We would certainly have an argument, but the gift would not be assured.'

'A gift, your eminence?' I asked.

'You have not heard? Baron Montcada has offered one-third of his estate in exchange for the salvation of his son. The Baron included in the bequest the condition of Francisco's "physical and spiritual recovery." It is the inclusion of the word "physical" that makes me pause before assenting to Father Adelmo's radical plan. I am inclined to try another avenue, to put Brother Vial's confidence in you to the test.'

'I am humbled by such an opportunity, your eminence.'

'As well you should be, Brother Lucas,' the Archbishop said. 'The landholdings and vast wealth of the Montcadas rival those of the royal family. Many parties stand to gain by Francisco's salvation, including you, Brother Lucas.'

'Me, your eminence?'

Archbishop Sancho placed his hand on top of mine. It felt cold and sweaty.

'I would not forget such a service,' he said.

Many parties stand to gain by Francisco's salvation, including you, Brother Lucas.

Including me, indeed. I imagined myself in the Archbishop's quarters. Sitting behind his desk. My desk. I would glide my hand over the solid oak, the smooth varnish like drops of water on my palm. On one side of the desk, I would keep quill and parchment, upon which I could pen correspondence to other archbishops, or perhaps the Holy Father in Rome. On the other side, a golden reliquary containing a finger, a few strands

63

of hair, maybe even the ear of some revered saint.

The Archbishop did not mention whether Francisco was one of the parties that stood to gain by his own salvation. Indeed, I do not think he was referring to Francisco.

Abbot Alfonso returned to Santes Creus the next day. I was sent to Poblet to gather Francisco. I carried a sealed letter from Archbishop Sancho to Abbot Rodrigo. I have already described my initial reception at Poblet and my impressions of Francisco and the conditions in which he was kept. Indeed, I was a bit jarred upon seeing my friend. I had not anticipated, I could not have imagined, the extent to which the demons had infested his soul and ravaged his body.

The morning of my arrival at Poblet, after visiting Francisco, I presented the letter to Abbot Rodrigo and Father Adelmo. Both men studied the document for some time, perhaps hoping to find a loophole, an ambiguity that would allow them to keep Francisco another week or two while clarification was sought from Tarragona. My eyes kept wandering to the scarred hands of Father Adelmo. They resembled claws more than hands, malformed, charred from applying the red-hot coals of repentance to his subjects. Having read the letter, I waited patiently, recognizing that the two men had no choice but to obey the Archbishop's unequivocal instructions. By midday, we had departed, Francisco manacled inside the wagon, as I rode above with our escort.

Father Adelmo watched us leave from the roof of the cloister. The black hood of his robe shadowed his face. But I could still see his eyes, blazing white with the Lord's fury.

It has been four months since Francisco arrived at Santes Creus. I have tried to follow faithfully Brother Vial's methods of exorcism. Waking for matins, I chant the psalms before walking to Francisco's cell on the second floor of the cloister. I read Scripture to him several hours each day. I finished the Bible and began again from Genesis.

I set aside a period each evening to transcribe Francisco's confession. When there is nothing to record, I write down my memories of Francisco – as Brother Vial said, a map of the soul, a map that one day, I hope, will show the path toward Francisco's salvation.

Francisco's physical condition improved rapidly. When he first arrived at the monastery, the wounds on his back were raw and pusfilled. Brother Vial provided herbs from the Levant, which have helped heal the marks of Father Adelmo's exorcism.

Francisco barely ate or drank and never spoke when he came to Santes Creus. After one week, he began to pick at his meals. Upon the advice of Brother Vial, I experimented with different foods. Francisco seems to prefer chicken. After a couple of months, he was eating full portions. He has gained weight. He is well groomed. The barber comes to Francisco's cell weekly to trim his hair and his reddish beard and cut his nails. Sometimes he looks like his old self.

Two months ago, Francisco spoke. He asked me to lower my voice so that he could sleep. Never have so few words brought me such happiness. Since then, Francisco has spoken more and more. He seemed a bit out of practice at first, never quite stringing together more than a few sentences. But he progressed swiftly so that in a few weeks we had full conversations. His memory is more or less intact. Quite surprisingly, Francisco did not at first recall my name, although he remembered that we had slept next to each other in the dormitory. He does know exactly where he is. He even asked about the health and whereabouts of some of his former brothers, most of whom remain at Santes Creus. He never mentioned Andrés. He never mentioned the crusade. Neither did I. Until two weeks ago.

I had always wondered why Francisco took the Cross. While Francisco was devout in his own manner, he seemed disinclined to follow the call of any man, no less an army. Nor had he ever evinced an interest in the military aspect of Christ's dominion. Moreover, as the heir of the Crown's most powerful vassal, Francisco's life in Barcelona was well set. I daresay every man in the kingdom, save the King, would have changed places with Francisco. And yet, Francisco chose another path – a dangerous and uncertain journey.

I had just finished the Book of Exodus for a second time when I asked him.

'Why did you take the Cross, Francisco?'

He did not answer. He stared straight ahead and did not acknowledge my presence for the rest of the day. Francisco has remained mute since I posed that question two weeks ago. He stopped eating as well and seems to have lost the weight he had gained over the previous months.

Since Francisco's arrival, I have lit a candle in his windowsill every afternoon before I leave. A candle of hope, a candle of courage. For the last two weeks, when I enter his cell in the morning, I have found the flame extinguished, the wick unused. As if Francisco can no longer abide God's light. As if he preferred outer darkness to reflect the condition of his soul.

Two days ago, I saw blood dripping from his closed fist. When he ignored my pleas to open his hand, I pried open his fingers. He was clutching the knife I had given him to carve his meat. The cut bore deep into his palm. I could see the bone. I confiscated the bloody knife and ran from the cell.

My heart was racing. I feared the worst – that I had unwittingly inflicted an irrevocable setback on Francisco, speaking of the Cross before he was ready. I thought Francisco would die before I could exorcise his demons. I thought his soul would dwell in the fires of hell for eternity.

I ran to Brother Vial. I found him in the kitchen, helping the servants and lay brothers prepare supper.

Brother Vial took my hand and led me into the parlor. We sat down on the bench. The strain of the previous months overwhelmed me. Indeed, I am ashamed to admit, but I cried for some time.

When I had recovered my composure, I told Brother Vial of my frustration and my fears concerning Francisco's future.

'Remember the woman,' I asked, 'who had suffocated her infants? You said she had wed the devil and that there was no chance of dissolution. Maybe Francisco has made the same unholy pact. Maybe he will never recover. Maybe he does not want to live. He could just as easily have used the knife to cut his throat instead of his palm.'

'Francisco's case is different from the murderess',' Brother Vial said. 'He has hurt no one but himself. He isolates himself, starves himself, lacerates himself. Why does he punish himself? Perhaps he holds himself responsible for some act, some terrible consequence.'

That's when I told Brother Vial that Francisco and Andrés were in Abbot Pedro's chambers the day of his martyrdom. I felt that I had no choice. You see, I thought it was Abbot Pedro's murder that haunted Francisco.

Brother Vial did not ask me whether I believed Francisco was responsible for Abbot Pedro's death. If he had, I would have told him how Francisco's eyes, as if hypnotized by some dark force, followed the razor.

68

'Do you believe, Lucas,' he asked, 'that Abbot Pedro was guilty of Noelle's murder?'

Expressing an opinion on such a matter could carry grave consequences. I weighed my words carefully.

'Did not Saint Benedict write, Brother Vial, that the faithful must endure everything, even injustice, for the Lord's sake? Isn't that what he wrote?'

'Yes, Lucas,' Brother Vial said, 'but some injustices cannot be endured. Abbot Pedro's fate is not what ails Francisco. The source of his possession lies elsewhere. Find out what happened after Francisco left Santes Creus, what happened to him on the crusade. To unravel the thread of Francisco's soul.'

'How?' I asked. 'I have already asked about the crusade. See how he responds?'

'Faith, Lucas,' Brother Vial said. 'Faith and patience.'

'Brother Vial, I cannot do this. Remember you told me that a man must recognize his own limitations. I do not know how to help Francisco. I do not know what the Lord wants from me.'

'The Lord does not demand very much, Lucas,' Brother Vial said. 'He demands everything. Blood and soul.'

Yesterday, on the first of November, I entered Francisco's cell. His food had not been touched and the candle had been snuffed out. I read for several hours before dozing off. Francisco's soft words woke me.

'Andrés was at the Citadel with me.'

I did not stir, trying to distinguish my own dreams from the substance of things. It was the first time. Francisco had spoken of Andrés or the crusade.

'Andrés was at the Citadel,' he said, staring blankly ahead. Then he turned over and closed his eyes.

I was unable to sleep that evening. I dozed momentarily but awoke abruptly with an image of Francisco approaching with a crown of thorns and open palms revealing the stigmata. In his agony, Christ must have looked similar to Francisco on that first day when I saw him in his cell at Poblet – emaciated, unkempt, excruciatingly vulnerable. I wandered barefoot in my quarters on the cold stone floor, clutching the beads of my rosary. I was trembling through the night, although whether out of fear or anticipation I cannot say.

When the bells rang, I dressed methodically, went to church for matins, then set out for Francisco's cell, ostensibly in the same manner as I had done the previous four months. I do not think I took one breath during that long walk.

I half expected to find him dead or gone, as if the Lord had finally taken him back. He was neither. He looked directly at me as I entered and started to speak as if no time had elapsed since his first words of yesterday.

CHAPTER 4

THE CROSS

It was never my intention to take the Cross.

Francisco did not look at me as he spoke. He was sitting on his bed mat, staring out the window, his arms wrapped around his knees. He rocked back and forth slowly, his rhythm uneven. I was standing, my hands clasped at my chest.

I was drawn neither to the sword nor the cloth. Martyrdom seemed so lonely, and the clergy rather boring.

Not to my brother. Sergio was eighteen when he announced his desire to take his vows – to join the Cistercian monastery at Poblet as a novice. My father was terribly upset – his firstborn, the Montcada heir, forsaking the society of men. He tried to press upon Sergio the importance of fulfilling his worldly responsibilities. He could do nothing in the face of Sergio's fervor for Christ, though. Except change its direction – he convinced Sergio to take the Cross as a warrior instead of a monk. Sergio would go on the crusade to reconquer Jerusalem from the infidels. He would return in a couple years to assume his rightful place as the son of my father, the King's most powerful vassal. My father had no intention of permanently surrendering Sergio to the Lord. I wanted to go with my brother, but my father forbid it. I was only fifteen.

All of Barcelona celebrated the launching. King Jaime led the festivities. Banners were held aloft – red and gold, brown and silver – the colors and arms of the most noble families – Berenguer, Díaz, Morera, Múñoz – and of the military orders – Knights of the Temple, Knights of the Hospital of Saint John, Knights of Calatrava. Minstrels plied their lutes for a coin or two from the honored citizens of the great city. Clad in black robes, priests from as far as Val d'Aran raised their hands to shout their blessings over the departing knights. The mendicant Orders gathered on the steps. They chanted psalms and swung censers of burning incense. Several of the clergy, overcome by emotion and the heat of the July sun, fainted where they stood, easy targets for the pickpockets that mingled amongst the crowd.

Five hundred knights from all parts of Spain, dressed in full battle armor, pranced up and down the dock – receiving the applause of lay people, both high and low, and the benedictions of holy men. The soldiers seemed giants, invulnerable. The Bishop of Barcelona, Arnau de Gurb, raised two fingers in blessing. The yellow rubies that lined his vestment shimmered against the sun's rays as he christened the ship *María de la Cruz*.

Sergio held my hand before he ascended the ramp. His smile serene. I was proud of my brother.

We had shared the same bedchamber growing up, drunk from the same cup, prayed side by side. I do not think I had been separated from Sergio for more than a day since my birth.

He put his cool hands on my cheeks to wipe away the tears, the same hands that had taught me to ride and to shoot a bow.

'God loves you, Francisco,' he said.

The ship capsized soon after launching. A new ship, untested, built at the shipyard at Drassanes, not one mile from where it went down. I was holding a shell to my ear, listening to the ocean depths, when the ship disappeared into the morning glare. Teams of sailors boarded fishing boats and rushed toward the empty space. In vain. The knights, still in their armor, were unable to swim. All five hundred drowned. Sergio's body was never recovered. God's love can be severe.

Francisco laughed. It was short, but unmistakable. I must have started or made a sudden movement, because Francisco looked up. He wore an amused expression, almost condescending, not quite smiling.

Excuse me, Lucas, but even you can see the humor in the situation. Five hundred knights thrashing around in the ocean. It was a ridiculous sight.

I crossed myself. I felt afraid. Lord, give me courage to serve you. Was I in the presence of a demon? It was Francisco's voice, but the words . . . Remember your station. Remember your mission. Remember who you are. I closed my eyes tightly and tried to picture the dark grain of the wood Cross hanging in my cell.

A great lamentation rose up from the dock. Fear and anguish. It was as if God were passing judgment on the entire kingdom – rejecting our most precious offering – our sons and brothers. Monks, beseeching Saint Michael, protector of mariners, fled in terror – back to the safety of their monasteries. Mothers wept. Fathers gnashed their teeth. I stood alone wading into the sea – separate from the throng. A few lazy waves lapping up on my shins. And then silence. Still water.

I always wondered what was going through Sergio's head as he sank to the bottom of the ocean. Did he close his eyes as the light faded?

The Holy Father in Rome had declared that all those who fell on the crusade would be assured a place in heaven. But since Sergio's boat had barely left the shore, there was talk in the city that the souls of the drowned men were in limbo – an indefinite sentence in purgatory that could be ended only by the intervention of Santa Eulalia, patron Saint of Barcelona. Bishop Arnau said that Santa Eulalia would champion the most worthy souls before Our Lord Jesus Christ, which meant the sons of families that were generous enough to underwrite the construction of a new church at the monastery at Montserrat.

My mother believed that the number of prayers that reached the heavens would overwhelm our patron saint. She directed her entreaties to Santa Tecla, who had received the Gospel directly from Saint Peter, the holder of the keys to heaven.

When she was not kneeling in the chapel praying, my mother walked through the gardens mumbling the Ave Maria over and over again, barely lifting her head. On suspicion that an evil spell had been surreptitiously cast on Sergio, my mother dismissed the entire domestic staff.

Within the family, my father bore the brunt of my mother's mourning. Although she never said so, she blamed him for Sergio's death. Not without reason. If not for my father's insistence, Sergio would have been safely ensconced at the monastery at Poblet.

My mother moved her bedchamber downstairs where she could be closer to the chapel. She said that she would not share my father's bed until the proper penance was exacted for the sullied union that begat Sergio nineteen years previous.

My presence seemed painful to my mother's eyes. Perhaps the brotherly resemblance opened her wound afresh. The same pale skin, our blue eyes – which I studied in the looking glass, searching for the source of my mother's repugnance and of the crashing waves that changed my life.

Our estate in Montcada became a garden of sorrow. An aching longing for a time and place that were extinguished.

My mother left Montcada. The servants packed her belongings in twenty-four chests, which followed her wagon in a caravan to our residence inside the old Roman walls of Barcelona – the palace built by my grandfather on the street named for my family to commemorate our service in the conquest of the island of Baleares – the Carrer de Montcada.

Sullen, remorseful, my father paced through the castle corridors. Often he seemed not to recognize me when we passed in the hall. He would pat my head with a perplexed smile before averting his glance. I thought my father would surely suffocate, if not from sadness and guilt, then from the exorcist's concoctions of blue smoke that pervaded the house.

My father too found his escape, though. He took his entourage of knights and traveled north to the jousting tournaments – to the Loire, Marseilles, Burgundy, Cologne.

I remained in Montcada with the seneschal of our family, Lord Ferrán, and a staff of servants and tutors. Our shared room had become a shrine to Sergio. The white roses of condolence breathed a sweet sickly smell. The Scriptures open to the last page we had read the dawn of Sergio's departure –

Know that God hath overthrown me,
And hath compassed me with his net.
Behold, I cry out of wrong, but I am not heard.

My bedchamber – a crypt for my brother. And me – a tree up-rooted, cut down on all sides.

Francisco winked at me, his eyes glowing an unnatural shade of deep blue. He was smiling broadly, an inane, burlesque, diabolical expression. He looked completely mad. I measured the distance to the door just in case a quick retreat became necessary.

I did not leave my bedchamber for several weeks. Lying in my bed, I stared out the window at the tall, red grass tumbling in the wind. I read that page from the Scriptures over and over, as if some secret meaning lay behind the gold leaf and black ink.

Lord Ferrán ran the affairs of the family in my father's absence. He was responsible for the well-being and education of the Montcada line. With Sergio's death, Lord Ferrán focused his concerns exclusively on me. He believed that I had taken ill, and he instructed Doctor Don Mendoza to discover the cause. After collecting and examining my feces for ten days, the good doctor diagnosed a buildup of black bile, a species of melancholia. He prescribed cold baths and bed rest. He also forbade me to take the sun or to eat spicy foods. Lord Ferrán posted one of his assistants outside my bedchamber to monitor my condition and to discourage any inclination I might have to wander from my room.

Andrés Correa de Girona appeared in my doorway on the fourth Sunday of October, ninety-three days after the death of my brother. I had met my first cousin but once – eight years previous at the funeral of our grandfather. I recognized Andrés by his long blond hair, which reached to his shoulders and gave him a feminine air. At fifteen, though, his vein-lined forearms and broad shoulders belied the impression created by his flaxen locks.

'Still so skinny, cousin?' he asked, shaking his head. I was sitting up in my bed, pruning the petals of Sergio's rusted roses.

'Come, cousin,' he said, 'I have brought a present from my family.'

Andrés disappeared. I continued tending the roses. I expected Andrés to return when he realized I had not followed. The corridor remained silent, though, except for the sibilant blaze of candles that lined the hallway in tribute to my brother. After perhaps half an hour, I rose from my bed and peered down the corridor. The sleeping attendant lay sprawled in his chair just outside my room. No one else was present. I went back to my bed but briefly. The temerity of my cousin rather annoyed me – entering my room stealthily, without a proper introduction, and then insulting me in my weakened condition. I resolved to have a word with him, even if it required disobeying Don Mendoza's instructions. I returned to the hallway and walked its length cautiously. There was no sign of my cousin. I descended the stairs and opened the door to the courtyard.

Andrés was sitting atop his horse with his hands on the reins of another.

'Her name is Pancho,' he said.

The horse's black eyes were depthless, luminescent.

'I told my father,' Andrés said, 'she would be too much of a horse for you. He said that you would grow into her.'

We rode all day. Through the Lecaros' cornfields, my face and lips stung by the sheaths until I could feel warm drops of blood on my cheeks. Faster and faster. Across the tilled fields of the Garcías, the peasants dropping their plows and staring as if we were divine messengers. Through the King's dusky forest just outside the city. The horse's briny sweat mingled with my own. Farther and farther away. Across the muddied mountain pass to the cliffs overlooking the sea.

We returned well after darkness had fallen. Lord Ferrán was seated in the courtyard. A servant had apparently reported our departure.

'Welcome, Andrés Correa de Girona,' he said. 'Thank you for responding to my invitation. I trust in the future you will provide company to your cousin without scaring the serfs half to death and requiring formal apologies to our neighbors.'

Andrés shared my bedchamber over the next several months. He made himself quite at home. He took up three-fourths of the bed, confining me precariously close to the edge. Three days after his arrival, he picked up the open Bible.

'A beautiful passage,' Andrés said.

I did not respond. He turned several pages. Then, without consulting me, Andrés closed the Bible with an emphatic thud that sent a cloud of dust scurrying across the room. He buckled the binding's latch and placed the Book in the chest alongside our winter blankets.

My stomach muscles contracted as if I had been punched. I could hear my teeth grinding. The presumption of my cousin. His unabashed arrogance. As if Andrés could stave off the darkness by such a thoughtless, unremarkable gesture. As if he could close the chapter on the blackest night, push it off to the side, and then go on living oblivious to the destruction wrought by Sergio's death. I scowled at Andrés. He smiled back at me, a wide, simple grin. Perhaps, I thought, like almost all my noble brethren, Andrés could not read. He did not comprehend the significance of his action.

'It is unwise, cousin, to trifle in affairs that are not your business and that you do not understand,' I said, trying to maintain an even tone. 'Do not forget, Andrés, that you are a guest here.'

'Does the Good Book not say, Francisco, there is a time for every season?' he responded. 'It seems the time for that particular passage ended several days ago.'

I had underestimated my cousin.

Two days later, Andrés threw out the dead flowers that adorned the bedchamber.

'The stench of these flowers has grown tiresome, Francisco,' he said. 'Perhaps we should discard them?'

He did not wait for an answer. He gathered them up gently and carried the bushel into the hallway.

This time, I did not protest. I said nothing. I turned aside, held my breath, and concentrated intently on the Cross above my bed.

Despite Andrés' brusque manner, Lord Ferrán welcomed his presence. He could not help notice a marked improvement in my health. Andrés and I took a daily ride in the morning and often practiced archery after supper in the afternoon. Three weeks after Andrés' arrival, Don Mendoza diagnosed a dramatic betterment in the color and consistency of my bowel movements.

'Francisco, now that you are well,' Lord Ferrán said at supper that evening, 'we must turn our attention to the family's affairs. Royal, noble, and clerical delegations have requested permission to visit Montcada to pay their respects to your blessed brother, Sergio. Your father remains in France competing in the seasonal jousting tournaments. In his absence, you must receive the visitors. They will scrutinize you closely – to assess your character, to curry favor, to glean any weaknesses that might be exploited when you assume the mantle of the family. Andrés will keep you company during the interviews. Your cousin's presence will

81

demonstrate the allegiance of the extended family and the future strength of the clan.'

Lord Ferrán looked at me hopefully. I nodded. Andrés was yawning.

The visits began two days later. A noble delegation led by Baron Calvell de Palau arrived in the afternoon. Lord Ferrán ushered them into the Great Hall, where Andrés and I sat waiting. The seneschal made a formal introduction of our guests, then dismissed himself. Lord Ferrán had said that it was vital for Barcelona to see that the young heirs could stand on their own feet in council with the heads of other noble families.

Andrés and I did not intend deception. Lord Ferrán had created the opportunity by neglecting to specify in his introduction which one of us was Francisco. Baron Calvell spoke for some time expressing his grief over the tragic accident and his condolences concerning my brother. He looked back and forth from Andrés to me. Finally, he seemed to focus his attention on Andrés and henceforth directed his speech entirely in my cousin's direction.

When the Baron finished his lengthy soliloquy, there was a long, silent pause. His entourage looked anxiously at Andrés, who was stroking his chin.

'How many chickens do you maintain on your estate?' Andrés asked pointedly.

'I beg your pardon, Don Francisco?' the Baron asked.

Andrés repeated his question, his countenance deadly serious.

The Baron consulted in whispers with the other members of his entourage.

'One hundred and ten, Don Francisco, give or take a few,' he said.

Andrés nodded gravely in my direction, as if his suspicions had been confirmed. The members of Baron Clavell's entourage looked uneasily amongst themselves.

'Yes,' Andrés finally said, 'quite so.'

The Baron and his entourage left soon thereafter. As they departed, they studied Andrés and seemed disinclined to turn their backs on him. The Baron himself must have bowed ten times on his way out the door.

We conducted one interview a day. Two, three, four hours of listening to a continuous litany of irrelevant details and stale lies. The number of hectares and serfs held by the family; their favorable impression of King Jaime's health during their latest visit to the palace; the bishops and royal family members whom they counted as close friends; their profound sorrow upon hearing of my brother's death and the many prayers they had said in his name, 'blessed Sergio.'

Andrés and I found it difficult not to doze off. After several days of interviews, we devised a strategy. We would finish our morning horse ride with a race back to the estate. Whoever lost would have to play Francisco at the afternoon interview. Despite Andrés' boasts, we were well matched as horsemen, and the burden of playing the heir seemed to fall evenly between us.

Like vultures circling the corpse of my brother, the delegations descended upon Montcada. We gave them what they wanted – a quiet nod, a knowing smile. That seemed to please our guests as much as any speech we could have given. When our visitors ceased speaking and looked up, we knew a comment or question was expected. We readily provided one.

Nevertheless, Andrés and I knew well that Lord Ferrán would disapprove of our switching identities. When one of the servants relayed Lord Ferrán's request to meet with us after our morning ride, we suspected that he had learned of our peculiar arrangement.

'Do you have anything to say to me?' Lord Ferrán asked, when we stood before him.

'Lord Ferrán,' Andrés said, 'let me first say that our city friends are prone to great exaggeration.'

'I think not, Andrés,' Lord Ferrán said. 'You are much too modest. The two of you are the talk of Barcelona – the cousins whose good looks are exceeded only by their sagacity. They say the twins – yes, that's what they call you – the twins talk in parables and poetry. A formidable pair, indeed. Nobles might be prone to exaggeration, but they can always discern excellence. All of the Montcada vassals share in the glory of the new heir. Our fortunes rise and fall with those of the family. I know if Baron Montcada were here, he would be full of pride for the performance of both of you this last month.'

Lord Ferrán was beaming, ebullient. He was looking at us expectantly, as if he too, like our daily visitors, required a comment or question. I shuffled uncomfortably.

'Yes, quite so,' Andrés replied. He was looking down at his shoes.

Lord Ferrán never discovered our arrangement. Andrés and I continued racing our horses for several months. We could have continued for several years if my mother had not intervened.

She persuaded my father to send me to the monastery at Santes Creus. She said she would return from Barcelona when the younger had fulfilled the elder's unspoken vows. In Sergio's stead, I would serve a three-year sentence at the monastery – to assuage the Lord's wrath and perhaps my mother's.

That's where I met you, Lucas. When was that – ten years ago? I see you have remained at Santes Creus. Judging by your jewelry, I would say you have profited quite handsomely in the clergy. Tell me, Lucas, did Jesus Christ wear gold rings on His fingers?

But I have lost the thread of my explanation. After three years at the monastery, I returned to Montcada, to the old darkness. My parents were away, my father at a jousting tournament in Flanders, my mother at our residence in the city. Although I was home, I felt an unrelenting homesickness. It was an unquenchable ache. My brother dominated my dreams – Sergio on the ship with his quiet, unsuspecting smile, Sergio beckoning me into the still water. Sleepless or sleeping, my nights were haunted by the same images.

I had been home for one month when Sergio called me from his icy grave. It was a dream. I was a member of a cavalry regiment. We were galloping toward the Holy City. We rode for several days without resting. My fears subsided in the rhythm of Pancho's powerful and certain gait, and in the thunder that shook the earth from a thousand hooves. I was a soldier in a vast and mighty army that moved as one organism. My armor felt as light as skin and my body underneath like iron, impenetrable.

I put my hand to my chest. My cloak was wet. I thought that I was bleeding from the heart, a familiar wound. I looked down but saw no blood. The rest of my tunic was soaking, though. I thought we must be riding in the pouring rain.

I cupped my hands in front of me to gather water for my parched lips, but my hands remained empty. It was not raining.

Then I realized. We were on the bottom of the ocean, a battle-ready regiment in full armor. I tried to speak to the nearest knight, to question him, but he could not hear my voice through the misty water.

I looked to my left and right. The horses and knights advanced slowly, bogged down by the effort of moving their limbs through the heavy water. I tried in vain to make out the faces of the others. One of the knights next to me motioned for me to approach. Pancho and I galloped by his side.

It was Sergio. He spoke without emotion. 'I am lost,' he said.

He does not recognize me, I thought. I shouted to him over the tumult of the galloping horses: 'Sergio, it is I, Francisco, your brother.'

He stared at me impassively, then lunged toward me. His nails scraped across my chest. I managed to pull myself away. Sergio disappeared into the maelstrom of charging cavalry.

We continued for several hours until I felt a hand grip my arm tightly. I turned to confront this knight. His shining armor illuminated a path toward the East, toward Jerusalem. I could not make out his face. I peered into his helmet but saw only the vast black ocean, inscrutable, unending.

When I woke, I did not need a priest to decipher my brother's message. Sergio had spoken to me from purgatory. My brother's soul was in limbo. He had asked for my help. To lift him from the inferno through my sacrifice.

That faceless knight – it was me, one of Christ's nameless soldiers. My own face, my own future – uncertain, uncharted. I would sail to Jerusalem in search of redemption – for my brother and myself.

It was never my intention to take the Cross. I was called. From the abyss.

From the Abyss, indeed. Francisco would have done well to consult a priest concerning his 'brother's message.' The ways of the devil are infinitely complex and wicked. I suspect it was Satan who assumed the guise of his brother Sergio to lure Francisco to the Levant. Satan undoubtedly viewed the Montcada heir as a great prize and would do anything to woo him into that dark fold. The devil understood that Francisco, far away from his home, would be more vulnerable to doubts and temptation. Thus the paradox at the core of Francisco's decision to take the Cross – the paradox that makes me shudder as I realize the cunning, nefarious methods of Satan – Francisco joined God's army and journeyed to the Holy Land at the behest of the devil.

Perhaps another note of explanation is necessary. In an effort to divert attention away from his own spiritual trials, Francisco mentioned the jewelry on my person. I do in fact wear two gold rings – one on each of my middle fingers. I say so quite openly. I am proud of the rings and wear them as a symbol of my devotion to the Lord.

The first ring was a gift from Bishop Bisson of Lérida in gratitude for my negotiations with Baron Enrique de Penedès over the sale of an indulgence. It could be said that Baron Enrique's elder brother Don Jaume brought death to his own door. Don

Jaume had, over a five-year period, repeatedly refused to fulfill his promise, made to Bishop Bisson, to take the Cross. After a final, unsuccessful appeal to Don Jaume, Bishop Bisson excommunicated him. The Bishop's declaration disinherited Don Jaume from his father's estate and released Don Jaume's vassals from any obligation they held toward him. Don Jaume refused to recognize the measure and went so far as to take three priests from Lérida hostage.

During the crisis, the younger brother, Baron Enrique, sent an assassin, a Frenchman, to murder Don Jaume. The assassin disguised himself as a Dominican priest and stabbed Don Jaume as he was receiving communion at the cathedral in Penedès. It was reported that the silver chalice with Christ's blood fell over during the commotion, and the blood of Don Jaume mixed with that of Christ on the floor of the cathedral.

I do not pretend that such a drastic measure as employed by Baron Enrique is ever justified. It contradicts most clearly the teachings of the Lord. No matter that the Baron was acting, in an indirect fashion, as an instrument of divine retribution.

When Don Jaume passed, his brother Baron Enrique became heir to his father's estate and provided the diocese of Lérida with a chest of treasures. In that chest was the ring I wear on my right middle finger. Bishop Bisson gave me the ring, engraved with the coat of arms of the family Penedès, in recognition of my work in negotiating the exact terms of Baron Enrique's dispensation. I do not think it would be false boasting to say that I drove a hard bargain – one indulgence in exchange for seventy pounds of gold and silver. In short, I received for the Lord the greatest possible settlement, and thereby increased dramatically, if not assured, the Baron's chances of entering the Kingdom upon his own death.

Archbishop Sancho of Tarragona gave me the second ring. He sent it to Santes Creus just last week with a letter.

'I am not surprised to hear,' he wrote, 'of Francisco's recent progress under your direction. I have high hopes, Brother Lucas, for your advancement in the clergy. I never told you, Brother Lucas, but I was deeply impressed by your poise during our meeting in my chambers in Tarragona.' That was the exact word he used – 'poise.'

'Unfortunately, Bishop Martín of Tortosa is quite ill,' the letter continued. 'I am making a preliminary list of potential replacements. If your work with Francisco should be completed by the time Bishop Martín expires, I would certainly consider you a leading candidate for the position. I am enclosing this ring as a mark of gratitude for your efforts with Francisco and as a harbinger of Francisco's spiritual and physical recovery.'

I have always believed that I carried and conveyed a special quality. I never lost faith that the

Lord or one of his illustrious servants would recognize that quality and reward my fealty. Even before the Archbishop's letter, I would often pretend I was a member of the high clergy. Sometimes, when Abbot Alfonso was not looking, I would try on his felt hat and make believe I was giving a sermon to the faithful. I had studied his hand gestures during the service and would copy them in the privacy of chambers.

It seems both impossible and inevitable that my hopes, my grandest expectations, will be fulfilled. What were the words of Brother Vial – faith and patience. *His eminence, Bishop Lucas of Tortosa*. It has rather a nice cadence. I can picture myself accidentally running into Francisco on a visit to Barcelona with my entourage. We will chat for some time about mutual acquaintances, perhaps members of the royal family. We will share a long charitable laugh at the expense of some of our former brothers at Santes Creus. When the conversation subsides, Francisco will smile and invite me to spend a week in Montcada. I, in turn, will insist that he spend part of the summer on my own estate in Tortosa.

Regrettably, Francisco, possessed by demons, cannot appreciate the significance of these rings or the nature of my sacrifices over the last four months. He cannot understand that these rings represent my commitment to one of Christ's most important precepts – the power of forgiveness and the salvation by the Church of a sinner. Is this not the very kernel of our work, to show sinners the true path? To rescue those who have lost their way? Indeed, the Archbishop's gift symbolizes my fidelity to Francisco himself and the process of his redemption.

CHAPTER 5

ISABEL

Yesterday I gave away one of my rings as alms to a beggar family. They visited the monastery during the feast of the holy martyrs. The father of the family approached me as I made my way to the chapel for morning Mass. Ill-clad and foul-smelling, he was the kind of man who would call master anyone who wore shoes.

He fell to his knees, blocking my path up the steps and rousing me from my internal deliberations on Francisco's predicament. He spoke to me of his two young ones, starving for lack of bread. He asked that God have mercy on him and his family. I was moved by the plight of the man, and I knew that the Lord would approve giving the ring to the family – it could probably feed them for a full year. When I bestowed the ring, the man grasped my ankles and began to kiss my feet. The rest of the family remained withdrawn, the mother clutching her two children to her hips. They looked almost mistrustful, too foolish to understand the full implications of my generosity. The act created quite a stir in the monastery, and I could see that the young monks looked to me with a certain reverence that was perhaps appropriate under the circumstances. If Francisco noticed the disappearance of the ring, he did not mention it.

Francisco and I have continued our discussions. While Francisco appeared indifferent to my presence during his first months here, he now seems to await my arrival anxiously, impatient to start speaking, to take up his narrative exactly where he left off the previous evening. Francisco often paces the cell as he talks. At times he exhibits keen emotions, as if he were reliving the events he describes. He usually speaks for several hours without resting. He seems to feel a great sense of urgency. Frequently he begins speaking before I can settle in my chair and place on my lap the wood board carved to my specifications by one of the novices. On this miniature desk, I keep a Bible, an inkwell, a quill, and parchment, upon which I take notes that help me transcribe Francisco's confession in the evenings.

As I make my way to his cell after matins in the morning, sometimes I feel a vague sense of foreboding. Perhaps I am afraid that Francisco will say something that will alter my life, that I will come face to face with an insupportable horror, the selfsame that pushed Francisco into the arms of the devil. I pray that I will be strong enough to look that temptation in the face without flinching.

Faith, Lucas. Faith and courage.

★　　★　　★

Andrés' letter came not one week after my dream of Sergio. He wrote of a crusade that King Jaime would launch in the coming year. He suggested that we join the Knights of Calatrava, who were sure to accompany the King. I felt as if my brother Sergio were the true author of the letter, a proposal that seemed more a mandate than a question.

I met my mother at our residence in Barcelona the next day. I found her in a barely lit parlor. She was praying, kneeling before a wooden statue of the Virgin, inscribed MATER DEI, the Mother of God. Mary held an apple in her right hand, Eve resurrected, and a golden chalice in her left, the mark of the Church's function on earth, sharing the body and blood of Our Savior.

My mother's hands were empty, tiny and frail in my own. The three years since Sergio's death had taken their toll. She was still dressed in the black clothes of mourning. I had to help my mother off her knees and guide her to a chair, her back stooped, her eyes cast down.

I told her that I had seen Sergio. I told her of my dream and my intention to take the Cross. She listened without saying a word as if she already knew. When I finished, she pressed her arid lips against my forehead and left the room.

Through correspondence, Andrés and I decided we would travel to Calatrava, the headquarters of the military Order, from his family's estate in Girona. I had never visited Andrés' home, although

I had met his father, my mother's brother, on several occasions. He would stay with us in Montcada when he traveled to Barcelona to attend meetings of the King's Council. When I was young, he used to carry me on his shoulders, galloping through the courtyard gardens. I would grasp his blond hair with one hand, the other wielding my stick against imaginary foes, cutting off infidel heads. My mother would always interrupt our sessions, chastising her brother for trampling the flowers. 'Sir Francisco,' my uncle called me, 'a knight errant.'

Baron Correa had not been to Montcada for many years, though. He had grown disinclined to leave his two children and would dispatch in his stead the family seneschal to attend the King's court.

My uncle sent one of his vassals, Pere de Girona, to guide me to the Correa estate. The trip to Girona took two days. The night before my arrival, Pere and I camped in a sheltered grove of pine trees a half day's ride from the Correa home. We sat around the warmth of a flickering fire, both exhausted from the day's journey. Neither of us made an effort to untie our belongings to retrieve the smoked meat that we had brought on our journey. We preferred to bed hungry and cold, huddled in wool blankets, anticipating the warm shelter in Girona.

I remember the crunching of soft footsteps on the snow, a deer with two of its young peering at us

96

around our campfire. Pere and I must have seemed strange pilgrims, shivering, bereft in that white forest. With one stroke, I could have orphaned the two fawns, but I did not have the strength or will. I pulled the blanket over my head. When I let it down, the visitors had abandoned our camp, disappeared into the shadows of the forest. I lay staring into the fire, listening to the crackle of frozen branches. If the flames foretold a destiny in Syria, I did not see it. It was an unwritten journey, Lucas, unwritten, unread.

By dawn, fresh snow had covered the dying ashes. We mounted our horses and set off for Girona. We rode without rest and reached the Correa estate before noon.

The storm had finally let up when we came upon the castle. We stopped before the moat that surrounded the manor – more of a ditch really. Pancho and I could have leapt over the gap with a running start. My uncle had neither the resources nor the enemies of a Montcada. Pere stood on his horse shouting until a white-haired servant, roused from his nap in the stables, shuffled out to let down the drawbridge.

A small courtyard led to the manor – a timber structure, dusky brown, with two levels of colored glass windows. Four stone towers were evenly spaced on the shingled roof. One of the towers slanted forward as if scrutinizing new arrivals.

The old servant stayed my horse, Pancho, and helped me down.

'Welcome, Don Francisco,' he said. 'We were not expecting you until tonight. Baron Correa and Andrés are still hunting. I know the young master was anxious to welcome you. They should return shortly.'

Pere led my horse into the stable. The servant helped me brush the snow from my body, then led me inside the manor. After a brief struggle, I wrested control of my trunk from the old man and balanced its weight on my right shoulder. I followed him up the stairs to the second floor, where we turned right and walked halfway down the hall to an open door. He stood aside to let me pass.

I stood in the doorway for several seconds. The room was large and filled with light from the double windows looking out over the garden. To the right was a large wooden bed, with two green wool blankets folded at the base. I could hear the wheezing of the brick hearth just across from the bed. I walked toward the smoldering embers, inhaling the sweet wood smoke, until the heat burned my face.

While blowing into my cupped hands to thaw my stiff fingers, I turned to examine the other side of the room. In the corner, a white marble Cross with the figure of Christ writhing in agony hung over a small prayer pew. The Christ statue was looking toward the ceiling plaintively. His eyes were open wide, as if He were surprised to find Himself nailed to the Cross. Perhaps the Son of Man thought that at the last moment His Father would show mercy, that His own fatal prophecy would not be fulfilled. *My God, my God, why hast thou forsaken me?*

I walked to the window. The clouded glass blurred the vista. I opened a small pane to look out. The land was white and serene. I could see a mountain range several miles from the estate. Directly under the window, a manicured garden of waist-high bushes formed concentric circles around a fountain with a stone statue of the Virgin. Her eyes were closed and her hands were open in a gesture of submission.

A looking glass hung in the corner of the room. I approached and examined my face in the reflection, consoled by its familiarity, but unsettled by its severity, the sharp curve of my jaw, the faint vertical lines where the wind had burned my lips, the dark circles that ringed my eyes and the sea-green waves that danced within them. I draped my winter cloak over the glass.

The door opened slowly. Andrés stood with a wide, mischievous grin. The hunt had muddied his cloak and tangled his thick blond hair. It had been just three months since I last saw him. Yet I noticed a change in his demeanor. His tall stature, his broad shoulders and powerful hands no longer seemed the innocent attributes of an oversized, artless youth, but instead the instruments of a practiced warrior. As a fair maiden loses the blush at her blossom and learns to welcome the attentions her maturation provokes, so Andrés, at nineteen, had embraced his brute strength. He strode confidently across the room, his bold gaze and certain gait displaying the command he had taken of his willful and strapping limbs. That I had overlooked the evolution of Andrés' maturation testified to our proximity and to the unbroken nature of our time together. Andrés grasped one hand behind my neck as he studied my face.

'Francisco, my friend, you have been seeing ghosts again. That will not be tolerated in the Correa household.' Andrés was shaking his head, a tender reproach.

'Father,' Andrés said, 'come greet your nephew, Don Francisco de Montcada.'

Baron Correa, standing in the doorway, seemed a twin to his son. A hulk of a man, he had the same shock of blond hair, only streaked with silver. I recognized his smile, kind and earnest, which bore in the indentations of his cheeks the trace of a full life.

'Welcome, Francisco,' Baron Correa said. 'It has been many years – too many. You have been remiss in not visiting your uncle and cousins sooner.'

My eyes found a third figure in the doorway, a young woman. She wore a dark green velvet dress that fully covered her body. Flowered brocade decorated her sleeves and hem. Even so, I could see the outline of her figure – the rise of her breast curving down to the waist; her slender shoulders; the gentle contour of her collarbones visible through the smooth fabric; the

100

lissome neckline; her flaxen hair braided behind her head.

'Francisco,' Andrés said, 'I present my sister, Isabel.'

Her face was rather plain. Her nose perhaps too prominent, her skin freckled, her lips too thin. Yet the combination of her features was somehow quite pleasing. Even disconcerting.

Perhaps it was the color of her eyes – slate gray – the exact shade of my brother's tomb. Layer upon layer of stone. In that depth, Isabel, just sixteen, seemed to possess an awareness not shared by the other Correas, an understanding of that other, nocturnal side of human existence. When I met her gaze, I thought I was peering into the looking glass, into the twilight shadows buried in the recesses of my soul.

I suppose such a notion sounds ridiculous. True or false, it does not matter anymore, does it? But, at the time, there was a part of me that took this confluence of colors as a hopeful sign – that perhaps Isabel was no stranger to the darkness that resided in me.

'Francisco,' Andrés interrupted my thoughts, 'this is my younger sister.'

Baron Correa and Andrés were observing me curiously, waiting for a response.

'Forgive me, cousin,' I said. 'Andrés did not warn me of your gracefulness.'

Her lips parted, her cheeks rose, the glint of her gray eyes seemed to unfurl. It was a smile.

'Francisco,' she exclaimed, 'you are all my brother talks about. Now that you are here, perhaps Andrés will be able to converse on other subjects.'

Baron Correa clasped arms with Isabel. 'Daughter, we leave the two soldiers to discuss battle strategy and dress for dinner.'

Baron Correa and Isabel left the room, the Baron exiting with a deep, theatrical bow.

I turned away from Andrés' gaze. I opened the dark casket of my trunk and started sorting my belongings on the bed.

'I have news, Francisco,' he said. 'We received correspondence from Calatrava just two days ago. King Jaime will send the Order of Calatrava to the Levant with his own entourage. The King's illegitimate sons – two of them – will accompany our force to the Levant. The royal bastards.'

'The best kind,' I replied.

'We will set out for certain by autumn.'

'Thanks to the Lord,' I said.

I do not think I could have survived another winter in Montcada. Waiting to heed Sergio's grim call whispered in my ear every night.

Andrés began to laugh and edged his way toward me with open arms. He picked me up in a bear hug. As the breath was squeezed from my chest, I saw the miniature Christ looking directly at me, as if calling me to some unknown, unknowable fate.

'Then we wait for the bastards,' Andrés said.

★   ★   ★

A horn announced dinner. Andrés and I walked down to the Great Hall, on the first floor, where servants with basins of fresh water and towels attended to the washing of hands. Dirt from two days of travel was deeply embedded and only stubbornly abandoned my skin. Our company sat at the very end of the long oak table. The Baron occupied the head, Andrés and I on one side of him and Isabel just across, next to her father. Fireplaces carved into the two other walls provided ample heat for the room.

Giant tapestries covered two walls opposite each other. I was facing the martyrdom of John the Baptist in eight parts – from his captivity to his death. The first panel portrayed John, bound, imprisoned by Herod. In the second, Herod's niece, the beautiful Salome, danced for her uncle. The King was pleased; his eyes feasted on her graceful movements. Whereupon he promised with an oath to give her whatever she would ask, though it be half of his kingdom. In the fifth panel, she asked for the head of John the Baptist. The sixth showed King Herod sorrowful, as if John were his friend. For the oath's sake, he commanded that Salome's wish be fulfilled. In the eighth and final panel, Salome was smiling, holding up a platter with the head of the saint.

Baron Correa said grace to bowed heads before servants brought out bread and butter from the adjoining kitchen, quickly followed by a warm spiced wine. Two dishes of meat were served.

103

There was a large boar on a wood platter. It had been hunted by Andrés in my honor the day previous. Its mouth was stuffed with oranges, its eyes squinting at the diners contemptuously. The chief servant held the boar's head as Baron Correa carved the succulent meat. There was also a special dish of mutton stew, blended with rice and boiled in almond milk. I was famished from my journey and had to restrain my appetite so as not to appear impolite. A lighter fare of peas and beans cooked with onions and saffron was served after the meat, but I was never partial to the dish.

Baron Correa and I spoke of mutual acquaintances in Barcelona. He knew the Garcías, my neighbors. Baron Correa and Don García had served together on the King's Council, which fixed the amount of the annual tithe paid by Muslims in the new territories of Catalonia. One of the García sons had taken the Cross several years before. Baron Correa asked if the family had yet received word from the boy. I told him that they had not but that they remained hopeful of his return.

'Are you also hopeful, Francisco?' Isabel asked.

Yes, of course I am hopeful – these are the words that were expected of me, the words I should have spoken. But I did not.

'No, Isabel,' I said. 'I visit their house on occasion. It bears the scent of death.'

The conversation stopped sharply. It was a

disquieting comment. Casting my gloomy meditations during my first dinner in Girona. Idiot. I could not help myself.

Isabel was not deterred.

'What does death smell like?' she asked. A morbid question, but then I was responsible for its content.

'Isabel, let our guest eat in peace,' Baron Correa said. He smiled at me, a paternal, wary, lopsided smile, which seemed to counsel silence.

I was asked, though, and I would answer. I thought of the smell that permeated my brother Sergio's and my bedchamber in the weeks following his death.

'Sweet,' I said, 'as a room filled with incense and flowers.'

'What kind of flowers?' she asked.

'White roses,' I replied, 'just on the verge of decay.'

Our eyes met for an instant. Isabel, solemn, seemed to be contemplating my answer. Andrés was fidgeting with his knife. Baron Correa was pouring more wine into glasses that were already full.

An awkward silence broken by a burst of laughter from Isabel. Unrestrained, unbridled, limitless. I had never heard such a sound. She tried to stifle her laughter, placing her hand in front of her mouth. But it was useless. I stared at her in disbelief. Was this the same girl whose gray eyes seemed to grieve unflinching? How could she, seeing that darkness, knowing it, laugh at its very doorstep?

Except for Isabel's laughter, the room was silent. It seemed as if the entire company had ceased breathing. Baron Correa regarded me uncertainly, waiting for my reaction. Andrés was wincing. I was still gazing at Isabel, trying to comprehend this contradiction in her character. She stared back, her laughter cascading across the table, through the windows and the doors. I do not doubt that the serfs resting in their huts after their day of toil could hear the reverberations.

Alongside Isabel's laughter, I heard a remote, forgotten sound, retrieved from the dungeons of another lifetime. It was my own laughter, twisted, forlorn. It seemed to come from deep within my stomach and built in waves. Andrés and Baron Correa were baffled. They looked back and forth between Isabel and me. Gradually, they joined in the laughter, at first cautiously, and then with more abandon. The servants took their cue from their master. Very soon, every person in the dining hall was laughing with Isabel, as if she were the conductor of a musical composition that reached its meridian and then gradually subsided.

'Next time I smell roses I will surely think of you, Francisco,' Isabel managed to say between gasps.

Isabel reached across the table and placed her hand palm upward between the platter of blood-stained meat and the carafe of red wine. It occurred to me that Isabel intended to hold my hand in a gesture indicating her goodwill and the benign nature of her joking. I hesitated, though, lest I was mistaken – you can imagine the embarrassment if I tried to grasp her hand and she had not such intention. Isabel nodded to me, though, and her open smile encouraged my advance. I raised my hand cautiously and reached across the table to clasp her own. The meeting was brief – we withdrew our hands upon contact.

Andrés was never comfortable with the subject of death or dying. Perhaps he feared such talk would trigger my own spiral toward melancholy. He laughed with the others, but I could sense his unease. When the noise abated, he seized the opportunity to change the subject. He spoke of the future.

'Father, tell Francisco of Uncle Ramón's report from Calatrava. I fear he is skeptical of my rendition.'

Uncle Ramón bore no blood relation to the Correas. He was a close friend of the family, though, having fought with Baron Correa in the King's army against the Muslims. After participating in the campaign in the southern territories of Catalonia, Baron Correa retired to his estate in Girona and married. Ramón remained one of Christ's soldiers, eventually becoming the Grand Master of the Order of Calatrava.

In the commotion, Baron Correa did not hear his son's question. Andrés was forced to repeat himself to catch his father's attention.

'Yes, I am afraid Andrés' report is quite true,' Baron Correa responded. 'We received a message from Ramón two days ago. The Order of Calatrava will accompany the King's sons in the forefront of the expedition.'

Andrés held my arm. 'You see, my friend, we will be fighting the Saracens in short order.'

Isabel's laughter faded at the mention of the Cross. Her smile turned down, almost disdainful. She glowered at Andrés, although he did not seem to notice. Then she turned to me.

'Francisco,' she said, 'why do you join my brother on this mad adventure?'

Andrés sighed loudly and responded before I could answer: 'Isabel, be quiet. You know nothing of these matters.' Andrés' exasperated tone indicated that this was not the first time brother and sister had engaged the subject.

'Perhaps your friend can speak for himself, brother,' Isabel said.

'Yes, Isabel,' I said, 'on a good day, I can. I go with your brother on this mad adventure. We intend to be the heart of Christ's army. The heart and the soul.'

She studied me, trying to discern my intentions, perhaps even the nature of my faith. She spoke to Andrés, but her stare never left my face.

'Brother, I think your friend mistakes my youth for naiveté.'

'That was not my intent,' I stated, 'but if I misspoke, please accept my apology.'

Perhaps my tone had contained a certain sarcasm, but I did not intend to insult my friend's sister. Evidently, Isabel did not accept my apology. She continued to examine me without responding. She seemed to be waiting for a clarification. The heavy weight of her gaze perturbed me.

Andrés came to the rescue. 'Father, Isabel forgets herself again. Is it her place to approve or disapprove of my decisions or those of our cousin? Or even to question my course of action? Isabel, you are my sister. My younger sister. Not my mother.'

Isabel remained upright, at ease, unaffected by her brother's chastisement. Until the mention of her mother. Then her body sank back into her chair as if absorbing a blow.

Baroness Correa had died while giving birth to Isabel. The mother started to bleed shortly after the birth. The doctor was unable to stop the hemorrhage, and the young mother bled to death. Andrés was three years old at the time. He never spoke of his mother. I learned of her death and the surrounding circumstances from one of our colleagues at the seminary whose family also came from Girona. Andrés seemed to have banished the painful event from his mind. Not so Isabel. The tragic loss burned a sepulchral black into the soft ridges of her gray eyes.

This misfortune, then, this was the source of Isabel's understanding – consecrated on her birthday, in her mother's blood. This burden was the looking glass into which I peered when I first encountered Isabel.

Baron Correa perceived his daughter's distress and intervened swiftly to protect her. 'Andrés, you will watch your tongue. Isabel will always speak her mind at this table.' He then turned to me. 'You see, Francisco, my daughter believes that Christ was a man of action.'

'Then I would think, Baron Correa,' I said, 'that she would support her brother's desire to take the Cross. How much more active can one be than to fight under His banner?'

Isabel did not wait for her father's response. She had recovered sufficiently from her brother's comment and would explain herself. She addressed her father, but her comments were clearly intended for her brother. Andrés shook his head as if to protest his father's tolerance for his sister's liberties.

'Yes, Father,' Isabel said, 'Christ is a man of action. But there are different types of action, different motivations. Certainly not all action, even if cloaked in the guise of Christian service, derives its legitimacy from Our Savior. I fear, Father, that my brother's decision to take the Cross has more to do with a desire for martial glory than with the Lord's call.'

Andrés banged his fist on the wood table so that our plates and utensils jumped. Stunned by the sound, one of the servant boys dropped a clay pot full of mutton stew on the floor. The ceramic shattered into a thousand pieces that glittered on the stone floor. The boy stood to the side and bowed his head as if in recognition of his unworthiness to serve at his master's table. The dogs rushed past the boy to get to the fallen stew. Everyone except Andrés seemed absorbed by the distraction.

Over the din of the lapping dogs, Andrés spoke sharply to his sister: 'Francisco and I do not pretend to imitate Christ, but we will be men of action in the Levant. With or without your blessing.'

'Sometimes, Francisco, when my brother is at a loss for words, he will express himself with his fist.' This I already knew. 'And do you agree with my brother, Francisco?' Isabel asked.

I was in a difficult situation. Of course, I would stand by Andrés, but I did not want to offend my other cousin twice in the same evening, nor become the next subject of her interrogation. I managed just barely to find an acceptable medium. I avoided the topic altogether.

'I have never considered myself a man of action,' I said, 'except when I was very young and I encountered a dragon or a rare species of Cyclops known to inhabit the outskirts of Barcelona.'

Andrés laughed loudly and slapped my back.

'My daughter has never been bashful about expressing her opinions, Francisco,' Baron Correa said.

'Why should she be,' I replied, 'when she has much to say?'

111

He smiled at the compliment to his daughter. Isabel looked at me skeptically.

'You give my sister too much credit, friend,' Andrés said.

When Andrés knocked at my door in the morning, I was wrapped in a green wool blanket, watching the red dawn peer over the horizon. The remnants of the snowstorm had passed. The sky would be clear for the hunt. We met at the stable, where the servants had already prepared our horses and provisions for the day, my bow and arrows slung on the side of Pancho. Andrés and I were the first to arrive. Baron Correa and Isabel followed several minutes later. Isabel wore a purple dress and cloak with a silver clasp at the collar. Small embroidered shoes peeked out from below the hem of her dress. Her hood was pulled back. I could see the loose strands of her hair tucked behind her ears, except for one that stubbornly eluded her efforts and settled, curving, across her cheek.

Andrés looked at Isabel from head to toe and frowned.

'Father,' Andrés said, 'we go to shoot deer, not to dance. With her outfit, Isabel will chase away our prey before we even reach the woods. I do not understand why you humor Isabel and her ridiculous requests. A woman should leave the hunt to the men of the family.'

'Isabel, dear,' Baron Correa responded, 'your manner of dress is a bit unorthodox. Perhaps next time you can wear a more natural color. Andrés, you are as much to blame as Isabel for her vestment. She has little experience and cannot be expected to know the proper attire. As her older brother, you should have counseled her on such matters.'

'Thank you, Father,' Isabel said, glancing sidelong at her older brother.

We set out in single file with Andrés leading toward the mountain range that I had viewed from my window. We rode east, toward the sun. Its reflection off the snow created a blinding glare. For much of the ride I closed my eyes and ceded to Pancho the responsibility of following the party. As we moved forward, I lost myself in the steady, labored breathing of the horses. Isabel began the journey at the back, but I changed places with her several times so that we shared duties bringing up the rear. We kept a good pace toward the mountain range, and Isabel never fell behind or faltered.

Because I was so close to Isabel, I could hear her talking with her horse. It was a peculiar habit, not because she spoke to her horse – many knights do so regularly. Isabel seemed to be engaged in an animated philosophical conversation. She and her horse, Flacito, covered many subjects together but seemed to focus on the stupidity of the crusade. Judging by Isabel's responses, Flacito seemed even surer on this point than she.

'Flacito,' Isabel said, 'do you really believe those

who take the Cross are often men without direction or purpose?'

At several moments I had to restrain myself from refuting a point made by Flacito, reminding myself that horses do not have the gift of speech.

After half an hour, we met the second party, neighbors of the Correas – Guillem and Miguel Clemente, father and son. Two servants on foot accompanied them. I suppose Baron Correa invited his neighbors in an effort to forge a more beneficial relationship with a family that, after the Correas, was the largest landholder in Girona. The fathers greeted each other warmly. Despite Baron Correa's introduction, neither Clemente seemed to take an interest in or notice my person.

Miguel, the son, was twenty-nine years old, ten years my senior. He wore a thick black robe with fur collar and a matching silk hat. His raven curls, well oiled, protruded from his hat. He seemed quite pleased by Isabel's presence. He rode most of the way next to her. From where I sat on Pancho, I could not help but overhear parts of their conversation. Actually, it was more a monologue – Miguel did all the speaking – mostly about the important contacts of the family or the extent of their property. I believe he made an inventory of the entire estate he stood to inherit, down to the last pig. Isabel's responses invariably consisted of only one word – 'sí' or 'bueno.' But she spoke in an enthusiastic tone that suggested to me a partiality to Miguel. Perhaps, I thought, her inappropriate dress did not stem from inexperience, but instead from anticipation of Miguel Clemente's company. Perhaps Baron Correa and Isabel had more ambitious plans for the hunt than catching our dinner.

I do not doubt that Miguel has certain attributes that would make him an appealing husband and a convenient ally for the Correa family. Given Isabel's youth, I suspected that she would be swayed by the superficial benefits of the match. I could picture it – a fall wedding in the garden of the Correa estate, under the watchful eye of the Virgin statue, a bridal terrace of silver leaves, Isabel's hair tied up under a headdress de moda. Andrés and I would be fighting in the Levant by then.

It was a long ride up toward the mountains. Pancho's gait was frustratingly uneven, and Miguel droned on with his soliloquy. Circumstances finally forced Miguel to suspend his discourse. We reached the foot of the mountains, a thickly wooded area where the deer found shelter. The hunt was on, and conversation amongst the party ceased. We slowed the pace to survey our surroundings. The narrow birch trees created a maze for our horses.

We rode abreast of each other, as an army on the advance, one solid line through the forest. Miguel and Isabel were on the far right, Baron Correa and Señor Clemente in the middle, and Andrés and I on the left. For some time, we rode without crossing game. A tiny hare scurried to the left, but neither Andrés nor I deemed it worth the arrow. I had a strong and strange desire to make the first kill – strange, I say, because I am usually not one to find contest with other members of a hunting party.

It was Miguel, though, who spotted the first deer. He practically ran into it as we climbed over a ridge. The deer seemed as startled as we. Eyes opened wide, the animal bolted upright, paralyzed by the sight of intruders in its sanctuary. Miguel had aimed his bow before any of us had a chance to react. The arrow whistled through the air and lodged itself in the hind leg of the deer. The wounded animal remained standing and tried to hobble toward a patch of brush. To my surprise, the Clementes seemed quite pleased with Miguel's shot and in no rush to finish the job. Señor Clemente even congratulated his son.

My brother Sergio had taught me to hunt when I was old enough to ride and shoot. I had a natural facility with bow and arrow, and my skills soon surpassed Sergio's. I could take down a buck at a full gallop from one hundred feet.

Sergio always emphasized the importance of an 'instantaneous death.' That is, killing an animal with the first arrow to avoid unnecessary suffering and bring distinction to the entire hunting party. With this instruction in mind, I readied my bow. As I did so, Señor Clemente yelled at me to hold my arrow – the kill, he said, was Miguel's. These were the first words he had uttered to me. I ignored him and discharged an arrow that pierced the deer's neck and ended its life before its body hit the snow.

Señor Clemente approached me, his horse trotting, his right hand raised and curled tightly in a fist. 'The deer was Miguel's,' he stated. 'Miguel was the first to draw blood.' He shook his fist and repeated himself.

I did not protest. I did not say a word. Miguel cantered toward me. When he was at my side, he placed his bow against Pancho's saddle so that it was pressing slightly against my backside.

'If you were not the guest of the Correas,' he said, 'I might not overlook this indiscretion.'

'And if you were not the guest of the Correas,' I responded, 'I would return your bow in pieces.'

Miguel lifted his weapon slowly.

After this incident, the whole party took to the hunt with more purpose. I felled another deer from a distance. It was a difficult shot, most of the animal obscured by a tree. The arrow entered at the front of the neck and buried itself in the body.

When we reached the deer seconds later, the breath of the animal had already expired. Baron Correa, leaning forward in his mount and looking down at the dead animal, remarked that he did not think my equal in marksmanship could be found in all the province of Girona. Señor Clemente expressed his view that two clean shots cannot establish the skill of an archer – a true statement, but ill-said under the circumstances. I tied the body of the animal on the broad back of Pancho, and the party proceeded forward.

Miguel killed another deer, this time with his first arrow. Miguel told one of the servants to gather it from the ground. As the man approached the deer, Miguel used his rope as a lasso. He threw it around the torso of the servant, binding his arms to his body. He pulled the rope tight, then went off on a gallop, dragging the man behind him. I felt temporarily disoriented, stunned – as if what I was seeing could not actually be happening. Perhaps, I thought, Miguel was staging a joke in which the servant played a voluntary role. The sound of the man's body slashing through the snow reminded me of sledding with Sergio in the hills of our estate. I would wrap my arms around Sergio's neck and scream in terror as we jumped over bumps and shifted our weight to avert collisions with rocks and trees, sometimes just barely. Señor Clemente's shouting disturbed my reverie. The father was laughing and pointing in the direction of the servant, helpless, skidding across the ground.

Before I could collect my thoughts, Andrés took off after Miguel. I could hear the hoofs beating the icy ground and see the awesome figure of my friend, his back turned toward us, gaining quickly on Miguel. Andrés unsheathed his dagger and leaned forward on his mount. He seemed a lion ready to pounce, a warrior closing in for the kill. He held his dagger aloft. Señor Clemente stopped laughing.

Miguel Clemente would see another sunrise, though. Andrés drew even with his neighbor. In one deft stroke, he sliced the rope that bound the servant. The man slid a short distance before slowing and stopping in a snowbank. Andrés put away his dagger. He trotted toward the fallen servant and reached down to pull him to his feet. The man appeared to be uninjured.

Miguel galloped for several seconds before turning around. He came back to our party holding the cut rope and laughing.

'Baron Correa,' he said, 'I wish I had known of Andrés' sentiments concerning the landless. I would have brought along a serf or two as a gift.'

Baron Correa, his mouth open, stared dumbly at his neighbor. Isabel, who had been on the outside of the party, trotted toward Miguel. There was nothing extraordinary in her movement. That she carried a grave mission was unmistakable, though. One by one, our eyes turned to follow her path. When Isabel was directly in front of Miguel, she stood in her horse uneasily for several seconds. She seemed on the verge of saying something. But the words eluded her. Without warning, she slapped Miguel fiercely across the cheek. The sharp sound echoed through the valley, up into the mountains and then back down again.

Miguel stood dazed and disabled before his assailant. His hat had fallen to the snow. He seemed a child, mortified by an unexpected and public punishment from a woman just over half his age. He placed his palm on the injured cheek, trying to rub the sting away. Isabel did not move from her position. I saw out of the corner of my eye that Andrés was holding his hand to his dagger, lest Miguel attempt to retaliate against his sister. It was a precarious moment. Even my horse, Pancho, stood completely still, holding his breath.

Finally, Miguel's face broke into a joyless smile.

'Hysterical women,' he said, 'should remain at home when their men are hunting.'

Miguel dismounted, picked up his hat, and brushed the snow from the silk folds. He returned to his horse and rode back to his father.

That evening at dinner, we ignored the incident and the Clementes. No words needed to be spoken. Baron Correa praised my skill with a bow, but I felt only shame. I wished that I could have relived the moment when Miguel threw his lasso. Perhaps I could have shot the rope through and put an end to the masquerade before the servant suffered such an indignity. I sat at dinner, despite the long day, without hunger. I looked at Andrés and occasionally at Isabel, their noble actions highlighting my own feeling of inadequacy.

Baron Correa stated that Isabel had proved herself an able rider and announced that she was ready to carry a bow. Isabel was gleeful. With a mouthful of venison, Andrés grunted in protest. Baron Correa asked if I would give his daughter archery lessons.

'Father,' Andrés said vehemently, 'a woman has no place carrying a weapon. It is unseemly.'

'Was it unseemly,' Isabel responded, 'for Eleanor of Aquitaine to don armor before marching into battle against the Saracens in Syria one hundred years ago?'

'I thought, Isabel,' Andrés said, 'you did not approve of the crusade.'

'You are mistaken, brother. What I do not approve of is your motivation in taking the Cross.'

'Father, Isabel talks like a sophist. She condemns the very act she now holds up as a virtuous example.'

'Francisco,' Baron Correa said, temporarily ignoring the disputants, 'I fought side by side with Uncle Ramón for three years. The infidel soldiers sometimes greatly outnumbered our forces. No trial, though, could prepare me for the challenges posed by my own children.'

The Baron turned to Andrés.

'Eleanor was Queen of France and England, was she not, Andrés?'

'Yes, Father,' Andrés responded, 'but she was royalty.'

'If Eleanor could make war on the infidels,' the Baron said, 'then surely Isabel can carry a bow.

'Francisco, what say you?' the Baron asked. 'Will you teach Isabel to shoot?'

'Yes, Uncle,' I said, 'I would be happy to assist.'

Isabel kissed her father and thanked him. I felt as

121

if a great gift had been undeservedly bestowed on me. Andrés was shaking his head in silent protest.

Rolando Esteban was a faithful squire to his master. He was loyal, good-natured, hardworking. His lack of riding skills made him an ideal chaperon for my lessons with Isabel. At dawn, the three of us rode together to the mountains, where the trees provided targets for Isabel's practice. Rolando was invariably out of breath, struggling courageously to keep Isabel and me in sight. We never outran him, as that would compromise the honor of both Rolando and Isabel. But for all intents and purposes, Isabel and I rode alone, side by side.

The morning sun rose quickly. Except for our initial greetings, we did not speak to each other during the ride to the mountains. The sight of dawn flooding the mountains in its tawny wake seemed to render our conversation superfluous, an imposition on the flawless landscape. Even Isabel's discussions with Flacito were muted.

When we reached the woods, I demonstrated the proper form of shooting, exaggerating and separating the individual movements of the fluid motion – placing the arrow exactly perpendicular to the bow, drawing it straight back, fixing the target, and discharging. The lessons provided a balm, the sun casting its glow on my face and diffusing the somber haze of the days and nights in Montcada.

Isabel and I hardly spoke – only to discuss the mechanics of proper shooting form and to identify particular targets. I am not acquainted with feminine attitudes or activities, and I was not sure if the silence between us might be awkward for the girl. Toward the end of the first week, I tried to start a conversation. We were one hour from the estate, almost at the mountains, when I spoke to her.

'Miguel Clemente deserved that slap that you gave him.'

When Isabel did not respond, I presumed that my words had drowned in the wind. I repeated myself.

She was looking straight ahead toward the mountains.

'Yes,' she said. 'I heard you the first time.'

We were left in silence once again – the grunts of our horses, the snow grinding underneath their hooves.

When a person is learning to shoot, it is critical to acquire the proper form immediately. Bad habits are difficult to reverse, sometimes impossible. For this instruction, manual contact is often necessary – so it was when Sergio taught me and when my father taught him.

Isabel and I focused much of the first week on proper stance and the timing of her release. To correct the contortion in her posture, I would stand facing her, using my hands to adjust her hip placement. To redress her tendency to release prematurely, I would stand behind her, my chest pressed to her back, my hands placed on her hands to guide them. In this position, my cheek brushed against hers. I could hear her short breaths as she aimed her bow. Sometimes I would breathe the same air that she had just exhaled.

Over the course of a few weeks, Isabel's marksmanship improved dramatically. I taught her to shoot riding horseback, first trotting and then at a gallop. I lectured her on the intricacies of hunting – the identity of different footprints in the snow, the necessity of remaining still to discern the movement of game, the importance of the first shot. She always listened patiently, but I suspected that she knew more than she let on. I say this because I never had to repeat myself. Isabel seemed to acquire proper technique immediately following my corrections. She was almost too polite, as if she did not want to hurt my feelings by revealing the true extent of her knowledge, and, conversely, the pointless nature of my lectures.

Two weeks after our first lesson, Baron Correa permitted Isabel to carry a bow on the hunt. During the ride to the mountains, Baron Correa questioned me extensively on Isabel's marksmanship.

'Be patient, Uncle,' I told him. 'Your daughter's abilities will be manifest soon enough.'

Isabel lagged behind, seemingly indifferent. I knew that she was anxious to prove herself, though, if only to annoy her brother, who rode morosely by my side.

When we reached the woods, the party dismounted. Baron Correa pointed out various objects for Isabel – trees, branches, bushes. Isabel loosed an arrow at each target. Observing his daughter's ability, Baron Correa increased the difficulty. Isabel responded gallantly to the challenge. She missed a few targets, but on the whole, her performance was quite satisfactory.

When Baron Correa was done testing his daughter, he put his hand on my shoulder and pronounced his judgment: 'Nice, Francisco. Very nice work.'

Andrés was skipping rocks across the snowfield, pretending to ignore his sister's display.

We mounted our horses and rode forward. Baron Correa spoke of the seasonable weather, but no one seemed to pay much attention: I managed a few curt responses, but I was focused on the landscape, watching for any movement. It was not long before we came upon several deer grazing in a valley. They noticed our presence as well and made for the nearby woods. We all looked to Isabel, but she needed no prodding. She was off at a gallop. She drew her arrow back as she came upon the straggler. Then she released the hemp string. The deer tumbled in the snow and came to a crashing halt.

The blade had pierced the shoulder, but the deer was only wounded, lying on its side, voicing a pitiful, rasping cry. Andrés galloped toward the animal, dismounting with dagger in hand. He pulled its floppy ears back and cut clean across the throat. The deer fell silent; its head dropped in the soft snow. Andrés walked back to his horse, glancing at his sister, slowly wiping each side of his bloodied dagger on the sleeve of his cloak. Isabel did not notice her brother, though. She seemed entranced by the scarlet puddle of blood that soaked the white snow. Her hands cupped firmly over her mouth. Baron Correa finally pulled her away.

Every morning, Isabel collected the leftover food from the evening meal in a large leather sack. When we returned from our archery lessons, she rode to different parts of the estate, distributing food to families of serfs who were unable to work because of sickness or injury.

Baron Correa had ambivalent feelings concerning his daughter's charitable activities.

'Isabel,' he said, at dinner one night, 'I am pleased with your visits across the estate. The family should demonstrate its benevolence to our charges.'

'Thank you, Father,' she said. 'I have made many friends.'

'Yes, Isabel.' Baron Correa raised his index finger. 'I wanted to speak with you about this very issue. I have received reports of your contacts with our serfs. My darling, friendship exists between people of similar classes. For example, your brother and Francisco are friends. Their friendship is based not only on mutual affinity, but also on the similarity of their circumstances, their opportunities, their acquaintances. If two people shared an affinity but lived in different worlds, friendship would not be possible. It would be unnatural. Sympathy, yes. Alms-giving, yes. But not friendship. Because of your youth and gender, these complexities may be difficult to grasp. Look to your brother's and my example when you become confused. Do you understand your father, Isabel?'

'I believe I understand you, Father,' Isabel said. 'Andrés then could be friends with Miguel Clemente, but he could not be friends with our stable hand Ernesto, because Ernesto occupies a station below him.'

'Exactly, my dear,' Baron Correa stated triumphantly.

'Andrés,' Isabel said, 'could I ask for your guidance on these issues from time to time?'

Andrés had been focusing his attention on the food on his plate and was taken off-guard by his sister's question. He hesitated for a second, then said, 'Certainly.' Baron Correa was smiling broadly, well satisfied.

'Brother,' Isabel said, 'perhaps I could bother you with a quick question?'

'Yes, Isabel.' Andrés did not look up from his food. 'What is it?'

'Would you prefer the friendship of Ernesto or Miguel Clemente?'

'Andrés,' Baron Correa stated, 'has been concentrating on his meal, my dear. Perhaps we should explain the context. The issues are quite complex.'

'No, Father,' Isabel said. 'I believe my brother, as a man of nineteen years, will understand intuitively these matters.'

There was only a brief moment of indecision before Andrés answered. He scrutinized Baron Correa's face, as if the answer could be found in his father's guarded smile, then he made up his mind.

'Ernesto, of course,' Andrés stated. 'Miguel Clemente is a scoundrel.'

With those words, Andrés resumed eating, angling a suspicious glance in the direction of his sister.

'Yes, Father,' Isabel said, 'these issues are decidedly complex.'

Baron Correa did not again raise the issue of friendship between Isabel and the serfs during my stay in Girona. He was concerned for the safety of his daughter during her trips to different villages, though, and he instructed Andrés to escort her. I accompanied my friend and his sister on these tours of the estate. When Isabel realized that she had two escorts, she began to collect other materials – cloth, tools, candles, shoes – which Andrés and I, like wandering merchants, would carry in her trial.

Isabel was well known among the Correa serfs, and her visits were always welcome. She seemed to know all of them by name. She would walk arm in arm with the peasant girls and their mothers, engaged in animated conversation concerning a sick child, a dying crop, a quarrel between siblings, even the potential matches for a young member of the household. As I had never really known a peasant, I was fascinated by her discussions and would often try to eavesdrop.

Isabel and her companions would stroll down the main thoroughfare, weaving through horse – drawn carts, a flock of hissing geese, peasants returning from the open fields. On both sides of the path, black smoke poured from the roofs of the thatched huts, doors open for the traffic of children and animals – pigs, hens, cats – who lived in the shelter of their owners' homes. Piles of dung lay next to the larger huts, and the smell of manure permeated the street. The ring of the smith's hammer mingled with the barking of dogs and the crying of babies. It was a turbulent scene, but Isabel seemed quite at home.

The accident occurred on a Monday, three weeks after our first archery lesson. While Isabel made her rounds with the villagers, Andrés and I remained just outside the hamlet, practicing switching horses in midstride. This difficult exercise attracted a sizable audience from the village, particularly among the children. Andrés and I tried our best to entertain them. We would bring our horses to a gallop side by side. When we were exactly even, Andrés would stand in his stirrups, grab Pancho's saddle, and pull himself behind me. I would then reach for the grainy mane of his horse and leap into the saddle. Done well, the maneuver was exhilarating. The villagers would clap and yell their approval. Even the horses seemed to enjoy the challenge. Pancho would shake her head and whinny after our successful exchanges.

After an arduous, slightly tangled exchange, one of our spectators, a young boy, told us that the 'señorita' had departed to a nearby village. We rode after Isabel, hoping to intercept her before she reached her next destination. When we were halfway there, we caught sight of her. She was sitting still on her horse in the middle of a frozen lake that, according to Andrés, served as their swimming hole during the summer months.

'Ah, my impatient sister waits for once,' Andrés said.

But Isabel was not waiting. As we descended toward the lake, the hazardous nature of her situation became clear. The ice had thinned in the afternoon sun, and the weight of a mounted rider had caused fissures across the surface. Isabel was afraid to move lest the ice give way.

When we reached the lake, Andrés sprang from his horse and ran toward his sister. I spurred Pancho forward and seized Andrés by the shoulder just before he stepped onto the ice.

'The ice will not support your weight,' I said. 'You will fall through before you reach her. I will go.'

Andrés hesitated. He covered his face with his clenched fists. Then he stepped back to the shore. I dismounted, maintaining my hold on his shoulder lest he change his mind.

'Sister,' Andrés yelled, 'be still. Francisco comes for you now.'

I handed Andrés my cloak and then edged out on my hands and knees, crawling toward Isabel. A thin layer of freezing water on the surface of the ice soaked my clothes – my knees, my shins, my gloved hands. I spoke to Isabel as I approached her, telling her that it would be all right, that the ice would hold. When I was ten steps from her, I told her to dismount slowly and lie down on her stomach. She moved both legs to one side of Flacito but was reluctant to release her grip and test the ice.

'It will hold you,' I assured her, until she slid down the side of her horse and stood uneasily on the ice.

From the far side of the lake came a horrific sound. It began as an almost imperceptible rumble. The vibrations grew into a low thunder underneath the dark glass. Then the surface fractured. It sounded like the loud creaking door of an old stone church opening painfully after decades of disuse. A large and visible crack made a straight path for Isabel from the far side. Isabel stood immobile, balancing herself on a solid floor that would soon vanish. Her face white with fear, she glanced at me – imploring, as if I could change the course of events.

The crack gained speed until it was directly beneath Isabel. It paused briefly underneath her, as if it could not decide whether to break, and then continued to the other end of the lake. There was a brief, silent lull.

Andrés, grasping the transient respite, called from the bank. 'We are saved, saved!'

Then it happened. Isabel disappeared. The ice underneath her gave way. She was gone without a trace, both she and Flacito, swallowed up by the black lake. I moved quickly to the edge. The thin ice held my weight as I scanned the darkness for Isabel and shouted her name – as if she could answer. The cold water lapped against the edge of the ice, spilling onto my hands. Andrés was shouting. I could hear him approaching but his frenetic questions seemed to fade farther away.

It beckoned me – that frozen blackness. Or was it death itself? I slid over the ice and into that hole. My body was on fire from the freezing water. I could barely breathe. I kicked my legs to keep myself afloat and looked up at the blue sky, the bloodless clouds, aloof, impartial, gliding overhead. I curled my knees into my body, brought my arms together, and dove down into the murky water.

I opened my eyes underneath, but it was pitch black. I remained underwater for as long as my breath held out, and then returned to the surface. No sign of Isabel. Isabel's horse surfaced near me. It seemed to be moving in slow motion, slapping its legs against the water's edge, smashing the ice in the process and expanding the dark region. Andrés had somehow reached the edge of the hole and was shouting wild, incomprehensible words.

I took a deep breath and dove again. I pulled myself down with long strokes of my arms. The lake was surprisingly deep. It took several seconds to descend. I could see nothing when I reached the bottom. I swam underwater in a circle trying to cover as much space as I could. I reached around me like a blind man but felt only water. Isabel was nowhere.

I exhaled my last breath slowly. I felt a sharp ache, as if a vise were tightening around my chest, crushing it and my spine. Even amidst this pain, I did not want to ascend. How could I return and face Baron Correa and explain that his daughter was dead? How could I deliver that merciless sorrow to the Correa home?

The pain slowly subsided, as if someone were loosening the vise, and, despite my somber thoughts, I felt a strange feeling of peace. I was so tired. That icy grave seemed a restful end.

I wondered where Isabel and I would be found when the ice thawed in the spring. Perhaps we would be close to each other – almost touching. I could hear my own heart beat in the silent vacuum of that hole, and I could see myself suspended and floating as the icy water began to lay claim to my body. I wondered whether my brother had felt the same sensations when he descended the ocean. I wondered what the Correas were having for dinner that evening.

I stretched my arms to their full length and sighed silently as if I were going to sleep. It was a placid surrender. When my right arm was fully stretched upward, my hand brushed against a solid mass. I thought it was a piece of ice floating downward, but when I reached up with the other hand I was holding a delicate ankle. It was Isabel.

The sun must have been shining directly above the lake, because when I pulled Isabel to me, I could see her face clearly. Her eyes were closed. Her blond hair swirled around her face. Her skin appeared as porcelain, as smooth as the figure of Christ that hung on my wall at the Correa estate. She was beautiful.

The desperate screams of Andrés penetrated into that silent space and awakened me as if from a dream. I looked up, in the direction of the voice, toward the sunlight. I was still alive. Andrés was calling me back to the world.

I hooked my arms under Isabel's shoulders and kicked the water underneath. We headed for the light. Our ascent seemed to last several minutes. Or was it days?

Save me, O God; for the waters are come in unto my soul.

We finally reached the surface, an explosion of ice and fire. Isabel was a stone. I needed all my strength to bring her body to the edge. Andrés was waving at me frantically. I pushed her toward him. He grabbed her arms and dragged her onto the solid surface. I followed her, crawling out from that black burial chamber.

For several minutes, I lay back on the ice and watched my friend trying to raise the dead – his own sister. Andrés was shaking her savagely and shouting her name. His cries seemed to come from within me, a pain that trespassed the icy numbness and pierced my chest like a barbed arrow. I closed my eyes and wished that I had never brought her body to the surface. I wished that I had remained in Barcelona and never come to the Correa estate.

She woke abruptly. Her gray eyes opened wide – bewildered, terrified – as if she were seeing the world for the first time in all its sad, wretched beauty. And then she began gasping for air and coughing fiercely, exhaling a gush of water. Andrés was holding his sister's arms to steady her. The clear water flowed from her mouth as if she had swallowed half the lake. As I looked at her pale, blue face, my chest tightened. I felt a strange pressure behind my eyes, as if tears were building that some internal force refused to relinquish. I stretched my hand forward on the ice and touched the water, expelled and warmed by Isabel's body.

Isabel's coughing gradually subsided, and Andrés let her limp body down onto the ice. He undid the front clasp that held his cloak and draped his sister in that brown robe. He told me to watch Isabel as he went for the rope I kept on Pancho's saddle. He thought we could tie it around her waist and pull her toward the shore. As Andrés crawled away, Isabel began to shiver. I clutched her close to try to thaw the chill from her body and ease her shuddering – but in vain, as I too was soaking wet and freezing.

I watched my friend maneuver his massive body to avoid falling through the ice – creeping, rolling, clambering – until he had made it to the shore. On land, Andrés sprinted toward Pancho to retrieve the rope. Before he reached my horse, another crack erupted. I followed this new breach as it traveled almost instantaneously in a zigzag pattern across the lake, blocking our path to the shore. The surface underneath Isabel and me shifted until it was slanting downward toward the intersection of the two fissures. It seemed as if the ice over the entire lake would collapse in a heap.

When I looked again to the shore, Andrés had gathered the rope and turned back. He raced onto the ice but fell through the surface near the bank in a shallow recess of the lake. He was cursing and slapping the water with his gloved hands.

'Francisco, I am useless,' he shouted. 'The ice will not hold me. Listen, you and Isabel must come to the shore yourselves. You must crawl together. Now! Can you do that?'

I did not respond. I did not know the answer. Perhaps I could make it to the shore. Perhaps. Isabel was another matter. She was lying on her side, exhausted. She seemed unable to raise her head.

'Isabel,' I said, 'we must move quickly. The ice will give at any moment.'

She looked at me vacantly. She mumbled something unintelligible. I slapped her cheek.

'Isabel, time is against us. We must crawl to the closest side of the lake.' I could see that she was trying to understand my words, but it was as if I were speaking in a foreign tongue.

'Spread yourself over the ice,' I said, 'so that no body part places too much weight on the frail surface and breaks through.'

I stroked her hair and repeated myself several times until she nodded. She did not move, though. I shook her and pushed her forward, until she started crawling. I followed directly behind.

She moved weakly, uncertainly, resting at frequent intervals. But she made steady, if slow, progress toward the shore. When Isabel came to the new fissure, she stopped. It was the most dangerous point of our path. She was reluctant to cross it. But we had no choice. I told her to continue onward. With as much conviction as I could muster, I told her that we would soon reach the shore. She started forward gingerly. When she was directly over the crack, I could hear the ice breaking underneath the surface – the layers cracking one after the other. Isabel awaited her fate perfectly still – her lips pursed together, her eyes closed tightly. She was too tired to offer any other resistance. I watched her intently, concentrating my attention on her furrowed brow, as if I could somehow hold her above the surface through sheer will.

The creaking sound became high-pitched. It squealed and screeched. Then the noise faded, until it stopped altogether, leaving in its wake a restless hush. Isabel opened her eyes warily and, without moving her head, surveyed the platform beneath her. The ice had held.

'Go, Isabel,' I said. 'Go now.'

Isabel took my cue and scrambled just beyond the crack.

She looked back at me, and I motioned for her to proceed to the shore before I moved forward. If I fell through, the breach could well take her with me. She refused to move, though. So I slithered along the lake over the crack. The rumble began again and surged, until the entire lake was humming. I quickened my pace. In my haste, I allowed my right hand to place too much pressure on the surface. It pierced the ice, and dove into the freezing water. The small hole remained contained, though. I pulled my hand back carefully and continued. When I reached Isabel, we nodded to each other. I squeezed her hand lightly.

Andrés was shouting encouragement from the shore – 'thirty more feet, you can make it.' We set off again, this time crawling side by side. 'Fifteen feet,' Andrés yelled. 'Almost there.'

I was looking down when I felt the snow under my fingers. We had reached land.

Despite my immersion in water, my mouth was

parched. I dropped my face to the earth and scooped snow into my mouth. When I looked up, I saw Isabel's ashen face. Her teeth chattered, her body shook violently. Andrés' brown cloak had soaked through. Isabel would not last long outside in her condition. Andrés and I exchanged anxious glances, then quickly prepared our two horses for the return journey. Isabel's horse was gone, entombed in that faithless lake.

We decided that we could make the best time if Isabel rode with me on Pancho. The weight of Andrés alone was a strain for most horses, no less an extra person. Andrés helped me up into Pancho's saddle and placed his sister behind me. Isabel wrapped her arms around my ribs and rested her head on my shoulder. In this manner, we made our return to the Correa household.

At dusk, after an hour's journey, we reached the estate. Isabel and I were welded together in a cold, deathlike embrace. Andrés and several servants lifted Isabel and me off Pancho as if we were a fragile crystal statue. They placed us in front of the fire in the Great Hall. We were frozen in the same position we had held during the ride – Isabel clasping me from behind, her chest fused to my back. Icicles dangled from our hair like ornaments from a solstice celebration. Behind us, Baron Correa paced back and forth as the flames oscillated in an agitated, macabre dance. When the fire melted the ice that bound us one to the other, Isabel's body slipped to the floor. She lay there, broken. Baron Correa picked her up in his massive arms and ascended the stairs. Andrés helped me to my feet.

For the first three days, the Correa house was in turmoil. The house servants rushed back and forth with blankets and cold water in a vain effort to stem the fever that raged through Isabel's body. She fell in and out of this world. Her delirious cries could be heard throughout the household, even in my room with the door closed. Most of what she said was incomprehensible – words and phrases strung together in an indecipherable pattern. She seemed to be experiencing again the moments of terror on the frozen lake. She shouted my name several times. She called to me as if I were the one drowning and not she.

While we had rescued her body, her mind remained trapped in the nightmare of that ruthless oblivion. Andrés sat outside her room with his sword on his lap as if guarding his sister from the angel of death. He did not eat or sleep. Her father sent for a doctor from Tortosa, but it would be several days before his arrival and by that time her fate would be determined.

I recognized the slow onslaught of the same darkness that had engulfed my house in Barcelona. The Correa estate was being pulled down into that corrosive mourning. I knew the signs. I felt it in myself and through the house, in the family and the servants – silent tears, desperate questioning, looks of disbelief, mumbled prayers. I felt as if I was reliving the past. Four years ago, lying awake in my bed, listening to whispers in the hallway, the preparations for services in Sergio's honor, the aftermath of an ineffable sadness, like a Cross branded forever on your forehead.

A ray of light that had flickered was now being suffocated. The darkness was returning as if it had never left, as if it had always been waiting its chance to reassert itself. Isabel's death seemed unbearably inevitable. First Sergio, then Isabel – two icy graves.

On the fourth day, the fever broke. I was not present at the time. One of the servants subsequently told me her first words – 'Is it snowing?' – as if nothing had happened, as if the world had not approached the abyss and then stepped back.

Andrés relayed the news to me immediately. I did not notice him entering my room. Gaunt and haggard from three sleepless days of fasting, Andrés put his hands on my shoulders and spoke.

'Isabel will live.' That was all he said.

After he left the room, I stopped pacing and stood staring out the window. The sun was just breaking over the mountain range. The trees stretched out after a long night. The white snow glistened in the velvet light.

I walked over to the pew and knelt. I clasped my fingers together and said a prayer of thanks. Then I looked up to the figure of Christ. He was staring past me, preoccupied by his own suffering.

That afternoon, I entered the sick chamber for the first time. Isabel's bed was in the middle of the room. The walls were bare, white-washed. A jar of water and an empty cup stood atop a small wooden table. There were two chairs, one at her side, the other at the foot of the bed. Andrés was fast asleep in the latter.

I walked slowly to her side. She was propped up against pillows, glancing out the window. I sat down next to her bed. Isabel turned to face me. She smiled softly but did not speak. She was still weak. Her pale skin was flushed from the struggle to survive, tiny beads of sweat graced her forehead, her chest rose and fell unevenly. I picked up her left hand in my own and placed her palm on my cheek. I pulled myself toward her, resting my head on her stomach. Her yellow hair fell across my face. I could taste the bitter lake on the fine strands. She placed her hand on my head as I wept silently into the folds of the coarse wool blanket that covered her.

Isabel did not stir from her bed over the course of the next week. She slept through the day and evening, except for one hour at mid-day when she poked at the foods prepared in accordance with the instructions of the doctor Don Eximen de Tortosa. The doctor arrived two days after the fever broke. With Isabel sleeping soundly, Don Eximen struck a contemplative pose, scrutinizing his patient, his right arm on his hip, his left hand smoothing his long, unruly beard.

'Food,' Don Eximen said.

'Excuse me, Don Eximen?' Baron Correa said.

'Food,' the doctor repeated. 'The girl needs food.'

After delivering this prescription, naming several of his favorite dishes, and collecting a handsome fee, the doctor departed the estate. He had to return to Tortosa, he said, to tend to the illness of a 'distinguished, very distinguished member of the royal family.' His assistant, Brother Tagle, remained behind to administer 'spiritual nourishment' to Isabel.

The week passed smoothly – Isabel gradually regained her strength until she was able to take short walks in the garden. Andrés and I acted the part of ushers on these excursions – one of us on each side, our arms linked in hers to provide support. Isabel did not speak at first, focusing all her energy on circumnavigating the garden. Andrés and I would usually discuss the merits of different weaponry – whether, for example, a man with shield and sword would best a man with similar abilities but armed with crossbow and mace; or whether a man on horseback with lance but no shield would defeat a man with bow and arrow, horseless, but a marksman. On several instances, I had to interrupt Andrés to avoid any mention of the crusade or the Saracens, especially when he began

143

to use examples of weapons favored by the infidels. Neither of us wanted to provoke Isabel's reaction in her weakened condition. As her strides became longer each day, however, she took an increasing interest in our conversation.

During one of these excursions, a commotion broke out just outside the rock wall that enclosed the garden. A bull had escaped the pen. We could hear the servants trying to trap it in the meadow, shouting at each other and the bull. At the time, Isabel had been discussing her plan to enlarge the estate's chapel as a present to her father on his forty-fifth birthday. Andrés, bored with the topic and eager to join the fray, asked if he could be excused to chase the wayward bull. It was a novelty to hear Andrés ask permission of anyone, no less his sister. I suppose her brush with death gave Isabel a temporarily elevated status.

Upon hearing Andrés' request, Isabel glanced at me with raised eyebrows. 'Did my brother just seek permission to depart or did I lapse back into delirium?'

'It could only be a relapse,' I responded.

Andrés frowned, looked straight ahead, and then pretended to ignore us. Isabel left her brother in this torturous limbo for another minute before kissing his clenched cheek.

'Dear brother,' she said, 'one faithful arm will support me. Go where your heart calls you.'

As Andrés dashed off, we laughed at the absurd figure he cut, squeezing his bulk through the wiry branches, then scrambling over the rock wall.

Isabel and I continued around the garden. We tried to carry on the discussion, but whatever issue we engaged seemed irrelevant. My voice sounded shrill and hollow. Soon, Isabel and I were pacing the stone walkway with not a word. I tried desperately to think of a new, fertile subject. My mind was blank, though. Andrés' absence grew heavier, disconcerting. The distance between Isabel and me became tangible and oppressive. Our steps quickened. I tripped over a raised bed of herbs, the brown leaves frozen, barely managing to prevent myself from falling headlong into the snow. I resumed walking, but my legs and arms felt unwieldy. The sound of the snow crunching under our feet accented the untenable awkwardness of the situation. Surely, I thought, the hardships of war must be easier than this excruciating silence.

'I believe it will snow tonight.' Isabel said, temporarily salvaging the situation.

'Yes, it would seem so, Isabel.'

'Even now the clouds descend upon us,' she said.

I looked to the sky and saw only blue. 'Perhaps,' I said, 'we should inform your father so that he can instruct the servants to gather more firewood.'

'A fine idea,' she responded. 'I will tell him.'

I tried to think of a clever response to sustain the dialogue. I racked my brain, but the issue was exhausted, defunct. We were left where we began. I bit the inside of my lip until I tasted blood.

'My brother enjoys the chase,' Isabel finally said.

'Yes,' I responded, seizing upon the subject. 'Andrés and I used to race almost every day in Montcada.'

Isabel seemed not to hear me, though. She continued speaking, her tone becoming more familiar, the timbre of her voice keener. 'My brother is an explorer. He would make a great pirate if he had been born under different circumstances. He takes the Cross for the same reason he ran off just now. For the adventure.'

Isabel was studying me again. I glanced at her, then looked away, focusing on the path ahead.

'But not you, Francisco. Your nature differs markedly from my brother's. You did not chase the bull. You remained here with me. It is not adventure that you seek in the Levant.

'I would say it must be Christ, then,' Isabel continued. 'That you take the Cross to glorify His Name. Only you lack the severe, humorless manner that soldiers of Christ invariably adopt. And if that were your purpose, I doubt you would be such close friends with my brother. No, I do not believe you take the Cross for adventure or for Christ. And yet, you will risk everything on the crusade.'

'I think you have misjudged me, Isabel,' I responded. 'Your brother and I are not so different as you believe. I too take the Cross in search of adventure. I cannot imagine living the life of my father before I have had a chance to explore the world.'

She nodded thoughtfully and walked several more steps before speaking. 'I do not believe you.'

She spoke as if she were stating a fact. She was so certain of herself. Isabel did not believe me. This sixteen-year-old girl did not believe me. What right did she have to question me on this of all subjects?

'Well, Isabel, because God wills it.' I spoke in a patronizing, acid tone the rationale of our ancestors, the first crusaders. It had become the refuge of idiots and fanatics. As soon as the words escaped me, I regretted having spoken them. My anger at her presumption dissipated. The bitter taste of my sarcasm lingered in my mouth.

I did not see Isabel's reaction. I felt the muscles of her arm grow taut. She stopped walking and stood transfixed. She seemed to be considering my statement, absorbing its meaning slowly. When she was done, she unthreaded her arm from mine and ran ahead toward the house. I stood still for several seconds, cursing myself. Then my arms and legs propelled me after her.

I caught Isabel at the closed door, where she was fumbling with the latch. I grabbed her arm. She tried to turn away, but I held her fast. She was crying. I spoke her name.

Isabel.

My intonations betrayed me. The graceful sound, the manner in which the syllables of her name banded together. There was in my voice an unpracticed intimacy, an unforeseen reverence.

Isabel's lips curled downward in a sullen scowl, but her eyes were soft. She stopped struggling to free herself.

I expected a cold slap. No, I did not expect it. I hoped for that release, her touch, even jagged. She would not give me the satisfaction. Her wounded eyes held the same unspoken question. I groaned. I held my breath. With images of my dead brother flooding my mind, I tried to answer her.

'I take the Cross for a ghost, Isabel, a dead man.'

I stopped speaking. I had never talked about Sergio – even with Andrés. It was a private matter. But Isabel reached out and pulled my cloak forward as if to encourage me, and I continued.

'I take the Cross for my brother. Sergio waits suspended between heaven and hell. He waits for me . . . for me. Only I can tip the scales in his favor. I must fulfill his ill-fated mission.'

She reached for my hand and held it tightly.

'Maybe your brother is already in heaven,' she said, 'and your sacrifice is unnecessary.'

I paused and looked beyond the garden, toward the horizon and then back at Isabel. 'The demons who keep me awake at night, they tell me of Sergio's agonies. They whisper secrets of the sea that will carry me to the Holy Land. They call me forth to meet my destiny.'

'You could remain in Girona with us, Francisco,' Isabel said. 'You are safe here. No demons are allowed on the Correa estate.' She smiled weakly.

'Yes, I saw the sign when I came to the estate several weeks ago,' I said. 'Regrettably, my demons are illiterates, a band of ill-mannered, uneducated tormentors. They have little respect for the ordinary courtesies.'

She gave a short laugh, but there was no solace. I offered her a handkerchief. She wiped her face and returned the cloth. The sweet tears woven indelibly into the fabric. I kept that holy relic under my metal shirt, until it was lost forever in the battle of Toron.

With the back of my hand, I tried to wipe away her tears. She turned my hand over and placed her lips on my palm.

Brother Tagle, Don Eximen's assistant, forbade Isabel from venturing outside over the next two days on account of a snowstorm that blanketed the manor. I wanted to see her, but not in the company of others. I hoped in vain that Isabel would escape her confinement for a rendezvous in the garden. I remained in my room peering through the colorless glass, waiting for her appearance. I declined Andrés' invitation to go sledding and faked a bout of nausea to avoid successive meals. I was both prisoner and sentry, confined to my quarters, and keeping steadfast vigil over my captive in the garden, the stone Virgin. I tried to remember the exact words of my conversation with Isabel, but it was in the silent spaces that I lived during those two days – the silent spaces between our words, the awkward gestures that chased away old shadows like the hushed breezes that swept the snowdrift from my windowsill.

After two days, the storm ended. It was dark outside when I exited my quarters and trod soundlessly down the hallway to Isabel's room. I stood close to the door and heard the baritone voice of Brother Tagle. He spoke of God's love for all living things.

'Jesus Christ,' he said, 'saved your life. Only through His love can you be completely healed.' He read from the Scriptures.

'I opened to my beloved, but my beloved had turned and gone.'

Though Brother Tagle was the reader, I felt it was Isabel who spoke those words, a rueful condemnation. I touched my palm to the rough grain of the closed door. I could hear her breathing.

'I adjure you, O daughters of Jerusalem, if you find my beloved, that you tell him, I am sick with love.'

CHAPTER 6

UNCLE RAMÓN

I was walking down the staircase when a party of three knights entered the Correa manor. Stamping the cold from their feet, they watched me descend. When I set foot on the landing, two of them tackled me. My face pressed hard against the cold stone. A knife held against my throat. My empty fists pried open. My body searched roughly down to my ankles.

'He has no weapon, Ramón,' one of my attackers said. 'Speak up, man. Who are you? What is the nature of your business in these parts?'

Andrés' appearance at the end of the hallway afforded considerable relief. Unfortunately, he seemed more interested in greeting my assailants, hugging them warmly, than in rescuing me. Finally, he seemed to notice my presence.

'Uncle Ramón,' he said, 'the man who polishes the floor is my friend Francisco de Montcada. We are your newest recruits in the Order of Calatrava.'

As the knee was lifted from my back, I raised myself.

'Delighted,' I said, as I rubbed my sore cheek. I offered my hand. It was nearly broken in Ramón's tight grip.

Uncle Ramón was no more Andrés' uncle than he was my own. Just the same, everyone seemed to call him by that title, probably in reference to his avuncular nature. Ramón was the Grand Master of the Order of Calatrava and the leader of some one hundred knights. He was a formidable soldier and an imposing presence. He was not a tall man. But he was powerful. He carried most of his weight in his chest and shoulders. He had a distinguished bald head, broad and wrinkled. A scar running across his cheek delineated his profession. His thin lips seemed too delicate for his ribald language and his penchant for imbibing sweet wines, two activities frowned upon by Abbot Vincente of the Cistercian monastery adjacent to the fortress in Calatrava. Abbot Vincente seemed to enjoy analyzing Ramón's spiritual defects.

'Ramón,' Abbot Vincente often said, 'is too much in love with life for a man of God.'

Although he smiled easily and laughed at times with abandon, Ramón had sad brown eyes with tiny flecks of gold, as if the death of each of his soldiers had made its mark. His eyes were framed by thick black-gray brows and creases that spread out like sunbeams.

In Calatrava, Ramón passed his days with the young knights, teaching, teasing, advising. He seemed to view the Order as an extended family.

He quickly learned all of our names, our strengths and weaknesses. As Abbot Vincente said, Ramón could know the core of a person after seeing the direction and number of creases on his face.

'Ramón sees too much for his own good,' the Abbot stated. 'It is better to leave certain things to God.'

This may have been true in general, but not in Ramón's profession. In the pitch of battle, a commander must know who can be counted on, who will run in the face of overwhelming odds, who will stay and fight. In short, Ramón was a man who, by the natural order, leads other men, and those who followed him would do so even unto almost certain death.

Ramón had two bodyguards – Bernard and Roberto – although Ramón preferred to call them his deputies. They were the men who had tackled me in the Correas' foyer. They never left Ramón's side, and they eyed strangers who approached him like watchdogs. In temperament and personality, the two men were very similar – brooding, vigilant, and fiercely loyal to their master. I never saw them smile or frown, except when they were drunk. Andrés used to joke that Bernard and Roberto reminded him of the two lion statues that guarded the palace entrance in Barcelona.

Uncle Ramón's need for bodyguards – there had been several attempts on his life – did not stem from his leadership of the Calatrava, but from more secular activities. It was said by some that

Ramón's 'indiscretions' would eventually catch up with him. Some men certainly wanted him dead – the husbands, fathers, and brothers of the women in question. I had my first taste of combat defending Uncle Ramón against the swords of paid assassins hired by an angry father. Actually, not really. Andrés and I were more bystanders than active participants.

They were Italian – a group of eight – all dressed identically in orange robes with gold epaulets and wide-brimmed, triangular black hats. Ramón had invited Andrés and me to accompany him and his bodyguards to the market outside the fort in the town of Calatrava. It was shortly after our arrival at the fort. I think Ramón wanted to make amends for our unusual introduction. Andrés and I ambled through the bustling market sampling the wares. We were clothed in the white robes of the Order with only daggers at our sides. I had dropped my finger in a jar of olive oil when Andrés tapped me from behind. I tasted the oil before looking up. The street was empty. The sounds of bargaining and haggling over prices had ceased. The merchants had deserted their stalls.

The Italians came four on each side. Their leader stepped forward. He had a tall face, a high, discerning forehead. Underneath a fine, bladelike nose, he had cultivated a long, waxed mustache that ran perpendicular to his narrow face.

He removed his hat, took a deep bow, and introduced himself as 'the venerable Gian Paolo

Manzella of Siena – soldier, spy, bon vivant, raconteur, renegade, traitor, confidant, and paid assassin.'

He then made a sound as if to clear his throat, and one of his colleagues handed him a scroll tied in a red ribbon. The venerable Manzella undid the ribbon ceremoniously, opened the scroll, and began reading solemnly in broken Catalán. It was difficult to decipher his words, but I gathered that the Count of Anjou had tried, convicted, and sentenced to death Uncle Ramón for the 'defilement' of his daughter, the Lady Mireille.

Uncle Ramón was leaning against a stall at the time and nibbling a fig. I heard him exclaim, 'Yes, Mireille, a lovely girl.' He smiled warmly at his Italian counterpart, who flared his nostrils disdainfully and then finished reading: '. . . signed the Count of Anjou, Marceau Dourmant, the fourteenth day of April, the Year of Our Lord 1268.'

I clutched my dagger. My heart was pounding.

The eight Italians unsheathed their weapons on cue from Señor Manzella and approached our position. We were surrounded. Ramón and his bodyguards seemed at ease, though, as if encountering assassins in the marketplace was a common occurrence.

'How is Mireille?' Uncle Ramón asked.

'Oh, she is fine,' Señor Manzella responded, twirling his mustache. 'Married to that same uncouth German. What a waste for such a beauty.

155

Six kids now. Brats, all of them, one worse than the other.'

Ramón shook his head, as if to say it was a shame, and sighed sympathetically.

When the Italians were almost upon us, Ramón and his bodyguards took out their swords. They hesitated an instant before charging toward one side. Andrés and I followed in their wake. It was difficult to get a clear picture. Squawking chickens were batted around and fruit stalls were turned over. When the debris cleared, two of the Italians lay dead, strewn across squashed fruit and exotic fabrics. The surviving six, including the venerable Manzella, were running in the opposite direction out of town. One was clutching a wounded arm. Another was limping.

Ramón shouted after them, 'Please give my regards to Mireille.' Under his breath, barely audible, he said, 'A lovely girl.' He finished the fig he still had in his hand, and we returned to the fort.

Unfortunately, we had no figs for Uncle Ramón during his visit to the Correa estate. Andrés' father had not expected his former comrade. Otherwise he would have sent for the finest from Granada. Ramón was a connoisseur.

I was still recovering from my unpleasant reception, massaging my neck, when Baron Correa called to Ramón from the top of the landing. He must have heard the commotion. He bounded down the stairs, taking two at a time.

'Ramón,' he said, 'you seem to have misplaced your hair on some battlefield.'

'Has it been so many years?' Ramón smiled.

They kissed on both cheeks and repeated the gesture several times, studying each other as if cataloging the minute changes in their faces.

'Your father and I,' Ramón said to Andrés, 'fought together in southern Spain against the infidels. I owe my life many times to his sword.'

'Come, daughter,' Baron Correa said to Isabel, who was standing at the opposite end of the hallway, 'greet your godfather, the godfather of both my children. We could ask for no truer friend.'

Isabel peered around the stairwell, then walked cautiously forward to kiss Ramón.

'I last saw you when you were so high, Isabel,' Ramón said, gesturing to his waist. 'You have grown into an elegant woman, like your mother.'

Isabel curtsied but said nothing. She understood that Ramón's arrival would mean the departure of her brother and me. She would not pretend to welcome this development, no matter her relation to Ramón or her father's affinity for the visitor.

Dinner was served in the Great Hall. It was a festive evening. A steady parade of servants traveled back and forth from the kitchen carrying various dishes – fish, mutton, vegetable soup, venison served with a savory sauce of herbs ground to a paste and mixed with wine, ginger, cloves, and cinnamon. The animal had stumbled upon our hunting party just yesterday. Uncle Ramón and

Baron Correa sat at opposite ends. Isabel sat on her father's left, next to me. Bernard and Roberto, Ramón's bodyguards, sat on each side of him. They jostled the servants who tried to get close enough to serve Ramón. Finally, the servants gave up and asked me to pass along Ramón's portions.

Baron Correa instructed Andrés to go down to the basement to retrieve a crate of wine imported from France. When Andrés returned and our cups had been filled, Ramón glanced quickly around the table.

'To the King's son, the bastard Fernando Sánchez,' Ramón shouted before downing his cup in one gulp and slamming it down on the table.

The bang of ceramic meeting the thick wood table was followed in an instant by the two empty cups of his bodyguards, Bernard and Roberto. Roberto's cup shattered over the table, but none of the three men seemed to take notice. Isabel raised herself from her seat beside her father and supervised the servants in cleaning the mess and replacing the offending vessel. Ramón used his sleeve to wipe the trickle of red wine that rolled down his chin.

'I have received a dispatch from the King,' Ramón said. 'The old man finally steps down from his throne and sees that all is not well in the world.'

Baron Correa leaned forward and whispered in a voice that carried to every crevice of the dining room so that even the dogs, slanting their heads, turned their attention from the food on the table and glanced confusedly at their master. 'Ramón, I wish you would be more careful in choosing your words. You have enemies enough. We would not want a false report to reach the King's ears indicating that any disrespect was accorded him in my home.'

Baron Correa motioned to the servants and frowned at Ramón. The servants, in turn, bowed their heads, pretending not to hear Ramón's colorful remarks or their master's plea.

'Rest assured,' Ramón stated, 'that the King is my personal friend. I love the man like a father. He has many exemplary qualities. He can be as lazy as a twenty-year-old mare, though. I say that with a filial affection.'

Upon speaking, Ramón again raised his cup, which had been filled by a servant, and pronounced a toast: 'To the King and whatever children he may have.'

Bernard and Roberto raised their cups, and the three men drank again, as the Correas and their servants looked on. Baron Correa threw up his hands and instructed one of the servants to retrieve more wine from the cellar.

'The fall of Antioch to the infidels,' Ramón said, 'made a deep impression on the King. They say the Saracens butchered every Christian in the city who could not be sold or bartered. A crusade will be launched from Barcelona this summer to retake the city and avenge our brethren. The King himself will lead it with the assistance of his two bastard sons, Fernando Sánchez and Pedro Fernández. Don Fernando asks that the Order of Calatrava take their passage alongside the royal army. I have never met Don Fernando, but I have heard he is a skilled and brave warrior. At the very least, he is wise enough to choose my knights to serve at his side. The Calatrava fight like lions in the defense of Christendom. Isn't that so, Andrés?'

'Yes, Uncle Ramón,' Andrés responded ardently. 'All of Spain knows there are no more bold or daring knights than those of the Calatrava.'

This, of course, was the right answer and probably true. Ramón, Bernard, and Roberto raised their cups, downed the contents, then looked at Andrés expectantly. He glanced into the murky liquid, put the cup to his lips, and drank until the vessel was empty. A good portion of the contents fell on his cloak, but Ramón was satisfied.

'Andrés,' he said, 'I can already see you will be a fine warrior.'

Andrés flushed a deep shade of red and mumbled something unintelligible, as if this were the highest compliment he had ever received.

'I regret, my friend,' Ramón said to Baron Correa, 'that my visit will be so brief. I have been called to the palace to make arrangements with Don Fernando. We must leave tomorrow morning for Barcelona and then on to Calatrava to train my soldiers. Andrés and Francisco, in the next week, you will proceed to Calatrava, ten days' journey

160

from here. Enjoy your last days of freedom. Soon you will belong to me, Knights of Calatrava.'

Andrés winked at me, vindicated, ecstatic. After a servant girl placed a platter on the table, Andrés took her by the waist and danced around the company to the rhythms of Uncle Ramón's clapping. Bernard and Roberto, following their master's lead, banged their wooden spoons on the table. This orchestra of three was surprisingly euphonic, and several of the other servants joined the dance. Baron Correa glanced philosophically at his son. Isabel, expressionless, stared straight ahead. Andrés finally tired and sat down. Dinner continued.

'Father,' Andrés said, 'tell Francisco about the time Uncle Ramón saved your life.'

'Has your father been telling lies, Andrés?' Ramón asked.

'Please, Father,' Andrés said.

'Very well, Andrés,' Baron Correa said. 'It was twenty years ago, my last battle before I returned to Girona. The infidels had just surrendered Seville to the Christian forces. The Castilians were busy celebrating in the streets of the city. Our regiment from Aragón – some one hundred soldiers – occupied a fort on the outskirts of Seville. The Muslims were supposed to have withdrawn all their forces in compliance with the terms of surrender. We did not expect to see any more combat. We were wrong. Not a week after victory, one of the infidel generals and his force surrounded the castle at dawn. Maybe he thought we had hid some treasure in the fort. Or perhaps he just wanted to kill some Christian knights before retreating.

'The infidels must have carried fifty ladders into battle – each as tall as the castle walls. Before we could organize our defense, the infidels advanced on the castle, leaning the ladders against the walls. Their soldiers climbed quickly. We ran frantically around the parapet, pushing off the ladders before the infidel soldiers could climb to the top. They fell backward, like trees cut down in the forest, the men dropping to the ground. We were greatly outnumbered, though. It seemed that for every one ladder we pushed down, two more would rise.

'As I scanned the outside walls,' Baron Correa continued, 'I spotted one of the infidel climbers fast approaching the castle tower. I sprinted to the tower and reached the ladder just as the infidel stepped onto the surface. Neither of us had drawn our weapons.

'The infidel and I began to wrestle on the edge of the tower. After a struggle, I managed to push him off the ledge. Our armor had become tangled, though, and I fell to the ground with him just outside the castle walls.'

'I was not injured from the fall. In fact, one the infidels helped pull me up before he realized I was a Christian knight. I was standing amidst a crowd of Muslim soldiers, who looked me over curiously. I drew my dagger and waited. I figured I could take at least two of them with me. They formed a tight circle around me, but did not attack.

'One of the infidels finally stepped forward. He must have weighed twice as much as me. He was a giant. He pulled his dagger. We circled each other. The crowd of Muslims around us grew. Many of the infidels seemed to neglect the siege to witness our one-on-one combat.'

'The Christian soldiers watched the action from the tower,' Ramón said. 'We shouted encouragement down to your father. I think he was trying to negotiate safe passage for himself.'

'If I did speak,' Baron Correa said, 'I was giving myself last rites. The infidel was stronger and faster than me. He slashed me twice across the chest, almost cutting through my chain mail. He was chasing me around the circle. Fortunately, he slipped, or you and Isabel would not be here. I pounced on him, stabbing him in the stomach – a deathblow. His comrades dragged his body from the circle. They seemed to be in the process of choosing another combatant for me, arguing amongst each other, when Ramón appeared in the circle. I thought he was an angel who had jumped down from the heavens.'

'What did you do, Uncle Ramón?' Andrés asked. 'Did you fly from the castle walls?'

'I had tied a rope under my shoulders,' Ramón said, 'and a group of our comrades lowered me to the ground.'

'Before I could think,' Baron Correa said,

163

'Ramón grabbed me by the chest, and we were yanked through the air. We smacked hard against the stone wall, but continued to ascend. The infidels had crossbows, but they did not shoot at us. They were too stunned to do anything, except cheer, paying homage to Ramón's bravery. There were a few more skirmishes that morning, but their force soon departed.'

'Did your father tell you,' Ramón said, 'that he asked me to marry him as we were still suspended in the air, pressing against one another?'

'Be quiet, Ramón,' Baron Correa said.

'Your father makes war sound entertaining,' Ramón said. 'I will tell some true stories from the crusade.'

With a mouth full of food, Ramón described animatedly several battles in the Levant. Andrés and I listened rapt. We interjected questions when Ramón glossed over details of the fighting. Bernard continued proposing toasts, to which we all drank. Except Isabel. She remained silent, withdrawn.

'Isabel,' Ramón said, 'you look as if the angel of death had paid a visit to your home. This journey will bring only glory to your brother and to the Correa name. The great army being assembled by King Jaime will smash the will of the Saracens. In a few years, we will reconquer Jerusalem. Then I will invite you and your father to come and pray with me at the Holy Sepulcher. I promise.'

Ramón's words did not have their intended

effect. Isabel remained stone-faced. Ramón realized he would have to employ a more drastic measure to coax Isabel into the spirit of revelry. He paused in contemplation for a moment, then started clapping and urging the servants to join him. He motioned for the two musicians to play. They began strumming their lutes, investing the meter with a lilting, lyrical air. When the spry melody had reached a pitch, Ramón walked over to Isabel and offered his hand. She accepted reluctantly, and Ramón and his goddaughter were soon dancing around the table to the rhythms of the proffered beat. The tempo accelerated, the skill of both dancers tested. Isabel moved her feet and whirled her dress with an elegance and charm that hypnotized guest and servant alike. The folds of her dress, resplendent with gold and silver, swayed with an infinite harmony. Her face a shadow of impenetrable grace.

Captivated by the music, Isabel finally exhibited the trace of a smile, her cheeks rising. Ramón, sensing his opportunity, spun her through the cavalcade of servants. When they were finished, Isabel curtsied graciously. Ramón sat down, his sweated brow, if not triumphant, at least displaying a measure of relief.

'Fill the cups, my friends,' Ramón said breathlessly. 'This is a night of celebration.'

And it was. Isabel remained staid, but she wore her smile, hardwon by Ramón. The evening passed in a blur. The sweet wine spread through my body, into my chest, my arms, and then my fingertips. My mind was swimming, and I felt an abiding affection for every person in the hall. I do not remember the number of toasts that were declared. To the Queen Mother, to the Apostles and all their mistresses, to Jesus, Joseph, and Mary, to Samson and Delilah, to Genghis Khan, and to Isabel and her simmering beauty. That last one was Roberto's – the first words he had spoken the entire evening. In fact, I think they were the most words I ever heard Roberto speak. Ramón and Baron Correa were too drunk to take notice of the impropriety. I glanced at Isabel, who looked straight ahead and pretended not to hear Roberto's compliment.

I gave my own toast – 'To Roberto, who has the soul of a poet but hides it well.' I smiled at Isabel as I raised my glass. She returned my gaze, her gray eyes flashing indignantly, as if it had been I, and not Roberto, who had taken inappropriate liberties.

Despite the pleasure of the evening, a melancholy nostalgia rumbled down my chest and lodged in the seat of my stomach. Ramón's news meant that I would soon be leaving the Correas. I had passed almost three months at their estate, and I felt a lightness in my heart that I had not felt since Sergio's death. The loneliness, so resilient, bottomless, in Montcada, had faded. Its wintry shadow no longer lingered in the moonlit hours. Its daggers no longer woke me at dawn. I looked at Isabel on my right. She was conversing with her brother. I knew that I might never see her again. I wondered whether she understood this. I had an urge to speak to her intimately, as I had in the garden, but we were not alone. The boisterous nature of the evening provided a measure of privacy, though. I seized a particularly turbulent moment – Uncle Ramón was standing on the dining table demonstrating the proper form to parry a sword thrust – to speak to her.

'Are you happy for your brother and me, Isabel?' I asked.

'If you will find what you seek, Francisco,' she said, 'then I am happy for you.'

'Pray tell, what is it that I seek?' I said. 'I have forgotten in this haze of wine and merriment.'

'Ghosts and demons, Francisco. You said so yourself.' Isabel spoke those words not bitterly, but decisively. Our conversation ended. Daughter and father excused themselves not long after our discourse. Isabel did not even glance at me as she departed the table and made her way up the stairs on his arm.

Those who remained drank until the first glimmer of natural light entered the dining room. With a wan and tired smile, Uncle Ramón announced that it was time to retire. Andrés was already asleep, his head resting on his outstretched arm across the table. His mouth was open and drooling on the stained brocade before him. Roberto and I walked arm in arm, supporting each other up the stairs. When we reached the corridor, he said good night, before collapsing facedown on the stone. A group of servants that must have been surreptitiously following us carried him away. I lumbered into my bedchamber, said good night to my stolid companion on the Cross, and lay down on my bed fully clothed.

The Grand Master and his entourage had already left the estate by the time I awoke in the early afternoon with a splitting headache and a parched tongue. Andrés kept me busy over the next few days – making an inventory of items for our journey, dragging me to the marketplace, bargaining for provisions. As we prepared for our departure, I barely spoke to Isabel. I yearned for her presence, but I did not know what to say to her. There was nothing to say.

On a coarse, cloudless day, Baron Correa and Isabel stood in the courtyard to see us off. My breath rising in the crisp air. I thanked Baron Correa for his hospitality and extended an open invitation to visit Barcelona. He hugged me warmly.

'Francisco,' he said, 'you will always be a son to me.'

'And you a father,' I responded.

'When you saved my daughter's life,' Baron Correa said, 'you saved my own. She is the light in this dark abode.'

I nodded to Isabel and told her to continue practicing archery. I presented her with my bow as a present. She had often admired its delicate craftsmanship. She said that the gift was too generous, but I insisted that she accept it. Isabel moved toward me. I took a step back and remained frozen. She kissed both my cheeks, then put her arms around the back of my head and pressed her cheek into my own. It was only an instant, but I closed my eyes and sealed the smell of her skin across my brow.

The evening of our arrival at the fortress, Ramón spoke to the new recruits in the refectory.

'In the Year of Our Lord 1099,' he said, 'a ragged army of one thousand five hundred starving knights laid siege to a city populated by more than one hundred thousand people. The Egyptian governor reinforced the local garrison with a special contingent of handpicked Arab and Sudanese soldiers. The city was Jerusalem; the army Christ's own. Our brothers, now in paradise, were victorious. In one month, they breached the walls and conquered Jerusalem.

'How was this done? How did these knights accomplish such a spectacular victory?'

'God's intervention,' one of the recruits answered.

'A partial answer,' Ramón responded. 'Christ inspired the knights. But the first crusaders were also stronger, quicker, more disciplined than their adversaries. Never forget the reason we train so rigorously. One day you will serve God in the same manner as the first crusaders.'

Primary training for a Knight of Calatrava lasts two years. The first year, the novitiate, is devoted to the more spiritual aspects of knighthood – learning the liturgy and the Rule of the Order. The second year, after taking vows, the knights concentrate on the physical and military aspects of our calling.

The armada of King Jaime would not wait for the twenty new recruits of the Calatrava to finish our regimen, though. Ramón said we would have to prioritize our instruction. Fortunately, Andrés and I had learned the liturgy as monks at Santes Creus.

'The infidel soldiers,' Ramón said, 'generally do not measure our knowledge of the prayer offices.'

We would spend only eight months at the fortress. Eight months in which Ramón molded us, transformed us into soldiers.

The blacksmiths woke us at dawn the morning after our arrival. The old men came into the dormitory and measured our limbs, our shoulders, the crowns of our heads. They avoided meeting our glances. They did not even ask our names as they scrawled figures in their notebooks.

When they returned with our armor three months later, seven of our number were already gone. Three left voluntarily. Ramón dismissed the other four. I envied them at the time. No longer having to endure the grueling, endless sessions of training. The days and nights which melded together so that when the bell struck to wake us, I could swear I had just then laid my head to rest. Roused from my moment of peace to run the mountain trail before dawn. Through the forest, over the black streams and jagged rocks. Ramón and his bodyguards always leading the way. Every step. Returning to the fortress for morning prayer. My stomach churning. The first few weeks, I threw up every day in the courtyard. My comrades surrounded me, retching, spitting, trying to catch their breath before proceeding to the chapel.

After breakfast and a short rest, we would simulate battle, sparring with wooden swords and shields. One partner would collapse from exhaustion, only to be spurred on by an instructor until the fallen one had raised himself to continue. I can still hear the cries of our instructors, men who had retired to the cloth after many years of fighting – *until death, men, a martyr's death!* We would shoot arrows at swinging wooden shields, fastened by leather cords to a high branch. My shoulders would burn, my fingers numb and bloodied. Marching the full day without rest, without water. My hands and feet raw. My legs and back stiff and tender.

One morning, I walked to Ramón's chambers during our rest period. I could feel Andrés' anxious gaze follow me through the dormitory into the courtyard. I intended to resign from the Order, to explain my situation to Ramón – *Uncle, I can no longer continue. My body cannot endure this punishment. I am finished.*

I stood before Ramón unable to speak. He was mending his boot, stitching the leather seam, ignoring my presence. He finally looked up and watched me for several minutes. He put his hands

171

together so that only his fingertips were touching.

'Do you think, Francisco, that your sorrow is unique?' he asked. 'Do you think there is another course you can take to salve the pain?'

I returned to the dormitory without speaking a word.

After a couple months, the hard skin grew back over the blisters. My muscles ached, but the strain had become familiar, almost comforting. When I lay down at night and closed my eyes, I was riding through the forest in Montcada. I could feel the blood course through my limbs, the warm vibration of pulsing sinew.

I slept. I woke. I ran. I prayed. I ate. I fought. I listened. My doubts and fears, the past and future receded.

The morning the blacksmiths returned was different. When we woke, rays of light illuminated the tiny particles of dust that floated gently through the chamber. It was the first time in three months I had not seen dawn's first light. I could smell the sweet dew rising in the courtyard. They placed the armor on our bed mats, then helped dress us, making adjustments to fit the armor more closely.

Over a long undershirt of quilted cotton, I wore a hauberk, forty thousand metal rings forged together in the furnace. The chain mail covered my chest and my arms, and extended to my knees. A mail coif, open-faced, was pulled over my head and hung down over my neck. A thick cotton pad attached to the crown provided a cushion for the great helm, a flat-topped metal bowl that fit snugly over my head. Mail leggings ran down to my feet.

Over my armor, I wore a white surcoat – a loose-fitting sleeveless robe. White, the same color as the habit of our Cistercian brothers, representing the simplicity and purity of our holy mission.

My sword weighed ten pounds, measured three feet long, almost half a foot wide at the hilt. I carried in my belt a smaller, pointed dagger, so sharp I cut the tips of my fingers brushing its edge.

Finally, a long triangular shield, made of wood, covered with boiled leather on the outside and padded with cotton on the inside. The edges of the shield were rimmed with metal to enhance its strength.

Viewing my comrades strutting through the courtyard fully armored, I remembered our mission, my mission. We were God's soldiers. In that service, I would save my brother's soul. I grasped the solid handle of my sword – the blade, gleaming, exquisite. One day to be stained with blood. But not that day.

Ramón assembled the recruits in rows alongside the other more experienced soldiers. Over one hundred knights ready for battle. Each knight dressed in identical armor – in accordance with the statutes of the Order and in the spirit of brotherhood – each of us equal in the eyes of God. Ramón walked silently through our ranks, perusing the shiny armor of the recruits. Then he walked to the front and faced us.

'Very pretty,' he said. 'We should conduct a beauty contest, only we have no qualified judges. You will have to settle for a foot race. Roberto and Bernard will assign each of you a partner. They will tie a leather cord between your wrists. You are responsible for your partner. You will run the mountain trail as you have every morning. Except today, you will wear your armor. And your partner will run beside you. There are fifty flags on the summit. Each team will retrieve one and return. You must complete the course with your full set of armor, including your sword and shield. The cord between partners must not break. The first two knights who plant their flag in the courtyard will become lieutenants in the Order of Calatrava.'

A lusty cry rose up from the ranks of the veteran soldiers. A commission of lieutenant in the Calatrava was a great prize – an honor recognized in clerical and lay circles. Roberto and Bernard went through the lines teaming more experienced soldiers with the newer recruits. Ramón had other plans for Andrés and me.

'Bind the cousins,' Ramón instructed Bernard. 'In the Levant, Andrés and Francisco will fight twice as hard side by side. They will run together today.'

Bernard wrapped the cord tightly around my wrist, then tied it to Andrés.

'Just like racing horses in Montcada, cousin,' Andrés said, 'only this time we both win.'

The key to moving quickly was coordination.

174

After a short awkward interval, Andrés and I learned to time our stride so that our middle, attached wrists were moving forward and back together. We ran the forest smoothly, then up the mountain trail. The others had more difficulty adjusting. We joined a group of five other teams who broke away from the pack. Sunyer de Jaca and Carlos de Casabas, two of the swiftest soldiers, led the group until they tangled and fell in a rock field. As the teams ran past the former leaders, we slowed to see Sunyer's shinbone, splintered, sticking out of his skin. White film and blood splattered on Carlos' new armor. Sunyer stared confusedly at his leg. Carlos was speaking softly, trying to console his partner. Several of the teams approached their fallen comrades to lend assistance. Bernard, running in front, yelled at us to proceed up the mountain and leave the injured to the medical attendants.

On the steep slope, two of the teams in the lead group fell back. They had gone out too quickly and could not sustain the pace. The distance amongst the teams spread as we made our way toward the peak. As Andrés and I approached the rows of flags, only two teams ran before us.

In the first heat of competition, the armor seemed not to hinder our speed. The chain mail, fashioned in the most advanced workshop in Iberia, afforded a full range of motion. The helmet fit comfortably and did not obstruct my vision. I was not accustomed to carrying the extra weight, though, nearly sixty pounds. On the downslope, I felt a twinge in my thigh muscles, which became sharper and more frequent as we descended. My shoulders strained under the heavy mesh, the sword and shield strapped across my shoulders. I fell as we entered the forest. My legs gave way. I pulled Andrés with me as I tumbled through the brush. My helmet smacked against the rock face before I landed on a patch of soil. My cheek rested on a cool pillow of dead leaves. Breathing the musty earth, I glanced at my wrist, stretched backward, still bound by the leather cord. Andrés sat next to me. His chest was heaving beneath the metal links, his face damp with sweat.

'Has nap period ended?' he asked.

I raised myself and brushed the leaves from my armor. Bernard was screaming at us from below.

'Take your time,' Andrés said, frowning. 'Who wants to be a lieutenant anyway?'

We began to jog, my limbs heavy as if we were running underwater. Bernard ran alongside us, shouting obscenities. We went faster, trying to keep pace with him. Twigs and branches crushed underneath. Through bushes, over tree roots, deeper into the forest. I looked to my right. We had pulled even with Galindo and Marcos. Galindo, glass-eyed, white foam on his lips. Blood coated the front of his armor. Three feathered arrows had pierced his stomach. The metal mesh ripped, exposing the torn flesh lining the inside of his stomach. I looked ahead, running as fast as I could away from that diabolic apparition. When I glanced back at Galindo, the arrows had disappeared, his armor undamaged, pristine. He and Marcos were struggling through the tall grass. They tried to stay with us, but faded as the fortress came into view through the trees.

Andrés and I were gliding breathless. We climbed the last hill to the entrance of the fort just behind Alejandro and Sancho. Our instructors shouted encouragement when we entered the courtyard. Ramón cross-armed, solemn, as if standing in judgment of our efforts. We collapsed next to the stake that Andrés planted in the ground. We were the second team to finish.

The others arrived in bunches, staggering, limping into the courtyard. After the first dozen teams had finished, Andrés and I had recovered sufficiently to sit up and cheer the rest of our brothers. When the last stragglers arrived, Ramón and his bodyguards left to help evacuate Sunyer to the infirmary. In Ramón's absence, the regular daily activities were canceled. We attended services in the chapel, ate breakfast in the refectory, then returned to the courtyard to wait for news of Sunyer's condition.

We would wait most of the day. Ramón returned at dusk.

'Congratulations to all of you,' he said. 'You ran courageously. I have some unfortunate news. The doctors could not save Sunyer's leg. They amputated this afternoon below the knee. Sunyer braved the surgery stoically – as a Knight of Calatrava. He rests now. Keep him in your prayers tonight. Alejandro and Sancho, come to my quarters after the compline service.'

As I lay on my bed mat that evening, I thought of Alejandro and Sancho receiving their commissions as lieutenants in the Order. They had been only ten paces ahead of Andrés and me when we entered the courtyard. We might have caught them if I had not fallen. I thought of Sunyer. His leg a bloody stump now. His fortunes changed in one instant, one false movement.

The next day, the bells rang before sunrise. As I dressed for our morning run, I noticed that Alejandro and Sancho were not in their usual places. I scanned the dormitory but did not see them. Perhaps, I thought, they had spent the night celebrating their victory with Ramón in the taverns of the town. Our Grand Master had a weakness for the spirits.

We filed into the courtyard, assembling in rows. The rain fell bitter. We stood in puddles, the fog rising in the half-light just before sunrise. The whispers amongst comrades ceased gradually, our attention focused on the two soldiers before us. Fully armored, they stood facing us, holding swords above their bowed heads. One of the soldiers grasped the blade in his bare hand. The metal had cut into his palm, so that the blood trickled down, the crimson rivulets washed in the rain through the chain links, into the mud.

'We ran the mountain trail yesterday.' Ramón was walking between the rows of soldiers. He spoke softly so that we had to strain to hear his words. 'A race. The prize – a position of leadership in the Calatrava. Tomorrow, in the Levant, we will run the gauntlet of infidel arrows. The stakes . . . life and death.

'Look upon your brothers Alejandro and Sancho. They have waited all night for you. To show their remorse. They finished first yesterday. But they cut the cord that attached them while running in the forest. They did this to speed themselves to the finish.

'Alejandro and Sancho are lucky. They live. They live because it is today and not tomorrow. And because the Grand Master of the Calatrava is merciful. The infidels are not. In the Levant, disobedience means death. Abandoning your partner . . . death. Fighting alone instead of beside your comrade . . . death.

'Andrés and Francisco, congratulations. You are first lieutenants in the Order of Calatrava. You will lead the run today.'

Not all of our training involved strenuous physical activity. For two hours each afternoon, we studied. The master engineer of the Order instructed us in carpentry and building. The first weeks, we sawed oak logs into beams, boards, and bars, which we used to construct long spikes, ladders, a battering ram. After several months, we learned to design

179

and build elaborate siege engines – towers on wheels with a gangplank – that could be brought against a castle during an assault. A doctor gave us two weeks of instruction in medicine – cleaning and binding wounds, making splints for broken bones, mixing syrup of roses to counteract dysentery. The veterans lectured on battle strategy, the past tactics employed by Saracen generals, the strengths and weaknesses of their soldiers, their weapons. Muslim soldiers often wear little if any armor, but they carry sophisticated weapons. They rely primarily on the mechanical crossbow, which can propel an arrow with enough force to pierce armor from one hundred feet.

'The infidels fear to look us in the eyes,' our instructors explained, 'so they prefer to fight from afar. Bridge the distance, men. Bridge the distance between you and the enemy as fast as possible. Close combat will render the crossbow useless.'

Ramón assigned one servant, two squires, and four horses to each knight – two warhorses, in the event one was felled, one packhorse to transport our armor, and one riding horse. The servant would carry and prepare food during journeys. The two squires would care for our horses and help us don our armor before battle, a process that usually required the three of us working together. The chain mail was unwieldy, and the blacksmiths placed buckles and straps in locations impossible for the wearer to reach. We spent an hour every day with our squires, dressing and undressing for battle, getting quicker each time.

We also conducted maneuvers with the foot soldiers of the Calatrava – mostly peasants trained to fight with spears and bows in support of the knights. They, along with the squires and servants, took their meals and found shelter in another wing of the fortress.

Periodically, Ramón expounded on what he called the 'art of war.' 'A true warrior,' according to Ramón, 'is always an artist. In Christ's name, he wades into the swamp of human passions – rage, terror, shame, euphoria, valor, reverence. He wades into chaos, seeking to create order – the Kingdom of God within himself and on earth. The warrior lies sleepless before battle, before creation, uncertain of the morrow. He might be anxious to prove himself – for ephemeral glory – the recognition of his peers. But the only lasting reward is his faith.'

During our last week in Calatrava, Ramón explained the unusual circumstances of our departure. By letter, King Jaime had requested a 'purely aristocratic contingent' from the Calatrava – only knights. Our servants, squires, engineers, and foot soldiers would not accompany us to the Levant.

Considerations of space aboard the fleet, the King's letter stated, made the inclusion of the Calatrava's common soldiers and servants 'impracticable.'

'We are all disappointed to leave our faithful

comrades,' Ramón said at supper. 'Nevertheless, the King has assured me that our needs will be met. A dearth of knights exists in the Levant, alongside a surplus of squires and foot soldiers – a body with no head to lead it. The King promises that upon our arrival in the Levant, he will provide unstinting support to our force – including servants, two squires for each knight, and five hundred foot soldiers from the armies already stationed in the East.

'In any case, we have no choice in the matter. We must abide the King's instructions.'

I was sitting across from Ramón. Toward the end of supper, I overheard him whispering to Bernard. 'The King,' he said, 'probably needs five ships for his sycophants and courtesans.'

Two days before we set out for the docks of Barcelona, we were inducted into the Order of Calatrava. We received our swords, blessed by Archbishop Emmanuel of Toledo. The ceremony began at dusk with a ritual bath. Purified by the sacred water, we dressed in white, linen garments with a hooded robe. We knelt barefoot before the altar, upon which we placed our weapons and armor. We remained in that uncomfortable posture until dawn without uttering a word. A group of Cistercian monks from the adjoining monastery chanted verses from the Holy Scriptures through the long evening and kept the candles and incense burners continually lit. A turbid cloud of purple incense spread through the monastery. An excruciatingly boring evening – eight hours remaining still like an idiot in that silly costume. The night passed painfully.

At dawn, the Archbishop entered the church. A fat man, sweat across his forehead, his hair combed straight forward in the style of the Roman emperors. He said Mass, coughing periodically when the mist of incense became overwhelming. Then he laid his hands on the altar and blessed our weapons in the name of Jesus Christ. After Mass, Uncle Ramón performed the dubbing. He struck our cheeks with the side of his sword and declared each one of us a Knight of Calatrava. The harder blows Ramón reserved for those who were dozing after the sleepless night. Their heads jerked back from the sting. One of my brothers fell over from the impact.

Andrés was fast asleep, his neck jutting forward, his blond hair hanging over his face. I was surprised he could remain kneeling in such a state. I tried unsuccessfully to rouse him, whispering across the cathedral, but the sound was captured by the hollow spaces under the apse. Andrés received the cruelest blow, the sound vibrating through the great cathedral. Even the Archbishop seemed to wince at the echo. Ramón was no doubt disappointed in Andrés, a lieutenant in the Order, a leader amongst our brethren.

On bended knee, we spoke our vows. Poverty, chastity, obedience. We promised to defend the

183

Church against its enemies, to protect widows, orphans, and the poor. It was almost evening when the ceremony finally ended and we made our way to the Great Hall for a celebratory feast.

I recognized the opportunity presented by Francisco's broaching the subject of his induction ceremony. Francisco, I believe, broke his vows in the Levant. I am certain that this transgression is at the root of his possession. I seized the chance to question him concerning his conduct on the crusade.

'Poverty, chastity, obedience,' I repeated.

'The very words we spoke, Lucas.'

'Do you know their meaning, Francisco? Do you understand the implications of the commitment you made before the Lord, His Son, and the Holy Spirit?'

'The words are simple, Lucas.'

Francisco must have felt as if the light of the Lord were directed at him, such was the intensity of my gaze.

'And you obeyed those vows, Francisco?'

Francisco seemed not to hear my question. His eyes scrutinizing his palms, his attention focused far away. What were the words of Isabel concerning Francisco's search in the Levant? Ghosts and demons.

'Francisco de Montcada,' I said sternly, 'while you fought in God's name, did you obey your vows?'

He smiled. Actually, half a smile. The same

ironic expression the first time I saw him in Abbot Pedro's quarters.

'Would that I had broken only one of those vows – or all of them. My deeds are much blacker, Lucas.'

'Tell me, Francisco. I am here to confess you. To offer God's forgiveness. Tell me of this darkness.'

'A starless twilight, Lucas, beyond redemption.'

CHAPTER 7

NOTE TO THE FAITHFUL

'A starless twilight. Beyond redemption.' I repeated Francisco's words to Brother Vial.

Brother Vial scratched the thin strands of hair on the side of his head.

'Your friend sounds a bit arrogant, Lucas,' he said.

'I do not understand, Brother Vial.'

'No one is beyond redemption,' Brother Vial said. 'A man who makes such a claim could just as easily maintain he is beyond damnation.'

'But, Brother Vial,' I responded, 'you said that in cases in which the subject has wedded the devil, dissolution is impossible. Isn't that what you said about the woman who had suffocated her two children?'

'Do you always remember everything I say?' Brother Vial said.

'For the most part.'

'Well,' he said, 'I suppose I did speak words to that effect.'

186

'Brother Vial,' I said, 'the Scriptures say, *he that shall blaspheme against the Holy Ghost hath never forgiveness, but is in danger of eternal damnation.*'

'Does the Good Book say that, Lucas?'

'Indeed, Brother Vial, it does. Perhaps Francisco is guilty of an eternal sin. Before his martyrdom, Abbot Pedro said that Francisco was in spiritual rebellion, that he was a man at war with God.'

'Did Abbot Pedro say that, Lucas?'

'Indeed, he did, Brother Vial.'

'A man at war with God . . .' Brother Vial mused. He was tapping his leather sandal against the stone. 'Francisco seems more a man at war with himself than with God.'

'I do not understand, Brother Vial.'

'Nor do I, Lucas.'

As much as I admire Brother Vial, I would concede that his lack of seminary training sometimes handicaps his understanding of more spiritual issues. A man at war with himself . . . Brother Vial probably heard the phrase during his sojourn in the Levant – picked it up from some unlearned knights in a tavern in Acre. To be charitable, it is a rather naive assessment of Francisco's condition. How can a man be at war with himself? True spiritual conflict takes place between the Lord and Satan. Between the Church and the devil's minions. Our souls merely provide the field of battle. Indeed, in God's name, I struggle with Satan every day for possession of Francisco's soul.

Perhaps Brother Vial's experiences as a warrior

have also softened, even skewed, his ability to stand in judgment of his comrades. When I related Francisco's report concerning the unwholesome activities of the Grand Master of the Calatrava, Brother Vial laughed generously.

'Yes,' he said, 'that sounds exactly like the great man.'

'The great man?' I asked incredulously. 'Then you made Ramón's acquaintance in the Levant?'

'Everyone who spent time in the Levant knew Uncle Ramón. He had a grand appetite for living.'

'Then you know of his corruptions.'

'Excuse me, Lucas. I do not follow.'

'The violations of his vows. Francisco's report indicates that Ramón engaged in drunkenness and fornication. Worse still, he permitted, indeed encouraged, his knights to follow his depraved activities. My cheeks flush with indignation when I think of the young, impressionable souls put in his charge. We have uncovered quite a scandal, Brother Vial. I will write an immediate dispatch to the Archbishop of Tarragona concerning these most unfortunate revelations.'

'Lucas,' Brother Vial said, 'you have a formidable mind and a prodigious memory. I daresay you know the Psalter and Scriptures by heart. The truth often lies beneath and beyond the words, though. The character of a man shuns simple equation. A knight might remain true to his vows, resisting every temptation, and yet his heart becomes a frozen pasture. He carries out his duties grudgingly and never exerts himself beyond his obligations. Another knight breaks his vows repeatedly, and yet his heart overflows with love. In battle, he refuses to desert a wounded comrade, though the enemy outnumber him ten to one. Who is worthier in the eyes of the Lord? Make such judgments at your own peril. As Christ said, *for with what judgment ye judge, ye shall be judged; and with what measure ye mete, it shall be measured to you again.*

'I would put aside any plans to write the Archbishop concerning Uncle Ramón. Your mission concerns Francisco and his salvation. There is someone you can write, though, someone who might help spur Francisco's confession.'

'Who would that be, Brother Vial? I will write him immediately.'

'Her, Lucas. Andrés' sister. What is her name?'

'Isabel?'

'Yes, Isabel. Send for the girl.'

'Brother Vial, I am confused. Would you place temptation before Francisco in his vulnerable condition?'

'Lucas, would you place a pitcher of water before a man who had walked through the desert?'

Brother Vial stood up, folded his arms underneath his robe, and walked into the courtyard. I hurried after him. When I reached him, he was gazing at the purple flowers around the cistern. I tugged at his robe to get his attention.

'Brother Vial, with all due respect, I believe

it would be a grave error to bring the girl to Santes Creus. She will constitute an unnecessary temptation, an extraneous obstacle to Francisco's convalescence.'

'Temptation, Lucas, is not only the province of the evil one. Does not the Lord place life and death before every person?'

'Indeed, Brother Vial, he does.'

'Both will tempt a man. We will tempt Francisco with life.'

'But, Brother Vial, Isabel has not seen Francisco for six years. She has certainly married. Her husband will probably not permit his wife to travel the countryside alone.'

'Then we will send an escort, Lucas.'

'Yes, Brother Vial, but Francisco will provide a painful remembrance of Isabel's lost brother. I doubt she will accept our invitation.'

'The girl will come.'

That was all he said before disappearing into the chapel for the afternoon office. I feel deeply troubled by our conversation. I fear Brother Vial underestimates the potentially pernicious and disruptive influence that Isabel could exercise on Francisco's recovery. Abbot Pedro used to say that a woman can never be trusted. 'Remember, Lucas,' he would say, 'you yourself were in this world but one hour when your own mother abandoned you in a barn stall.'

Perhaps I was mistaken to recount Francisco's confession to Brother Vial. I wish I had at least omitted Francisco's trip to the Correa estate in Girona. Then Brother Vial would never know of Isabel.

I cannot very well disobey Brother Vial's injunction to send for Isabel. As the prior of the monastery, I outrank him. But Brother Vial's authority derives from his moral and spiritual prestige, not his position. And, of course, his connections – especially to his cousin, Archbishop Sancho of Tarragona. It would be most unwise to defy my mentor. Tomorrow I will send for the girl. The consequences, if they be negative, will be on Brother Vial's head.

Perhaps Isabel will decline the invitation. That would be most desirable. I suspect she will be loath to embark on what would probably be a ten-day journey from Girona to Santes Creus – assuming she is still in Girona. Perhaps she married a gentleman from other parts, and the invitation will never reach her. Indeed, it is quite silly for me to worry about the effect of her visit on Francisco, an event that in all likelihood will never occur.

Francisco's physical condition continues to improve. We take long walks around the courtyard most every day. Once a week we venture forth from the monastery and roam the hills around the sanctuary. Francisco never speaks on these outings. He seems quite taken, indeed invigorated, by the natural beauty of our surroundings. His spirits seem to lift for the rest of the day.

Francisco's confession continues. The intensity of his demeanor during our sessions has not abated. It seems to build every day. Sometimes Francisco trembles as he speaks, as if he were approaching some terrible abyss, perhaps the very root of his infection.

Francisco's case is such a critical affair for the Church. I cannot help but smile when I imagine the great works, the charities, that could be promoted with the bounty offered by Baron Montcada – one-third of his estate in exchange for his son's salvation. I hope my work here will bring forth a monument to God's glory. Indeed, the Church has placed an awesome trust in me. I feel as if the eyes of Rome are focused on Santes Creus.

I write weekly to Archbishop Sancho, describing Francisco's progress. We seem to grow more and more familiar with each correspondence. I believe the Archbishop considers me a personal friend. Last week I received a letter from the Archbishop. He informed me that Bishop Martín's condition worsens. 'Regrettably,' the letter states, 'Tortosa will soon have a vacant post. I hope that your work with Francisco concludes before I must name a replacement.'

The seal of the Archbishop's letter had already been broken when the Abbot's personal servant delivered it to me. That's just as well. Abbot Alfonso might as well know of the Archbishop's regard for me. Perhaps he will show the proper appreciation for my abilities that I sometimes feel he lacks. Indeed, he seems to have grown more solicitous of my needs since I received that correspondence. Yesterday the Abbot inquired if I might prefer fine Egyptian cotton to the worn and rough material of my current robe. Before I could answer, Abbot Alfonso summoned Brother Mario, the monastery tailor, who took my measurements and will cut the cloth this very week.

My fortunes appear to have changed forever. The future holds immense possibilities. Sometimes, in the night, I close my eyes and picture again the Archbishop's quarters – the gold chalice brimming with wine, the silken vestments. It seems just a matter of time before the Lord calls me forth to a more hallowed station.

Last night I dreamt that a simple priest in a foreign land many years from today, perhaps one hundred, was reading a copy of this manuscript. Brother Vial's suggestion that these pages might serve as a map of Francisco's soul seems prescient, if a bit shortsighted. I suspect this manuscript will provide more than that – a map not just of Francisco's soul but of others similarly afflicted. I wonder if Brother Vial regrets his decision to cede responsibility for the exorcism. Perhaps it was inevitable that I would take charge. As my own star rises, Brother Vial's will probably grow dimmer. Indeed, I feel a bit sorry for him. I suppose that is why I share details of Francisco's confession with Brother Vial – to give him a sense of involvement, though it is peripheral. To his credit, Brother Vial evinces no jealousy. He never fails to praise my approach and to encourage my efforts. Just this afternoon, Brother Vial approached me in the parlor.

'Patience, endurance, and restraint,' he said. 'These are the Lord's most powerful weapons against the wiles of the devil. All these qualities, Brother Lucas, you have exhibited in the last four months, waiting for Francisco to begin his confession. Where the violent methods of Father Adelmo at Poblet failed, the more peaceful approach of Brother Lucas has succeeded. I am proud of you.

'Perhaps,' Brother Vial continued, 'when Francisco has been saved, I will cede to you responsibility for other cases of possession. You will find the same approach you employed with Francisco no less effective with other troubled souls.'

'Brother Vial,' I said, 'I would welcome such an opportunity. I do not wish to boast, but I believe I have established an impressive record as prior, a record that will testify to my diligence and my uncompromising devotion to Santes Creus. Did you notice the hedges that surround the monastery? Many visitors have commented on the manner in which the green bushes soften the gray stone. I overheard Abbot Alfonso tell visitors the idea for the plantings was his own. Perhaps he has told the same to you, Brother Vial. I would not contradict my Abbot. Nevertheless, I would point out that a man's memory is frail. Sometimes individuals hear a suggestion, forget its source, then propound the notion themselves.'

Brother Vial put his finger to his lips to stop me speaking. He grasped me by both shoulders and smiled softly.

'Brother Lucas,' he said, 'you are at the beginning of an arduous journey. It is my fervent hope that after your experience with Francisco, you will find yourself closer to the Lord than you have ever been and that you will reject the false prophets of ambition and vanity that tempt all men. Perhaps, Brother Lucas, when I scale down my official duties, you will become the chief exorcist at Santes Creus and prove a more fierce and implacable adversary of the devil than I could ever be.'

Those were his exact words. *A more fierce and implacable adversary of the devil than I could ever be.*

I thanked Brother Vial for his kind words. I was a bit embarrassed by his lavish praise and his future plans for my advancement. But I was not surprised. Does not the devil employ the same schemes to deceive, to possess, to destroy God's children? And do we, His loving servants, not employ the same methods to foil the darkest and most clever plans of the devil? The very same methods I have used to provoke, to draw out, Francisco's demons, so that one day I, the instrument of the Lord, will crush them. Indeed, this manuscript provides a faithful and precise record of these methods and of what Brother Vial calls this 'arduous journey.' Sometimes I imagine monks from all over Spain traveling to Santes Creus – by wagon, by horse, by foot – to copy this manuscript and to meet its author. Perhaps they will view the document as a model, a manual for combat with the devil. The whole Christian world might one day know Francisco's name – and my own. *Brother Lucas de Santes Creus. Bishop Lucas. Blessed Lucas. Saint Lucas.* I really must focus more energy on my penmanship.

In light of the potential for wide dissemination of the information contained herein, I feel it imperative to provide background concerning the glorious crusade against the infidels. You see, I fear Francisco's version of events might give my esteemed reader a distorted impression. He is, after all, still possessed.

Satan begot the incubus. Six hundred years ago, the poisonous weed of Islam sprouted in the deserts of Arabia. Muhammad's armies spread the scourge east into Persia, north into the Holy Land, west and south across Africa. The darkness cast its shadow into Europe. The Moors carried the affliction across the Straits of Gibraltar into Spain.

For three hundred years, Christian lords have fought sultans and caliphs for control of the Iberian Peninsula. Indeed, the Christian kingdoms of Spain, led by Aragón, Castile, León, Navarre, and Portugal, have put aside their border disputes and petty quarrels and found common cause in the struggle against the infidels. In the last decades, the Christian armies have driven the Moors farther and farther south, conquering Valencia, the Algarve, Córdoba, Murcia, and Seville. Granada is the last infidel stronghold in Spain. God willing, the Christian armies will soon push the savages back across the Mediterranean into the dark regions of Africa.

Unfortunately, the heathen still rage in the east. The abomination continues. The godless occupy, profane, and desecrate the land where Christ lived and died – a holy relic. At first, God's army experienced miraculous victories. In the Year of Our Lord 1099, the crusaders conquered Jerusalem. Indeed, the Lord wrought fire and brimstone on the devil's children. The knights put every person in the walled city to the sword. They say the blood ran up to the soldiers' ankles.

The international military Orders established their headquarters in Jerusalem. The Knights of the Hospital of Saint John claimed the Church of the Holy Sepulcher – built at Golgotha, the place of skulls, the site of the crucifixion. In addition to fighting the infidels, the Hospitallers provide shelter and medical care to pilgrims visiting the Levant. The Knights of the Temple received their name from their base of operations. The conquering lords awarded the Templars the land underneath the old Jewish temple. The crusaders had burned the building to the ground after locking inside the Jews seeking refuge from Christ's fury.

Indeed, the warrior monks have set a high standard of piety and devotion. They take the same vows as ordinary monks – poverty, chastity, obedience. The Church in Rome has granted all the crusaders remission of their sins in return for their service.

Francisco's Order, the Knights of Calatrava, has a long and illustrious history fighting the Moors on the front lines of Andalusia, Muslim Spain. I am proud to write that one of my own, a Cistercian monk named Ramón Sierra, the abbot of a Navarrese monastery, founded the Order. In the Year of Our Lord 1159, Abbot Sierra traveled to Toledo on business. While he was there, he learned that the Moors were set to attack the nearby City of Calatrava. The situation was desperate – the Moors greatly outnumbered the city's defenders. Abbot Sierra, with the permission of the King of Castile, organized the defense of the city, recruiting an army of soldiers and monks from his native province and the surrounding territories. In the face of Abbot Sierra's formidable force, the Moors decided not to attack the city.

Inspired by the fortitude of his recruits, including men of the cloth, Abbot Sierra established a Christian army at the fortress in Calatrava. A few years later, Pope Alexander III issued a Papal Bull recognizing the Knights of Calatrava as the first religious and military order native to Spain. Frey Garcia, the Grand Master of the Order, swore allegiance to the King of Castile and sought affiliation with the Cistercian monks.

The Cistercian Order accepted the request from Calatrava. Thereafter, the Cistercians and the Calatrava have viewed each other as brothers and partners in service to the Lord – the Calatrava will do with the sword what we cannot accomplish with the Book.

The Order of Calatrava is renowned for the military valor and skill of its members and for their spiritual devotion. The members are not permitted to hunt, hawk, play dice or chess – activities that are considered frivolous diversions from prayer and spiritual development. Fornication is punished with flogging, and, in some cases, expulsion from the ranks. Regrettably, it appears that under Uncle Ramón's stewardship, the Calatrava relaxed considerably its monastic discipline. Let us hope that the current Grand Master has restored the spiritual precepts that have traditionally undergirded the Order.

The Calatrava played a critical role in the reconquest of Spain. In response to setbacks suffered by the Christian enclaves in the Holy Land, the Calatrava have more recently turned their attention east. Six years ago, when King Jaime organized an army from Aragón to sail to the Levant, he invited the Calatrava to accompany the armada. After receiving the blessing of King Alfonso of Castile, the son-in-law of King Jaime, the Knights of Calatrava accepted the invitation. Francisco and his comrades joined King Jaime's crusade. Indeed, this manuscript provides a chronicle of

Francisco's pilgrimage, a journey that took place at a time of great turmoil in the east. In the several years preceding Francisco's departure to the Holy Land, the Sultan Baibars led his infidel hordes as they swept through the Levant conquering Christian territory, slaughtering and enslaving the inhabitants. By the time of Francisco's arrival, the Kingdom of Jerusalem did not even include the City of Jerusalem. The Christians were confined to a narrow strip of coast along the Mediterranean, from Jaffa to Acre to Tyre.

In the Year of Our Lord 1269, Hugh, King of Cyprus, acceded to the throne of the Kingdom of Jerusalem, crowned in the great cathedral in Tyre. Hugh was a king in waiting – most of his land occupied by the infidels. Perhaps for this reason, Hugh chose to reside on the island of Cyprus. He installed a constable in Acre to administer the affairs of the city. Unfortunately, the absence of the King and the weak hand of the constable created a confusion of authority in Acre, the largest city in the truncated kingdom. Without the King's presence to unite the Christian knights, fighting broke out amongst various factions. The Venetians fought the Genoans over trade privileges. The grand masters of the different military Orders made conflicting claims concerning ascendancy in military affairs.

As problematic as the internal divisions of authority in Acre was the presence of a large number of Christian convicts who had their sentences commuted in lieu of settlement in the Levant. While many in this flock have turned to the Lord, there remain a minority that cling stubbornly to their evil ways. Indeed, a priest from Poblet who recently visited the Holy Land told me that his pockets were picked twice during his two-week stay in Acre. In addition, he said that he had to make lengthy detours to avoid treading on streets sullied by the presence of pagan and Christian women selling themselves.

Perhaps the failure of our Christian soldiers and traders to unite in the name of Christ and to stamp out the licentiousness in their presence explains why the Lord would allow Baibars' army to wreak havoc on our Christian outposts and to occupy the Holy City. With the threat he poses to Christendom, Baibars might actually prod our knights into the life of true warrior monks – poverty, chastity, obedience, and, if necessary, martyrdom. Perhaps, then, that is God's will, His just punishment, His design.

That Baibars is an agent of Satan there can be no doubt. His evil deeds are well documented. I will mention just a few episodes lest the uninformed reader be led astray by Francisco's inattention to the crimes of the infidels. Indeed, I shudder when I think of the barbarous acts committed against our brave soldiers.

Safed is a name that should connote horror for every Christian. In the Year of Our Lord 1266, Baibars laid siege to the Templar castle of Safed.

After a valiant but doomed defense, the Order of the Temple negotiated safe passage in exchange for their surrender. The documents were signed and delivered to the respective parties. Baibars' personal seal was set down on the deed, guaranteeing the inviolability of the Christian knights. When the unsuspecting knights, their Templar banners raised to God, exited the castle walls, Baibars' soldiers fell on them. Those who were not immediately killed were subsequently skinned alive and decapitated. They say that Baibars himself participated in the torture of many of the knights and delighted in the anguished cries of his victims.

The next year, the Kingdom of Acre sent a delegation of Christian ambassadors to the castle of Safed, which Baibars had converted into a Muslim fortress. The ambassadors were to propose a truce between Christian and Muslim forces. The sight of a thousand Christian skulls surrounding the castle did not deter these bold men from fulfilling their mission. Baibars was unyielding, though. He offered our ambassadors, after their long journey, neither bread nor water, and he rejected every attempt at compromise. It was probably just as well. There can be no peace with Baibars or his soldiers. The infidels must be rooted out and completely destroyed.

Perhaps my venerable reader holds a more hopeful view of the potential for a peaceful settlement in the Levant. To obliterate any such illusions, I give one more example of the treachery of the infidels.

As my reader is no doubt aware, the Christian City of Antioch fell to the Muslims in May, the Year of Our Lord 1268. Less widely known is the extent of atrocities perpetrated by the infidel soldiers in the wake of the city's capture. The following account I received from a knight from Aragón who was present in Antioch during its capture. Through God's grace, this soldier managed to escape the city amidst the chaos of the ensuing massacre.

The first order of business for the Muslim commanders involved the execution of Christian soldiers. The lucky were beheaded. Others died more slowly – lashed, mutilated, burned, quartered. After murdering combatants, the infidels turned their attention to the other inhabitants of the city – women, children, old men. Eyes were gouged out, noses and ears cut off, young girls and boys violated, most unspeakable. Statues of the Virgin were desecrated – spat upon and smashed. There were reports of Saracen soldiers defecating in the churches and holy sanctuaries.

Those Christians lucky enough to find hiding were subsequently rounded up and sold as slaves. Every soldier in the Sultan's army acquired a slave or two, and a surplus still remained which was sold in the markets of Cairo. They say that because of the great number of captured Christians, the price for a girl fell below that for an aged goat.

This was the carnage, the evil, confronted by the armies of Christ. That our forces might have committed some excesses is regrettable. Under the circumstances, though, such unchristian behavior by Christian warriors is understandable. With this note, I return the reader to Francisco's life, his confession, his sorrows.

CHAPTER 8

THE KINGDOM OF ACRE

lmost two months we had been at sea.
Seven out of ten of the ships in our armada,
including the vessel of King Jaime and his
entourage, had been forced to turn back because
of the relentless and pounding storms. In our ship,
forty men had taken ill with dysentery and died;
their bodies were quickly hurled into the sea to
avoid the contagion. One unfortunate soul was
thrown into the gray swell before his last breath
had expired, his hollow eyes righteous, uncompre-
hending. Our sleeping quarters reeked of death –
the guts and bloody excrement smeared indelibly
on the worn floorboards, seeped into the cracks,
like a shiny coat of varnish.

When the fortress city loomed over the horizon
in November, the Year of Our Lord 1270, there
was an outbreak of joyful weeping even amongst
the hardest knights. The winter sun sanctified the
stone walls of the Templar citadel that guarded
the entrance to Acre. Gleaming towers announced
the majesty of the city as if it were Eden itself.

The three boats from Spain glided into the harbor, every man on deck mumbling grateful prayers. Knights streamed forth into the city like ants swarming over the remains of a dead animal. It was not the glorious entrance Uncle Ramón had described many times belowdeck during the rough waters. But it was triumphant – we were alive.

The Calatrava had lost seventeen men. Eighty-seven knights were left in our entourage. We stumbled on the stone steps leading to an open plaza, where the constable and other notables of the city greeted the commanders. Representatives of the three major orders – Templars, Teutonic Knights, Hospitallers – were present to welcome their brethren and escort them to their quarters.

News spread quickly amongst our ranks that several thousand infidel soldiers surrounded the walls of the city. One knight whispered to his brothers, who passed on the news until we all knew. We had arrived in a city under siege. The fears engendered by this information dissipated, though, as I perused the strangeness of our surroundings, its secrets, which distracted and seduced my attentions.

Alongside the Knights of the Cross stood the city's natives, dressed in wondrous garb – white turbans, twisting headdress, purple shoes with upturned points, golden armbands shaped like demonic serpents. Curious onlookers gazed at us as if we were refugees who worshiped at some primeval altar. Young boys, half naked, were hawking coarse bread and perfumed potions that left a foreboding aftertaste. Bejeweled prostitutes poised in the shadows like a somnolent, dreaded promise.

Burning incense created a haze that permeated the narrow streets. The red stone, pockmarked, salty, rose in gilded churches. Soaring towers brooded over a doomed city. The raw wind we drank – swallowed it like desert wanderers, covetous after months of breathing the fetid air of the ship's quarters. A briny balm pervaded the city – the scent of my brother's deliverance and my freedom.

The Calatrava had no representatives in Acre. We were orphans, but fortunate to be affiliated with the Hospitallers through the blood of Uncle Ramón, the fourth cousin of Baron Gustav Bernières of Rouen. Baron Bernières was the Deputy Grand Master of the Hospital of Saint John, the most powerful military Order in the Levant.

The Baron was surrounded by an entourage of knights, battle-weary soldiers in full armor, eyes distant and preoccupied, white Crosses sewn on their black tunics. I felt like a boy amongst men who had experienced the trials of combat and had seen up close the face of death, whereas I had only viewed it from a ship, a safe harbor. They treated us courteously, but there was about them an intimation of disdain, or perhaps bitterness for the uninitiated, as if they begrudged our innocence.

The Baron arranged for our knights to be

quartered at the Hospitaller Ward. Their Order had suffered heavy losses in the recent offenses by Baibars, and they were pleased to adopt the new arrivals. Moreover, of the three hundred or so Hospitallers that remained in the Holy Land, the majority were guarding the castle fortress in the north, the Krak des Chevaliers.

Toward the center of the city, the Hospitallers occupied a massive compound surrounding a pillared courtyard, palm trees sprouting from a floor overlaid with Arab mosaic – peacocked birds, green and yellow patterns on white tile. The Calatrava were housed on the second floor in the eastern wing of the quarter. We slept ten to a room, on straw mattresses, the ocean breeze whispering to us in our dreams of glass castles reaching to the heavens; fair women with copper hair and glazed skin; invisible foes, gargantuan, invulnerable.

The Hospitaller knights, mostly French and German, slept in the western wing, their foot soldiers in the stables sharing the straw mattresses with the horses. The Hospitaller foot soldiers were peasants from all the Christian countries of Europe. Some were native to the Levant. Most did not possess a horse and had little armor – perhaps a shield – maybe a helmet stolen off the head of a dead enemy. But many would fight with a bravery unsurpassed by their noble brethren.

Don Fernando Sánchez, the bastard son of King Jaime, to honor his father's word, provided the Calatrava with squires from his own force.

They transported our armor to the Hospitaller compound. The Hospitallers gave us horses from their own stables.

Meals for the knights were served in the refectory. We ate in pairs, each person assigned the task of monitoring the diet of his partner – to verify that he ate enough to regain the strength for battle, although this mandate was superfluous for the Knights of Calatrava. For the few weeks we remained in Acre, we ate voraciously, rapturously, even when full, to stifle illusive pangs of hunger, the ghosts from our last weeks at sea. Together, the knights from both Orders could fill the long cedar tables in the Great Hall only by half – the echo from grace reminding our fellow knights of their missing and dead brethren. We ate two meals a day. Sesame bread with olive oil, mashed chickpeas, and melon in the morning. For dinner, rice, honeyed bread, and every other day skewered lamb. The wine flowed plentifully during both meals.

There was a hospice across the courtyard from the refectory. True to their original mission in Jerusalem before Saladin reconquered the city from the crusaders, the Order of the Hospital maintained a ward in the western wing of the compound to administer to the sick and provide shelter for pilgrims to the Holy City. In truth, most of the ward's occupants were native Christians displaced by Baibars' recent advances. There was a separate wing on the third story for knights who had suffered grave wounds in battle. One of the

Hospitallers told us that the incurables were taken to die there. Exploring this sector one morning, Andrés and I walked by the gates, peering into the darkness behind the iron bars, hearing moans, intimate, breathing the rancid stench of rotting flesh.

We took turns manning the gates and towers of the city. Each Order had responsibility for a different section. Baibars had surrounded the fortress city, but he had made no move to breach its defenses. In the night, we could see the bonfires of the infidels, like a thousand fireflies beating against the city gates. We could hear the sound of their laughter, smell the pungent spices of their roasts. When we looked up, it was to a star-filled sky full of premonitions.

Three and a half months after our arrival, we woke to find that the infidels had disappeared, packed their tents and marched off, a pilgrimed caravan into the night. Baron Bernières said that Baibars' decision to withdraw derived from his intelligence concerning the arrival of a large force in the city. But Uncle Ramón, in private, surmised that the infidel generals had merely turned their attention north and would return.

With the siege ended, the gates of the city opened. Moribund streets sprang to life with a parade of merchants, their wares in tow. We could hear the procession from our windows in the Hospitaller compound – traders making their way to the market.

Our commanders relaxed the vigilance of our

regimen. Baron Bernières and Uncle Ramón gave one day of leave to their knights to explore the city. Andrés and I departed the compound after breakfast. Initially, we tried to avoid the crowds, ambling through side streets, disoriented in the maze of alleyways. Winding streets became so narrow I had to move sideways, hugging the wall. Buildings leaned one toward the other, each one planted in the other's light. The sun disappeared as if we had passed a door into night.

We ducked under an archway into a dark tunnel. I glided my fingers over the cold stone. A stream of water ran over my boots. A man was begging silently, his palm thrust forward. I stepped over him. The street opened. The sun returned.

Black robes hung from a line above the street, dripping water and soap onto the cobblestone. The smell of lye stung my eyes.

An old man, shirtless, stood in a window, a thin patch of white hairs on his chest. He stared down at Andrés and me. I saluted him playfully. His face remained unchanging, impassive.

We could hear the sounds of the market – shouts, grunts, laughter. A foreign strand of music weaved gentle amidst the tumult, teasing us forward.

Walking around a bend, we found ourselves in the middle of a fantastic carnival. All colors of men – white, black, brown, olive, yellow, red. Smiling welcome, they waved us toward them and their stalls, as if we were old friends. Each one was speaking a different tongue, some harsh, others soothing, like a Tower of Babel. They wore costumes from every land. A man in flowing white robes and the Arab kaffiyeh wrapped around his head was talking with a Frenchman, fitted in the tights and blouse fashionable in European courts.

Amongst these different men, the haggling proceeded, solemn and thoughtful, as if they were philosophizing. The negotiations turned fierce, then tender, and back again.

Shops were selling all manner of merchandise – panther skins from India, crimson silks from Mosul, paper from Samarkand, the parchment thick and creamy. Other stalls displayed spices and other delicacies – open sacks of cinnamon, saffron, rhubarb, anise, capers, cloves, dates, pistachios. Pungent aromas penetrated beneath the skin so that even the hairs on my arms stood straight. A red so red I could swear I had never seen that color.

We entered a plaza. Two giraffes from Yemen milled about languid, as if they had passed most of their days in just such a place. Children squealed. They reached up, proffering bread to the animals. The noble beasts did not bother to look down at the clamor beneath them.

With the promise of cold water mixed with fresh lemons, an old man selling pieces of the True Cross managed to lure Andrés and me into his shop. The cold, tart flavor pressed against the back of my throat, bitter tears momentarily blurring the scene of this sacred sale. When we had drained our cups, we turned our attention to the bloodstained pieces of timber. They resembled wood chips recently axed, the bandaged finger of the man's mute assistant suggesting the origin of the dried blood. Andrés and I, callow, clothed in the robes of a strange order, must have seemed easy targets. I suppose the fact that we picked up the chips – just to view up close the ridiculousness of the scheme – sparked the old man's hopes.

'For true believers such as yourselves,' he said, 'I will give two pieces away – one gold dinar each.'

We left soon thereafter, but the old man, having invested fresh lemons already, followed us through the stalls, maintaining a one-sided dialogue in which he kept lowering his price – he reached three wood chips 'soaked in His blood' for half a copper – until we finally dashed off to lose him, hiding around a corner in the busy market, panting, laughing.

After a few blocks, we found ourselves before a shop selling articles from different warriors who had traversed this remote land, their weapons strewn across the walls in homage to their lonely sacrifice in deserts long forgotten. There were feathered arrows that must have been over one hundred years old; a round, studded shield that bore the scars of many sword blows; a broken lance, the point dulled from its service to the Lord. I unsheathed a hooked Muslim dagger that the owner claimed was from the Abbasid's royal guard in Baghdad. Andrés tried on the round helmet of a Mongol warrior. He looked like Genghis Khan come to Acre.

The shopkeeper wanted five silver dirhams for the Mongol relic. Andrés offered three. In the end, he bought the helmet for four. Four silvers for the memory of this warrior, a brave man or coward we knew not, nor on what field of battle he drew his last breaths. Perhaps, I thought, my own helmet, rusted and bloody, would one day hang on the same wall.

Three stalls down the same Mongol helmet was selling for two silvers. We went back to the original shop, where the man pretended not to remember us. We were engaged in a heated argument with him, demanding the return of two silvers, when a commotion broke out in the Venetian quarter. Reluctantly, we abandoned our efforts and went to see the source of excitement.

It was the advent of a new batch of slaves. The arrivals were chained together, walking from the pier toward a semicircular stone stage on the very edge of the market, wooden benches aligned before it. It was a doleful procession, a lurid circus – white-haired pagan girls from Georgia; voluptuous women from the harems of Arabia; tall, unbroken ebony men from deep Africa; sinewy Orientals, captured by the Muslims east of Persia.

The chief slave master was a Venetian of about forty years, a straggled beard like a patch of weeds covering his several chins. His brown eyes darted around the stage viewing his potential patrons. A gold medallion that bore the emblem of the Roman Pope hung from a thick chain and danced on his belly. Several rubied rings, gold and silver, seemed to be strangling his fat fingers. He was assisted by six of his countrymen – sailors all, faces leathered by the wind.

When the Venetians had herded their captives onto the stage, they unlocked the chains to allow for more thorough examination by prospective buyers, who climbed on the scaffold to inspect the stock. There were locals, and others in Arab kaffiyehs who had traveled many miles. A group of Templars were examining one of the Arabian women. They held her hair up to the sunlight, studying the raven strands. An Arab merchant was using a string to take the measurements of one of the Africans – the shoulders, the width of his chest, his biceps.

Don Fernando was viewing the Georgian girls. The bastard son of King Jaime was a man of thirty-four years, with dark hair, close-cropped, with a pointed beard and a goatee. He was medium height, well built. He could be recognized from a distance by the purple cape he always wore. His close-set eyes, coal black, carried a perpetual look of worry, as if he were making critical internal calculations. Perhaps he was thinking of whom he would have to kill to succeed to the throne, or simply to remain alive.

When Uncle Ramón had introduced Andrés and

me on board early in our journey, Don Fernando recognized my name. He ignored Andrés.

'This is young Montcada, then,' he said, scrutinizing my face. 'I have heard of your brother's untimely demise. So you have become the heir to the Montcada estate. The last becomes the first. The words of Our Savior.'

At the slave market, Don Fernando's look of worry was replaced by a pensive, earnest expression. He was examining the group of Georgian girls, looking at their teeth, their eyes, their posture. He focused his attentions on one in particular, a slender creature, maybe thirteen years old, maybe less. Don Fernando placed his hand gently on her cheek, and glanced at her, a paternal smile. Then he turned to one of the Venetian assistants and asked that he pull down the girl's smock. It was brought down to her waist, the silken down from her femininity just visible. The man behind her motioned to Don Fernando, asking whether he wanted the smock removed altogether. Don Fernando, musing, shook his head, then cupped her left breast and squeezed it, as if he were measuring the freshness of an orange in the markets of Barcelona; the girl impassive, perfectly still, like the stone statue of the Virgin in the Correas' garden. Don Fernando brushed his trimmed beard with one hand, nodded thoughtfully, then retreated to take his seat in the gallery, surrounded by his eight lieutenants and four courtesans.

The bidding began when one of the African men was brought to the front of the stage. A Genoan merchant, well dressed, with hose, red jacket, and skirting, made the first offer. He raised his hand, three fingers spread, and said, 'Oro' – three gold pieces. With the opening bid, a slew of cries, raised hands, cryptic, alien words, erupted from the crowd. The slave master, sitting in a solid wood chair at the side of the stage like a bishop on his throne, followed the progression of prices dispassionately, judiciously, pointing to the current highest bidder with raised fingers as if he were blessing one of his subjects. Several Arabs in the gallery jostled one another. The bidding reached a high pitch. I placed my hands over my ears to shut out the frenzied shouts. Then it was over. Sold. To the first bidder, the fashionable Genoan, for nine dinars. The chains were again placed on the African, and he was led off the stage to his new master.

One of the Georgian girls was next – the selfsame whom Don Fernando had examined so closely. She was brought to the front of the stage, her smock once again lowered to her waist and then pulled back up. The girl stood transfixed – looking toward the sea, as if she might capture a glimpse of her father, mother, or some other refuge. An enchanted gaze that engendered a wistful quiet amongst the gallery, a silent prayer to this pale madonna and our own homelands, real and imagined. I turned my thoughts to Isabel and clutched inside my robe the cloth that held her tears against my skin.

It was a rapt spell, but it was interrupted, exiled by the onslaught of savage cries from the gallery. The price for the girl rose quickly, the stares from the bidders primitive, hungry, untamed. Don Fernando seemed oblivious to the prospective transaction, twirling his purple cape, laughing with his lieutenants. The sale was about to close at seventeen gold coins when Don Fernando finally turned his attention to the stage and put forth his proposal. He said that he would trade two of his courtesans – 'straight from the royal court of Barcelona' – for the five Georgian girls.

'I give you my word,' Don Fernando said, 'the two girls are virgins. The Crown of Aragón be my witness.'

The slave master thought that he had misunderstood and had his assistant translate Fernando's offer. When he had heard again the proposal in his native tongue, he looked perplexed, and questioned Don Fernando: 'But these women that you offer, they are of the Christian faith, signore, no?'

Don Fernando responded forthwith, 'As was Mary Magdalene.'

The slave master raised himself from his chair, pacing the stage, squinting, scratching his head, like King Solomon deciding the fate of the newborn claimed by two women. He rubbed his hands together, called over one of his colleagues, consulted in agitated whispers. Then he descended from the stage to observe more closely the two proffered women, who were laughing amongst their company and seemed willfully oblivious to the proposed transaction.

'Sí.' One word from the slave master, a nod from Don Fernando, and the deal was done. The Venetian shouted to his assistants, and the group of Georgian girls were chained and led down to Don Fernando's party.

The two courtesans made no movement from the royal contingent. Three of the Venetian sailors came down from the stage and stood tentatively outside the circle of Don Fernando's retinue, waiting for his signal. Andrés and I, drawn by a wrenching curiosity, squeezed our way through the throng of people to the margins of the royal party.

Don Fernando spoke to the two women: 'My elegant nymphs, I have some unfortunate news. You are now the property of Venice.'

He looked away from them, spoke with one of his lieutenants, then looked back, as if he expected the two women to have withdrawn already.

When he saw that they had not moved, his tone became more severe. 'Listen, my beauties. I have grown weary of your company. Perhaps you can use your charms to captivate other masters. Leave me now.'

The two women laughed uneasily, perhaps hoping the Don was playing an elaborate but harmless jest. As the Venetians moved closer, though, the two courtesans recognized the gravity of their position.

'But Don Fernando,' one of the women said, faltering slightly, 'we are your courtesans, royal courtesans.'

He looked at the speaker thoughtfully. 'No,' he said, 'you were royal courtesans. Now you are the property of these gentlemen. I advise you to make the best of your new condition. You were whores anyway. Remember that. And remember to have faith. Circumstances can change. Isn't that so, young Montcada?'

Don Fernando glanced at me, a smile, almost compassionate, if not for the edge of his lips, downturned, mocking, and a glare in his eyes that expressed a lifetime of unwholesome yearning, unsated ambition, and unspoken fury. I looked only a moment into the furnace of those eyes until I could hold his gaze no longer.

The women prostrated themselves, falling to their knees, clutching the legs of Don Fernando. He looked down at them, a vague sense of disappointment crossing his face, a beleaguered distaste for the whole affair. Then he motioned for the Venetians to enter his circle and take the women away.

The two women refused to retreat. One of them shrieked hysterically. The other appealed to one of the Venetians, who looked at her blankly. She kept repeating details of her lineage, maintaining that she was third cousin to the Bishop of Barcelona, as if that fact would immunize her from such an undignified fate. The Venetians finally picked the two women up, carrying them over the shoulder toward the back of the stage.

As this drama unfolded, there was a furtive laughter from the royal entourage. The remaining courtesans laughed the hardest, perhaps in relief that they had not been picked by their master. Don Fernando was straightening out his tunic, ruffled by the clutching of the two sold women. In his party, he alone was quiet, his expression transformed, calculating, apprehensive once again, as if he were contemplating vital affairs of state or perhaps matters of succession. When one of the Venetians brought down the document of exchange, Don Fernando signed as if it were a treaty between Aragón and Navarre. When he was done, his entourage departed with the new acquisitions.

I had the absurd impulse to buy the two women back and send them home to Aragón. Absurd it was because Andrés and I had left most of our coins back at the Hospitaller Ward. The two of us rummaged through our pockets but could come up with only four silver pieces. Despite our lack of funds, I asked the slave master how much he wanted for the 'Catalán virgins.' He looked at us keenly, suspiciously, as if we were meddling in affairs in which we had no business. After this short perusal, he chose to ignore my entreaties altogether. Within minutes, the two women were resold to a merchant for sixty-three gold coins.

The bidding began immediately on the next group of slaves. I turned toward the sea, my fists clenched, the chill of the westerly breeze on the cold sweat that cloaked my body.

The next week, Uncle Ramón called the Calatrava to a meeting in the Hospitaller Ward. Flanked by his bodyguards, Bernard and Roberto, Ramón stood in the corner of the courtyard under the refectory. The smell of pressed olives wafted down from the open windows.

'My brothers,' he said, 'soon we go to battle. The bastard Don Fernando has grown impatient in this den of debauchery. He has consulted with the Deputy Grand Master of the Hospital, Baron Bernières, and persuaded him to strike at the infidels. After all, we did not come halfway around the world to sample the whores, did we?'

I let out an inadvertent laugh. Don Fernando, eager to strike a blow against the infidels, the sword of Christ, protector of Christendom. It was amusing.

'Do you have anything to add, Francisco?' Ramón asked.

'No, Uncle,' I said. 'Please excuse me.'

'Baron Bernières and Don Fernando,' Ramón continued, 'have decided to attack Baibars where he is most vulnerable – the castle of Toron, thirty miles march from Acre. The Muslims seized the fortress three years ago. Today, only a small garrison holds it.

'Conquering the castle would be a great victory for Our Savior. Its possession would provide our armies a base of operations to protect the kingdom and to strike at the infidels farther east.

'Don Fernando and his forces – two hundred knights and more than one thousand foot soldiers – will depart for Toron tomorrow. We will accompany Baron Bernières and his four hundred knights the next day.

'Our combined forces will lay siege to the castle. We will not starve the castle's inhabitants into submission. We know from our spy, a Christian Arab who resides in the fortress, that the castle's reserves of food and water could last several months. The Baron hopes that the stranglehold will convince the entrapped populace and soldiers of the inevitability of the castle's fall, so that their commanders will negotiate a bloodless surrender. The Baron will offer safe passage for all the inhabitants in return for the complete evacuation of the castle.

'The Baron, as the commander of the largest force, will assume overall command of the Christian armies. He has requested that the Knights of Calatrava join the expedition.

'Prepare yourselves, my friends. We march on Toron in two days' time.'

It was decided then. I yearned for battle, for the taste and smell of war to liberate Sergio's soul and lift the shadow of my burden.

CHAPTER 9

A FIELD OF BLOOD

The mounted soldiers made the journey to Toron in one day. We rode horses provided by our Hospitaller brethren. Don Fernando's squires transported our armor.

At Toron, the Hospitallers and Don Fernando's army laid siege to the castle – surrounding its walls, preventing entry or exit. The Calatrava set our tents one mile from the other Christian camps. We were situated on the edge of a forest, just out of sight of the castle. Uncle Ramón had volunteered our services in helping construct a siege tower. Our Grand Master seemed to have expertise in all aspects of combat, including engineering. For two weeks, Ramón directed the Hospitaller engineers and their crews, some five hundred men, in designing and building the tower.

The Hospitaller engineers had transported from Acre fifty iron rods and the four corner beams of the tower – thick wood, over one hundred feet long, long, enough to reach the tallest tower of the castle. The Hospitallers had received the measurements of

Toron's towers from the Christian knights who had surrendered the castle three years previously.

In a flat field, the Hospitallers set out the materials. The first day, under Ramón's supervision, the engineers fit the iron to the wood. The rods held the beams apart, making a square. Ropes tied around the four corners held the beams together. The engineers tightened the ropes toward one end, the wood bending, the four beams straining toward each other. Laid out near the forest, the frame of the tower resembled the carcass of a giant beast, with iron ribs and the ropy residue of hanging flesh.

The Hospitallers distributed axes. The Knights of Calatrava found ourselves cutting down trees in some remote forest in Syria. Teams of two worked each side of the trunk. We cleared whole groves, then moved on to the next. My back and shoulders burned from the toil.

The Hospitallers carried the felled timber to another workplace. There the engineers cut, sawed, and shaped the trees into solid beams. The rasping sound of the saws mixed with the coughing of workmen inhaling the dry sawdust.

Another group carried the cut wood to the skeletal tower, as if providing food to the dead beast. In the main camp, Ramón consulted with the master engineer of the Hospitallers, perusing sketches, inspecting the labor, shouting instructions. The constant thud of hammers made it difficult to hear Ramón. Spikes carried in the teeth of the engineers were soon fed to the machine, swallowed whole. The wood planks spread out each day, concealing the empty insides of the tower. The animal came to life slowly.

In an adjoining field, the engineers had placed long vats of vinegar. Animal hides from Acre lay soaking in the tubs. When the hammering subsided, the skeleton no longer visible, the Hospitallers carried the hides to the tower. They nailed the skins to the smooth wood, making a fur coat that eventually covered the entire structure. Ramón said it would prevent or at least slow the spread of flames from burning arrows.

On the last day of construction, another contingent of Hospitaller engineers arrived from Acre with four wooden wheels, each as tall as my chest, and iron axles. The Hospitallers fixed the wheels to the flat end of the tower, providing legs to the engine.

As the final work proceeded, Ramón sent the Calatrava into the forest to clean ourselves. We bathed in the river, washing away the grime of our labors, preparing ourselves for an altogether different task. We returned a couple of hours later and beheld our creation – the tower standing vertical as if it had waked from sleeping. Andrés said that he had not thought a whole army could raise the tower. Ramón later told us that a mechanical contraption, an invention of the infidels, had borne most of the weight.

We stood there for some time, examining the

soaring edifice, paying homage to the colossal creature. It was in fact a death machine, a carriage to transfer the Christian soldiers onto one of the castle towers. More than one hundred knights would approach the castle in midday protected by this wood and iron shelter. The interior of the engine had three stories connected by two openings and rope ladders nailed to the uppermost ceiling. The top floor had a plank that would drop to the surface of a castle tower, a ramp from which the knights would charge the Muslim defenders. The forty knights on the top floor would be the first wave to attack, reinforced and replaced by the knights below. Under fire from the Muslims manning the walls, hundreds of foot soldiers would wheel the tower so that the four wooden wheels would move us into the battle.

And battle there would be. Uncle Ramón had met with Baron Bernières and Don Fernando that morning. The two other commanders had lost patience with the infidels. The Muslim generals had rebuffed the generous offers of safe passage. The latest indignity enraged all the Christian knights. The infidels had stripped naked our emissary and sent him tied and blindfolded on the back of an ass trotting to the Christian forces.

The three commanders decided to attack the castle in two days' time. That gave us one day to wheel the engine to the front lines. Ramón relayed the battle plans. Following an artillery barrage from the catapults, the three armies – the Calatrava, the

Hospitallers, and Don Fernando's force – would attack simultaneously. The Calatrava and Hospitallers, would join forces against the western walls of the castle. Our combined force would rely on the siege engine to lead us into battle. Don Fernando's army would strike from the east.

Five hundred Hospitaller engineers spent that night with spade and hoe, leveling a wide path for the siege engine to travel straight to the castle. At dawn, they attached ropes and pulleys to the great machine. Hospitaller crews took turns hauling the tower toward the castle.

The Calatrava had armored before daybreak. On our warhorses, we guarded the tower, providing protection in the event the infidels tried to send a raiding party to fire or dismantle the machine. They sent no one, though. We spent a full day and the better part of a night watching the grueling struggles of the Hospitaller crews, the slow movement of the tower – step by step. Every quarter hour, the Hospitallers suspended their efforts in order to clean the mud from the wheel axles.

A light rain began to fall at dusk. One of the engineers slipped in front of the tower. I could hear his ribs collapse, crushed like a bundle of twigs on an anvil. Just before dusk, we reached Baron Bernières' camp. It had taken twenty-two hours to move one mile. As our squires pulled off our armor, we could smell the remnants of meat roasting on the spit from the previous night's supper. Looking in the distance, we could see the outline of the fortress, but we paid no mind to that stone apparition. Our bodies craved sleep, our eyes closing fast.

We lay but a couple hours under the canvas tents that were set up before our arrival. One of the Hospitaller foot soldiers woke us with sorrowful melody on his flute – a siren's elegy – a solemn call to battle. We yawned and shook our heads to drive away the troubled spirits that visited us in our sleep. The rain had ended, and a rainbow appeared – 'Noah's golden rainbow,' Uncle Ramón called it. The burnt reds, emerald green, the blue and yellow streaked across the valley.

Through a delicate fog, we glimpsed the castle. The gray stone appeared aloof, indifferent, as it had seen soldiers from many nations march before its walls, only to be buried in the shadows of its formidable facade. The walls reached to the sky, anchored by round, open towers, manned by Saracen archers. Standing on top of the parapet of one of the towers, a man peered out toward our encampment. Perhaps he was a knight just like me, or maybe one of their commanders counting our numbers, measuring our strength. It was my first sight of an individual enemy, an infidel, admittedly from a distance – more a silhouette than a man. But even so, I felt a wave of apprehension and excitement – that very day, I might come face to face with this nameless soldier.

Arrow slits – thin, vertical holes – graced the stone walls in horizontal rows, a menacing pattern that would enable the Saracen archers to shoot at the approaching enemy while remaining hidden. There were larger slits for the mechanical cross-bows that would be used against the siege engine and catapults. Sheltered galleries ringed the walls, making it possible for infidel patrols to circle the entire castle and gauge an enemy's vulnerability. At points the galleries jutted out, concealing large slots in the floor from which burning oil or rocks could be dropped on soldiers attempting to scale the walls.

The squires carried our armor to a patch of dust and gravel just beside our tent. They helped us dress for battle – smoothing the kinks in our chain mail, fastening buckles, tightening straps. Ramón told us not to wear our leggings. The heavy weight of the chain mail would restrict our movement on foot.

French Hospitaller servants served us a breakfast of bread and wine, a wretched, lukewarm concoction, tasting more like vinegar than spirits. The servants looked disdainfully at us, as if it were we who should be serving them. After tasting that foul liquid, I emptied my cup into the earth.

'This wine tastes like shit,' Galindo Fáñez said.

'Ça va,' one of the French servants made the mistake of responding.

'Merde, merde,' Galindo said with a thick Catalán accent, pointing to his cup.

'N'importe quoi vous dites, vous allez mourir

avant midi.' This second mistake was near fatal for our French server.

Whether, as a general matter, Galindo understood French, I do not know. But he understood the gist of those words – no matter what you say, you will die before noon. Galindo grabbed the speaker by the hair, twisted him to the ground, and pressed his sword to the Frenchman's neck.

'I may die in the coming battle,' Galindo said, 'but not before I get a decent cup of wine.'

The sneer vanished from the Frenchman's face. His cheeks blanched. His eyes wide, fastened on the fist that held the sword before him.

No doubt if the Frenchman had understood Galindo's sensitive nature, he would have chosen his words more carefully. Galindo had revealed this nature the first day of our training in Calatrava. We were in the barn, hanging on a metal bar placed across the stalls. It was a test of strength. Ramón himself counted off the seconds as we clasped the bar. Galindo was one of three trainees who fell before thirty.

'Do not worry, girls,' Ramón said to this group of three, 'Bernard and Roberto will get you into shape.'

Grand Master or no, Ramón had insulted Galindo, who took off, rushing headlong toward our master. It seemed he would tackle Ramón from behind. Ramón must have heard the footsteps or sensed Galindo's approach. He rotated his body and brought down his elbow on Galindo's head just before their collision. Galindo went sprawling, his face planted in a pile of mud.

'Galindo,' Ramón said, 'one day you will be a Knight of Calatrava. Until then, try to remain on your feet.'

In our makeshift camp at Toron, Galindo was on his feet. He was standing on the Frenchman, dumping a jar of wine on his head.

'Kill him,' Enrique Sánchez said. 'Kill the bastard.'

All of us, including Galindo, turned to Enrique in surprise. He was the youngest of the knights, barely eighteen. He was amiable, well liked by all our comrades, known more for his exploits in love than in our martial contests.

He had almost been expelled from the Order several months before our departure. It was the feast of the Assumption. Many of the knights visited the town's festivities, some the local tavern. We made our way back to the fortress after nightfall, singing ballads and dancing. Enrique could not be found. We thought he had returned with an earlier group. He had – a group of two. We came upon them in the refectory. Esmeralda, a whore from town, rushed to greet Ramón.

'What sweet boys you hide up here, Ramón,' Esmeralda said.

We were in the company of the head priest of the Order, Padre Dioniso, who had been awakened by our singing. Barefoot, his pale, bony shins sticking out from his robe, the padre was lecturing us on the evils of consuming spirits when even he was silenced by the scene before us. Enrique was lying flat on his back on one of the wooden tables – naked, except for a leather pendant around his neck, a gift from his companion.

'Padre Dioniso,' Ramón said, 'may I introduce Esmeralda, one of Calatrava's most beloved residents. Of course, you know Enrique.'

That Enrique would be expelled from the academy the next day was assumed by all in the company. The other soldiers, including me, retreated hastily to our quarters, leaving Ramón, Enrique, and Esmeralda to face Padre Dioniso's wrath. We learned what happened several days later. According to Galindo, Esmeralda was well acquainted with Padre Dioniso. She referred to him as 'el lobo,' the wolf, and snarled playfully. Despite Esmeralda's familiar salutation, the padre maintained that he had never met the girl. The padre launched into a diatribe against fornicators, bringing Esmeralda to tears with a vivid description of the torments that awaited her in hell. When he was done, he began slapping his own face. He did so repeatedly, red welts rising on his cheek, until Ramón stayed his hand. Sobbing, the padre fell to his knees and confessed to an illicit liaison with Esmeralda. He kissed Uncle Ramón's feet and begged him to be merciful. Uncle Ramón agreed to keep Padre Dioniso's secret on condition that Enrique be allowed to remain at Calatrava. In order to maintain appearances, Padre Dioniso pleaded with Ramón to allow a minimal punishment for Enrique. Ramón told the padre that, given the unusual circumstances, he would need the permission of Enrique, who magnanimously agreed to the imposition of an extra hour of silent prayer in the afternoon for one month.

Any magnanimity Enrique displayed toward Padre Dioniso was absent that dawn before the battle. 'Kill the French bastard,' Enrique repeated, as he unsheathed his sword with one hand and twirled Esmeralda's leather pendant in the other. He seemed determined to perform the deed himself if Galindo's resolve faltered.

Chance saved the Frenchman's life. Uncle Ramón and his two lieutenants, Bernard and Roberto, arrived before Galindo or Enrique could draw blood. Our leader had been at a strategy meeting of the various commanders.

'Taut nerves after a difficult journey make for short tempers,' Ramón said, as he rode upon his company. 'This man is not your enemy. Save your blade for the infidels.'

Galindo and Enrique did not move.

'Do you mean to practice on our hosts then?' Ramón said, laughing. 'Very well. Galindo, hold him down so Enrique can cut his throat. Why stop there, though? Let's kill all the servants.'

Galindo and Enrique peered uncertainly at Ramón, then at their prisoner, then back at Ramón. Finally, Galindo stepped off the Frenchman, who scurried away. Enrique returned his sword to its scabbard. We resumed our preparations, glancing occasionally at Galindo and Enrique with a vague mixture of disquiet and respect.

'Ramón, what reward,' Pancho Jerez asked, 'to the knight who kills the greatest number of infidels?'

Pancho was a fine warrior – a skilled swordsman, highly effective with a joust. But his opinion of himself greatly exceeded even his able talents. He tried to get the other knights to call him El Cid. He offered me a belt of fine leather if I would refer to him by this nickname and persuade Andrés to do the same. We ended up calling him El Cidiota, the Idiot.

'Just fight, Pancho,' Ramón said. 'Leave the counting of the dead to the Lord.'

We pulled our white tunics over our chain mail. I grasped tightly the cloth that I had received from Isabel in the garden of the Correa estate. Then I placed it under my chain mail against my chest.

When we were armored, Ramón marched the company toward our Hospitaller brethren. Baron Bernières rode amongst them – a handsome man, tall in the saddle, with fine sandy hair that extended to his shoulders, and a light brown beard, closely trimmed. He spent considerable time each morning grooming himself. At the refectory in Acre, he came to each meal as if he were dining with the King, his robes pressed, his brown hair glistening with oil. I heard some of his knights refer to their master in whispering tones as 'the immaculate one.' It was a moniker infused with an irony unflattering for the commander of several hundred knights, particularly one who had only recently arrived in the Levant and had yet to prove himself on the battlefield. His chief credential derived from his family name. The Baron was the brother of François Bernières, the Archbishop of Paris. Even the morning of the assault, I remember seeing the Baron seated just outside his tent, trimming his eyebrows, as his squire held up a looking glass.

For sure, the Baron was no warrior – even I, never having fought a battle, could see that. He was too pretty. But, as Uncle Ramón stated, the Baron's great virtue lay in the fact that while he might not have been called to the sword, he surrounded himself with men that were, including our Grand Master, Uncle Ramón.

At the behest of Baron Bernières, the Calatrava composed a separate contingent within his Hospitaller regiment. A scout from the camp of Don Fernando had informed the Baron and Ramón that his troops were set to begin their assault on the opposite side.

The Calatrava stood behind the catapults with the Hospitaller knights, sharpening our swords, making final adjustments to our armor. Facing the castle, the siege engine stood next to the armies, observing our preparations, waiting for its occupants.

The catapults – twelve of them – had been pulled under cover of darkness to within striking distance of the castle walls. Carts full of stones lay astride the machines. Forty soldiers and engineers, led by a captain, operated each contraption. Like the rapt maiden audience to a jousting contest, we watched the Hospitaller crews prepare the machines and load them. I had never seen such advanced instruments – catapults constructed by the finest engineers in Acre. A long, sanded beam balanced on a metal axle. The longer end of the beam was tied down, impatient, ready to spring forward, its leather pouch holding a great stone. On the other end, several ropes hung loosely, to be yanked down in unison to propel the missile. Carved and stained into each beam was the name each crew had given to their machine – the Minister, the Lion, Paris, the Apostle.

The firing began as the sun's glare became visible in the metal helmets worn by the Hospitaller knights. We could hear the rocks whining through the air almost disappearing into the clouds, only to descend and crash into the castle – an awful, terrifying thunder. The Saracens on the walls responded with a salvo of arrows that fell well short of our position.

The bombardment by catapult was unrelenting. The whistle of the missiles as they descended toward the castle was disconcerting even to the Christian knights huddled in the opposite direction of the trajectory. The impact shook the foundations of the fortress' walls and the earth beneath us. I looked to my right at Andrés.

He was staring solemnly at the awesome display.

'Holy Mother of God,' he said, under his breath.

The Saracen archers, out of range of their targets, disappeared from the towers. It seemed impossible, but the walls remained standing. Smashed, riven, cracked, but the walls remained. That is, until an unexpected development led Baron Bernières to change our battle plans.

Without warning, a sizable breach appeared in the outer wall. I suppose we should have suspected a ruse, given the nature of the opening – the two sides almost parallel, as if a knife had cut a swath out of the wall. Perhaps sensing the potential for a rout, the Baron ordered one of his deputies to charge the castle with a company of knights. On horseback, the Hospitallers – around eighty men – approached the gap cautiously but unmolested. Ramón sensed something amiss. He was standing just in front of me.

'Baron,' Ramón said, 'the gap – it's too clean. I fear an ambush. Call your men back. We should abide by the original plan. The siege engine will bring us right to the castle walls.'

The Baron smiled good-naturedly at Ramón, but with a hint of condescension.

'I never thought,' the Baron said, 'to see the Grand Master of Calatrava lose his nerve in the pitch of battle.'

From our position, we could see through the

breach. The Hospitaller knights rode into the gap. After a brief interval, we could hear exultant cries from the Hospitallers within the castle, their warhorses stamping triumphantly in the deserted courtyard. 'Glory be to God,' came the shouts from inside the castle, which were echoed by their brothers outside. It was as if our foes had vanished into the mist.

Jubilant, the Baron looked to Uncle Ramón at his side.

'Perhaps, my friend,' the Baron said, 'the infidels realized the futility of resisting such an overwhelming force.' He patted Uncle Ramón on the back.

When the gate slid across the opening – wrought iron, perhaps twenty feet high – there was a moment of harrowing confusion and disbelief amongst the knights trapped inside the castle. The Saracen soldiers reappeared on the walls. Instead of facing us, they were looking toward their captives in the castle's interior.

The shouts of victory from the Hospitallers did not end immediately. Many of the knights did not seem to comprehend the significance of the changed circumstances. The warhorses were the first to realize the danger of the situation. They began to buck and neigh furiously. The Saracens seemed to savor the excruciating, palpable sense of uncertainty. For several minutes, they made no move against their guests, who would soon recognize the strategic blunder they had made. The Saracens had disassembled the wall themselves, seducing the Hospitaller knights and their commander with the prospect of an easy victory.

I glanced at Ramón. His eyes were closed, but in his sullened grimace, I saw the fate that awaited our brethren. The knights with whom we had shared quarters and food for almost four months – eighty of them – they were dead men, lured into the castle only to end their lives as target practice for the expert Saracen marksmen who manned the walls with their crossbows.

The sound of the slaughter commenced with the swoosh of infidel arrows, piercing armor. One of the trapped knights charged the gate and swung his sword at the iron bars – a ferocious but hopeless gesture, the clang echoing through the valley. The knight's horse was felled underneath him, and he struggled to his feet. I could see his hands gripping the bars. He was shot from behind. He slumped forward, his arms through the holes of the gate so that his lifeless body was still standing, suspended.

We watched, helpless, afraid to look each other in the eye, as if it were somehow our responsibility, or there were something we could do to stop the massacre. What could we do?

Uncle Ramón urged the foot soldiers operating the catapults to resume firing. He shook several of the captains violently, but they just stood there, paralyzed, straining to hear the affliction of their comrades – the frantic cries for help, screams of pain, the moans of the dying. And then all that was left was a perfidious silence.

Baron Bernières looked as if he had traveled through the nether regions of hell and beheld his own self. Ramón tried to capture the attention of the Baron and focus him on the battle before us.

'Baron, you are our commander,' Ramón said. 'We await your orders.'

But the Baron stared silently ahead, beyond Ramón, a vacant smile on his face.

'Baron,' Ramón persisted, shouting in his face, 'I recommend that we employ the siege tower.' Ramón repeated himself, until the Baron finally nodded as if to be rid of a nuisance.

Before Ramón could dispatch Roberto to relay his orders, one of Don Fernando's scouts stumbled into our circle. His eyes wild with the grim reflection of combat, he approached the Baron and Ramón, escorted by one of the Hospitaller knights. He reported that Don Fernando's first battering ram had been set ablaze by burning oil dropped from the castle's ramparts.

'The second ram is in place, though,' the scout stated. 'Don Fernando is confident that he can protect its advance with his archers.'

The scout waited for a reply, but the Baron stared fearfully at him as if he were the ghost of one of his men come back to haunt him. It was a disagreeable, awkward moment, the brave scout baffled by his reception. When it was apparent the Baron would not respond, Ramón spoke.

'Tell Don Fernando,' Ramón said, 'our lives depend on his success. Give the scout water, Roberto. Send him back to Don Fernando with news of the temporary setback we have suffered here.'

After the scout's departure, Baron Bernières staggered forward. Uncle Ramón caught him before he fell in the dust and sat him down amidst his Hospitaller entourage.

'My lord,' Ramón said, 'with your permission, I will assume command of the force until your recovery.' The Baron did not reply. The Hospitaller knights that surrounded them, including the Baron's deputies, deferred to Ramón's judgment, looking down in embarrassment for the behavior of their commander.

Ramón instructed Colonel Pierre Delacorte, the Baron's first deputy, to prepare the Hospitaller crews to wheel the siege tower into battle. Ramón then directed the Hospitaller foot soldiers to carry the clay pots of Greek fire to the front line of catapults.

Greek fire was invented in Byzantium some six hundred years ago. Our Greek brothers closely guarded the secret of its composition, until the Muslims stole it or stumbled upon it in the last century. It is made of sulfur, saltpeter, and oil, and mixed in clay pots. In Calatrava, Uncle Ramón had told us of its destructive powers. Ramón had been made to endure the fire-and-brimstone barrage of that substance during the Saracens' unsuccessful siege of Margat. At that time, Ramón was a knight in the Order defending the castle against an army from Egypt. The siege lasted half the year, the starving knights reduced to eating their mounts, and then the dead amongst them. According to Ramón, one of the order's priests issued an extraordinary dispensation allowing the consumption of the dead in order to save the living. The priest himself refused to partake of Christian flesh and died a few days later, his body and blood victim to his own edict.

Before advancing on Margat, the Saracens bombarded the castle by catapult – with Greek fire that exploded on impact with a cloud of fire and smoke. Several of Ramón's comrades died in the flames; others suffocated from the smoke. The defenders were on the verge of surrender. The Saracens had wheeled their siege engine a few steps from one of the castle towers. Their soldiers were beginning to scale ladders leaning against the castle walls. As Ramón was mumbling a final prayer, the Saracen engine imploded. Ladders fell, the climbing infidel soldiers hurled to the ground.

The Christian sappers had dug a mineshaft under the castle walls. When the siege engine reached the shaft, it broke through the earth. With the onset of the summer heat, the campaign season ending, the Saracen commanders decided to withdraw. The siege was lifted, and Margat remained in Christian control. Of the original one hundred seventy-five knights who guarded the castle, twenty-one remained alive, including Uncle Ramón.

I do not know why Baron Bernières had neglected to use Greek fire in the initial salvo. He had been anxious to breach the fortification before Don Fernando's men, and he probably believed that the stone missiles would speed penetration of the castle walls.

Uncle Ramón said that we would return to the original battle plan. The Hospitaller crews operating the catapults would continue to launch stones in an attempt to breach the western wall, but would set aside an interval of time to load clay pots of Greek fire. This interval would precede and provide cover for an assault of the siege engine against one of the castle towers. Ramón said that the Greek fire would create enough turmoil within the castle to divert the attention of the Saracens from our attack.

Once the Greek fire was carried up to the front line of catapults and launched toward the castle, the tenor of the battle changed dramatically. Sailing over the castle walls, the Greek fire exploded, sending smoke billowing up from the interior. Small fires broke out along various sections of the castle's walls where wood had been used in the construction. The noise and commotion within the castle raised the morale of our soldiers, breaking the stupor into which many had sunk after the slaughter of our brethren.

The siege engine was wheeled almost to within

range of the Saracen archers when Uncle Ramón gave orders that the Calatrava were to ascend to the top floor of the tower. We would be the first to hit the ramparts. The Hospitaller knights were to occupy the lower floors, acting as reinforcements. Before entering the siege engine with his men, Uncle Ramón ceded operational control of the battlefield to Colonel Delacorte, the Baron's first deputy.

'Colonel,' Ramón said, 'I order you to remain alive in order to oversee the battle.'

'Ramón,' Colonel Delacorte stated, 'my survival, as yours, is in the hands of Jesus Christ. I hope that He looks with favor on both of us today.'

We followed Ramón into the siege engine, single-file, then climbed the rope ladder that connected each level. It was a difficult ascent because of the extra weight in armor and weaponry each of us carried – some sixty pounds. The darkness deepened as we ascended, moving farther away from the entrance, the only source of light in the tower. The skin on our palms rubbed off on the coarse twine. I could feel warm drops of blood on the rope. Upon reaching the top level, Ramón took hold of my arm and guided me to the left front corner of the engine. I stood there, sightless, clenching fast my sword and shield.

It seemed an interminable period before the other knights filled the lower levels of the tower.

We could hear the scrape of their boots on the wooden floor. Ramón spoke over the rumble.

'Once inside the castle, men,' he said, 'you will be offered all manner of Muslim cuisine. Be chivalrous, and eat what they serve you. We would not want to offend our hosts by declining their most precious delicacies.'

Amongst our company, there was a restive laugh, a long, unnatural sigh, a release of hidden fears. Most of us would probably not survive the assault. When the gangplank was lowered, the Knights of Calatrava would be the first Christian soldiers to set foot inside the castle. Our casualties would be very high – they always were for the first line of attackers – usually fifty percent, sometimes one hundred.

'I have received intelligence,' Ramón said, 'from our spy concerning the secret existence of a harem in the castle. He says it contains the most beautiful women in Arabia. Perhaps I could seek a special indulgence from the Bishop of Acre to allow the victorious knights an opportunity to enjoy the local fruits. They say he is a very understanding man who has a taste for that sort of thing. Or maybe I should seek the kindly intervention of the Pope. What say you, Francisco?'

The laughter was harder, drawn out, more inclusive – even the devout forgetting themselves and joining Ramón's congregation.

'I would say,' I responded, 'thank you, Uncle Ramón. If I live, I will pay a visit to this harem. If I live.'

'Francisco,' Ramón said, 'you are a gracious boy. But you brood unnecessarily. Your approach to life is rather grave. I think a visit to this harem would be just the right medicine for you. Yes, I am certain of that. Bernard . . .'

'Yes, Uncle,' Bernard replied.

'Remind me,' Ramón said, 'once we have taken this castle that Francisco is to be the first knight to enter the harem.'

Ramón continued speaking, teasing various knights, making fun of Baron Bernières' elaborate wardrobe – 'I was surprised that the Baron did not wear his golden epaulets to the battle. They were quite becoming back in the refectory in Acre. Don't you think so, Andrés?' – any topic but the battle in which we would soon be engaged. Ramón's words did not banish the fear – the dread that would grip my heart when I thought of running down the plank onto the castle tower. But those terrible moments of isolation diminished, fading in the glare of Ramón's valor, in the casual, undaunted tone of his voice.

There were some knights, veterans, perhaps just as brave as Ramón, who guarded the source of their courage jealously as if revealing or sharing it would diminish its strength. Ramón offered his bravery as a deep trough from which we all could drink freely.

When the engine was full, the Hospitaller foot soldiers began wheeling the tower forward, under increasing fire from the Saracen defenders. The flanking boards, nailed to the sides of the siege engine that morning, fanned out from the structure like a set of wings. They provided protection for those on the ground, but the Saracens were still able to pick off at regular intervals the soldiers who wheeled us. We could hear their grunts under the heavy burden, the woeful cries of the wounded, the urgent calls for reinforcements when their casualties mounted. The sounds of war sometimes drowned out Ramón's discourse, but he kept speaking.

The movement of the tower was agonizingly slow. At several points, the engine stopped altogether. I lost track of time – had it been minutes, hours, or days that we remained in that dark chamber? I had no idea where we were in relation to the castle – whether we were close or many feet away from the battle. We could hear the constant thump of arrows against the tower – the wood splintering. Sometimes we could see the glint of an arrowhead protruding inside the engine. The heat from the burning arrows raised the temperature to a suffocating, almost intolerable degree. The sweat from my brow dripped down into my eyes, but my helmet was fixed in place, ready for battle, and I dared not take it off to relieve the painful sting. My throat ached from dryness.

If the engine caught fire, there would be no escape. The tower would make an impressive funeral pyre for the Knights of Calatrava. I wondered how they would report our demise in Spain. They could not say that we died before engaging the enemy – that after all our training, after King Jaime had personally requested our presence in the Levant, that not one infidel fell under the mighty swords of Calatrava. No, they would create a more glorious ending.

How would my parents take the news? It would kill my mother. One son dies by water, the other by fire. Two martyrs in the family. My father would run faster, travel farther, from one jousting tournament to another. He could not, though, escape the bitter reality that his seed had been extinguished.

Fortunately, the fire did not enter our chamber. The vinegar-soaked hides that coated the tower proved an effective antidote to the flaming arrows. I doubt that hell itself was hotter than that chamber, though.

The soft words of a comrade diverted my attention. I recognized his voice. Enrique Sánchez, Esmeralda's young lover, was reciting the prayer for the dead.

The Lord is my shepherd; I shall not want.

Before Enrique reached the second verse, most of my neighbors had joined him. I did not chant the prayer, although I derived some comfort from those familiar verses, humming along to the soothing meter.

He leadeth me beside the still waters.
He restoreth my soul.

Still waters sometimes rage underneath. I thought of Isabel's struggle under the ice, her gray eyes, her smooth hands, her silver tears. Her silken cloth pressed against my chest, drenched in my sweat, perhaps soon in my blood. I wondered what she was doing at the moment – practicing archery, gossiping with the serfs.

Thou preparest a table before me in the presence of mine enemies . . .

Mine enemies – these nameless soldiers who waited for me. The mind can become trapped in the dread of the approaching trial, the gnawing suspicion that death waits just beside you. The darkness inside the engine would be for many of my comrades the very shadow of death closing fast.

The knights on levels below accompanied Enrique's prayer – a funeral dirge – a chant of suns forever setting. The whole tower swayed with the rhythmic ballad and the slashing arrows of the infidels.

I could hear Ramón, just beside me, fidgeting uneasily with his armor. I suspect that he was uncomfortable with the recitation of such a somber, pessimistic prayer. He probably thought it would contribute to a certain resignation not compatible with the fierce mood required for a swift and brutal assault on the tower.

Ramón did not attempt to stop the ballad, though. I do not think he could have if he tried. Instead, he joined in the rendering. His bold voice overshadowed Enrique's melancholy tone and injected a note of defiance. Somehow, under Ramón's direction, the sorrowful melody transformed into song of combat. The prayer became a petition not for us but for the infidels who would soon die under our swords.

We knew that we were close to the castle walls when we could hear the shouting of the infidels, peculiar, enticing words, and smell the distinctive sulfurous smoke from the explosions of Greek fire that beset the Saracen defenders. My sword was shaking in my hands, clattering against the cedar planks. I squeezed the handle with both hands, but I could not stop the tremor.

I am going to die, I thought. Andrés and I will join my brother before the day is done. Perhaps in seconds. What happens if my legs will not move forward when the gangplank lowers? Must I reach the castle tower in order to redeem my brother's soul? Must I kill one of the infidels? Or simply die with honor? Is that enough to lift Sergio's soul to paradise? Is that enough for my own deliverance? Lord, please give me the strength to serve You.

The gangplank made a loud thud when it landed on the tower. A blinding sunlight flooded the chamber. My eyes hurt from the effort to see. I heard shouts from all around me, 'Go, go, go!' The men in front of me shuffled toward the exit. The first wave of knights hit the gangplank greeted by the crisp sound of crossbows snapping, savage howls, horrific screams. Our sanctuary had been ruptured.

When my eyes adjusted, I could see the ramp. It sloped slightly downward, a thick wooden board

251

– ten feet wide, fifteen feet long. A walk of death. Over the shoulders of the knights before me, I could see several Saracens. They were kneeling, aiming their crossbows at the opening. The castle's stone tower was round, crenellated, so that the Saracen archers could aim their crossbows in the gaps of the fortification.

Our knights spilled out, pushed onto the plank. They ran down the ramp, frenzied, hunted. Galindo Fáñez was holding the sword that only hours before had pressed against the neck of our French server. He was moving ponderously down the ramp. He held his shield in front of him and raised his sword timidly. The arrows tore into his shield, dismantling it, until he was holding only the leather handle. Then the arrows ripped into his hauberk, screeching through the metal mesh. Galindo stopped suddenly and turned toward the engine, distracted, as if he had forgotten something – in his face, a doleful confusion.

When Pancho, El Cidiota, stepped out onto the plank, he hesitated for a split second, perusing his adversaries. In that instant, an arrow bored into his neck. An arc of blood cascaded from the wound. The stream fell like rain past the edge of the plank. Pancho pitched forward facedown on the plank.

Enrique Sánchez was next. With Esmeralda's leather pendant dangling from his neck, he dashed down the ramp.

'For you, Esmeralda,' Enrique shouted, 'with all my soul.'

Enrique was shot in the stomach. He continued down the ramp until he stumbled onto the tower.

Still the incessant commands – 'Go, go, go!' – echoed in the chamber. Just outside, the screams of the dying.

Ramón and his deputies stood to my right. They were advancing slowly toward the opening. Andrés and I moved directly behind them.

We were close to the entrance. Our turn would come in seconds. I could hear the Hospitaller knights below. They were ascending the ladder to fill the places left by our dead comrades.

And then we stood before the light, a crystal-blue sky. We were in full view of the enemy, a company of twenty or so Muslim archers spaced evenly around the circle. Not one seemed to be injured. Most were in the act of reloading their crossbows.

This was the moment of which Ramón had spoken during our exercises in Calatrava – the 'window of vulnerability.' It was crucial, according to Ramón, to close the gap between the archers and us as soon as possible. At a distance, the Saracens could pick us off one by one. In close combat, the Saracens would have great difficulty defending themselves against our heavy swords. If we could reach them before they reloaded, if we could reach them before they aimed their crossbows, we would stand a good chance.

Followed by his two deputies, Ramón stormed down the plank. The Saracens seemed intrigued, puzzled by the fierce cries. They looked up from their weapons to the charging knights. Ramón's sword came down like a tornado. His victim's head snapped back, severed from his body. The man remained standing, frozen in the act of loading his crossbow, as if the loss of his head were only a momentary setback. Slashing, thrusting, Bernard and Roberto fell upon a trio of archers to the left. They reached the group before crossbows were raised.

Andrés and I followed. Ramón's wild cries resounded in my heart. I sprinted forward, anxious to find a destination for my sword. As I crossed the bridge, I looked down to the earth, one hundred feet away. The broken bodies of my brothers were splayed on the dusty ground. When I looked up, I fixed my sight on one of the infidel defenders. He was just toward the right on the tower. I ran toward him. He was putting an arrow in the chamber of his crossbow. I heard my own voice – a foreign, barbarous cry. The Saracen placed the arrow in its shaft. He pulled back the bow. Before raising his weapon, he glanced up at me. His black eyes desolate. My sword came down on his head, splitting his skull like a coconut under the knife. The warm, gray juices spattered like myrrh on my burning cheeks.

The man crumpled forward. To my left, a Saracen trained his crossbow on me. I raised my shield to defend myself. He released the arrow. It flew toward me slowly. It seemed to take several seconds to reach my shield. It punctured the wood easily. The arrow blade slowed and stopped just before reaching my chest. I jettisoned the shield and charged him. He was reaching for his dagger when I ran him through with my sword. The blade, razor-sharp, plunged into his stomach with no more resistance than if I had thrust the weapon into the sea.

The sword's removal was more difficult. I tried to pull it up with one hand. The dead man resisted, his entrails clutching the instrument as if it belonged to him. As I was struggling to extricate my sword, I saw out of the corner of my eye one of the Saracens charging toward me with an axe at his side. It occurred to me that I could let go of the sword and use my own dagger to fend off the attacker. But a dagger is a weak defense against an axe. I thought I could wrench the sword free in time to block the imminent blow. I put both hands on the hilt. I placed my foot on the dead man's shoulder. I pulled with all my might.

The Saracen was quicker than I anticipated. He was upon me before I could salvage the weapon. His axe coiled back, ready to spring toward me. I braced for the impact, as if somehow my taut muscles could deflect the blade. I did not feel afraid. Not anymore. The fear had not disappeared. It was simply pushed to the side. There was no space for it.

The axe did not strike, though. My assailant staggered. He dropped his weapon and fell forward. He wrapped his arms around me. As his grip slackened, his body slid down my own. I saw over his shoulder the hilt of a dagger welded to his back. Ramón stood about ten feet away, his right hand open, as if gesturing to this unimagined embrace. When the Saracen fell to the ground, I resumed the battle to loosen my sword. It finally came free, the blade coated in a scarlet sheen.

No Saracen stood before me. I turned around and beheld the exit of the siege engine – a glorious sight. The arrows of the Saracens were no longer concentrated on the opening. Our knights rushed forth fearlessly. The fresh soldiers chased down the few Saracens that remained alive. They killed some by sword. Others they threw off the tower. The screams of the condemned men echoed through the valley like a flock of raving seagulls.

I fell to my knees. I closed my eyes. The victorious shouts of my comrades enveloped me.

Blessed Sergio. I am alive. Thank you, Lord. Thank you for giving me the courage to serve you.

When I opened my eyes, I saw Uncle Ramón on bended knee. He was stroking gently the head of one of our fallen knights. It was Roberto, his deputy. Dead.

Enrique lay beside Roberto's body. His moans drew Ramón's attention. He was breathing in short gasps. He had taken two arrows in his stomach. His intestines were oozing out of his chain mail and staining his tunic. He had fouled himself, the stench from his guts and excrement overpowering.

I approached him, unseen, staring at his ashen face. Ramón held his hand.

'Enrique, it seems,' Ramón said softly, 'you may enter the harem before me. Do not hog all the beautiful women.'

Enrique coughed, blood sputtered on Ramón's cheeks.

Ramón bent over him and grasped his hand. 'I am proud of you,' Ramón said. 'You fought with valor, Enrique. I will visit your family to tell them of your heroism and your sacrifice here.'

I do not think Enrique heard Ramón's words of consolation. He was wheezing heavily and seemed to be focusing on the clouds just beyond Ramón.

'Please say goodbye to Esmeralda,' Enrique said. 'Pay her a coin or two. I never did settle with her.'

Enrique's mouth dropped open. His cheeks froze in place. His eyes locked in a vacant gaze. A martyr's death. His last words homage to a whore, lying in his own shit, so noisome I was forced to turn my face.

Ramón touched my arm. 'Francisco,' he said, 'where is Andrés?'

The air drained from my body, leaving a hollow cavity in my gut. I had forgotten Andrés. I had last seen him crossing the ramp, his jaw set fast, his sword raised. *What if he is maimed? What if he is dead? What will I do? What will I say to Isabel?*

I pushed my way through a crowd of knights. I grabbed the white tunics of my comrades. I spun them around to inspect their faces. They spoke to me from far away, perhaps of the battle, their words unintelligible. I looked at the corpses on the tower's surface. *No, it cannot be. Please, God.* I called his name. No answer came. Then I looked up and saw him.

Andrés was standing on the parapet, looking north, away from the castle. He seemed to be studying the cliffs of a distant mountain, as if he were looking for a suitable line of ascent, a path to take him beyond the horizon, far removed from the killing at Toron. A gust of wind filled the void in my stomach. I called to Andrés. He turned around, looking straight at me. He did not seem to recognize his friend. His thick forearms were covered in blood. His white surcoat and his face were streaked black from the smoke.

'Francisco,' he finally stated, almost a question, as if he had difficulty recognizing me.

The world had changed – the rage of combat, watching comrades cut down like animals to the slaughter, the ease and arrogance of killing another man, the elation of victory. Hope and fear set free.

'Yes,' I said, 'I am here.'

I left Andrés on the parapet and walked toward the center of the tower, where Uncle Ramón and several Hospitaller deputies were huddled on bended knees. They were taking account of our losses and discussing the battle plan.

Ramón was counting our casualties on his

bloodstained fingers. Thirty-nine knights from the Order of Calatrava had been killed or seriously wounded in the assault. Forty-eight of us remained.

'Jesus Christ,' Ramón said, 'has been merciful.'

Ramón told the Hospitaller deputies to use their foot soldiers to evacuate the dead and wounded. Then he turned his attention to the battle. He drew an imaginary map of the castle on the stone floor, which became the basis for planning the tower's defense, each man pointing to the invisible diagram as if it were drawn on parchment.

'The Saracens will be forced to devote much of their resources to containing and attempting to crush our intrusion,' Ramón said. 'We will create as much trouble as possible to ease the pressure on Don Fernando's strike from the east.'

Before issuing specific orders, Ramón reviewed the structure of the castle's tower. There were three entrances, he said, three points from which the Saracens could counterattack – a winding staircase carved into the stone, going down into the bowels of the castle, and two tunneled staircases on each end, which led down to galleries where Saracens patrolled the walls and maintained communication with the other towers.

Ramón instructed the Hospitaller deputies to bring up twenty of their best archers. 'Assign five archers to defend each stairwell,' Ramón said. 'The passages are narrow. I doubt two men could climb the stairs at a time, so it should not be difficult to defend. The ten others will fire from the tower into the castle courtyard. The Calatrava will send scouts down the middle staircase to probe the Saracen defenses in the tower's interior.

'Any questions?' Ramón inquired, but he did not seem inclined to answer any, and none were asked.

One of the Hospitallers spoke to an aide, who rushed down the engine to deliver Ramón's orders. After several minutes, Hospitaller archers ascended the tower, manning the inside parapet and firing into the castle's courtyard, setting off a scene of pandemonium. Muslim soldiers, dragging their wounded, ran for cover behind the archways and pillars that ringed the castle. The other Hospitaller archers formed a phalanx at each entrance to the tower, firing periodically at the Saracen soldiers who tested our position.

The Calatrava knights who had not overheard Uncle Ramón's orders were quickly informed by their colleagues of our mission. We congregated around the center of the tower peering into the opening. It was a dark passage. The slender stairs were visible from the surface for the initial descent only – and then they wound around into the unknown.

As we contemplated our new situation and waited for Ramón's order to descend the staircase, Marcos Vicens declared solemnly, 'Uncle Ramón, Alejandro and I volunteer to be the first knights to enter the passage.'

Marcos and Alejandro were identical twins. Most of the other knights could not distinguish between the two brothers. At Calatrava, Ramón had them wear different-colored ribbons around their wrists so that he could tell them apart. Marcos wore blue, Alejandro red. Alejandro once told me that the ribbons made him feel like livestock. His father, he said, had used a similar system to keep track of which cattle were sick or needed extra feed.

I could see the difference between the two brothers. Marcos' cheeks were slightly fuller than Alejandro's. Marcos stared you straight in the eye during conversation, whereas Alejandro always looked to the ground. I told Ramón this in the hope of obviating the need for ribbons. Ramón responded with an affable laugh.

'You are a sensitive soul, Francisco,' Ramón said. 'You may want to lose some of that delicacy before we arrive in Syria.'

I did notice Ramón studying the two brothers over the next days, though. One week after our conversation, Ramón told Marcos and Alejandro that they were forbidden to wear ribbons on their wrists, or, for that matter, any ribbons at all.

On the castle tower, Ramón tilted his head in surprise as he examined Marcos. We were all a bit puzzled by his proclamation. I do not think Marcos had volunteered for anything in his entire life, including membership in the Order of Calatrava. Marcos and Alejandro's father had four sons. The first became heir. The father pledged the second son to the Church and the third and fourth, the twins, to Christ's army. In Calatrava, Marcos and Alejandro seemed ill-suited for combat. They always fulfilled their responsibilities but often performed mechanically. When our instructors turned their backs, Marcos and Alejandro would slacken the pace of whatever activity in which we were engaged – archery, sparring, running. Marcos showed more passion for playing the flute he kept under his bed mat.

Despite his distaste for the regimen of martial life in Calatrava, Marcos had volunteered for a perilous expedition in Toron. The first soldiers to breach an enemy stairwell face an uncertain journey. They are often the necessary sacrifice, experiments from which those who follow learn the position of enemy booby traps – murder holes from which Saracen archers remain sheltered and fire through a window at enemy soldiers; wooden stairs that can be quickly removed in darkness and cause a knight to fall to his death on the hard stone.

Perhaps, I thought, Marcos had received a sharp blow to the head that affected his judgment. Or maybe at a weak moment as the siege engine approached the castle, he made the Lord a promise to serve the Cross more courageously, in exchange for divine protection.

Just before Marcos and Alejandro descended, Ramón gave final instructions – listen carefully for corridors running alongside and on top of the passage, beware the murder holes, take each step slowly and with great caution. Marcos and Alejandro paid strict attention to our master, but they knew everything he said. We all did. We had trained for such circumstances, simulating descents into hostile castles in the towers of the fortress at Calatrava.

Marcos and Alejandro started down, treading lightly on the stone floor. They carried their swords poised before them. Their backs were pressed against the wall so that they could see as far down the stairs as possible. After a few seconds, they disappeared from our sight.

We huddled around the entrance, waiting, listening intently for any noise from the passageway. Over the clamor of small battles conducted by the Hospitallers in defending the tower, we could hear nothing. The long period of silence raised our hopes. Perhaps, I thought, the Saracens were in such disarray after the tower's conquest they were neglecting the defense of the tower's interior. Perhaps the two brothers had made it unscathed into the belly of the castle.

When we finally heard a noise, it was unmistakable – the sound of an arrow shot from short range penetrating chain mail and entering flesh. There was a groan, and then Alejandro's voice calling to Marcos. They must have been far down into the castle. The words were barely audible.

'Marcos,' Alejandro said, 'stay where you are. I will come and get you.'

There was a distant lull and then the splash of liquid, as if several buckets of water had been dumped inside the stairwell.

'I cannot see!' It was Alejandro's voice, terrified, chilling. 'I am blinded!'

That could only be the effect of oil. The Saracens frequently employed the substance against besiegers trying to scale or breach the fortress walls. I had never heard of its use inside a castle's confines. It seemed that the infidels intended to burn the intruders alive.

Ramon grabbed Bernard by his tunic. 'Get Alejandro, Bernard,' Ramón said, 'and return immediately. This hole is a deathtrap.'

Bernard's face revealed neither fear nor concern. I never understood the man. Either he concealed his feelings skillfully or he had none – a perfect soldier. He walked down the stairs nimbly, silently, like a phantom.

'Alejandro,' Ramón shouted down the stairwell, 'help is on its way.'

Before Ramón finished his sentence, we could hear the eruption of flames, the hissing, the seething crackle, the anguished screams of Alejandro.

Ramón slammed his fist against the stone floor. 'Damn it,' he said. 'Goddamn it.'

The sound of Alejandro's cries echoed through the entrails of the castle as if it were the voice of Jonah calling from inside the great whale.

'Help me, Uncle!' he pleaded. 'I am burned alive!'

'Alejandro, stay where you are,' Ramón shouted down the stairwell. 'Help will reach you soon enough.'

After several more minutes, Ramón became restless. He paced the tower in a small, distracted circle, unnerving all the knights accustomed to Ramón's equanimity. He stopped walking before the entrance to the stairwell and called out to Bernard. There was no answer. Following a short pause, Ramón resumed his confused circle. He stopped abruptly. He pulled out the dagger strapped to his shin. He would rescue the stranded knights himself.

'Uncle,' Andrés said, 'I will retrieve Alejandro. Your place is here, commanding the soldiers.'

Of course, Andrés was right. Ramón was directing the defense of the tower. His absence, his death, would have caused an unacceptable absence of leadership. But Ramón was not prepared to expose Andrés or any of his other less-experienced knights to the perils of that passageway. Not yet. Ramón ignored Andrés' words and proceeded with his preparations, tightening the straps of his wooden shield against his forearm.

'Uncle,' Andrés raised his voice. 'I will go.'

'No,' Ramón said, not even looking at Andrés. 'I have seen the inside of more dangerous passages than this one. I will not be long.'

'Uncle Ramón,' I said, 'you cannot leave the

men here. Andrés and I will retrieve Marcos and Alejandro. We can do the job. We were trained for this.'

Ramón turned an annoyed glance on me.

'Uncle, Francisco is right,' Andrés said. 'You cannot leave the men without a commander. Would you put us in the hands of Baron Bernières?'

Andrés' question caused Ramón to halt his preparations. He glanced pensively at his group of knights – those who had survived the assault. Ramón turned his back on us and walked toward the archers, who were firing a steady stream of arrows into the castle's interior. He was peering at the castle courtyard. The Knights of Calatrava gazed at his broad back, waiting for a decision. Alejandro's sobbing continued, rising up from the stairwell like a melancholy haze.

Ramón called forth one of the archers manning the tower and took his weapon. Then he walked back to the circle of his knights. He handed me the bow with a sheath of arrows.

'The attack,' Ramón said, 'will come from above, from a shaft in the ceiling. You will have to kill with an arrow. Francisco, put your sword in its scabbard. Andrés will cover you with his. If oil is poured from above, even if it be well in front of your position, flee up the stairs, and be done with it.'

Andrés and I moved to the opening. Ramón clasped both of us by the shoulder.

'Uncle,' Antonio de Figueres said, 'let them go. I never saw an archer with Francisco's skill.'

Antonio spoke his compliment in the past, as if it were an epitaph, as if he were speaking fondly of a fellow knight who died many years ago. His appeal had its intended effect, though. Ramón released both of us, and we began our descent.

The passageway was dark and cool. A moist film coated the outer walls, glistening with the little light that remained from the entrance above. The sodden moss that grew between the stone tablets exuded a musty trail. Andrés and I took turns leading. Very soon, we were walking in pitch dark. The tumult of the battle faded. Drops of water fell from the ceiling, echoing through the corridor. My bow was taut and ready. Our muscles strained with vigilance. We expected an ambush at any moment, from any direction.

After each step, we paused and peered into the darkness. We felt our way down the jagged walls. It was not long before I felt the presence of someone or something, perhaps one of the enemy crouching in wait, maybe just an insect or a cobweb. I reached out carefully. I felt only air. Still, I sensed that we were not alone. As I was moving my boot to the next step, a narrow window opened just above me. A glimmer of light fell into the black corridor. I was momentarily frozen, silently cursing my legs for not moving.

In that instant, I saw a rope emanate from the glare. It fell loosely around my chest – like a lasso used to rein in a wild horse. Before I had a chance to react, the noose tightened around my neck. My body was jerked into the air. I wanted to cry out to Andrés behind me. I could not breathe, though. I flailed my legs, trying to gain a foothold in a crag of the wall. My neck burned. My temples felt as if they would burst. My eyes rolled back in my head.

Then I was falling. The pressure pounding my temples released. I hit the ground, tumbling down the stairs. For several minutes, I was gasping for air and coughing violently. When I caught my breath, I could see Andrés standing above me.

'Are you injured?' he asked.

I moved my limbs. They seemed intact, unbroken. But I was too disoriented to know for certain.

'I am still alive, anyway,' I responded, my voice rasping. 'How did the rope break?'

Andrés motioned to his sword. 'Your body was swinging,' he said. 'It took three strokes to connect.'

He helped me to my feet. We continued slowly down the stairs. Andrés took the lead. After just a few steps, he leaped backward. He raised his sword to strike. I readied my bow. Just ahead we heard a squeaking, pitching sound as if a cable were lurching back and forth on a rusted axle.

Andrés poked his sword forward. It was a swinging body that he touched – Bernard. We could tell by the embroidered Cross stitched to the front of his tunic, a gift from his sister. Ramón had allowed his deputy this exception from the requirement of conformity in all aspects of uniform. Bernard was hanged – my death that would have been but for Andrés' intervention. He had not reached Alejandro and Marcos. This fearless warrior dangled like a trinket in the forgotten alcove of some remote cathedral. I took my dagger and reached out to cut the rope that bound him. Andrés stopped my hand.

'Leave him,' he whispered. 'The Saracens will know our exact location if the body falls.' I obeyed Andrés' injunction, although I suspected that the infidels already knew exactly where we were, each step that we took. Alejandro's moaning stirred us forward. His voice was getting closer.

After rounding another bend in the staircase, we came upon Marcos and Alejandro, a hideous sight. A shaft of light from above illuminated the two men's bodies. Marcos was already dead. Several arrows had pierced his shoulders and chest. One of the arrows had entered his bare head and stood straight up like a feathered decoration. He was sitting on the stone floor, holding his helmet in both hands – he had probably removed it to see more clearly the dark passage.

Alejandro lay on his back. His hair stood up like tiny cinders, his eyebrows still smoking. His lips vanished, burned right off; his eyes pus-filled, unseeing, his ears malformed, his surcoat a rag of ashes.

'Who is there?' he said, his familiar voice frayed, sunken.

We did not respond immediately. Again, we were wary of alerting the Saracens to our location.

But Alejandro was desperate and terrified, and Andrés relented.

'Who is there?' Alejandro asked again. 'Saint Peter or Lucifer?'

'Alejandro, it is neither,' Andrés said. 'It is Andrés and Francisco. We will carry you back to safety.'

'No, Andrés,' Alejandro said. 'I am already dead. Please, please, let me go.'

'I do not know what you mean,' Andrés responded.

'Too much pain,' Alejandro said. 'Mercy.' Alejandro was weeping, a searing lament.

'What you ask,' Andrés said, 'is not possible.'

But it was possible. I pulled back the string of my bow. I closed my eyes. I released the arrow. Alejandro's weeping ceased. An eerie silence returned to the passageway. Alejandro's life ended – by my hand. But I feel no remorse. Not for that. Alejandro's might have survived a day or two, but not much longer. There was no valor or mercy in prolonging his life – or his death.

The light shaft stood ten feet ahead of us just above the stairwell – a sliding hatch from which the Saracens had ambushed the twin brothers. Marcos' body was slumped directly underneath the shaft. Alejandro was about seven steps higher. He had crawled up a little ways, a human flame, before collapsing on the stairs. We could see the slick surface where the oil had fallen and the path of Alejandro's grieved steps. A torch lay on the stairs, still burning – the incendiary device dropped on Alejandro after the oil had blinded him.

Two metal sheets that extended down from the ceiling blocked our view to that window. The rays of light filtered through the hole, affording a ghastly view of Alejandro's disfigured face – the gray skin blistered, melting, smoldering still. In the shadows, we could see the steam rising where the trail of fire had followed Alejandro.

From the shaft above, we could hear grunts of physical exertion, alien curses of frustration. The hatch was stuck, the Saracens trying frantically to slide it back over the opening – to extinguish the light in the passage that could guide us to their position. Andrés and I realized the urgency of the situation – that the Saracens would be vulnerable only as long as the shaft remained open. When it closed, the enemy would once again be hidden, and we blind, defenseless.

In whispers and gestures, Andrés and I communicated our plan. Andrés would bolt past the window. We assumed that the illuminated area – approximately eight steps – comprised the boundaries of the Saracen's visibility. If Andrés could take two steps at a time, he would be exposed, unprotected, for two to three seconds. That's how long we thought it would take him to pass through the light. His presence would bring the Saracens into the opening, to fire at the moving target and then to become targets themselves. Andrés' quickness, we hoped, would take our adversaries by surprise, so that their arrows would find only stone. After the Saracens shot their arrows, I would slide down, my bow already taut, to fire straight up into the open hole. One shot, one Saracen life would be enough – for now, that would be enough. Afterward, I too would leap down the few steps into the dark shelter.

We moved gently down the steps, stopping just before the rays of light. We were both crouched, straining to hear the movement of the Saracens above us. But the noise had ceased – a bad sign – the Saracens were aware of our proximity. They were waiting for us. I drew back my bow. Andrés prepared to bound down the stairs, bobbing his head up and down as if to establish a rhythm before sprinting forward. He turned to me and nodded. He was gone in an instant, springing forward into the light. He seemed suspended there for several seconds, like a deer hurdling in the bright snow, caught in the sights of some weary hunter.

As Andrés passed the threshold, I heard shrieks from above, the snap of bows, the crash of arrows. Whether any of the arrows had found their mark, I could not see. Andrés continued down the stairs, swallowed back into the safety of the shadows.

As soon as the arrows were fired, I moved underneath the shaft. I used the wall to balance my weight and to steady my aim. Looking straight up into the light, I saw blurred figures leaning over the opening. I released the arrow. It passed through the two metal sheets. I rose quickly and ran down the stairs. Just behind me, several arrows ricocheted off the stone floor. It took another second before one of the Saracens let out a soothing groan, a hymn of vengeance.

As soon as we were past the shaft, a commotion broke out above us. We heard the sound of hurried footsteps in the passage overhead. Perhaps the Saracens were alerting their comrades below of our intrusion, or sending for reinforcements. We would not wait for them.

Andrés was wounded – an arrow sticking out from his thick forearm. Not fatal – unless the Saracens had tipped the blade with poison. Shot at close range, the arrow had penetrated deeply. It bulged from the other side of his arm. That was just as well. It would be easier to push the blade through when the time came.

Andrés looked at the arrow, perturbed but unwincing. He was a stoic man. I took his hand and smelled the blade for poison. It was clean. I motioned for Andrés to sit down on the stairs. Andrés braced his arm in the wedge between steps. With a swift blow from the butt of my dagger, I snapped off the end of the arrow. Andrés cursed at me between gritted teeth. I tore a strip from my robe and tied it tightly around his wound. We would worry later about extracting the blade.

We continued our descent, until a terrible explosion knocked both of us off our feet. The stone tablets that lined the walls scraped and screeched against each other. Rocks fell from the ceiling. It seemed an earthquake. As if God Himself had seen enough and decided to bury both armies in the rubble of our war machines.

When the reverberations subsided, we proceeded downward urgently, anxious to exit the dark tomb that seemed on the verge of collapse. We came upon an opening, a doorway around the bend. I slung the bow over my shoulder. I drew my dagger and walked down to investigate. It was a small balcony facing out into the castle's courtyard. One Saracen stood guard, looking away, his hands on the railing. I walked back to Andrés. Our best course, we agreed, was to draw the Saracen toward us, into the stairway. With this object, Andrés tossed his sword just outside the open door. It bounced off the stone, the clang echoing through the stairwell. As we anticipated, the noise brought the Saracen guard rushing in from the balcony, his sword at the ready. He looked down first. Then up at Andrés and me. He did not seem surprised. He spoke strange words, perhaps a greeting. I shot him in the chest. He fell backward. After a second, he turned over and began crawling toward the balcony. I shot him again, in the back, between the shoulder blades. His head dropped to the stone floor.

With our passage cleared, we stood just to the side of the balcony's entrance and peered outside. We could see clear across the castle to the source of the great thunder. Don Fernando's battering ram had demolished the castle gates. Knights from his entourage were riding through the gap, trampling the Saracen foot soldiers, smashing skulls, tearing flesh and sinew, dispatching our foes like insects under a boot heel. The Muslim lines broke, their soldiers fleeing for cover.

Don Fernando himself, the folds of his purple cape buffeted by the wind, led his brigade. His lieutenants surrounded him, but he was riding fast enough to outstrip them. He surged forward, into a horde of defenders, like Moses parting the Red Sea. Don Fernando wielded his sword with a savage expertise, crushing, crashing, slicing his way toward every crevice of that castle.

Don Fernando approached the mosque, chasing infidels seeking refuge in that imagined sanctuary. One of the Saracens jumped from a second story onto the Don's horse. I saw the man. I cried out, to warn the Don. My words were lost in the distance, the din of battle. It was a bold, deft move by the Saracen. He ended up behind Don Fernando, his dagger drawn to the Don's neck.

Don Fernando must have seen his assailant in the air. With his right hand, the Don had raised his sword in front of him to block the Saracen's dagger. With his other hand, he drew his own dagger from its sheath. He thrust it behind him, into the ribs of his attacker. The Saracen rode with the Don for several strides before falling off his mount, left in the dust, jettisoned like flotsam on the open seas.

Don Fernando looked a king, dashing, invincible – Charlemagne, Richard the Lion-heart, King Louis of France.

For Andrés and me, there was no need for further action. We stood on the balcony, watching the rout, unable to tear ourselves away from the macabre scenes and the satisfaction we felt at the destruction of our enemies – the killers of my comrades – the murderers who had made Alejandro into a human torch and me into his executioner. In the beginning of the siege, the infidels had been offered safe passage in return for giving up the castle. Their leaders had declined. Now their soldiers would live with the consequences.

I do not know at what point the nature of the rout changed – whether there was a specific act, an order spoken, a signal given, an implicit understanding. Once the boundary was crossed, though, it disappeared forever in a river of hushed screams and ineffable sorrow. Conquest became massacre, and then murder. I know, Brother Lucas, because I witnessed these events.

The infantry followed our cavalry, a deluge of fury into the dirt courtyard. The Muslim soldiers who tried to resist were quickly overwhelmed and put to the sword. Of those who did not resist, some were killed anyway. Most were taken prisoner, their hands bound by leather cord, their weapons, armor, medallions stripped, stolen, claimed as spoils by the hungered mob.

Our soldiers formed two parallel lines several feet

apart, two Christian columns. They herded their Muslim counterparts, forced to run the lawless gauntlet to the western edge of the castle, just under our position. Every so often the black mark of fate would fall on one of the prisoners – ripped from the grisly parade, set upon, torn to pieces like a rabbit plucked down amidst a pack of wolves.

Eventually, the living prisoners – perhaps sixty – were collected in the castle corner. They were no longer soldiers, just a huddled, wretched mass. The others, the wounded and dead, lay alongside the bodies of Hospitaller knights and horses from the initial, failed attack. Mounds of flesh littered the courtyard.

The meridian sun radiated a specious light on the Muslim prisoners. Andrés and I remained riveted on the narrow balcony, dazed sentries, transfixed to our post as if we had stumbled on some ancient, unhallowed coliseum. We were voyeurs, with a perfect window overlooking that dark vision.

After taking refreshments with his lieutenants in the shade of a small grove of fig trees in the far corner of the castle, the Don strode forth toward the captives. Prisoners and guards turned toward the royal retinue. A dreaded silence descended upon the castle, so that the Don's deliberate footsteps could be heard even on our perch and seemed to pronounce dire sentence with every measure. His lieutenants organized the prisoners in rows for inspection, the Don just on the outside conversing with his men. Hands were shaken, hugs exchanged, salutations, congratulations, 'glory be to God.'

Six rows of prisoners stood in the courtyard – a heathen, ragged brigade. Don Fernando walked leisurely, examining each man, occasionally asking questions through an interpreter, an Arab Christian from Acre. We could not hear the conversation, but from the Don's amiable demeanor, he could have been asking their birthplace or the names of their parents. The Don selected five of the Muslims, silver-haired, higher in rank than the others. They were led out of the castle, hostages, who would be ransomed later or killed in the event their value was overestimated. The other prisoners remained standing as the Don's entourage set up chairs in front of their ranks. The Don sat in the middle flanked by his lieutenants. Perhaps, I thought, we would witness another slave auction. Or maybe Padre Albar, the personal confessor of Don Fernando, seated to his right, would deliver a stern lecture to the infidels on the perils of eternal damnation for those who rejected the Savior. We waited, we and the prisoners.

Orders were given, indecipherable from our position. One of the Muslims was led just in front of the Don, as if to pay homage. He was pushed to his knees, his mouth moving hurriedly, perhaps begging for mercy or praying to some infidel deity. One of the Don's knights, his sword unsheathed, glinting, walked slowly behind the kneeling captive. The air was damp and heavy, and I breathed it in shallow, vigilant gasps.

There was not a sound in the castle when the Don lifted his arm, then brought it down swiftly in a swooping motion. The sword seemed to follow the same arc. A clean strike, sundering neck and head, the blood from the void bubbling, spouting, sprinkling forth like some mountain spring gone awry. One of the squires, a sneering grin, picked up the head, its black eyes bulging in disbelief. The squire raised his arm triumphantly, as if displaying a trophy to the crowd of knights and soldiers, who erupted with a rabid cheer.

Two more Muslims were already being led to the fore. Two by two. And then two more, the headless bodies dragged off and piled on top of one another, entwined in a gentle, grotesque embrace.

One of the youngest prisoners, a beardless boy with torn tunic and mournful countenance, looked up to the balcony as he was escorted to the executioner's ground. Was he looking at me? I could not be sure. I had thought myself invisible, but his gaze, unblinking, seemed to pierce that veil. In his eyes, a knowing accusation, as if I were somehow accountable, as if the bystander had become the executioner. To that spurious charge, I tried to proclaim my innocence.

I am a servant of God, a soldier of Christ. I fight for my brother, for his salvation. Christ's army stands before you, on a holy mission to wrest from the infidels this sacred ground, this earth soaked in His blood.

279

I opened my mouth to speak the words, to shout them. My voice failed, though, drowned in a wave of confusion that rose from my stomach like an arrow shot from inside me.

I reached into my hauberk for the cloth that held Isabel's tears – to remember another place; another world. But it was missing, lost in the fighting.

I looked down at the blood on my sword, my hands, my surcoat. I held my breath and ground my teeth until the ache subsided, until I could breathe again.

I looked back to the mud pit, to the boy kneeling, like a parishioner waiting for the priest to place the body of Christ on his tongue. The priest as executioner. The sword struck below the neck, embedding itself in the boy's shoulder. He fell to his side, like a wounded, flailing deer.

The knight lifted his weapon another time and swung. He missed again, hitting the collar, shattering the bone. The sound reverberated like a stone from a catapult smashing into the castle wall. The boy's face twitched spastically. He grunted. A leering, vicious laughter burst forth from the Christian troops, who strained to see over their comrades this grim spectacle. The executioner became flustered, and began to hack at the boy's neck. The crowd howled louder with each blow.

When the boy's head rolled forth, the surrounding soldiers roared their approval. The Don, exhibiting the imperious smile of a gracious host, clapped animatedly. The squire playing jester wove his fingers through the dark curls, picking up the boy's head. He whirled it around like a windmill, heaving it high up into the air. The boy's head seemed suspended, as if it would take flight. But then it fell back to earth into the crowd of knights and soldiers.

Two by two. And then two more. I watched, benumbed, unhinged, swept away.

Don Fernando organized a midnight Mass in the castle to commemorate the triumph of our forces. Uncle Ramón refused to attend the ceremony. He told Don Fernando that the execution of unarmed Muslim prisoners tarnished the reputation of the entire Christian force and invited retaliation against Christian prisoners in Muslim jails. Under Uncle Ramón's instructions, the Knights of Calatrava withdrew to our tent headquarters. We sat around a fire, drinking spirits to celebrate our victory. We drank to mark our survival and to dull the images of comrades dead and dying. I rubbed the dried blood from my hands, like copper crystals collecting in my palms. Still dressed in my armor, I fell asleep on the soft ground.

I woke in the dark, my body tensed, ready to fight, the tinny taste of blood on my tongue. A lantern burned in the corner of the tent. My comrades were asleep. They looked like corpses, gray, open-mouthed, still bloodied from combat. I stood tentatively, my neck stiff, my back aching.

I could see Andrés just outside, sitting on the ground, rocking, his knees pulled to his chest. I left the tent and approached him.

Andrés was gazing toward the castle. I sat near him.

'Is that how you imagined it, Francisco?' he asked.

'Imagined what?' I asked.

'War,' he said.

'I never imagined anything, Andrés.'

I touched my neck, tender where the rope had burned my skin.

'Could we take a walk?' he asked.

We did not speak of a destination. We headed toward the castle, to the site of our witness. Drawn inexorably to a field of blood. We passed the entrance, nodding brusquely at Don Fernando's knights, ignoring their hard glances.

It seemed like daytime in the courtyard, so bright was the fire from torches and their reflection on the yellow stones. We stood in the shadows of an archway, behind the pillars that led to the castle's mosque.

Tiny, decrepit, Padre Albar spoke from a wood platform hastily erected in the middle of the castle courtyard. Behind the padre sat Don Fernando, the torchlight casting a fierce glow on his visage.

As Padre Albar recited passages from the Scriptures, the foot soldiers dragged the headless corpses and other body parts along the side of the castle, just past the mosque, to a bonfire outside the castle walls. The continuous procession splattered a bloody path through the mud. The padre motioned to the fire, preaching a solemn warning, a grave prognostication, a biblical incantation.

He will thoroughly purge His floor, and will gather the wheat into His garner; but the chaff He will burn with fire unquenchable.

The flames sparked and cackled with the fresh blood and exhaled a sweet, sickening smell of roasting hair and flesh that clung to our clothes and armor for several days. Andrés and I could not eat meat the following week, so pungent was the remembrance of that carnal aroma.

After his sermonizing, Padre Albar offered communion to the Christian knights, bowed, silent, drinking from the silver chalice the blood of Christ, dark and viscous. Our comrades, a tribe of cannibals, with Don Fernando its chief, his lips smeared red by the sacrifice.

Andrés and I shunned that ritual. But we watched. From behind the marble pillars that guarded the mosque, we glimpsed the ghoulish shadows of our comrades, forever changed by the dim gloom of the acrid smoke and the dance of a thousand fires.

Perhaps Francisco's account of the execution of infidel prisoners troubles my sensitive reader. Indeed, after leaving Francisco's cell yesterday afternoon, I found it difficult to eat supper. The red beans that covered my plate resembled miniature heads, the bloody remnants of the beheadings at Toron.

Abbot Alfonso commented on my loss of appetite.

'Brother Lucas,' he said, 'you have not touched your food.'

'Indeed, Abbot Alfonso,' I responded, 'I have not.'

Lest my reader feel sympathy for the infidel victims, though, let us remember the systematic atrocities committed by the Muslims not just against Christian soldiers, but also against civilians, as in Antioch, where the Saracens murdered women and children. I have heard numerous accounts of infidel hordes preying on pilgrim caravans, raping, torturing, killing young and old.

I would not claim that such actions by the enemy justify or excuse excesses committed by Christian armies. Nevertheless, the infidel crimes help us to understand the righteous anger harbored by some Christian knights and the zealous, perhaps over-zealous, manner in which they sometimes dispose of their Muslim captives.

But let us not flinch from the cruel realities that our martial brothers confront in the Levant. Last night after supper, I relayed Francisco's account of the executions to Brother Vial. He listened patiently, nodding periodically as if the story were familiar. When I finished speaking, he rose and paced a small circle in the parlor.

'When we captured Beaufort castle,' he said,

'we held over two hundred Saracen soldiers. The Christian commanders convened a meeting to decide the fate of our prisoners. The Hospitaller deputy called for their immediate execution. A heated debate ensued. The other generals, motivated by more practical considerations, preferred to ransom the captives. I thought execution an unnecessarily severe measure and cast my vote in favor of ransoming the prisoners. The Hospitaller contingent was outnumbered. The final tally authorized negotiations with the infidels. Eventually, we traded our captives for much-needed food supplies and ten thousand silver dirhams, an amount that could sustain the castle for a full year.

'Two weeks later, fifty Hospitaller knights set off for Acre for reassignment to the northern territories. The Muslims set an ambush not one mile from the castle. When we heard sounds of battle, I organized a rescue party. By the time we reached the plain, forty-seven knights were dead. The three survivors said that they saw amongst their attackers the same men they had guarded in the stockade.'

Brother Vial stopped pacing and squinted hard at the craggy rock face just behind me.

'I never again set an able prisoner free,' he said. 'A soldier who releases his enemy only to fight him the next day is a fool.'

It was rather disconcerting to hear my mentor, normally so serene, speak in such a bitter tone about such a disagreeable affair. I sometimes forget that Brother Vial spent most of his life as a soldier.

I have never understood warfare. A thousand times I have read the Ten Commandments. *Thou shalt not kill.* The mandate seems rather simple. After receiving this injunction, the Israelites went on to slaughter their enemies – razing whole towns and killing all the inhabitants – in order to conquer and then defend the Holy Land. And they did so with God's blessing and assistance. Perhaps killing is justified when it serves a higher purpose. We, the heirs of the biblical Jews, follow the same path – slaying the heathen in God's name, redeeming His land with our blood.

War certainly implicates complex issues. I daresay that we, members of the cloth, who understand most clearly the spiritual parameters of battle between God and Satan, should hesitate before imposing the same standards of conduct on brothers of the sword, who do combat on a very different battlefield. Compassion and mercy, which glorify God in the monastic setting, might have the opposite effect in a theater of war. Perhaps, as Brother Vial suggests, emancipating captured enemy soldiers is neither merciful nor compassionate, but plain stupid. I suspect Richard the Lion-heart understood this harsh truth. After taking Acre in the Year of Our Lord 1191, he ordered the execution of all two thousand five hundred Muslim prisoners. Richard's army hacked the prisoners to pieces in sight of Saladin and his Muslim armies.

The Lord knows I am no expert on military strategies against the infidels. It seems to me, though, that once you commit to fight a holy war against Christ's persecutors, you must kill them. Evidently, this fine point is lost on Francisco, who seems, in his description of the Toron executions, to disapprove of Don Fernando's actions. I wonder what Francisco expected when he chose to take the Cross. Did he think that God's army could persuade the Muslims to abandon the Holy Land after a few demonstrations of military prowess? Did he think that if Don Fernando released his prisoners, they would leave the territory and exchange their swords for plowshares? And what difference does it make whether you kill your enemy while storming a castle tower or later after the battle has been won? In either case, you accomplish the same purpose – killing infidel soldiers, freeing the Holy Land of the devil's children.

Quite frankly, I was a bit annoyed with Francisco and his sanctimonious attitude toward Prince Fernando, whose able leadership produced a glorious victory for Christendom and for Aragón. Indeed, Prince Fernando's actions, by drawing the Saracens away from the Calatrava's position, probably saved Francisco's life.

When I entered Francisco's cell this morning, I did not greet him. I had to restrain myself from launching the stern lecture I had replayed many times the previous evening. It was, in fact, an instruction on the spiritual perils of hypocrisy and ingratitude.

'Perhaps, Francisco,' I said, when I had settled in my chair, 'we should focus today on your actions and not seek to cast aspersions on the brave men who lead the crusade.'

Francisco did not respond. He was sitting against the wall with his eyes closed. After a minute, he stood up and walked to the end of his cell, leaning on the windowsill.

Andrés and I skulled back to our tent from the castle. From our camp, we could see the red flames, a bonfire of our enemies. Andrés sat on his bed mat, humming softly, just a whisper. I laid my head down and closed my eyes. Soon I was lost in the sparks and hiss of the fire – a hot, angry night.

When I opened my eyes, the dark had receded to a damp gray. I could hear the birds, a hushed conversation that whined and twisted free until all that was left was the crying of children. Not a call for attention, but a haunted melody.

The infidel women and children, we were told, had fled the castle before the siege began. I looked to my comrades, searching their faces for some explanation. No one would meet my glance.

'Uncle Ramón,' I called. He was still sleeping. 'Uncle Ramón.'

He opened one eye.

'This had better be good, Francisco,' he said. 'I was in bed with a dark-haired beauty.'

'The children,' I said.

Ramón studied my face. Then he jerked up to a sitting position and cocked his head inquisitively. A dark shadow crossed his face. He bounded to his feet and reached for his hauberk.

'Francisco and Andrés,' he said, 'we return to the castle. Dress for battle.'

Ramón set a brisk pace. Andrés and I had to sprint to catch him. I cursed my trembling fingers as I struggled to buckle my belt. My sword rattled against the skirt of my chain mail. The cries became louder, hideous shrieks of ruin and damnation.

The trail to the castle sloped uneven through the mud. The earth scarred black, still smoking. Patches of grass singed, like tiny embers. Andrés had stopped abruptly. I reached his side and pushed him forward. He resisted, an uncertain smile, pointing down at some unnatural intrusion. A blue flower, solitary, grown mistaken in that barren country.

As we approached the gates, I had to rub my eyes and squint through the fog to see the strange sentinels who guarded the castle. Four heads on the end of wooden stakes. Children, three boys and a girl, with fierce grimaces that belied their innocence, and blood-stained eyes that followed our movements. I walked that gauntlet as fast as I could. But Andrés stopped just underneath the girl and peered up at her tenderly, as if he would ask that little head if she was thirsty and then offer a drink. I shouted his name, but he was preoccupied with that imagined conversation. I was forced to walk back under the watchful eyes of those four gatekeepers and to pull my friend through the castle portal.

Inside the fortress, the rancid smell of battle permeated every crevice and choked the air from my lungs. The prayers of the condemned pierced the fetid mist. The shrill cries swallowed the colors, so that the world could be seen only in black, white, and gray. For an instant, I caught a glimpse of one of the infidel girls running naked, the white, spectral skin of her delicate shoulders. She was looking back at an unseen assailant. Then she vanished.

Ramón had already exchanged words with one of the soldiers at the entrance. He escorted us along the sidewall to the threshold of a heavily guarded room. One of Don Fernando's aides recognized Ramón immediately and ushered us inside.

The room had no furnishings except for a long, rectangular table with wooden benches. The white-washed walls were bare. Don Fernando sat at the head of the table with his lieutenants spaced about him. Platters of venison exuded a noxious aroma that seemed indistinguishable from the smell of rot and death that pervaded the castle.

'Uncle Ramón, it is a pleasure,' Don Fernando said. 'I trust you were greeted by our youthful hosts as you entered the castle.' The laughter of the Don's lieutenants grated against the solemn labors perpetrated by those same men.

'Don Fernando, if you refer to the four heads on stakes, we saw the display,' Ramón said gravely.

'The women and children,' Don Fernando said, 'were hiding in an underground tunnel during the battle, praying to their pagan gods. My soldiers found them last night after Mass.

'Young Francisco and Andrés,' Don Fernando continued, 'welcome. Are you Ramón's first deputies now? You have taken advantage of the tragic deaths of your comrades. I applaud your initiative. Please enter.'

I took a step forward and slipped on a slick patch of blood on the stone floor. I was able to regain my balance before falling, but, even with their heads riveted on the food before them, Don Fernando's lieutenants had seen the misstep and were snickering at my expense. Men, so avocated, never miss a sudden movement, not in wartime.

'Don Fernando,' Ramón said, 'there is an important matter about which I would like to speak to you in private.'

'Ramón,' Don Fernando responded, 'I trust my men with my life. They can hear whatever matter concerns you. But first you must join us in this celebratory feast. Then we shall talk.'

'Don Fernando,' Uncle Ramón said, 'I must decline your invitation. We are here on business.'

'What business would that be, friend, on such a glorious day?'

'I must protest,' Uncle Ramón said, 'the manner in which your men have treated the Muslim women and children. I would ask that you instruct your deputies to see to the protection of all prisoners under your guard and put an end to the abuses against civilians.'

'Abuses?' Don Fernando asked. 'Are you aware of any abuses, Pablo?'

Pablo González, the Don's first lieutenant, was seated just to his right. He glanced at Ramón. His dull brown eyes seemed lifeless, incapable of absorbing light or displaying emotion.

'No, master,' Pablo said, 'I know of no such abuses.' Then he resumed eating.

'And you, Francisco,' Don Fernando said, 'have you seen these alleged abuses?'

'Don Fernando,' I said, 'I have heard the cry of innocents.'

Don Fernando's lips curled in amusement as he examined my face.

'Innocents?' Don Fernando said. 'The word is alien to me, Francisco. It was my impression that there are no innocents amongst the infidels. Perhaps we should consult Padre Albar on this interesting theological point.'

'Don Fernando,' I said, 'I use the term in reference to the Muslim women and children. They are noncombatants.'

'Don Fernando,' Ramón said, 'the actions of your men bring dishonor on all the Christian forces.'

'No, Ramón,' Don Fernando said sharply, 'you are mistaken. I honor my men by giving them the freedom they have justly earned after risking their lives in this great struggle.'

'Don Fernando,' Ramón said, 'I cannot countenance these activities.'

'Then go home, old man,' Don Fernando said. 'This is not your war.'

Don Fernando waved his hand as if shooing a fly away, then turned his attention to his meal. He seemed to forget our presence. Not so his men. They understood the potential consequences of speaking such words to the Grand Master of the Calatrava. Every one of his lieutenants stopped eating and looked up. Uncle Ramón's jaw was hard and shadowed, the crooked vein on his bald head throbbing. He grasped the handle of his sword. Almost simultaneously, Don Fernando's men swept plates and mugs from the table in a frenzied clatter. They put their hands to their weapons, although none were drawn. They looked to Uncle Ramón, expectantly, hungrily, and then back to their master, waiting for a signal, like obedient dogs anticipating the distribution of scraps from the table.

I could feel the eyes of Don Fernando's lieutenants on my person, scanning my armor, looking for its vulnerable points. I counted their number – twelve of them . . . three of us. We would have been slaughtered. Our bodies left to decay in that loathsome pit.

I felt for the hilt of my sword.

Don Fernando's methodical chewing was the only sound, the only movement in that chamber. He continued to eat his meal peacefully as if he were in the comfort of his own castle, indifferent to the explosion of violence that threatened to erupt.

'Ramón,' Don Fernando said, not looking up from his plate, 'has life grown so tiresome that you would forfeit it to defend a few infidel whores?'

In the breathless hush that followed, Ramón carried the weight of all our fates. He looked at Andrés and me. He scrutinized us carefully as if he were calculating the value of our lives. Then he shook his head slowly and eased his grip on his weapon.

The moment had passed. Don Fernando's men relaxed their vigilance, although they watched Ramón from the corner of their eyes. Ramón turned slowly, outmaneuvered, overrun, and left the chamber. Andrés and I followed in his wake.

We walked back to our tent without exchanging word or glance. We never spoke of the confrontation or what we had seen at the castle, not to each other, not to our comrades.

When we arrived at our tent, Ramón ordered the men to prepare to march back to Acre. Maybe he thought that by putting distance between our force and Toron we could disassociate ourselves from the crimes committed by Don Fernando's army. Maybe he thought he could silence the silent howls of those children.

We left early that afternoon, carrying our wounded – four men – in a covered wagon. Two of the wounded died en route. We buried their bodies in full armor on the side of the path, marking the mounds with branches tied, torn, wrenched into a Cross. After reciting the prayer for the dead, we rode off, leaving the gravesites to the local scavengers. No one looked back.

Two days after we left Toron, we reached Acre. The sun had not yet risen. The streets were deserted. We slinked back to the Hospitaller Ward, fugitives with the bitter taste of our flight like a film on our lips.

I had great difficulty listening to Francisco's description of the bloody events at Toron. The whole affair is quite upsetting. Indeed, I felt feverish and weak when I left his cell. As I made my way down the winding stairwell, I almost stumbled on the steep steps.

When the bells rang, I did not go to prayer services. I spent the entire afternoon in my quarters, reading and rereading sections of this manuscript, a record of Francisco's confession, a map of his soul. I was seeking the source of his possession, some pathway, a trail that would lead through all this darkness.

I could not concentrate on the written words, though. My thoughts kept returning to Francisco's account of Toron. The black ink spread like blood on the parchment. Images of the battle mingled amongst the letters. The dark stairwell Francisco descended into the bowels of the castle. Don Fernando's soldiers breaking through the gates, trampling the fleeing infidels. The head of the little girl on a stake, her olive cheeks smooth, unsullied.

In short, I was troubled, confused and troubled. I sought out Brother Vial for advice. I found him sitting alone in the parlor gazing at several flowers he had picked from the courtyard.

'Brother Lucas,' he said, 'you look as if you have seen a ghost. Are you unwell?'

'Brother Vial,' I said, 'could we speak of Francisco's confession?'

'Please, Brother Lucas, share your concerns.'

'I fear, Brother Vial, that Francisco has lost his bearings,' I said.

'You have lost your bearings, Brother Lucas?' he asked.

'No, Brother Vial, I speak of Francisco. In his description of the battle of Toron, he cannot distinguish between Christian knights and their infidel counterparts. Horror seems to taint everyone and everything.'

'War is most unpleasant, Brother Lucas.'

'I spent the afternoon reading over Francisco's confession,' I said. 'I must have read his account of the battle of Toron ten times. I was searching for the map of his soul, some hint of light. I did not find any. It seemed more a map of hell.'

'What's all this talk of maps, Brother Lucas?' Brother Vial asked.

'Excuse me, Brother Vial?'

'You referred to a map, Brother Lucas,' he said. 'Has the monastery received a new shipment of manuscripts from Barcelona?'

'Brother Vial, I am speaking of more weighty issues. I refer to the map of Francisco's soul.'

'A map of Francisco's soul?' he asked.

'Brother Vial, surely you remember our conversation not five months ago when you told me the reason you transcribe the confessions of your subjects. In the parchment, you said, you find the map of the subject's soul, a map that reveals the source of possession and the path toward salvation.'

'Ah, yes, the map of the soul,' Brother Vial said. 'I remember. An old man's memory sometimes fails him. Forgive me, Brother Lucas.'

'Brother Vial,' I said, 'I searched for the map of Francisco's soul in his confession. I found only blackness.'

'Brother Lucas,' he said, 'perhaps I misspoke in the conversation to which you refer. I meant a map of the exorcist's soul. Your soul, Brother Lucas, not Francisco's.'

'My soul, Brother Vial?'

'Yes, Brother Lucas,' he said, 'your soul.'

'Brother Vial, surely you jest?'

'Brother Lucas,' he said, 'the soul of a man is not a subject for jesting.'

'I am certain, Brother Vial, absolutely certain

that you spoke of the map of the soul in reference to the possessed.'

'An interesting idea, Brother Lucas,' he said, 'but not mine. I do transcribe the confessions of my most stubborn subjects. When I read the manuscript, oftentimes I am surprised to find in the parchment the map of my own soul, my own confession. In certain cases, Brother Lucas, the exorcist must examine himself, undertake his own spiritual journey through dark, untrod forests.'

'Brother Vial,' I said, 'I am confounded.'

'Brother Lucas,' he said, 'sometimes we must be confounded, before we can find our way.'

Brother Vial sat up slowly, put his hand on my clenched fist, then made his way out of the parlor. I sat by myself for a while. I did not feel restful, though. In truth, I felt quite angry with Brother Vial. I suppose my feelings were unjustified. I cannot blame Brother Vial for his memory loss. Perhaps he is becoming senile. He certainly speaks nonsense. Of what use would a map of my soul be? I am not possessed; Francisco is. I decided right then that I would not consult Brother Vial again and that I would seek the answers I needed in prayer. I stood and walked through the courtyard to the church.

In a dark recess of the chapel, I knelt before a statue of the Virgin. I looked up to the wood sculpture of Mary. The Mother of God – gazing upon the Lord's creation, mourning the loss of her

Son, grieving for the innocents. The wood grain visible through the peeling paint.

That's when it happened. A most unfortunate incident. Just an instant. Maybe longer. I do not know. I glanced at the blue enamel of Mary's eyes, chipped, sorrowful, turning gray. Through the glaze, I imagined I could see the ocean waves – and the horizon, perhaps the same vista Francisco saw on his journey to the Holy Land. A storm seemed to be brewing in the distance. The sky melted into the ocean, the waves leaping to meet the ashen clouds. The boundaries between elements blurred. I could no longer distinguish land from water, sky from sea. I felt dizzy, disoriented, lost in the vortex of that gray space, the apocalypse. The clouds running into the ocean. Goodness bleeding into evil.

I wiped the sweat from my brow. I could hardly breathe. The stale air was choking me. I rose and headed for the courtyard. The straight line of the aisle became crooked, though. The location of the door kept shifting. I knocked into an iron candelabrum, dodging the falling flame just barely. When I reached the door, one of my brothers tried to lend a supporting arm.

'Brother Lucas, what is the matter?' he asked.

I pushed him away, then staggered into the courtyard. I found refuge under the canopy of the cistern. I splashed water on the back of my neck. Indeed, I dipped my head in the cold water and held on to the rail until the spinning subsided.

When I looked up from the basin, I noticed a small congregation of monks staring at me from across the courtyard. I must have seemed quite a spectacle. I had to act rather quickly to dampen the curiosity of my anxious brothers. Despite the unsteadiness of my legs, I managed to stand up straight. I washed my hands leisurely, straightened my robe, and walked precisely to the nearest bench. I sat down and pressed my palms together, pretending to pray silently. My brothers soon lost interest in my activities and dispersed.

When I was finally alone, I took slow, deep breaths. The cool air revived me. In short time, I felt much better, quite myself. The unpleasantness had passed. I was able to reflect with more lucidity on Francisco's account of Toron.

Over the years, I have heard stories of the battle of Toron – the boldness of the Christian forces, the barbarism and cruelty of the infidel defenders, placing their civilians before them so that our knights could not fire for fear of hitting a woman or a child. I daresay it would be difficult to find a loyal subject who had not learned the words of at least one of the several songs that commemorate the bravery of the Catalán knights, in particular Prince Fernando. It was upon Fernando's triumphant return to Barcelona that King Jaime gave his son the title 'El Conquistador de Toron, Defender of the Faith, Prince of Barcelona.'

Needless to say, Francisco's recollections did not comport with the more established version.

In recounting the treatment of Muslim civilians, Francisco divested the army of Christ of its spiritual and moral authority, obliterating the distinction between Christian and infidel soldiers. As narrated by Francisco, the battle of Toron seemed a dark, godless abyss.

How can I account for the discrepancy between Francisco's version of events and the better-known characterizations with which you, my venerable reader, are no doubt familiar? There is of course a simple explanation – the demons that possessed Francisco sought to spread lies and blasphemy in order to foster doubt amongst the faithful.

And yet, I cannot deny that Francisco had been an eyewitness to the battle. Nor can I deny that his description of the siege was consistent in certain respects with the more established histories. It is well known that the Knights of Calatrava captured the northwest tower of the castle before Prince Fernando's forces stormed the eastern gate.

Francisco's account was also straightforward and vivid. As Francisco described the bonfire that consumed the Muslim corpses, I could almost smell the burning flesh, a remote yet familiar scent. When I was still a servant at Santes Creus, before the arrival of Francisco, there was an outbreak of fever in the monastery. Fifteen of the brothers succumbed to the illness. To extinguish the contagion, the Abbot instructed the servants to cremate the corpses. The naked bodies of the dead were dragged from carts and fed into the fire in the plaza just outside the gates of the monastery. A putrid scent enveloped the square. The flames whistled louder with each new body, until a constant, low scream pervaded the monastery, overwhelming even the survivors' lamentation.

But why did I dwell on such dark memories? Why did I feel unsettled by Francisco's tale? After listening to Francisco's account, I found myself, for a brief moment, questioning the virtue of Prince Fernando's crusaders, admittedly a small group in the context of the larger Christian force.

And then I caught myself and remembered the warning of Brother Vial, the warning he spoke before I set out to gather Francisco from the clutches of Father Adelmo at Poblet. It was the hand of the devil – setting forth temptation in the form of doubt. Doubt in the righteousness of Christ's own army. I can assure you, it was a humbling moment – the realization that even I, a child of the Church, a child of God, the second-youngest prior ever appointed at Santes Creus, was vulnerable to the devil's seduction.

Preoccupied by these troubling thoughts, I was walking the courtyard leading to my quarters when I saw Isabel. She was sitting in the parlor talking to Brother Vial.

CHAPTER 10

ISABEL

To spare my mentor further embarrassment, I tried to avoid a confrontation with the girl. The less attention focused on the spectacle of a female in the parlor, the more likely to minimize the scandal. Despite his worldly experience, Brother Vial sometimes displays poor judgment.

I pulled the white hood of my habit down over my head and quickened my pace toward the church. Alas, Brother Vial recognized me.

'Brother Lucas,' he called, 'we have a special visitor today.'

'Brother Vial, is that you?'

'Yes, Brother Lucas, come and meet our guest.'

There was no escape. I approached the parlor on the stone footpath that cut across the courtyard. Inadvertently, I strode off course onto the grass carpet. I could feel the cool blades brush the skin in the gaps of my sandals.

'Doña Isabel Correa de Girona, I present Brother Lucas.'

'Welcome to Santes Creus,' I said.

'Brother Lucas is the prior of the monastery,' Brother Vial said, 'and Francisco's confessor.'

'How was your journey, Doña Isabel?' I asked.

She stood and bowed slightly. She seemed to be my height exactly, so that our gaze was unmediated. Evidently, she did not hear my question. Or perhaps she did not deem it necessary to respond.

'With your permission, Doña Isabel,' Brother Vial said, 'I will excuse myself for afternoon service.'

I grabbed Brother Vial's sleeve as he turned to leave.

'Surely, Brother Vial, you would not leave a woman alone in the parlor.'

'No, Brother Lucas, I would not. I leave her in your capable hands. The two of you can discuss Francisco's condition.'

'But Brother Vial,' I said, 'the appearance of the prior talking alone with a female might cause consternation amongst members of the flock.'

'You place too much value on appearances, Brother Lucas.'

I watched Brother Vial's broad back as he walked through the courtyard, then disappeared around the corner pillar. I turned to face Isabel. Most uncomfortable.

'I trust our messenger proved a faithful guide?' I asked.

Her glance was direct, her eyes sharp, her posture

erect. She did not seem to grasp the improper nature of her presence in the holy sanctuary. Nor did she feel a compulsion to engage in pleasantries.

'Brother Lucas, how is my cousin?'

Francisco had said that her eyes were gray, the same shade as his brother's tombstone. A peculiar tombstone indeed. From my vantage point, I could not discern their color. Her eyes seemed green, then blue, then yellow.

'The devil is stubborn,' I said. 'He will not yield his prize easily. Nevertheless, we make progress.'

Tiny brown freckles settled across the bridge of her nose and marred the clarity of her white skin.

'Francisco speaks, then?' she asked. A restive glance in the wake of her question betrayed her even tone. I delayed just a moment before answering.

'Yes, Isabel, Francisco speaks.'

Isabel looked away before I could gauge the impact of the news of Francisco's improvement.

'I trust your husband approved your visit to Santes Creus,' I said.

'I am unmarried, Brother Lucas.'

'I am sorry.'

'I am well occupied caring for my father.'

'Is he unwell?'

'He became sick following my brother's death. Did you know Andrés?'

'I made his acquaintance many years ago at the

monastery. A fine young man. Devoted in his own manner.'

'Devoted to adventure, Brother Lucas. Ill-suited for monastic life.'

'We all have our calling, Isabel.'

'He died at the Krak des Chevaliers. My father received a letter from Prince Fernando, who commanded the Christian forces at the castle, commending the bravery of my brother. He died the day before the castle fell.'

I had to restrain an urge to wipe away a fragment of yellow crust lodged in the corner of her eye. She had obviously failed to groom herself before our interview. Locks of hair, uncombed, iridescent, escaped from under her hood and fell over the side of her face. Brother Vial once said that women help men to recognize the beauty of God's creation. Women, he said, make the blue deeper, the green greener; 'the red catches fire.' A quaint hypothesis. I tend toward the view that only through prayer can we approach a full appreciation of the Lord's bounty.

'Do not despair, child,' I said. 'Andrés died in the service of the Lord.'

'Sometimes I wonder, Brother Lucas,' Isabel said, 'whether the Lord looks with favor upon those who raise their swords against an enemy so far away.'

'Child,' I said, 'your brother died for Christ. He was one of the chosen, a member of God's army.'

'Does God have an army, Brother Lucas?'

306

'He certainly does. Knights, monks, and priests who battle the devil's agents wherever we encounter them. A righteous army of the strong and courageous – the keepers of the divine legacy.'

'Isn't it the meek who shall inherit the earth, Brother Lucas?'

The girl could be irritating.

'Yes, Isabel, but the strong shall ensure the inheritance.'

The afternoon sun cast a mournful shadow across her face. Sorrow borne in the delicate lines that graced her forehead, probably imperceptible before her brother's journey to the Levant. She smiled wearily as if my conversation were tiresome.

'You must have faith in the divine plan, Isabel.'

'I cannot see what role my brother's death plays in such a plan. It seems quite meaningless.'

'I understand your distress, child,' I responded tenderly. 'I understand more than you can possibly know.'

I did not tell Isabel that I too have experienced injustice, born into the world almost certainly of noble blood, yet without a name. A common servant I became. We cannot comprehend the path the Lord has chosen for us.

'Remember, child,' I said, 'our suffering brings us closer to Christ. Our tears run into the river of blood that flows from the stigmata. It is there that we find communion and peace. Your brother, just as Christ, died for you.'

'Forgive me, Brother Lucas. I have not studied the Scriptures or spent the hours of spiritual devotion that you have. I know that I am unlearned in these matters. But I do not understand why these men had to die for me. If it were my choice, I would have preferred that they live.'

'They do, Isabel. Your brother lives in paradise. He looks down upon you right now.'

I spoke fervently, but the girl seemed not to be listening. Her attention focused on a patch of weeds that sprouted between two stone tablets on the floor of the parlor. An embarrassing distraction. I would speak with Brother Eduardo, who is responsible for the proper maintenance of the monastery grounds. The Lord's work requires an uncompromising discipline that must extend to all members of the monastery and to all tasks, from the holy offices to the most mundane chores.

'Sometimes, Brother Lucas,' she said, 'I feel that I must be missing some critical wisdom that explains these matters. It seems to me that a martyr's death brings only anguish to those who live after him. Perhaps he will enter paradise. To those who survive, he leaves only suffering. Even Christ Himself. Imagine, Brother Lucas, the Virgin Mary watching as her Son writhes on the Cross. If He chose life, He could have made water into wine as an old man, healed the sick, given sight to the blind.'

A faint bitterness tarnished the gentle edge of her voice. Isabel was making a motherly reproach, chiding her brother for taking the Cross. As if Isabel were Mary, chiding her Son for the imprudence, indeed, the selfishness of His choice.

'Isabel, you are not thinking clearly right now,' I responded. 'Christ chose the Cross so that He could share our condition, so that He could show us the path through suffering, through death, to eternal life. So that He could take our sins upon Himself.'

'I never asked Him to take my sins upon Himself,' she said, 'and I am not sure what good He accomplished in doing so.'

'Isabel, you speak dangerous words. You do not know what you are saying. I suggest you take time to reflect before speaking on these matters again.'

The girl needed a warning. Her next interlocutor might not be so understanding. Moreover, one of the monks might overhear her. It would not be the first time one of my brothers eavesdropped on a private conversation and relayed the content to Abbot Alfonso, or, worse, to an overeager inquisitor passing through Santes Creus.

'I am sorry, Brother Lucas. I speak recklessly because I grieve for my brother.'

I took a cloth from my cassock and wiped the beads of sweat from my forehead. I tried to smile at the girl, but I suspect it seemed more a grimace. The Lord's work is strenuous.

The bells rang for holy office. The chimes provided a welcome respite from our discussions and an opportunity for the girl to recover her composure. Regrettably, many of my brothers could not resist the impulse to gaze upon our visitor as they walked past the parlor. Some of them probably had never set eyes upon a female of Isabel's gentility. Brother Mario stopped cold and stared at the girl.

'Brother Mario,' I said, 'the Lord calls you to prayer.'

He remained transfixed, open-mouthed, like a village idiot.

'Perhaps, Brother Mario,' I said, 'you would enjoy an extended visit to one of the monasteries in the new territories of Catalonia. The Church needs volunteers to spread the Word amongst the Moorish villagers. I think you would be well qualified.'

The boy joined his brothers forthwith, and the chapel doors soon closed. Isabel and I were alone.

'I suppose, Isabel, you wonder why I sent for you.'

She was twirling a lock of hair in her fingers, periodically placing the end in her mouth. She seemed to be concentrating intently on the task as if she were weaving a basket. I cleared my throat rather loudly. Isabel withdrew the hair from her mouth and tucked the wet strands behind her ear.

'Perhaps, Isabel, you have asked yourself why you are here.'

'I know why I am here, Brother Lucas.'

The girl could be presumptuous.

'Pray tell, Isabel, why are you here?'

'When can I see Francisco, Brother Lucas?'

'Patience, child. We were speaking of your visit to our humble sanctuary. The purpose of your presence here.'

'I am here to visit my cousin,' she said.

'Yes, you are, Isabel. Perhaps, though, you do not fully appreciate the situation. Santes Creus is not a castle, and your cousin is not in the habit of receiving visitors. While we have made progress in battling Satan, Francisco is still possessed by the dark one. His soul and body remain in mortal peril. I would not be surprised if he does not recognize you. I daresay if not for our efforts, he would probably be dead. The slightest negative influence could jeopardize his recovery.'

'What kind of influence am I, Brother Lucas?'

'I trust a good one, Isabel. You have been called to assist with Francisco's exorcism. To tempt Francisco with life.'

Those were Brother Vial's words when he suggested that we send for the girl – 'tempt Francisco with life.' In truth, I remained skeptical. Isabel might tempt Francisco, but toward what purpose? Did not Eve tempt Adam with the apple? Perhaps Isabel had her own purpose in coming to Santes Creus. It would be foolish to discount the possibility that she might seek to take advantage of Francisco in his weakened state to bring about a marriage. Any girl, particularly a twenty-four-year-old spinster, would covet the fortune of Francisco, whatever his condition. I resolved to inquire as to Isabel's intentions.

'Isabel, I know you must be tired after your long journey. Could I bother you with a few questions?'

'Please, Brother Lucas.'

'How would you describe the nature of your relations with Francisco?'

'We are first cousins.'

'Yes, I know, Isabel. But how would you characterize your feelings for Francisco?'

'I am fond of my cousin, Brother Lucas.'

'Exceedingly fond or just fond?'

'I am not sure what you mean, Brother Lucas.'

'Perhaps, Isabel, you could describe the background of your association with Francisco.'

'I am sorry, Brother Lucas. I have not the slightest idea what you are talking about.'

The girl was not as forthcoming as I had hoped she would be.

'Very well, Isabel. We shall start at the beginning. Where did you meet Francisco?'

'At the estate of my father in Girona.'

'And that's where you became, as you say, fond of Francisco?'

'Yes, Brother Lucas.'

'And did he become fond of you?'

'Yes.'

'How do you know? Did you ask him?'

'No.'

'Did he tell you?'

'No. Not in words.'

I could picture Francisco at her father's estate – before the crusade. His pensive gaze, the sadness on the borders of his quiet smile, a smile that could easily be misinterpreted.

'Sometimes, child, we have an affinity toward another person that is not reciprocated.'

'Francisco once told me there is a moment that holds both night and day.'

'I am afraid, Isabel, I do not follow.'

'Five o'clock in the morning. Maybe later. The second before dawn.'

'Isabel, I do not understand.'

'Francisco said that in that instant he could sometimes see his brother.'

'Are you quite sure, Isabel?' I asked.

'Sergio's image in the half-light,' she said.

'Francisco never spoke of such an image to me.'

'One eye focused on Sergio,' she said, 'the other on dawn breaking over the horizon.'

'It does sound like something Francisco might say.'

'In that silence, we recognized each other,' she said.

'Where, Isabel?'

'A place where life and death intersect.'

I recalled the circumstances of Isabel's nativity – born astride a grave. Her mother died in childbirth. A cruel inheritance, indeed.

'Are you feeling well, child?'

'A restless loneliness,' she said.

'Our hearts are restless, Isabel, until they rest in the Lord. The words of Saint Augustine.'

'Then Francisco came to Girona,' she said.

'Yes, he told me of his visit to your family's estate.'

'Francisco understood,' she said.

'What did he understand, Isabel?'

'The desolation that follows in death's wake.'

'Are you speaking of Francisco or yourself, Isabel?'

'It had marked us both,' she said.

'Do you mean under the ice?' I asked. 'Is that what you mean with these cryptic references? Francisco told me of your accident over the lake. How he dove in the freezing water. The two of you crawling to safety as the pond's surface crumbled.'

'Francisco cast a pale light,' she said.

'A light?' I asked.

'Amidst this death,' she said.

'Francisco was casting lights?'

'A pale light that pierced my solitude,' she said.

'Francisco rescued you,' I said. 'Perhaps now you seek to save him? Is that what you mean to say?'

'One eye focused on night, the other on day.'

'Isabel, are you listening to what I am saying?'

'Until Andrés' death.'

'This hardly seems a conversation,' I said.

'The pale light extinguished,' she said.

Her little speech was beginning to grate on my nerves.

'Speaking of the pale light,' I said, 'the sun seems to be setting. Perhaps, Isabel, we should retire.'

'And then night, Brother Lucas. A long night for Francisco.'

A long conversation. Or rather soliloquy.

'Now only I hold the candle,' she said.

'Actually, Isabel, your hands are empty. Perhaps you are tired after your journey.'

Isabel was gazing rather dramatically toward the pastel shadows encroaching on the parlor. I slapped my hands to my knees and rose to my feet. She finally glanced up.

'Shall we go, Isabel? You will need your sleep. We will meet with Francisco tomorrow morning.'

Isabel stood slowly and followed me as I left the parlor.

She certainly has a morbid disposition. I could see why Francisco and she might be drawn to one another. Both seem to share an unwholesome fascination with the macabre.

'Brother Lucas, could I ask you a question?' Isabel spoke as we navigated the courtyard.

'Certainly, child.'

'Are you here to fulfill an obligation?'

'No, child, I serve the Lord from love, not from obligation.'

'Brother Vial told me that you have been with Francisco for almost five months.'

'Indeed, I have,' I answered.

'Thank you, Brother Lucas, for your devotion to Francisco.'

'Servants of the Lord do not seek gratitude,' I said. 'The work provides its own compensation.'

As we walked the narrow passage through the courtyard plantings, I was forced to veer closer to Isabel, so close that I could feel the soft rustle of her silk dress against my white robe.

'Can I ask another question, Brother Lucas?'

It seems the girl did not know when to shut up.

'Please, child.'

'Perhaps I overstep my bounds, Brother Lucas, but is your presence here related to the reward Baron Montcada has offered for the salvation of his son?'

'I am not sure to what you refer, Isabel.'

'It is said that Baron Montcada has offered one-third of his estate to the Church in exchange for the salvation of his son.'

'It is said by whom, child?'

'Perhaps I have been misinformed,' she said. 'Girona is rife with rumors.'

Isabel has no business knowing the intricate workings of the Church, no less the substance of a private exchange between the diocese and a member of its flock. The girl is simply not capable of understanding the full ramifications and intricacies of such matters. Nevertheless, I did my best to explain the situation in order to dispel any misconceptions she might entertain.

'Isabel,' I stated, 'you are not misinformed.

316

Baron Montcada has made such an offer. It is the desperate plea of a father who has already sacrificed one son to the glory of God. You would not have the Church ignore the Baron's plight, would you?'

'Is that what you meant, Brother Lucas, when you said the work provides its own compensation?'

'I do not think the direction of your questioning would please the inquisitors, Isabel. The Church has answered the request of one of its most devoted followers, Baron Montcada. My superiors sent me here in the service of the Lord. To banish the demons that afflict the soul of the Baron's son.'

In mentioning the inquisition, I did not mean to threaten the girl, but merely to warn her for her own good. If she did not become more careful in her discourse, Isabel might well find herself facing one of its tribunals. I would have thought the subject terminated. I was wrong.

'And what do you gain, Brother Lucas,' Isabel asked, 'if Francisco is saved?'

'Excuse me, child?' I said. Such audacity.

'What temptation,' Isabel continued, 'keeps you so long tending to my cousin, Brother Lucas?'

We stopped walking and stood facing each other, not two feet apart. The girl's stare was fixed, her teeth clenched. Our dance was over. Isabel had dispensed the mannered cloak of our diplomacy. Her insolence provoked an anger that took me by surprise. It was with an effort and God's grace that

317

I resisted an impulse to slap her. When she saw on the morrow the progress Francisco had made under my care, I was certain she would bitterly regret the manner in which she had doubted my intentions. But for that moment, she was unaware of my sacrifices. She did not understand the keenness of my emotions in this matter.

Yet, there was more in her expression than a brazen challenge. In the dark shadows under her eyes, in the slight twitch of her eyebrow, I perceived the markings of a solemn, unhealthy introspection. The girl has certainly experienced her share of loss. When her father dies, Francisco will be her most intimate and perhaps only link to the past. I felt a pang of compassion that subdued my anger and drew me toward the girl. My proximity to Isabel was such that I could smell the gentle scent of lavender – the dried leaves that perfumed her clothing. I quite forgot myself and reached out to comfort her, stroking her forearm. It was several seconds before I looked away, distracted by several of my brothers exiting the church. When I looked back, Isabel had turned toward the main gate and was walking through the courtyard. I had to move quite quickly to catch up with the girl. I escorted her to one of the private chambers reserved for our patrician visitors.

When I returned to my quarters, I lingered in the anteroom to my bedchamber, considering my conversation with Isabel. The girl's questions suggested that I had been less than forthright about Baron Montcada's offer and the personal benefits I might expect in the event of Francisco's salvation. But I have made no secret of Archbishop Sancho's solicitude for Francisco's welfare or his appreciation of the difficulties of my mission.

I would not claim that I am indifferent to the Archbishop's favor. I doubt any man is completely immune to the material temptations. Brother Vial had said as much on more than one occasion. What if I want to rise in the clerical hierarchy? Is not my ambition compatible with the work of God? Is not the success of my mission – the salvation of Francisco's soul – consistent with my plans for clerical advancement? Indeed, the higher I rise the more good I can accomplish.

And what right does Isabel have to speak to me of temptation? Has Isabel ever felt an aching emptiness in her stomach that would not be filled that day, nor the next, nor the day after? I have, and I have not forgotten. Born an orphan, a lowly servant. A godforsaken existence of filth and hunger. And servitude to these very people, her people, who were oblivious to my sufferings, who treated me as if I were just another animal on their estate. I have not forgotten.

Then, amidst this daily degradation, the Lord dangles before you not only food and a warm place to sleep, but much more – a life of privilege, the life that Isabel, Andrés, and Francisco so carelessly assumed as their birthright, then seemed

319

indifferent to its benefits, contemptuous of those who sought its blessings.

What if I wanted a crumb from their table? Would God condemn me for that? Would God judge me for wanting to better my condition? Who would not choose such a life and follow it to its logical conclusion, higher and higher, farther and farther away from that wretched poverty?

The next morning I met Isabel in her quarters. She was sitting in her chair, much the same as I had left her. Her bed mat was unruffled, the blanket folded to the side.

'Good morning, Isabel. Santes Creus gets quite chilly at night. I hope you managed to stay warm.'

I addressed her in an amiable manner, determined to show her that her insulting remarks had no effect on me. She returned my courtesies, but cut short a discussion of recent weather conditions. She seemed altogether uninterested in conversation. Nor did she partake of the tea and biscuits Brother Dominic, the porter, provided on my instructions.

I set out on the same solitary walk I had taken every day since Francisco's arrival at Santes Creus some nine months ago. Only this time, I could hear the soft beat of footsteps behind me. I led Isabel through the courtyard, up the stairs, and down the long corridor. When we reached Francisco's cell, I nodded reassuringly at the girl.

'May God be with us, child,' I said.

As soon as I opened the door, Isabel tried to maneuver past me into the cell. I stayed her, holding fast her arm just underneath the shoulder. I did not want to startle Francisco with the sudden sight of his cousin.

He was facing away from the door, seated in the middle of the cell, looking out the window.

'Francisco,' I said, 'you have a visitor. Isabel Correa de Girona stands beside me.'

Francisco did not turn. He made no sign that he had heard me.

'Francisco,' I said, raising my voice, 'Isabel Correa, your cousin, visits you from Girona.'

Still no reaction from Francisco. Most peculiar.

I released my grip on Isabel's arm. She walked slowly around in front of him. I followed her closely. Francisco continued to stare out the window, ignoring the girl. She touched his cheek, studying his face. Isabel's emotions finally overcame her cool reserve. She fell to her knees and placed her head in Francisco's lap. She clutched his legs tightly as if he were a phantom that could disappear at any moment. The girl was sobbing softly, her nose running onto Francisco's newly laundered cloak.

Francisco clenched his fists and closed his eyes tightly – a pained expression, as if Isabel's fingers were shards of glass. He raised his arms above his head. I thought he was preparing to strike the girl. But then he turned his body away from her, his torso twisted in an unnatural, almost violent manner.

Isabel sensed Francisco's discomfort. She loosened her grip and looked up confusedly. Her glance unguarded. Tears suspended.

'Francisco,' she said, 'it is me.'

Her voice seemed to exacerbate his condition. His face contorted anew. She let go of his legs, pulling her hands back, but remained kneeling before him.

'Francisco,' I said, 'will you not greet Isabel? She has traveled many miles to visit you.'

His sealed lips uncoiled.

'Has she come to view the corpse, Brother Lucas?'

'Francisco,' I said, 'what are you talking about?'

'Tell Isabel, Brother Lucas, that Francisco de Montcada died several years ago in Syria. An ignoble death.'

'Francisco, this is no time for jesting.'

'I agree, Brother Lucas,' Francisco said. 'Isabel should know the truth.'

'Isabel,' I said, 'do not pay attention to this momentary nonsense. Francisco's confession proceeds quite rapidly. I can assure you that we have made enormous strides in beating back the demons. One day I hope to write Baron Montcada with news of his son's complete recovery.'

'Brother Lucas,' Francisco said, 'I am not Lazarus, and you cannot raise the dead.'

Francisco could be quite ungrateful. I felt the blood rising to my cheeks.

'By the grace of God, Francisco, you live,' I said.

'I can assure you, Brother Lucas, the Lord does not deem me worthy of His grace.'

'The Lord's grace,' I said, 'gives hope to those who suffer, faith to those who doubt.'

'My faith disappeared several years ago,' Francisco said, 'drowned in the blood of children.'

'A man can live without faith,' Isabel responded.

Francisco turned hard toward the girl.

'Perhaps he can, Isabel. But he cannot live without faith or honor.'

'You spoke to me once of your brother Sergio,' Isabel said. 'You told me that his soul was in limbo. You took the Cross for his salvation. Is not that honorable, Brother Lucas?'

'Yes, Isabel,' I said, 'quite honorable.'

'There is no honor in murder,' he responded.

'Francisco,' I said, 'I have listened to your account of the battle at Toron. I have recorded every word. Excesses were committed. The isolated acts of overzealous comrades do not taint the nobility of your mission, nor of the combined Christian forces.'

'Nobility? I can still smell the stink of burning flesh from our victory. Sergio's soul did not rise on those ashes.'

'It rose on your service to the Lord,' I said. 'Saint Michael must have taken notice of your bravery when he weighed your brother's soul.'

'A coward cannot tip the scales of Saint Michael,' Francisco said.

'A coward,' I said, 'would not have traveled one thousand miles to fight the enemies of Christ. You were a member of a glorious crusade, Francisco. I do not understand how you can speak of yourself so.'

'You will, Brother Lucas. You will understand all. Come to my cell tomorrow morning. I invite you as well, cousin, with Brother Lucas' permission. The death of your brother, Andrés – that's the subject of tomorrow's session – a somewhat tragic tale. It is a story of cowardice and shame. My own.'

Isabel reached forward and grasped Francisco by the front of his robe.

'You speak lies,' she said.

He studied her for several seconds. Then he laughed. Or was it a demon, so strident was that sound?

Isabel fell back as if struck by a blow. She clutched her hands to her chest.

'Tomorrow, Isabel, you will see me as I am and not as you imagine. Then you will flee this place and leave me to my demons.'

Brother Vial told me that the suffering of others sometimes helps us to overcome preoccupation with our own predicament. Isabel was badly shaken. As I looked at her, prostrate on the floor, I put aside my own distress concerning Francisco's condition. I mustered all my strength to raise the girl, placing her arm over my shoulder and leading her out of the cell and down the corridor.

'Isabel,' I said, 'do not heed Francisco's words. It is the devil who speaks in his stead.'

As we walked, Isabel stumbled on the uneven rock. I was forced to call Brother Dominic to help carry the girl down the narrow stairs.

I left Isabel at her quarters and returned to the courtyard. I spent the remainder of the day in silent prayer and meditation. By the time I returned to my chambers, the sun had already set. My supper had been laid out on the table in the antechamber. I was not hungry, though. I found it difficult to sit still. I clasped my hands behind my back and paced around the antechamber. I stopped across from the broken shard of looking glass placed in one of the window panels. Sometimes, when I become discouraged with Francisco's progress, I contemplate my reflection. Its familiarity is a source of comfort – its certainty, the determination I find in my expression, the distinguished crease that runs between my eyes. Sometimes I imagine myself wearing the long crimson robe of a bishop or a cardinal. I practice blessing my subjects with two outstretched fingers. Yes, I think, that is my future. That is I.

That evening was different, though. My reflection seemed remote, alien. It felt as if I were looking at a stranger. I turned away from the looking glass. I assumed the self-assured smile that always reminded me of my plans, my hopes, my ambitions. Then I glanced back suddenly at the mirror. The effect was the same, though. There was something foreign in my eyes – a gnawing insecurity, a vague, restless fear. Looming behind my reflection, I could see that gray vista – the sky bleeding into the ocean, black into white. My stomach began to churn. I got down on my knees before the iron crucifix set on the windowsill and clasped my hands together. *Help me, Lord. I am lost.*

Just before the call to matins, I drifted off to sleep. A loud knocking at the door woke me. I tried to ignore the noise, hoping my visitor would give up, but the pounding only intensified. I lit the candle beside my bed and dragged myself to the door. It was Abbot Alfonso.

'May I have a word, Brother Lucas?' he asked.

'Yes, Abbot Alfonso,' I replied. 'Please enter.'

'Prince Fernando has requested a timetable in his latest letter,' Abbot Alfonso said.

'A timetable for what?' I asked.

'The Prince,' Abbot Alfonso said, 'wants to know when Francisco will be fully recovered. He wants a date certain. Francisco is still progressing, yes?'

'Yes, yes,' I responded. The events of yesterday seemed a nightmare. I was certainly not ready to discuss the encounter or its implications concerning Francisco's condition.

'The Prince,' Abbot Alfonso said, 'has asked

whether Francisco recalls his experiences in the Levant – the battles, his imprisonment – the details.'

Abbot Alfonso looked at me expectantly, but my mind was occupied with thoughts of the impending interview with Francisco.

'Prince Fernando,' Abbot Alfonso continued, 'lost many of his men in the service of the Lord. He has great concern for the well-being of the survivors and holds a special place in his heart for Francisco. The least we can do is provide him a report. With good news, I hope?'

Prince Fernando – the same man who oversaw the massacre of women and children at the castle of Toron – was concerned about the welfare of Francisco.

'Yes,' I said, 'of course, we can provide a report to assuage the concerns of the Prince.'

'Well, then?' Abbot Alfonso asked.

'Please write Prince Fernando,' I said, 'that Francisco remembers the events of the crusade as if they happened yesterday. His memory for even the smallest detail is quite remarkable. Write the Prince that Francisco's condition improves, but still I can give no specific date for his recovery. The Lord's work is fraught with uncertainty and spiritual peril, Abbot Alfonso.'

'Brother Lucas,' the Abbot said, rather irritably, 'spare me the sermon. An estimate will suffice.'

'Abbot Alfonso,' I replied, 'God does not work on a deadline.'

'Are you feeling well, Brother Lucas?' he asked. 'Perhaps you need a rest from your toils, a break from your work with Francisco?'

'And will the devil,' I asked, 'also take a break, Abbot Alfonso?'

Abbot Alfonso took my candle from my hand and held it just in front of my face. I could feel the heat on my cheeks.

'I worry about you, Brother Lucas,' he said. 'In the last month, you have changed considerably. I have passed you more than once in the corridor without your recognition, as if you were entranced by some black sorcery. Even your appearance has altered. Your cheeks are gaunt, your complexion has grown pale. You spend all your time in Francisco's cell or pacing in the courtyard. You have neglected your duties as prior of Santes Creus. I wonder if your work with Francisco has undermined your loyalty to the monastery.'

'I am sorry, Abbot Alfonso, if I have disappointed you,' I said. 'I can only say that my devotion to Francisco's exorcism merely reflects my fidelity to the Church.'

'Let that be so, Brother Lucas. Be careful, though. If you put your hand in the fire, you will sustain a burn. If you put your soul there, you risk eternal damnation.'

The call to matins occurred as the Abbot exited my quarters. I dressed quickly, pulling my brown robe over my head and fastening my sandals.

As I proceeded down the corridor to Isabel's

quarters, I suspected that the girl would decline to revisit Francisco's cell. I certainly did not relish hearing an account of Andrés' death. I could only imagine that Isabel viewed the prospect with dread. If asked for spiritual counsel, I would have advised Isabel to leave Santes Creus and never return.

Isabel had no intention of leaving, though. She was already dressed when I arrived.

'I am ready, Brother Lucas,' she said.

I led her once again up the stairs to Francisco's cell. We stopped just at the entrance. I took a deep breath. It would not have surprised me if Satan himself had been standing behind that door.

'Faith, Brother Lucas.' These words Isabel spoke to me as I undid the latch and opened the door.

Faith indeed, Isabel Correa.

CHAPTER 11

THE KRAK DES CHEVALIERS

Francisco had moved his chair closer to the window, perhaps to enhance his view of the monastery's garden. Or perhaps to exclude Isabel and me from his line of vision. Indeed, he did not seem to be looking down into the courtyard, but instead staring at a gray patch of sky. He gripped the armrests tightly, the blue veins visible on the back of his hands. He did not respond to my greeting or acknowledge our presence. Isabel and I sat down on the cold stone behind Francisco. We spoke a few words. I inquired if she was comfortable. She said she was. Then we waited. As the sun rose, its shadow crept over the floor. I followed its progress across each stone, across Isabel, across me. An hour, two hours, three – I do not know how much time elapsed before Francisco began again his confession.

Almost forty knights of Calatrava had been killed at Toron – both of Ramón's deputies – Roberto and Bernard. Andrés and I assumed their posts.

We were the next-highest-ranking officers – first lieutenants. We had earned that distinction by winning the foot race over the mountain trail during our training in Calatrava.

Our Order occupied less than half the space in our chambers. No one bothered to collect the unused mats, though, and their presence fostered the illusion that our dead comrades were merely delayed and would return shortly.

Andrés' wound healed rapidly, but not his fighting spirit. He spoke little during our few weeks in Acre and never left the compound. He walked around the courtyard during the day, his eyes glazed, his blond hair spread haphazardly across his shoulders.

Baron Bernières and Don Fernando arrived in Acre a few days after us. Don Fernando's men returned to their quarters on the outskirts of the city. Our Hospitaller comrades settled across from us in the eastern wing of the compound. To mark our victory at Toron, they conducted daily celebrations after morning Mass. In the Great Hall, spigots of wine remained open from dawn until dusk. Knights reveled into the evening hours.

As guests in the Hospitaller headquarters, the Knights of Calatrava could not decline the invitation of our hosts to join the festivities. In their strident mirth, my brothers sought to disavow their memories of Toron. I could not forget, though. Padre Albar standing before a bonfire of corpses in the castle courtyard. The Word of God proclaimed in a field of blood.

The merrymaking of my comrades grated like a knife against stone. My head pounded. I had to loosen my collar to breathe more freely. On the fourth day of celebration, I left the Hospitaller compound. I went alone, without asking Ramón's permission, without informing anyone, even Andrés.

I wandered through the streets, losing myself in the anonymity of the city. When I reached the port, I sat on the dock, dangling my feet just above the waves that washed against the stones. I looked out at the harbor, at the sailors loading cargo – the same exotic goods from the market bound for Christian Europe. The men rolled laden barrels up ramps into the ship's hold. One of the barrels escaped, whirling backward. Sailors jumped into the water to avoid being run over. The barrel splintered against the dock. Pearls, yellow, white, black, scattered like marbles across the stone.

At dusk, I returned to the compound. As I walked through the streets, a group of monks came up behind me, jostling, pressing on both sides. Their brown habits were frayed, worn ragged from their sojourns. Belts of rope kept their rags in place. Their bare feet had blistered, crusted in dried blood and dirt. They were pilgrims on their way to Muslim-occupied Jerusalem, relying on the Lord's protection and their patron – one Francis of Assisi. I had heard his name at Santes Creus.

Accounts of his passions had reached Aragón, inspiring others to follow his example. Those men called by the saint had established a new monastic Order and taken the name of their master – Franciscans.

Censers burning incense swung to and fro. The sharp perfume pervaded the narrow street. One monk carried a wooden Cross, groaning under the burden. Their leader, grim-faced, shouted in Italian, reciting the miracles of Francis. He spoke of the five wounds which appeared on the saint's body – the stigmata of Christ. The scars blackened, the same color as the nails that bore into Our Savior.

Saint Francis of Assisi, dead not fifty years. His side discharged drops of blood even after his death. The monk set forth the evidence, describing the condition of his master as if he had seen the blood with his own eyes. He pointed his finger at shopkeepers, at passersby, at me. He looked sideways, across his shoulder, down his long arm, as if he were an inquisitor inquiring as to our doubts, our deeds.

'Likewise,' he testified, 'one of the twelve companions of Saint Francis, whose name was Friar Giovanni Cappella, apostatized and finally hanged himself by the neck.' The monk's voice resonated, cracked and shrill. 'This being a cause of humility and fear even amongst the elect.' He nodded his head, severe and knowing. 'That no man can be certain that he will persevere until the end in the grace of God.'

A week after his arrival in Acre, Baron Bernières summoned Uncle Ramón for a meeting. As Ramón's new deputies, Andrés and I accompanied him.

When we entered his chambers, Baron Bernières sat regal on a gilded chair. He wore a silk sash across his shoulder and a garland of leaves on his head.

'Ramón,' the Baron said, 'welcome. Congratulations to the Knights of Calatrava for our glorious victory.'

'And to you, Baron Bernières, and your men,' Ramón responded.

'Ramón,' the Baron said, 'unfortunately, I have called you here to discuss some troubling news. Yesterday I received a letter from the Krak des Chevaliers. Don Lorgne, the castellan, reports that the Muslim commander Baibars has laid siege to the castle. The state of affairs is rather disappointing. You would think with such a massive fortress they could protect themselves.'

The Baron called forth his first deputy, Colonel Delacorte, who nodded at Uncle Ramón and unfurled a parchment. He began to recite:

'Greetings from the Krak des Chevaliers, Baron Bernières. Unfortunately, I write in desperate circumstances. Baibars' forces have surrounded the castle. In the last several days, the infidels have transported catapults to lay siege to the fortress. Barring the arrival of significant

334

reinforcements, the castle will fall before summer.

'Accordingly, I am requesting that you lead all Hospitaller knights under your command to the Krak. Our survival depends on your swift journey north. God willing, we will see each other under more favorable conditions.

'Don Lorgne, castellan of the Krak des Chevaliers, the twenty-fourth day of March, the Year of Our Lord 1271.'

Colonel Delacorte rolled up the parchment.

'Ramón, do you know how many years the Hospitallers have occupied the Krak?' the Baron asked.

'I do not,' Ramón said.

'One hundred and thirty,' the Baron said. 'Constructing and reconstructing the castle over decades, we have built an impregnable fortress. Two sets of walls protect the castle – a fortress within a fortress. Eighteen towers guard its approaches. There is even a windmill. A whole city for God's army. Do you know how thick the walls are? Twelve feet. Twelve feet of solid stone.

'Did you know, Ramón, that the castle has survived four major earthquakes? Did you know that the Hospitaller knights defending the Krak have repulsed twelve attacks by the Muslims? Saladin, after conquering Jerusalem in just thirteen days, led an expedition to the Krak to mount a siege against the fortress. He recognized the importance of the

335

castle. Whoever occupies the Krak controls the flow of goods between the Mediterranean and the inland cities. Do you know what Saladin did after observing the castle defenses? He turned around and left. He never returned. Even the great Saladin recognized the futility of attacking such a fortress.

'And now we have a castellan who panics because a few infidel regiments have surrounded the fortress. It's disgraceful. I'm sure, Ramón, you can understand my hesitancy in sharing internal correspondence which casts an unfavorable light on one of my fellow Hospitaller officers. And yet I have no choice. With the Grand Master of the Hospital out of country, I am responsible for the defense of our castles, and though the castellan is a bit hysterical, I cannot ignore his appeal. If we do not relieve the castellan, I fear he will surrender the castle without a fight.

'You see, Ramón,' the Baron continued, 'I left most of my knights at Toron to guard the castle. I have a mere one hundred knights – that's all the able-bodied men I have at my disposal. It's quite ridiculous to think of such a force coming to the rescue of our excitable castellan. My small contingent could hardly affect the course of any battle.'

The Baron continued to examine Ramón.

'If we can enlist the powerful combination of forces that conquered Toron . . . well . . . then the probability of steeling our castellan and rescuing the fortress would increase rather dramatically. I meet with Don Fernando to request his assistance later this afternoon. I am hopeful that both of you will agree to fight under my command. I do not see that you have a choice. If the Krak falls, no one in the Christian Levant will be safe from Baibars' soldiers.'

Ramón was stroking his beard thoughtfully, and he did not provide the ready assurance the Baron seemed to expect.

'Surely, Ramón,' the Baron asked, 'you do not plan to partake of our hospitality, eat our food, drink our wine, while we fight to protect your well-being?'

'Baron Bernières,' Ramón responded, 'the Calatrava will not turn their backs on comrades in need. We will fight by your side. As Don Fernando may join the expedition, though, I feel it is my duty to protest the treatment by his soldiers of the Muslim prisoners at the castle of Toron. I trust you are aware of the cruel manner in which Don Fernando's army dealt with the civilian population. The actions of his men besmirched every Christian soldier who took part in the siege.'

'Ramón,' the Baron said, 'this is neither the time nor the place to bring up petty conflicts or jealousies between you and Don Fernando.'

'This matter is not petty, Baron. Nor does it stem from my personal feelings toward Don Fernando. The treatment of civilians by Don Fernando's soldiers at Toron was incompatible with our mission.'

'Ramón,' the Baron responded, 'I find it distasteful that you raise this trivial issue at such a critical juncture. How will Don Fernando perceive such an attack?'

'Let us hope, Baron,' Ramón said, 'the Don will perceive it as an inducement to change his behavior and that of his regiment.'

'Considering the results, I thought Don Fernando's regiment behaved rather well at Toron.'

'Baron Bernières,' Ramón said, 'as you are reluctant to pursue this matter with the Don, I have no choice but to lodge my protest with your superior, the Grand Master of the Hospital, and with King Jaime, the Don's father, upon my return to Aragón.'

'Ramón,' Baron Bernières said, 'you can seek redress from Jesus Christ for all I care. Just prepare your men for the journey.'

After Andrés and I gathered our brothers in a corner of the courtyard, Uncle Ramón told them of our mission.

'The infidels,' he said, 'have laid siege to the great castle of the Krak des Chevaliers. Its capture would be a devastating blow to the armies of Christ. In a few days' time, we will march north to go to the aid of our Hospitaller brothers at the fortress.

'We lost nearly half our number at Toron. More of you will perish beneath the walls of the Hospitaller castle. Know this. The Lord measures every drop of blood shed in defense of His Kingdom.'

In the afternoon, I crossed paths in the courtyard

with Don Fernando. He was coming from his own meeting with the Baron. I noticed his purple cape from a distance and tried to avoid a confrontation by changing direction. He called before I could elude his gaze.

'Ah, Francisco,' he said. 'How is the heir to the Montcada fortune?'

'I am well, Don Fernando.'

'Tell me, Francisco,' he said, 'how is the Princess?'

'I know no princess in these parts.'

'Do you not serve the illustrious, the renowned Princess Ramón of Calatrava?'

'I know of no such person.'

'My spies,' Don Fernando said, 'tell me that your master has a story concerning my conduct at Toron that he intends to tell my father. If Ramón thinks I will stand by while he sullies my reputation, he knows little of my character.'

I did not respond. I had seen enough to draw my own conclusions as to Don Fernando's character.

'Very well, Francisco,' Don Fernando said, 'I have good news on another front. There is an opening on my staff. I invite you to join my entourage. I have plans for you, Francisco.'

'Don Fernando, I am flattered by your consideration, but I remain faithful to the Calatrava and my master, Ramón.'

'I admire your loyalty, Francisco. One day I hope to be its beneficiary. Reflect on my offer, though.

339

I fear there is not much of a future for our Uncle Ramón.'

We left the city three days later, just before dawn. Uncle Ramón explained that the stealth of our departure stemmed from a desire not to alarm Acre's residents, most of whom considered the Krak des Chevaliers invincible, a symbol of Christian might in the Levant. News of the Krak's predicament might well have spread panic through the city, already teeming with rumors of infidel advances.

The Krak stood at the northeast boundary of the Christian territories, approximately one hundred and sixty-five miles from Acre. According to Colonel Delacorte, Hospitaller knights generally made the journey from Acre to the Krak in two weeks. Because of the dire situation at the castle, we would make the journey in five days.

Only mounted soldiers could travel with such speed. Accordingly, foot soldiers and archers were not included on the expedition. Nevertheless, the consolidation of forces fielded a formidable force – over two hundred and fifty knights, several hundred mounted squires, and another one hundred professional calvary soldiers drawn from the local populace, Orthodox Christians by religion, Arabs by ethnicity. The natives looked like the men we had just fought at Toron. They also spoke the same language – two facts that caused uneasiness amongst my brothers. I had heard stories of native Christian guides leading our knights into ambushes. But I had also heard stories of Hospitaller and Templar knights slaughtering whole Arab villages, only to find out later that the residents were Orthodox or Jacobite Christians. So I would not judge certain natives if they felt more allegiance to their neighbors than to their Christian comrades. This reluctance to pass judgment, though, did not lessen my concern or my vigilance. In the night, we would never turn our backs on the Arab Christians.

One of these native Christians approached Andrés and me outside Beirut. He stood before us, shifting his weight back and forth. Andrés put his hand to his scabbard.

'One day you go home,' the man said.

'God willing,' I said, 'we will all go home.'

He smiled, almost bashful, glancing back at the city lights.

'I am home.'

We rode twelve hours a day straight up the coast, bivouacking on the outskirts of the northern cities – Tyre, Sidon, Beirut, Tripoli. Ramón said that when the first crusaders came to the Levant, the Christian residents competed with one another to feed and shelter knights traveling into battle. Sentiments had changed. The local populace provided food and shelter, water and oats for our horses. But we paid for our provisions in coin, gold and silver, which the merchants counted carefully right before us.

We ate our meals around campfires. Instead of

staring into the burning embers, we looked to the distant lights of the city, listening jealously to the sounds of the night, the call of a friend, a scuffle outside a tavern, the laughter of a girl. We slept – immobile, dreamless – like dead men, too tired to ponder an uncertain future. We woke at dawn and set out before the merchants had set their stalls, leaving no trace of our presence. The city residents must have wondered if pilgrim soldiers or ghosts had visited them. After a couple of hours' riding, I could not remember under what stars we had lain or even if we had slept at all.

When we reached Tripoli, we received one of the Hospitaller scouts from the Krak. He had managed to sneak past the infidel lines and had arrived in the city only hours before us. Colonel Delacorte hastily arranged a briefing, attended by Baron Bernières, Uncle Ramón, Don Fernando, and their deputies, including Andrés and me. We met in the office of the city constable, who doubted the accuracy of Don Lorgne's report and seemed anxious for our departure.

'Even an army of fifty thousand of Baibars' finest soldiers,' he said, 'could not conquer the Krak. You are wasting your time.'

The constable did not wait for the scout's news. He said that he had business at the port – a Venetian merchant refusing to pay taxes – and departed hastily.

The scout from the Krak sat in the constable's chair surrounded by our entourage. Staring down at his clasped hands, he seemed reluctant to face his examiners.

'What is the status of the battle, scout?' the Baron asked.

'Not good, sir,' he responded. 'They never stop. They never stop coming.'

'Has the garrison repulsed the infidel attacks?' the Baron asked.

'Yes, sir, I think, sir,' the scout said. 'Well, no, sir. We had to retreat inside the inner walls of the castle. The infidel sappers dug underneath the foundations of the outer walls. One of the towers collapsed. Their soldiers rushed into the breach. A good number of our men were caught by surprise and did not have time to escape to the inner enceinte.'

'How many men were caught?' Colonel Delacorte asked.

'A good number, sir,' he answered. 'None were taken alive.'

'Can you estimate the size of Baibars' force?' Don Fernando asked.

'Very large, sir,' he said.

'An elephant is very large,' Don Fernando said. 'How many soldiers surround the castle?'

'Four thousand, five thousand,' the scout said. 'More soldiers than the eye can count, sir.'

'What is the condition of the inner walls?' Colonel Delacorte asked.

'They were still there when I left, sir, but the Muslims were hauling up their catapults to the top of the outer walls. From that position, their machines will be able to blast away at the inner enceinte until very little is left of the castle.'

'How many Hospitaller knights are defending the castle?' Ramón asked.

'At least sixty-five, sir . . . when I left. With another two hundred foot soldiers and archers. There are many wounded, some of whom will fight when Baibars storms the castle.'

When Baibars storms the castle . . .

I looked to Ramón, who seemed not to register the gravity of this prognosis. He had reached his hand forward and was gently touching the dried blood that stained the scout's tunic.

'An arrow?' Ramón asked.

'Excuse me, sir?'

'Your arm,' Ramón said. 'Was it an arrow?'

'Yes, sir. That's why Don Lorgne chose me as messenger. With one arm, I was no good as a fighter. I can still ride, though.'

Ramón nodded.

'Sir,' the scout said, 'I am sorry.'

'Perhaps,' Baron Bernières said, 'we should reconsider our mission. It is not as if . . .'

'That will be all, scout,' Ramón said, interrupting the Baron. 'My men will dress your wound and provide food for you.'

We did our best to contain the bad news to the small coterie of officers who had listened to the scout's report. But leaks occurred. When the sun rose the next morning, much of our army had deserted, disappeared into the bustling streets of Tripoli – all the native Christians, most of the squires. The Hospitallers, on a mission to rescue their own brethren, lost half their number. Don Fernando's army surrendered only a couple of knights. Don Fernando sentenced the two deserters to death. He said he would personally carry out the sentences after repulsing Baibars' attack at the Krak.

The Calatrava alone were intact. Our devotion to the Cross did not exceed that of our Hospitaller brethren. It was simply a loyalty to Uncle Ramón and my comrades – the men with whom we had lived, slept, eaten, and fought. If death waited for us at the Krak des Chevaliers, then so be it. I would have rather made his acquaintance than suffer the shame of deserting my brothers.

After meeting with Baron Bernières and Don Fernando, Uncle Ramón called his knights into a circle.

'As you already know,' he said, 'we have lost some of our Hospitaller friends. They were the weaker of our number. We are better off without them.'

Ramón spoke loudly, perhaps too loudly, as if he could make up in volume what he lacked in conviction. Some of my brothers looked anxiously to Andrés and me, as if Ramón had designated us to hear their appeals. Others were kicking dust or staring off into the hills. Ramón stepped back and surveyed the fifty-eight knights under his command.

'Remember what I told you when you first arrived in Calatrava,' he said, lowering his voice. 'A small band of knights, hungry, tired, and ill-equipped, marched down the coast of Syria and conquered Jerusalem in the Year of Our Lord 1099. With God's grace, we could vanquish an army of demons.'

We headed east into the hills of Syria. In the absence of all but a few squires, we strapped our armor on the backs of our horses. Several of the Hospitallers had spent stints at the Krak, including Colonel Delacorte. They acted as our guides. It was a sixteen-hour trip to the castle from Tripoli. We had planned on making the last stage of our journey in two days. After hearing the scout's report, the commanders decided we would ride until we reached the fort. We still had a force of two hundred knights.

Through misty valleys, we rode our horses. Untamed hills seduced us into forgetting our destination. We could hear the melodies of crickets and doves, the trickle of a creek. We passed a furtive colony of yellow flowers, stems straining against the cool wind. The stunned eyes of a rabbit glowed through the tall grass. A lithe Arab girl, bent over in the river, washing her clothes. Her long black hair, untied, skimmed the surface of the water. She did not even glance up at the army of knights who passed on the bank. I did not think of the battle that waited at the Krak. I could not imagine it in those placid hills.

346

Night fell like a soft cloak. Riding side by side with Andrés, I remembered our races in Montcada when he came to visit after Sergio's death. My brother Sergio. My brother Andrés. I thought of my father, probably competing at some jousting tournament in France or Germany, and of my mother, still in the black of mourning, seven years after Sergio's death.

An alien and distant noise interrupted my meditations. At first it sounded like rolling thunder. As we approached the castle, I recognized the distinct tenor of artillery.

'It seems,' Ramón said, riding just behind me, 'that Baibars intends to keep our brothers at the Krak from sleeping, lest they dream themselves to another place.'

It was not long before we could hear the sound of stone on stone – the projectiles from the catapults smashing into the fortress. The barrage seemed to escalate so that the streams, the crickets, the other animals – nature itself – became silent as if in homage to that great storm or in fear of drawing its ire. We alone continued on that path, toward the center of the tempest – over the protest of our faithful horses, who whinned uneasily and jerked backward when the earth trembled. My hands tightened around the reins.

As the sounds of battle became fiercer, the commanders rode to the front of our force. Their deputies, including Andrés and me, trailed just behind. Colonel Delacorte spoke to the three men in turn, first the Baron, then Don Fernando and Uncle Ramón. I could not hear their conversations. I watched, though, trying to ascertain information concerning our fate. After listening to the Colonel, Baron Bernières grabbed his deputy's hand and shook it vigorously. Don Fernando crossed himself, then kissed his closed fist. Ramón looked back toward Andrés and me. I could read nothing in his expression, though.

Perhaps a mile or two from the fortress around a ridge that concealed us from the enemy, Colonel Delacorte told the men to dismount. When the commanders and their officers had gathered around, Colonel Delacorte instructed the knights to don their armor. Between each other and the several squires that were left, we managed to dress for battle while Colonel Delacorte explained the plan of action. The humming of artillery forced the Colonel to suspend intermittently his discourse, but he continued when the noise abated. The precise, plainspoken nature of Colonel Delacorte's orders made many of us wonder regretfully how it came to pass that such a man as Baron Bernières was our commander instead of his deputy.

'We will not attack Baibars' force outside the castle,' Colonel Delacorte said. 'There is a secret underground passage one mile from the castle. It leads to the inner enceinte. We have kept the tunnel a secret even from our most trusted soldiers. Only the Grand Master and Hospitaller knights who have been stationed at the castle know of its existence. If you are captured, you must never reveal this knowledge.

'The entrance is marked by a pile of rocks atop a square stone. Baibars is unaware of the tunnel. The rocks remain undisturbed, the secret passage undiscovered.

'The pathway is narrow and will not accommodate our mounts. We will abandon them here. On foot, we will proceed rapidly, daggers drawn, to the entrance of the tunnel. We should reach the opening in ten to fifteen minutes.

'Ramón, I would request that your men deal with any infidel sentries who stumble upon our party.'

'We will do so, Colonel,' Ramón responded.

'Once the last soldier is safe in the passage,' Colonel Delacorte continued, 'I myself will pull the stone over the entrance.

'Before dawn we will be in the castle. The infidels will not understand the appearance of fresh soldiers. Baibars will think that God Himself dispatched a band of angels to defend the fort.'

Colonel Delacorte set off immediately, running cautiously toward the ridge. Baron Bernières and the other Hospitaller knights followed in single file. We all fell in line, reluctantly releasing the reins of our horses, abandoning the last vestige of a hope unspoken that somehow our path would bypass the besieged castle.

We came around the ridge noiselessly. It was my first glimpse of the castle. The Krak stood defiant amidst its enemies, deflecting the Muslim artillery in a symphony of sparks and flames that transformed night into day. The gray stone rising from the earth as if it were natural-born of that same rock that covered the landscape in Golgotha. A monument to the martyrs – those who had fallen in her defense and those who would fall. The round towers soared. Each block of stone conspiring to pierce the firmament, groaning under the burden of our righteousness.

I was running instinctively, entranced by the majesty of the castle, when Ramón tapped me from behind. He had grabbed Andrés' shoulder with his other hand. He pointed to the back of a man, a Muslim sentry, not thirty feet away. The sentry was moving quickly toward the infidel lines. We had been discovered.

Andrés and I sprinted after the man. We gained on him so rapidly it seemed that he was standing still. Andrés tripped him from behind. He was screaming, trying to attract the attention of his comrades. The din of battle drowned his voice. As Andrés held him down, I moved my dagger across his throat. The blade cut smoothly. Drops of blood fell like raindrops on my fingers. Andrés and I perused the area quickly for other sentries, but there were none. We ran back to our company and took our place next to Ramón.

Colonel Delacorte had already reached the passageway. One by one, our comrades disappeared, swallowed by the earth. I was the first of the Calatrava to enter the passage. I jumped into the open hole, my fall cushioned by the soft clay. I was helped forward by one of the Hospitaller deputies. The remaining soldiers soon filled the passageway.

When Colonel Delacorte pulled the tombstone over the opening, darkness enveloped us. The night was total. I was breathing heavily from our exertions and could not catch my breath. The smell of rank clay and damp air was suffocating. That tunnel seemed like a crypt, closing fast around us. I clutched Andrés' arm.

Two of the Baron's men lit torches that chased the darkness down the long corridor. My fears subsided gradually as I looked at the steady profile of Uncle Ramón just beside me. The knights leaned against each other, listening to the muffled sounds of the artillery barrage.

'Welcome to the Krak des Chevaliers, men,' Colonel Delacorte said. 'Keep your heads down and keep moving forward. We will space a torch every tenth person.'

Led by Colonel Delacorte and the Hospitallers, we began walking down the tunnel. The dimensions of the passage seemed to vary every few steps. At times we could stand straight up. At other times we were forced to kneel and even crawl through the cold stream of water that flowed on the floor of the tunnel. My gaze never left the torch carried by one of Don Fernando's deputies, exactly five men ahead of me.

As we moved forward, the crush of artillery

intensified. When the missiles hit the ground above us, the whole passageway shook. If we were standing, we would be thrown to the ground. Rocks and dirt would rain down from the tunnel's ceiling, so that we had to stop and cover our heads with our hands or, if we were quick enough, our shields. The pounding became so frequent that we did not bother to stand, even when we were able. We crawled through the mud and clay toward the inner castle of the Krak, toward the roar of combat.

When we reached the end of the tunnel, two of the Hospitaller knights from the castle helped pull us up into a gloomy alcove. My comrades stood uneasily, coughing the clay from their lungs, waiting for directions from our hosts. We had made it into the castle.

Other Hospitaller knights appeared. They seemed neither surprised nor pleased by our arrival, as if they were receiving guests at a funeral. They divided the new arrivals into groups of three men, then escorted us outside the dank compartment.

Andrés and I were grouped with Uncle Ramón. Our chaperon led us up a flight of stairs, through covered tunnels and vaulted passageways, and more stairs. The bombardment was unrelenting. I could not hear my own footsteps. At times the stone missiles landed close to our position, so that rocks and other debris fell just where, an instant before, we had been. The knight who led us seemed unconcerned, though, never altering his pace. We followed close to his side. When we reached the threshold of a large chamber, our escort abandoned us, disappearing into a dark passageway.

We took a step forward. We had entered a chapel, a sturdy fortress unto itself, with heavy vaults girding the lofty ceiling. The noise of battle diminished as we crossed into the sanctuary, a haven from the fighting. The fragrant haze of incense banished the acrid smoke that pervaded the castle city. Torches lit the painted walls – colorful battle scenes – Christian military victories interwoven with images of martyrs and saints. Shields and swords hung amongst the frescoes.

A priest in a hooded robe motioned for us to proceed toward the apse, where a knight was kneeling before a wooden Cross. His head was bowed in prayer.

Our other comrades arrived in groups and quickly filled the church. We gathered silently around the praying man, afraid to disturb his concentration. He stood finally. Brown hair extended down to his shoulders. Long sideburns flanked taut, riven cheeks. The white Cross of the Hospitallers was sewn on his black tunic.

My attention diverted to the chain around his neck, a string of translucent orbs. They resembled seashells, or the wafers of bread given by the priest at Mass. There must have been twenty.

I looked closer at these strange ornaments dangling across his chest. I rubbed my eyes and squinted through the mist of incense.

353

No earthly sea spawned these trinkets. Nor were they consecrated in any church. Don Lorgne was wearing a necklace of ears. Infidel ears.

When he talked, my comrades closest to him stepped back. Perhaps they were surprised that the savage could speak.

'That shield,' he said, pointing to a place high on the wall, 'was used by Sir Geoffroy de Joinville. If you look closely, you can see the arrow marks. One hundred years ago, Sir Geoffroy commanded a small company of knights that left the castle to collect tribute from a local village. They ran into a full regiment of infidel soldiers that were passing through the territory. Outnumbered and unprepared for battle, Sir Geoffroy chose nevertheless to engage the infidels rather than flee back to the safe confines of the castle. The fighting was ferocious. Sir Geoffroy himself stained his sword with the blood of one hundred infidels. The Muslim soldiers eventually overwhelmed the Krak's defenders. Sir Geoffroy and his entire company were killed on the battlefield. Out of respect for their worthy adversary, the Muslims left Sir Geoffroy's body and armor at the entrance to the castle the morning after the battle. His bones lie beneath you.'

His gentle voice betrayed neither hope nor fear. His tone never rose nor lowered.

'I am Nicolas Lorgne, the castellan of the Krak des Chevaliers. For ten years, I have lived within these walls – ten years fighting the infidels. Ten

354

years in the wilderness, defending Christ's Kingdom against the heathen. I have studied their tactics and learned their strengths and weaknesses.

'Baron Bernières and Colonel Delacorte, Ramón of the Calatrava,' Don Lorgne said, 'Jesus Christ will reward the courage of you and your soldiers who have risked their lives to come to our aid. The dire nature of our situation is obvious. You have heard the force of the Muslim barrage. Even with your arrival, their soldiers outnumber us ten to one.

'Baibars demands an unconditional surrender. That would mean death or slavery for every knight in the castle. To avoid this fate, we must convince Baibars that the siege will be too long and costly.

'Supplying his force requires the transportation of food and drink for five thousand mouths to this desert outpost. All the while, he allows his other enemies – both Christian and Muslim – to roam freely in the territories. If we can hold out into the hot summer months, Baibars might decide he cannot afford to continue the siege. God willing, he will withdraw his army.

'Muslim artillery poses the gravest threat to our survival. Every day, their catapults destroy more and more of the castle fortifications. If the Muslims break through the inner wall, the battle is lost.

'We have used secret passages to conduct several nighttime raids, dismantling ten catapults. In the last several days, the infidels have attempted to wheel catapults into the no-man's-land between the inner castle and the outer wall. From that proximity, the projectiles would carry a devastating force – even against the thick walls of the Krak. Fortunately, we have been able to destroy these catapults. The area is in range of our marksmen.

'To provide protection for a catapult inside the no-man's-land, the infidels are building a stone shelter. We have tried to sabotage their engineers – pouring burning oil on the shelter, dropping our heaviest stones – to no avail. Despite our efforts, the infidels managed to wheel a catapult under the shelter two nights ago. The catapult will be operational soon, perhaps tomorrow, and it faces the weakest section of the inner wall. We have no choice but to eradicate the position.

'At dawn, we will conduct a sortie to destroy the catapult and kill the infidels in the shelter. There is a postern with a sliding stone door opposite the catapult. I will lead a team of twelve men through the passageway. We will set fire to the catapult and then return to the inner enceinte. The entire operation will be over in less than five minutes.

'Our remaining soldiers will provide a hail of arrows to cover the attackers, but the soldiers on the mission will be vulnerable to the Muslim archers manning the outside walls and will meet resistance from soldiers guarding the catapult. I need twelve volunteers to form my team.'

Amongst some of the men, there was a restless shuffling of feet. Several knights even looked away from Don Lorgne, studying the chapel's decorated walls, as if they had not heard his appeal.

'I will fight by your side, Don Lorgne,' Ramón said. 'Who in the Calatrava will join me?'

Andrés and I and three other knights in our Order raised our hands. The other members of the Calatrava, observing their comrades, followed our example, some slower than others. Ramón selected eleven of us – including Andrés and me.

Don Lorgne had described the mission in stark terms. The chances of survival seemed less than even. Yet, he had also offered a chance for a noble death. If we remained behind, we would probably die anyway. Better to die beside Andrés and Uncle Ramón as warriors, rather than huddled in the castle, waiting for a missile to hit my position, or worse, captured by the Muslims to die more slowly.

'In a few minutes, at the first sign of sunrise,' Don Lorgne continued, 'the Muslims stop shelling to say their prayers. That gives us thirty minutes of peace. We have much to show you and accomplish in this short period.'

Don Lorgne instructed his deputy to give the new soldiers a short tour of the castle, to learn its general design and 'the nature of the infidel encirclement,' before the resumption of artillery made such movement impossible.

'The team of volunteers will assemble back in the chapel in twenty minutes. From there we will proceed to the postern and launch our raid. The rest of you will be spaced at different points on the walls to strengthen our defenses.'

When we left the chapel, the night had drained, leaving behind a worn gray. As Don Lorgne predicted, the Muslim shelling had ceased. We walked upright through empty streets and alleyways of the Krak. Small fires burned unattended. I stepped over the carcass of a dead dog, the rib cage partly buried in the dust.

We passed through a courtyard, a crooked path between craters still seething. Blue ash rose where infidel stones had rent the soil. A narrow passage under an archway led to the kitchen. We walked quickly through that chamber, but not before I could smell stale bread left on the open ovens and feel a pang of hunger. I had not eaten a full meal in two days.

We proceeded up a stairwell, then across a walkway. Several knights were leaning against the battlements. Most had painted faces. 'Blood and charcoal,' our guide said. They looked us over sullenly, silently. One soldier focused on me. A half-smile – half-greeting, half-mocking. *Who are you? The blood smeared across his cheeks, his forehead. Did you think to find meaning here, in this hell, to find light in this darkness? Is that what you were thinking?*

As I walked along the ridge, my left foot fell through a gap in the castle floor. I looked down and could see to the ground, corpses littering the no-man's-land. Ramón grabbed the scruff of my chain mail and lifted me up.

'Watch your step,' the deputy said. 'We drop burning oil through the slots, not our own soldiers. The oil will burn the face off a man in an instant.'

We entered a tower and climbed the circular staircase. When we had reached the summit, the deputy spoke again.

'We threw several infidels off this tower when the siege began. They were Baibars' spies who had been hired to work in the kitchen just weeks before the siege began. Don Lorgne discovered one of them making a diagram of the fort.'

From that vantage, we had a clear view of the Syrian mountains, a range of snow-capped peaks. A soft haze settled in the valleys. Small villages, still sleeping, dotted the landscape. Patches of forest sprinkled across foothills. To the west, I could see all the way to the ocean – no ships, no port, just a blue fire glimmering in the first light. Closer to the tower, white tents – the Muslim encampments – encircled the castle. They were concentrated on the south side, where the natural defenses were weakest – no steep incline prevented an assault. The Muslims occupied the outside wall and had wheeled their catapults on top of its towers. Groups of Muslim soldiers bowed their heads to the ground as if worshiping the might of their machines.

Looking back, I saw the castle in all its splendor, a city carved out of rock. Deserted streets snaked between buildings that, in the first rays of morning light, glinted like silver. The stones were so finely cut the mortar was invisible. Towers, rounded and squared, stood like a phalanx of sentinels against our enemies. Christian sentries stationed on the parapet resembled sculptures of ancient warriors hewn from the rough stone.

I looked east. The sun was rising, the orange and purple spilling across the dusty shoulders of the hills. A cold breeze stung my cheeks.

'Behold, Francisco,' Uncle Ramón said, just behind me, 'the beauty of God's creation. Even Baibars cannot stop the sun from rising.'

Before Ramón finished speaking, a whining sound arose in the Muslim camp. As the sound drew closer, it transformed into a strident whistle. I looked up and saw the massive boulder, as if the sun were hurtling from the heavens.

The impact threw me forward against the wall. The world turned black. I was floating, hovering tranquil amongst the clouds. I looked down at the battle, at my comrades on the tower, at the Muslim encampments. I saw an endless line of infidel soldiers riding humpbacked camels. Red turbans twirled around their heads. The cloth folded, winding like a snake, its tail flapping in the wind across each man's face. They must have come from Arabia, like vultures in anticipation of the fall of the great Christian fortress.

Whether this Arabian cavalry truly existed, I cannot say. A sharp pain in my head jarred me back down to the tower's surface. I felt dizzy. Struggling to sit up, I managed to wedge my back between the rock teeth. Andrés was kneeling in front of me. He was yelling in my face. I could not hear him. Only the soft echo of Ramón's words – 'the beauty of God's creation.'

I looked through the smoke and soot in search of my other brothers from the Calatrava. Diego Ponso stumbled toward me. His right shoulder and arm had been ripped from his body. Bloody and torn metal mesh tossed in the wind. One eyebrow raised, Diego's face bore an expression of righteous indignation, as if he felt that the infidels had broken a tacit agreement by loosing their catapults without warning on the tower. Diego fell to his knees. Then he keeled over like a tree freshly cut.

I looked down at my legs and noticed a shiny particle on my knee. It seemed a piece of cloth, perhaps velvet. I reached down to pull it off, but it was stuck to my leg. I examined it more closely. It was a dark curl of oiled hair, attached to a piece of chalky scalp, like a smashed eggshell. I recognized the lock of fine hair as belonging to the Baron. That was all that remained of him. The Baron Gustav Bernières, well groomed until the end.

Andrés was still yelling at me. I could make out his voice, but it seemed to come from a distance.

'The infidels have set their sights on the tower,' he said. 'We leave now before the next stone falls.'

He helped me to my feet. Other soldiers had arrived to carry the wounded down the tower's staircase. I walked the stairs with my arm around

Andrés' shoulder. When we reached the ledge, I was able to proceed unaided. The knights we had passed on the walkway had taken cover behind the stone walls, waiting for the next Muslim salvo. The Knights of Calatrava followed Uncle Ramón to the chapel, where Don Lorgne was waiting.

In addition to Baron Bernières and Colonel Delacorte, eleven members of the Calatrava were killed on the tower – eleven of my brothers. A devastating loss. Five of the dead had volunteered for the mission against the catapult. Uncle Ramón chose replacements from amongst the other knights.

We gathered in the nave of the church. Don Lorgne assigned two men to carry jugs of oil, two others to carry torches. If any of these men were killed before reaching the target, Don Lorgne said, the closest knight would be responsible for completing the duty of the fallen man.

'Ramón and I will lead you out of the postern,' Don Lorgne continued. 'Swords drawn, we will reach the infidels' position quickly. We will take no quarter and no prisoners.'

Don Lorgne bowed his head before continuing. 'Lord,' he said, 'give us the strength and courage to perform this mission. If we should not return to the castle, please let us join our brothers in paradise this very day.'

'Amen,' Ramón said.

Don Fernando and his lieutenants met us as we left the chapel. They would be responsible for raising and lowering the postern. They would also use crossbows to provide cover for the raiding party. We followed Don Lorgne down a staircase, then through a passageway to the postern. The stone door was massive – perhaps three hundred pounds. Using a rope pulley attached to a crank, one man could lift the door and close it. Don Fernando's first lieutenant, Pablo, took the handle of the crank.

We stood just outside the gate. My comrades were mumbling private prayers. The seams of his brow furrowed, Ramón was looking at his men uneasily, as if concerned he had forgotten to convey a vital piece of information. Don Lorgne was studying his blade intently.

The door creaked open slowly. I thought that after the trials at Toron, I would be immune to the fears before combat. I was wrong. My chest drained. I swallowed, thirsty for a breath, but inhaled an unwholesome, hollow air.

Don Lorgne was the first through the passageway, followed by Uncle Ramón. When I passed through the gate, I could see the catapult about forty steps away. A stone canopy held up at all four corners by wooden logs protected the machine and its engineers from our archers. There was a gap toward the back of the stone platform – the hole through which projectiles would be fired.

Don Lorgne and Uncle Ramón were running unmolested. We had caught the Muslims off-guard. Perhaps it was the boldness of the plan, or the stupidity. Sprinting across the no-man's-land, I had to leap over the rotting corpse of a soldier. Whether he was Muslim or Christian, I did not see. I could only smell the vile stench. My legs supported me faithfully, and I crossed the distance to the catapult in seconds.

Under the canopy were perhaps twenty Muslim soldiers. Half were sitting on the ground working on the catapult. Don Lorgne and Ramón were upon them instantly. The infidels had time neither to stand nor to defend themselves. As he wielded his sword, Don Lorgne let out a shrill cry, an infernal harmony that awakened within me an uncharted fury. Rage against the infidels. Rage against the whole peoples of Arabia.

On the other side of the canopy, one of the Muslims was standing. He held a jar to his mouth. His lips still glistened with nectar as I brought my sword down upon him. He crumpled. I stood over his writhing body. He was whimpering, muttering alien words, asking for mercy. I lifted my sword and smashed his skull.

Several Muslims tried to escape our onslaught by fleeing the shelter of the canopy. Don Fernando's lieutenants standing at the postern gate with their crossbows made quick work of them.

'Pedro and Miguel,' Ramón yelled, 'douse the catapult.'

Before my comrades had emptied the jars of oil, Ramón dropped a torch on the catapult. We stared into the fire, mesmerized by the flames. I wiped my forearm against my face; warm blood spread across my lips.

Don Lorgne broke the spell.

'Nine of you will break for the gate,' he said, pointing to my comrades. 'Sprint to the postern. Do not look back. The rest of us will follow behind you.'

It was all according to plan – a perfectly executed mission. My brethren set out for the castle with long, confident strides.

A moment later, they were dead, cut to pieces. Little pieces. Our brothers lay sprawled in the no-man's-land not halfway to the postern. We had taken the Muslims by surprise with our initial assault. They had responded in kind, ambushing our retreat.

'Christ have mercy,' Uncle Ramón said, looking at the bodies of his men, 'Jesus Christ.'

Uncle Ramón, Don Lorgne, Andrés, and I – we were the only knights on the mission who remained alive. As we contemplated our changed circumstances and listened to the crackle of flames consuming the catapult, we heard a thud on top of the canopy. Then another thud. The infidels were sending soldiers down onto the platform to finish us off. We could hear them just above us, whispering, crawling, planning our demise.

The Muslims concentrated the barrage from their catapults and archers against the castle battlements and the open postern gate. The intensity of the bombardment forced our archers to take shelter and provided cover for the Muslim soldiers who would carry out the assault on our position. We were alone.

'Gentlemen, our guests on the roof will drop in on us any second now.' Don Lorgne spoke calmly, as if he were telling another tale of some brave knight who died long ago. 'Fortunately, because of the small size of the opening, they can only enter two or three at a time. They will send a team at first – probably nine or ten men – to probe our position. Then, if we are still alive, they will wait, give us a chance to surrender, before sending another, larger assault.

'To live, we must take some of the infidels alive. Alive.' Don Lorgne repeated the word, paused, and then spit into the fire, as if the concept were anathema. 'We will use them as shields when we cross the pathway back to the castle. Not the first batch – too difficult to guard prisoners and fend off an attack at the same time.'

We spaced ourselves strategically under the canopy's opening and waited. The catapult was quickly reduced to a few smoldering pieces of timber. The barrage against the Krak continued unabated. The Muslims remained on the roof of the shelter just above us. Perhaps they thought if they waited long enough we would try to make a run for the castle. One look at our dead comrades erased any temptation we may have had along those lines.

Three soldiers finally jumped through the gap.

Two of the men were wounded before they hit the ground. Don Lorgne's sword swept through the air, slicing the face of one, cutting into the neck of another. Andrés inflicted the final blows with his blade. The third soldier lost his footing when he landed. Ramón thrust a dagger into his chest.

Three more came immediately. As they stumbled on their dead comrades, I plunged my sword into the stomach of one. Still gritting a dagger in his teeth, he held the hilt of my blade with both hands. Ramón and Don Lorgne dispatched the other two.

'Alive,' Don Lorgne said. 'Take the next group alive.'

We stood back as the three Muslims fell to the ground. They were, true to Don Lorgne's prediction, the last soldiers in the assault party. As they struggled to their feet, we held ourselves back – reluctantly obeying Don Lorgne's instructions. Neither side attacked the other. The three intruders shuffled side to side, waving their daggers in front of them.

Don Lorgne, Ramón, Andrés, and I did not stir. The vague foreboding I felt at the postern had evaporated in the course of battle. We looked at the infidels as if they were harmless rabbits that we would slaughter as soon as Don Lorgne gave the word. The Muslims glanced at the hideous poses of their dead comrades, then back at us. A pretty sight we must have made. We could almost see our bestial reflection in their eyes, in their dread.

Don Lorgne started speaking to them in their native tongue – Arabic. I did not expect to hear that foreign language from the lips of the castellan of the Krak. The infidels seemed unsurprised, though, as if they expected that the demons before them could communicate in any tongue, ancient or living.

I did not, of course, understand the words that Don Lorgne spoke or the negotiations that ensued. But I understood the gist of the exchange. Don Lorgne offered to spare their lives if they dropped their weapons. They refused at first. Adamantly.

Don Lorgne seemed unconcerned by their emphatic tones. He spoke with them perhaps a minute. The syllables of that strange language entwined off his tongue, the sentences strung together as if he had uttered but one soothing word, whose logic could not be refuted.

The Muslims' refusal became more tentative. They began to argue amongst each other. Don Lorgne stood by patiently, knowingly, as they debated his proposition.

When the three men tossed their daggers on the ground before Don Lorgne, he spoke again to them. I imagine he was reiterating the promise he had made, congratulating them on the foresight of their decision.

Don Lorgne had not lied to these men. Not exactly. They would not die by our hands. That much he had promised them, and we would keep his word. They were dead nonetheless. As soon as they fell through the opening in the canopy, they were dead. Ramón once said that a drowning person would cling to any branch, no matter how flimsy, that floats before him. What Don Lorgne offered our captives was a brief respite before the inevitable.

Don Lorgne spoke again to them. The three Muslims protested meekly, but they had already made their deal. They obeyed his instructions, pulling their robes over their heads. They threw the garments at our feet. One of the men wore a vest of chain mail. The other two were unarmored. Bare shoulders hunched forward, lean brown arms crossed against chests to hide their nakedness.

'Ramón,' Don Lorgne said, 'you and your men put on the infidel robes.'

We picked up the Muslim garments and pulled them over our white surcoats. Andrés had to rip the sleeves to make room for his muscled shoulders.

'And you, Don Lorgne,' Ramón said, 'what about you?'

'I am the castellan of the Krak,' Don Lorgne said. 'I cannot wear a Muslim robe in my own castle.'

Don Lorgne took a step toward the Muslims. They lurched backward, holding up their hands submissively. Don Lorgne laughed softly as if he were chiding wayward children. He crossed the barrier between the two parties without breaking stride. When he stood before them, he spoke again in Arabic. The three men hesitated, then turned away from us to face the other side of the canopy.

'Ramón,' Don Lorgne said, 'pick one of your deputies and walk to me.'

Ramón looked to Andrés. Together, they moved next to Don Lorgne, who positioned each of them behind one of the Muslims.

'Take out your daggers slowly,' Don Lorgne said. 'When I put my own to the neck of the man in front of me, do the exact same. Do not draw blood. We need these men alive.'

Don Lorgne whispered in the ear of the Muslims as he pulled out his weapon. In an instant, our three prisoners felt the sharp edge of daggers against their throats. There was a brief struggle. Don Lorgne whispered again in that unfathomed tongue until the Muslims stood still.

'Knight,' Don Lorgne addressed me, 'bring four shields from the dead infidels.'

I gathered the shields quickly, prying them loose from the stiff fingers of the dead. I brought them to Don Lorgne.

'We will walk to the Krak,' Don Lorgne said, 'in a tight circle. Each of us will take an infidel shield. That should thoroughly confuse Baibars' soldiers.

'I expect the trick will not take us all the way to the Krak. But it will confound the Muslims at first and carry us safely at least partway to the postern. When they start shooting, use our friends here and the Muslim shields to deflect the arrows. When we are close to the gates, we will make a dash for safety.'

Don Lorgne, Ramón, and Andrés pulled their

prisoners toward one another in a circle. On Don Lorgne's order, I stepped into the middle of the group, holding the infidel shield above my head. Don Lorgne spoke again in Arabic, and the Muslims locked arms, closing the circle.

In that awkward position, we stepped from the shelter of the canopy and began the uncertain walk toward the postern. It seemed as if a million eyes were upon us. Every step, we walked over the bodies of our dead brethren.

Don Lorgne again whispered to the Muslims. They began to speak out loud, and then, as Don Lorgne tightened the pressure from his blade, to shout in their foreign tongue.

I looked past the side of my shield at the Muslim ramparts. The infidels aimed their weapons at the circle but did not shoot. Even the Muslim catapults stopped firing in the confusion. Baibars' soldiers on the outer wall began shouting down questions, trying to discern the components, the purpose, the meaning of this strange cabal crawling beneath their position.

My Christian comrades were just as confused. With the hiatus in the Muslim barrage, they had returned to the battlements. They joined the chorus above us, screaming execrations at the Muslims across the way and at our cryptic ring moving slowly toward the castle.

Our circle shifted so that for a second I could not distinguish between the two armies. We were in range of both walls, vulnerable in every direction.

Faces snarling, teeth gnashing. Blue eyes, black eyes – the same loathing.

We were two-thirds of the way to the castle when an arrow from the Muslim ramparts was fired into our circle. It found the neck of the man held by Don Lorgne. The prisoner fell forward. Don Lorgne quickly pulled the body up and held it before him.

The shot signaled both sides that the reprieve had ended. The Muslims had no intention of allowing any of their enemies to reach the Krak, even if they had to kill their own men in the process. When it became clear that the infidels had turned against our circle, the Christians on the ramparts became our defenders. The break in artillery had enabled our knights to position themselves to shoot at the Muslims on the opposite wall. The Christians let loose a flurry of arrows that drew the attention of most of the infidels away from our circle. I looked up and could see the arrows colliding, flying back and forth between armies, darkening the sky.

Most of the arrows aimed at our position landed in the dirt. Enough found our circle, though, so that the three prisoners were soon dead. The arrows ripped and slashed through the hard flesh of the infidels. Don Lorgne, Uncle Ramón, and Andrés held up the lifeless bodies, which lurched and twisted with the impact of each arrow like shredded marionettes.

We were almost at the postern when Don Lorgne

tripped. There was an instant, a tanquil moment, when both sides ceased firing. They peered down at the fallen man who had come free from the circle. Don Lorgne pushed the dead body of his prisoner to the side. He did not try to recover. It would have been useless anyway. He looked up at his men on the ramparts. He spread his shirt with his hands so that the white Cross on his chest was visible to both armies. The necklace of ears tangled in front of his surcoat.

'Christ is King,' he yelled.

I do not know if his men heard Don Lorgne's final words. The Muslims had already unleashed a torrent of arrows that cloaked Don Lorgne's body in a jagged shroud.

Ramón must have recognized the opportunity, the distraction, afforded by Don Lorgne's misfortune. He told us to make a run for the postern. Ramón and Andrés dropped their dead prisoners. We sprinted toward the gate.

I ran, holding my breath, bracing for the cut of an arrow. *Christ is King, Christ is King* – those were the words I repeated each step toward the postern, as if Don Lorgne, with his sacrifice, had revealed the magic mantra that would hold the miracle of my survival. Don Fernando's lieutenants stood at the gate gawking, stunned at the sight of three comrades in Muslim robes bearing down on their position.

I was under the postern when I felt a sharp pain in my back. An arrow had pierced my shoulder. I fell forward into the arms of one of Don Fernando's men. Andrés entered the Krak right after me.

I looked behind for Ramón. He had been hit in the calf and the arm, but he was near the threshold. So near I could see the tremor in his lips when the stone gate slid shut.

Andrés leapt forward and tried to lift the massive postern. He groaned, he pleaded, he cursed the Lord. The door did not budge. He took out his sword and swung it against the stone. The collision broke the blade, which burst like a thunderclap.

By then, it was too late. I could hear on the other side of the gate the last whispered breaths of Uncle Ramón.

I gazed up at Don Fernando, his sword unsheathed, standing over the gate's pulley. The cable had been cut and was swinging back and forth.

'He was dead already,' Don Fernando said.

Andrés turned around slowly.

'Francisco,' Don Fernando said, 'tell Andrés that Ramón was dead. Tell him.'

His words sounded hollow, like a pebble dropped into a pool of water.

'Andrés,' Don Fernando said, 'I will reward your brave service here. Perhaps a new castle in Aragón or a position on the King's Council.'

Andrés' head was tilted down. His fists clenched. The veins in his forearms throbbing.

'Emotions run high after battle,' Don Fernando

said. 'You need time, Andrés, to collect your thoughts.'

Don Fernando began to back away. He glanced at his deputies, then motioned to Andrés. But they looked blankly at their master.

After a few steps, Don Fernando bolted toward the staircase. Andrés caught him not halfway up the stairs. He tackled Don Fernando, who reached for the dagger strapped to his shin. He thrust it at Andrés. As the blade scraped against his chain mail, Andrés grabbed the Don's wrist. He banged it against the stone until the dagger came free. Then Andrés brought his hands down around the Don's neck and began choking him.

When I saw Don Fernando's aides rushing to save their master, I tried to raise myself from the ground. I fell back down, though. The pain in my shoulder burning, as if the arrow had penetrated anew. One of Don Fernando's lieutenants used his shield to slam Andrés on the back of his head. Andrés fell forward. Don Fernando's other lieutenants dragged Andrés body off their master and down the stairs. They kicked him viciously. I lay on the ground, helpless, watching the beating of my friend. After several minutes, the Don's men realized that Andrés was in a realm beyond suffering. They left him facedown in the dust.

Don Fernando was sitting up, coughing furiously, holding his throat. His lieutenants reached out to him solicitously. He slapped their outstretched hands away and raised himself.

'Dump him in the hospital,' Don Fernando said, gesturing to Andrés. 'His friend too. And take their weapons. All of them.'

I do not remember the subsequent hours. As Don Fernando's lieutenants took turns carrying and cursing me, I passed out.

When I woke, I felt a sharp pain in my shoulder. I reached for the arrow. It had disappeared. A taut dressing had been placed on the wound, the blood staining the cloth. Night had fallen. I was in a corner of the Knights' Hall – the hospital. It was more a morgue, judging by the dead men around me. The torchlight illuminated their bodies. It froze them in their moments of death and cast blinking shadows against the wall.

Andrés was sitting in those shadows. The light flickering across his face. One eye swollen shut.

'Is Uncle Ramón dead?' I meant to make an observation rather than an inquiry. The words, disbelieving their speaker, queried of their own accord. Andrés did not respond.

'What happened to the arrow?' I asked.

Andrés looked down at me with his one open eye. 'The Hospitaller doctor removed it. We were lucky. The blade missed the bone. We cleaned the wound and wrapped it in a strip of cloth from the Muslim garments.'

A stillness permeated the hall and enabled me to hear Andrés clearly. The Muslim shelling had ceased.

'What happened, Andrés? Has the battle ended?'

'Don Fernando has taken command,' Andrés said. 'When he cut the rope of the postern, he killed his only remaining rival – Uncle Ramón. This afternoon, he led an entourage out of the castle to negotiate with Baibars. The cease-fire began just before his departure.'

I fell back to sleep. When I woke at dawn, the rigid corpses had been stacked against the wall. The living had gathered in small circles, trying to glean the latest rumors of what transpired during the negotiations. One of the knights said that Don Fernando and his lieutenants had returned to the fort just before sunrise, but had not revealed the outcome of their diplomacy. He speculated that the reticence of the Don's party could only be a bad sign. Another knight was more hopeful and pointed out that the continuing absence of Muslim artillery must mean that Don Fernando had reached an agreement with Baibars.

When Don Fernando appeared outside the chapel, a hush fell over the other knights. Surrounded by his lieutenants, he walked into the Knights' Hall and stood on one of the benches.

'Brothers,' he said, 'we mourn the loss of Baron Bernières, Don Lorgne, Ramón of the Calatrava, and the other brave knights who have died defending the castle in the last month. No more Christian blood will be spilled on this ground. I have a letter in my hand from the Grand Master of the Hospital, Hugh Revel.' Don Fernando held up a parchment. 'We received it yesterday afternoon following the heroic sortie against the Muslim catapult. In the letter, the Grand Master instructs Don Lorgne to negotiate the surrender of the castle in exchange for safe passage for the castle's inhabitants. With the death of Don Lorgne, I have become the commander of the castle. As a dutiful servant, I have carried out the Grand Master's instructions.

'Glory be to God,' Don Fernando continued, 'the sortie led by the martyrs convinced Baibars that the defenders of the Krak would never agree to an unconditional surrender. That Baibars would have to sit across the table from us as an equal. This morning, after hours of difficult negotiations, we were able to reach a settlement. The infidel king shouted. He screamed hellfire. But we did not back down. As soldiers of Christ, we looked Baibars in the eye. When he knew that he could not intimidate us, he changed his tone. My friends, we were able to exact significant concessions. The armies of Christ will have safe conduct to Tripoli. Baibars has agreed to supply horses for the wounded and our officers, and we will be able to keep possession of the sacred Christian relics that remain in the chapel.

'I know the frustration, nay, the humiliation that some may feel – abandoning this great outpost of Christendom to the infidels. But remember the words of the Lord: *I have set before you life and death, blessing and cursing: therefore choose life, that both thou and thy seed may live.*

'Your Grand Master instructs us to live, to

continue to serve God and battle for Jesus Christ. In many ways, dying as martyrs here would be the easiest alternative – the most selfish. The Lord demands more of you.'

I suppose we all suspected Don Fernando was lying. No one had seen the scout from the Grand Master. And the timing of his arrival was too convenient. We all chose to accept Don Fernando's report, though. It was a conspiracy of exhaustion and hope, which coalesced around the eloquence of Don Fernando.

I do not condemn Don Fernando for manufacturing a missive from the Grand Master of the Hospital – not for that. Perhaps we could have held out another couple of days. But the fall of the Krak was inevitable. Without a negotiated surrender, the Muslims would probably have massacred the surviving knights. The infidels despised the Hospitallers above all the other knights in the Levant – mostly because of their impressive record of military victories against the Muslims. Don Fernando had greater ambitions than to die in the dust of the Krak des Chevaliers.

To the extent it could be said that a man such as Don Fernando has a finest moment, his speech was that. We all wanted to live, even the most pious of the Hospitaller knights. Don Fernando provided the rationale to enable them to put to rest any guilt or misgivings they might have felt about abandoning their sanctuary. It would be, according to the Don, an honorable surrender.

Just two hours later, the Christian survivors of the siege were marching through the courtyard toward the gates of the castle. The first Hospitaller knights held aloft the standard of their Order – a white Cross stitched on a black banner.

The mounted wounded followed the Hospitaller knights. I was among this group, resting on a lame mare courtesy of Baibars, whose soldiers were already entering the castle. Andrés had refused the offer of a horse. He was holding the reins of mine. We had just started to move out when four of Don Fernando's lieutenants approached.

'Francisco and Andrés,' Pablo said, 'your commander, Don Fernando, wants a word with you in the chapel.'

'Tell Don Fernando,' Andrés said, 'we are presently engaged.'

The four men moved to block our path. Andrés tried to lead my horse through their tight phalanx. He pushed one of the lieutenants, who stumbled backward, then reached for his sword.

'Andrés,' I said, 'perhaps we should visit Don Fernando before departing the castle.'

'A wise choice, Francisco,' Pablo said.

Don Fernando's lieutenants escorted us back to the chapel. Andrés helped me dismount, and we walked into the building. Pablo followed us and stood next to his master. Don Fernando was sitting on a bench. His hands clasped in prayer, he gazed intently at the Cross.

'You may wonder,' Don Fernando said, 'what a man like me prays for.'

Andrés and I did not venture a guess.

'Victory,' he said. 'He prays for victory and the defeat of his enemies, the enemies of Christ.'

'It seems,' Andrés said, 'that Christ has not heard your prayers.'

'On the contrary. Ramón is dead, and here you are, Francisco and Andrés.'

'Are we your enemies, Don Fernando?' I asked.

'I will tell you a story, Francisco,' the Don said. 'It is a personal anecdote, but it is relevant to your situation.

'Just like you, Francisco, I once had a brother. Miró Sánchez. We were identical twins.

'Lucinda, one of the royal nursemaids, cared for us in the palace in Barcelona. She shared our bed, suckled us when we were infants, sang to us during thunderstorms. I slept on her right, my brother on her left, pressed against the soft folds of her dark skin.

'Every evening, Lucinda would leave two cups of milk on our night table, the sour cream squeezed from her own breast.

'We had just celebrated our tenth birthday. It was early spring. The cold of winter was lifting. We could see the tiny green buds on the trees outside our window. The yellow flowers sprouted through the crevices of the castle stones.

'My brother drank both cups of milk that night.

I went to sleep thirsty and angry, swearing at my brother.

'I woke in the dark. Miró was groaning. Lucinda was gone. I thought his pain was my fault – that I had placed a curse on him. I ran barefoot through the halls on the cold stone looking for Lucinda. She had disappeared.

'When I returned to my brother, he was trembling and coughing blood. I sang songs to take his mind off the pain. I told him that his sickness would pass.

'When the morning light came through the window, I was holding Miró's hand. His pale body wrought stiff. Steam rising from his blue lips.

'It took several years to find Lucinda. One of my half brothers, Nunyo Rodríguez, had paid her handsomely to murder the two of us. Nunyo was anxious to eliminate competitors to the throne. Despite her failure to complete the job, Lucinda found refuge at Nunyo's estate in Palau. She became nursemaid to his children.

'When I was fifteen years old, I sneaked into my half brother's abode disguised as a pilgrim. I played the part well. Smelling most foul after two weeks on the road, I wore a tattered brown smock.

'I found Lucinda in one of the upstairs rooms. She was humming a forgotten melody, watching a sleeping infant, one of my cousins. I envied his innocence. He accepted her tender care unknowing.

'She looked up as I approached. She smiled at

382

me. She could not help herself. You see, she still loved me. Then she glanced away, pensive. I could see her thinking, perhaps reliving that night five years previous. Her recognition. Then the terror. Her little boy had become a man.

'I gagged her, then cut her hands off. Lucinda watched me as she bled to death. She held out one of her stumps as if she would hold my hand. The baby woke. His crying concealed Lucinda's muffled screams. After she had passed, her hands still labored under the weight of her crime. The same fingers that had poured the poison twitching on the gray stone.

'I waited in the chapel for my half brother. I had heard he was quite devout. I was kneeling in the pews when he arrived in the afternoon. He was alone. That was more than I had expected. I thanked God for delivering him to me.

'"I suspect that for a coin or two, you could sing a spry tune, stranger," he said. "Are you a traveling minstrel?"

'"No, sir," I said.

'"Please accept my apology," he said. "Then you are a pilgrim traveling to the tomb of Saint James in Compostela?"

'"No, sir," I said.

'"Then you are a mystery, stranger. Please tell me, what is your business in these parts?"

'"I have come to mend the past."

'"You will find," he said, "that the past is better left to the Lord." He laughed freely, untroubled.

383

Then he put his hand on my back. "You need a priest, friend. I will call for one at your command."

'He smiled at me. A curious smile. Under different circumstances, we might have been allies.

'"You look at me with a peculiar familiarity," he said. "Do I know you, stranger?"

'"I am Fernando Sánchez, your brother," I said.

'His smile disappeared. He opened his mouth to speak, then thought better of it.

'I stabbed him in the chest. I stabbed again and again until there was no clean mark for my blade.'

Don Fernando waved his empty fist, as if he were reenacting the deed.

'It's a charming story, Don Fernando,' Andrés said. 'I do not mean to sound disinterested, but Francisco and I must get going.'

Don Fernando glanced up soberly.

'Francisco, you and Andrés will be going soon enough,' he said, 'but not where you think. I know the loyalty both of you feel for Uncle Ramón. If I let you live – either of you – you would do no less for Ramón than I did for my brother. I would be disappointed if you weren't already plotting my destruction.

'But it will never come. Not by your hands. I am not Lucinda, and I will not make her mistake. Baibars wanted some souvenirs to bring back to Aleppo to show his people that the mighty Krak des Chevaliers has fallen. I took the liberty of volunteering your services. You are, are you not, under my command since the tragic death of Ramón?'

'Yes, master,' Pablo interjected, 'the entire garrison is under your command.'

'Shut up, Pablo,' Don Fernando said.

'You must see it,' he continued, 'from my point of view. I waited five years to kill Lucinda. If I let you live, I would always be waiting for you.'

As Don Fernando spoke, Muslim soldiers had already moved into the chapel. Don Fernando pointed to Andrés and me. The Muslims surrounded the two of us.

'Goodbye, gentlemen,' Don Fernando said. 'I would say good luck, but luck will not suffice where you are going. I will report your courage in the face of death to your families. That should provide them some solace.'

'One day,' Andrés said, 'I will settle with you, Don Fernando.'

'Until that day,' Don Fernando said, 'enjoy the Sultan's hospitality.'

Don Fernando and his men walked past us as they exited the chapel. At the doors, Don Fernando turned to face us.

'While my lieutenants are fiercely loyal,' Don Fernando said, 'they are idiots. I would have liked a deputy with your savvy and fortune, Francisco. And your courage, Andrés. It is a pity.'

CHAPTER 12

THE CITADEL

The bells rang for sext. We had been in the cell for four hours. Francisco stood haggard in the afternoon shadows. His eyes focused inward, he seemed oblivious to our presence. Isabel was sitting next to me. Her body still, her mouth slightly ajar as if she would pose a question.

'It is a pity,' Francisco said, repeating Don Fernando's last words. His tone steady, as if he meant to recount an incident without apportioning blame.

'Andrés died at the Krak des Chevaliers,' Isabel said.

Francisco seemed not to hear her.

'Francisco,' Isabel said.

Francisco glanced away, toward the window. Isabel stood and walked in front of him. She grasped his free arm under the elbow.

'My brother died at the Krak des Chevaliers.'

Francisco pressed his palms hard against his eyes, as if he would blot out the image of those events.

'Don Fernando sent a letter to my father recounting Andrés' bravery during the siege. He died defending the castle.' Her voice trailed off until it was barely audible. It was not clear whether the girl was making a statement or asking a question.

'No, Isabel,' Francisco said.

Perhaps my esteemed reader thinks Francisco's response fostered hope in Isabel that her brother might still be alive. It was not so. A foreboding silence lingered in the wake of those two words. An intimation of horror.

'Isabel, it is best that we leave now. It will soon be supper.'

Her gray eyes fixed on Francisco, Isabel ignored my words. I offered my hand to lead her from the cell. She did not take it. There was nothing I could do. It was her choice. She would hear the truth wherever it might lead. She would know the circumstances of her brother's death.

Indeed, I think Francisco's cruel demeanor toward Isabel had been calculated to avoid just this moment – to drive the girl from Santes Creus. Perhaps he had wanted to spare her the painful details, or maybe spare himself the telling.

We brought up the rear of Baibars' army, traveling north to Aleppo. A company of armed guards surrounded the wagon that carried Andrés and me, chained together by the wrist. They fed us at night, after the day's march. Andrés split our provisions – one loaf of bread, a bowl of chickpeas, and a cup of water. Every other day, he would save some water to clean my wound. Then he would dress the cut with a new strip of cloth torn from one of our tunics.

On the third day, an infidel city appeared in the early light. A Muslim church – blue marble – with a slender tower, like a reed sprouting from a swamp. A bearded old man made his way slowly up the winding tower steps. When he reached the summit, he began to sing, a whining melody. The soldiers halted our caravan, then knelt down with two open hands spread before them.

'I guess no one ever told them about bells,' Andrés said.

Other men on other towers joined the chorus of lamentation, announcing the new day.

Andrés stood up in the wagon, glancing thoughtfully. His chains rattled.

'They probably wouldn't listen anyway,' he said.

Only once did one of our captors speak to us. I woke in the night, my shoulder throbbing. The cold wind cut through the wool robe Andrés and I shared as a blanket. Flies buzzed thinly over the blood oozing through the cloth. I heard whispering behind me. I turned my head toward the end of the wagon. One of our guards was speaking softly, urgently. He looked left and right. Then he reached into his cassock and pulled out an apple. He extended his arm, holding the offering in his closed fist. I could see between his fingers the red glittering. I hesitated, suspicious. What if he had poisoned the apple, coated it in some Arabian venom? Well, I thought, then nothing. Nothing at all. We were dead men anyway.

The guard pretended to bite the apple as if to show its purpose. Whispering strange words, he reached his arm forward again. Andrés had woken and was watching our benefactor warily. I held out my hand. The guard dropped the apple in my palm, then walked away. Andrés and I passed the apple back and forth furtively. When the caravan moved out, I was rolling the sweet pulp against my tongue.

Soldiers pulled us off the wagon at the gates of Aleppo. We walked between a mounted guard, parading through the streets. The Arabs ran from their homes, from the bazaar, from mosques. They cheered their soldiers, dropping pink flower petals in our path.

Andrés and I walked with our heads down, looking at the dirt, trying to avoid the sneers, the stones thrown by the crowd. I went down when a rock hit me in the head. The warm blood flowed evenly across my face and neck. When I opened my eyes, I was looking at the civilians gathered on the side of the route. The young and the old. They were laughing, shouting, spitting.

I saw Sergio standing next to an old woman. He looked young – a soldier – wearing the same armor as the day he left the port at Barcelona. He was staring at me. I spoke his name. He tilted his head forward. *Who are you?* It's me, Sergio, I said, your brother. The guards pulled me up. Walking forward again, I surveyed the spectators, searching for my brother. I shouted his name. The ignorant crowd laughed louder each time I called to my brother.

'Sergio is not here,' Andrés said, beside me.

Then I saw him again. He was leaning out of a second-story window. His hair grown gray. Deep creases running down the side of his face. His armor rusted. Sergio shook his head rueful. *Did you think to find salvation here?* A rock hit me in the chest. I stumbled, coughing fiercely. I managed to remain standing barely. I took the Cross for you, Sergio, I said, your salvation. He could not hear me over the jeers, the tumult of the procession. Sergio gazed down. *Look at you now.* He smiled, a pitying smile. *This is your salvation, brother.* The bone in my chest smarted. My eyes burned wet.

'Francisco,' Andrés said, 'remember when I visited you in Montcada. Racing those horses. What was the name of your mare? Pancho?'

Yes, I said.

'I wonder what the old girl is doing now,' he said. 'Probably eating grass in some pasture.'

I suppose.

'A green meadow.'

I looked up at the open window. It was deserted, a sheer curtain stirring in the wind.

We marched into the evening. I saw the same

faces in the crowd. The young and the old. They pointed toward the Citadel, glancing knowingly. All day we could see that fortress, a huge slab of stone suspended above the city. It waited patiently for Andrés and me.

The street finally spilled out before the massive fortress. The people, unsated, tried to follow the procession over the drawbridge. They broke through the ranks of soldiers. The guards became our protectors. They beat back the throng. But the crack of bones only excited the crowd, which surged toward the bridge. In the clash, some of the Arabs tumbled into the moat. The fallen splashed into the murky water, trying frantically to stay afloat. The struggles diverted the multitude as we passed over the bridge into the Citadel.

As we watched the fortress doors close, palace guards were already moving toward us. They seized us roughly, forcing us through a dark corridor. The shouts of the crowd faded. They marched us around corners, up stairs, down stairs, past other chambers, into the open air, a dirt courtyard.

A group of soldiers were leaning on their spears, conversing in the courtyard. They drew to attention as we approached. The soldiers parted as one man in their number stepped forward.

He examined Andrés and me. When he completed his second turn around us, he let loose a torrent of harsh, alien words. He was gesturing with both fists, baring yellow teeth, hissing spittle across my cheeks.

When his tirade finally ended, he was breathing heavily. One eyebrow raised indignant, he looked impatiently at the two of us, as if he were owed an apology. An awkward standoff. Two parties, two different views of the circumstances that brought us together.

'Greetings to you too,' said Andrés, pinioned by two guards. 'It's nice to finally see some hospitality in these parts. If it were just the same with you, my friend Francisco and I would like to take a bath before supper. A man feels grimy after such a long journey.'

Stroking his rough beard, their leader pondered Andrés' response. His eyes darted between Andrés and me. His smile twisted uncertainly. He didn't understand one word Andrés had uttered. The other soldiers poised keenly, waiting for the verdict of their superior.

It came swiftly. He pulled a wooden club strapped to his belt and struck Andrés in the stomach. His comrades took their cue from their commander. Kicks, slaps, jabs came from every direction. I tried to protect my head with my forearms, only to shift them down to my sides when the blows struck at my ribs.

A full punch hit me in the face so that I could feel the indent of each knuckle across my brow. I dropped to the ground. As I lay there, I looked over and could not see Andrés. He had disappeared. The soldiers who had surrounded him were dispersing in different directions, wiping

392

Andrés' blood from their fists, straightening their tunics.

Two soldiers hooked their arms under my shoulders and dragged me across the courtyard. We were headed toward the place where Andrés had vanished – a gate that opened to the underground. It resembled the hatch on a ship leading to the lower decks.

Then I was flying, plunging fast. The light, the voices became more distant, fading. I landed on my side. Every limb ached, so that I could not locate the source of pain. Andrés' voice cut through the dead air.

'Remind me, Francisco, never to visit Aleppo again.'

My head was resting on a patch of mud. The slime made a soft bed. Weariness took hold. I closed my eyes.

I was wakened by a hand rubbing my head. More hands on my body were gently pulling my robe over my head. Someone was trying to take my boots off. When I sat up, the hands pulled back. Shadows slid away through the mud. I stood and peered straight ahead. I squinted, my eyes adjusting to the darkness slowly. Andrés was lying on his back a few feet away. Just beyond him, figures were slinking to and fro.

'My name is Francisco de Montcada,' I said. 'My friend is Andrés Correa de Girona. We are Knights in the Order of Calatrava and subjects of King Jaime of Aragón.'

My voice echoed through the chamber, coming back fractured, unrecognizable. My words, my name, tangled with a shrill laughter pealing child-like. Specters circled us like a pack of wolves – their eyes gleaming ominously.

Andrés had waked. He was standing next to me.

'So this is hell,' he said. 'I imagined it hotter.'

'The guards make it cooler when new prisoners arrive.' A stranger's voice, just a few feet away. He was speaking fluent Catalán.

'You would be the devil, then?' Andrés asked.

'Even the devil would not enter this abyss,' the stranger said.

Shrieks pierced the darkness. The other prisoners deplored the efforts at polite conversation.

'They don't seem fond of us,' Andrés said.

'They have no opinion on your merits,' the stranger said. 'They treat all new arrivals thus. They covet your possessions. Many wear rags or nothing. Their clothing disintegrates during captivity. They want a new shirt, perhaps a pair of boots. Unless you want to donate yours, follow me.'

Andrés went first, trying to keep sight of our acquaintance. I kept my hand on Andrés' shoulder. We slogged through the mud, passing a cluster of prisoners, grasping, whining. I was glancing sideways, trying to gauge the nature of our new dwelling – cave, dungeon, inferno. Our acquaintance stopped at a rock wall. I ran my hand over the craggy edges.

'Welcome, Knights of Calatrava.' I could make out only the outline of the speaker. He was sitting against the wall. 'My name is Salamago de Huesca. You have already met Manuel. We are Knights of the Order of the Temple. I am sorry for your present circumstances. We are pleased to have the company of two more knights from Aragón, though.' His voice was grainy, wheezing between breaths. Yet his words marched forward, the deep pitch resonating certainty. 'We left Aragón seven years ago – five years fighting the infidels, almost one year in this hole – three hundred and forty-eight days. Perhaps you have some news from home. Manuel misses Barcelona terribly. Tell us, are the women of Aragón still fair?'

'More beautiful than any in the world,' Andrés said.

'What color hair do they have?' he asked.

'Brown, black, red, blond,' I said, 'whatever color you can imagine.'

'Precisely,' Salamago said. He exhaled a long breath. Manuel grunted affirmatively. Both men lingering over my response, basking in whatever visions they could conjure.

'Where are we?' Andrés asked.

'The ancient palace of Aleppo,' Salamago said. 'To be exact, you stand in the kitchen. At least, Manuel thinks so. You see that stone before you. Manuel claims it's the remains of an oven. I think it's where the Emperor defecated. See the stains? What do you think?' He paused for a moment, cleared his throat, and spit. 'Well, in time, you will form an opinion. What was I saying, Manuel?'

'The old palace becoming a prison.'

'Yes,' Salamago said. 'The infidels discovered these ruins decades ago. They say one of the Sultan's sons was fucking a whore in the harem when the floor collapsed. The son was killed instantly. The whore survived. The son's body cushioned her fall. She viewed her survival as a miracle and immediately took a vow of chastity in gratitude to the infidel gods. Even they could not protect her from the Sultan's wrath, though. He blamed her for the son's death and executed her personally. Subsequently, the Sultan moved the harem to more solid ground and found a new prison in this cave. Such are the vagaries of life. A whore miraculously survives a great fall, only to be executed. The Sultan loses a son but gains an escape-proof prison to house his enemies.'

'Escape-proof?' Andrés asked. 'How do you know?'

Salamago laughed, short and mirthless.

'Many men much smarter than me – knights, murderers, monks pickpockets, pilgrims – have studied this question,' he said. 'Let me spare you the trouble. Perhaps you recall your descent into the prison. You passed through the only entrance or exit – more than thirty feet up – a small gap in the roof. If you could fly, you could soar out of this pit and fight your way past the infidel garrison of two thousand men. Or you could dig a tunnel for the next ten years. But you would only hit the moat and drown us all.'

'A pretty picture,' Andrés said.

'It could be worse,' Salamago said. 'The prison is not without its virtues. Unveil the mosaic, Manuel.'

Manuel bent down on his knees. He used his hands to wipe away the mud on the ground before us. Salamago pulled two sticks from the wall and planted them in the crevice of a large stone. Then he began to twirl the sticks between his palms. Quicker and quicker, until sparks flickered. One of the sticks flared. Salamago cupped the fragile fire as he brought it close to the floor.

'Behold,' Salamago said. 'Beauty even in this underworld.'

Flames danced against the pearly stone. A blue river shimmered across the floor between Andrés and me. Flowers bloomed red and blue. Delicate palm trees swayed under the weight of their fruit. The sun burst yellow, a bright reflection casting its warmth on my cheeks.

'A man sculpted each one of these tiny cubes.' Salamago was holding a square stone between his thumb and forefinger. He had a shaggy beard soiled black. His ribs protruded jagged from his chest. 'This one is ivory,' Salamago continued. 'Some of the stones contain gold, silver, rubies. The guards value the precious stones. We barter them for food.'

Salamago snuffed out the flame with his bare

fist. The flowers and trees disappeared; the sun extinguished.

'And the other prisoners,' Andrés said, 'do they leave you and your mosaic in peace? You are only two men.'

'We used to number seven,' Salamago said. 'Five of my men were ransomed several weeks ago. The Templars sent a representative to the Citadel. He paid twenty gold coins per head. Unfortunately, he had only one hundred coins in his possession. He will be back for Manuel and me. Perhaps your friends in the Calatrava will ransom you before we are freed.'

'We will not be ransomed,' I said.

'The Sultan runs a profitable business out of the prison,' Salamago said. 'He invites representatives from all the knightly orders to come to Aleppo and buy back their prisoners.'

'No one will come for us,' Andrés said.

'How can you be sure?' Salamago asked.

'Most of our comrades in the Calatrava are dead,' I said. 'They died during the siege of the Krak des Chevaliers.'

'The great castle has fallen?' Salamago asked. 'When?'

'Only weeks ago. Andrés and I were taken prisoner.'

'How come there are only two of you?'

'The defenders of the Krak received safe passage in exchange for the surrender of the castle,' I said.

'Safe passage to this dungeon?'

'Francisco and I were betrayed by Don Fernando, the son of King Jaime,' Andrés said. 'He was responsible for the death of the Grand Master of the Calatrava, Ramón. We witnessed his treachery. He delivered us to the infidels to keep secret his perfidy.'

'Surely,' Salamago said, 'one of your surviving comrades will report your disappearance. They will investigate your fates.'

'Don Fernando,' I said, 'will make sure they do not have the opportunity to pursue the matter.'

'Then the Templars will have to buy your freedom as well. Manuel and I will insist on your inclusion in any transaction.'

'Francisco and I would be indebted,' Andrés said.

'It is we who are indebted to you,' Salamago responded. 'We have grown quite bored of each other's company. Besides, your presence will deter the Teutonic knights from attacking. Since the departure of the other Templars, our German brothers have been watching, waiting for the opportunity to strike. You can see them peering over the rubble of the parlor wall.'

I looked in the direction that Salamago had gestured. I could see only a black haze.

Salamago shouted into the darkness. 'Hello, scalawags. Perhaps you have noticed the advent of the Knights of Calatrava – Francisco and Andrés – fresh from the front lines.'

'The eight Germans occupy one of the Sultan's

antechambers,' Manuel said. 'It has enough timber to supply the whole cave for several winters. A couple of Englishmen discovered the wooden floor while digging for gold. They tried to conceal their discovery, trading the wood sporadically. A German scout chanced upon the English pulling up one of the planks. The next day, the Germans left their shelter on the other side of the cave and attacked. We watched the battle from here. The English fled within minutes. The Germans trade sections of timber as firewood to every faction in the prison.'

'Like all rich men,' Salamago interrupted, 'they are never satisfied. They look for their next conquest. If the Germans come for the mosaic, we will fight them to the death.'

'Salamago,' Manuel said, 'no talk of death. We should show Andrés and Francisco the rest of the prison.'

'The grand tour,' Salamago said, 'to help our friends understand the state of affairs in the netherworld. You take them, Manuel. I will remain behind and defend the fort.'

Salamago handed stones to Andrés and me. 'Just in case,' he said,

We walked a wide path – three abreast with Manuel in the middle. Our footsteps made no sound in the soft clay. Our prison mates became visible in the darkness. A silent gallery on both sides of the walkway examined Andrés and me, assessing, reassessing the implications of this new alliance of knights. Salamago and Manuel must have foreseen the consequences of our march – putting to rest any ideas amongst the other prisoners concerning the vulnerability of the two Templars and their two newly arrived countrymen.

I played my part, walking vigilant, soldierly. I passed the solid stone between my hands, feeling the rough grain. From hand to hand and back again.

'The Turks on the left,' Manuel said.

Five men were sitting in a circle. They looked up when we passed as if we had interrupted some discussion or a game of dice. Five heads turned, following our course.

'They jail infidels here too?' Andrés asked.

'All manner of men,' Manuel said. 'Muslim, Christian, Jew. French, German, Turk, Mongol. Knight, monk, criminal. Each faction bands together. The larger groups occupy a room, establish a shelter. We battle over the meager resources that mean the difference between living and dying.'

A man stood in the center of the path. He was naked. His body, smeared with mud and excrement, exuded a foul smell. He was twirling a straggled beard, the other hand on his hip. He mumbled to himself in a strident tone.

'He's a Franciscan monk,' Manuel said, 'captured on a pilgrimage to Jerusalem. We offered him refuge when we were seven. He refused. He said that he must accept the full weight of the Lord's judgment. He will die soon.'

He ignored us when we walked around him. He was speaking Italian and seemed to be carrying on a heated debate. The three of us quickened our pace to leave behind the noisome stench.

On the right, we passed a hut. The old walls of a palace room were still intact on two sides. On the other two sides, rocks were stacked high, enclosing the space.

'Venetian sailors,' Manuel said, motioning to the structure. 'We think there are twelve of them – the largest faction in the prison. They built a small fortress in the middle of the prison. They stay in there all day, except to find food or to relieve themselves. They dug a latrine on the edge of the cave a few feet away from the entrance. Most civilized. They are probably waiting for Venetian merchants to deliver a ransom.'

As we proceeded on that path, I lost track of the different groups Manuel pointed out. Mongols, Jews, Arabs, the two English who had fled the German attack. They waved sticks, like primeval tribes, growling if we got too close.

I saw the outline of a man, advancing slowly. He wore only a cloth around his waist. He approached stealthily, holding a stick, a small spear. I raised the stone, trying to warn him off. He kept coming, though. When he sprinted toward us, I cocked my arm. Manuel held my hand back before I could hurl the stone. The man released the spear. It flew to the side, a short, screeching sound. He yanked back the spear with a string attached to his wrist.

A small rodent dangled on the end of the point. The tiny claws were still moving.

'Well done,' Manuel said. 'Francisco and Andrés, you could learn from watching his technique.'

'How did he get his weapon?' Andrés asked.

'We carve spears and knives with stones, sometimes our fingernails and teeth.'

'To hunt mice?' Andrés asked.

'Mice, rats, snakes, insects.'

'Are there many?' Andrés asked.

'Not enough.'

The path opened up on both sides. A wide, barren circle.

'Look up,' Manuel said.

Pearls of light stole down into the underworld.

'The gates to the inferno,' Manuel said. 'That's where the guards dropped you.'

The hatch was almost as high as the bell tower of the monastery at Santes Creus. I looked down and saw the imprint of my body in the clay that had cushioned my fall.

'All of us entered through the same passage,' Manuel said. 'As Salamago said, it is the only entrance or exit.

'Every other day, the guards drop food through the hole,' Manuel said. 'Their garbage – a stale crust of bread, a chicken bone, rotten fruit and vegetables. As soon as the light streams in, the prisoners scramble for position under the hole. Even the Venetians leave their compound. It can

403

be quite dangerous. To entertain themselves, the guards sometimes shoot arrows into the crowd. The prisoners scuffle over a crumb. Salamago and I remain on the side, let the others do the fighting, and then pounce on a stray morsel.'

'Can you see the sky through the hatch?' I asked.

'I have seen the sun and the moon,' Manuel said.

'Every other day the guards open the hatch?' Andrés asked.

'Yes. That's how we keep track of our time in captivity – three hundred and forty-eight days.'

We walked a few more paces before reaching the end of the path, the edge of the cave – about two hundred steps from the mosaic at the other end. I could hear the trickle of water, like the lilting murmur of a flute. I touched my hand to the rock wall. The water fell across my forearm. I cupped my hands together, the water collecting in my palms. I brought my hands to my face. The cold water stung my eyes, spilling across my cheeks, down the back of my neck.

'Salamago says,' Manuel said, 'that the stones are weeping the tears we can no longer shed.'

I tilted my head and let the water flow into my mouth. It soaked my lips like a burst of rain on a parched field.

'We share the water,' Manuel said. 'The underground spring sustains us. It flows all year long.'

When Andrés and I had sated ourselves, we

walked back through the same gauntlet. The other prisoners had lost interest in the new arrivals. They resumed their activities – scavenging for sticks, stones, a tiny scrap of food overlooked by the other prisoners.

Salamago was pulling up one of the mosaic stones when we returned.

'Pure gold,' he said. 'This one will fetch a loaf of bread.'

It did more than that. Andrés and I were sitting against the cave wall when the light came unforeseen into the night. We followed the Templars toward the other end of the cave, toward the open hatch. Looking up, I could see the blue sky, the sun's rays falling in a halo on the floor of the prison. Salamago positioned Andrés and me so that our group formed a circle just on the edge of that halo. When the guards dropped the contents of the buckets, we stood our ground and watched the battles rage. In the presence of food, the factions came undone. Each man at war with the other. Except for us. While maintaining the circle, Salamago and Manuel snatched the pieces of food that bounced near us. They shared the spoils with Andrés and me. It wasn't much, and it tasted like horse manure. But we ate it just the same, grateful for any substance to hush the hunger pangs.

When the prisoners had finished combing the soil for scraps of food, they dispersed. Most returned to their shelters. The others withdrew to the shadows but remained close to the light source. Salamago kept our group on the edge of light. Three prisoners formed a line, each man holding some offering. Salamago was second. The guards lowered a bucket by a thick rope. The first prisoner stepped into the center of the circle of light, directly under the hatch. He placed a stone in the bucket and watched it ascend. Crossing his hands, he muttered a prayer.

While the man stood supplicant, the guards passed the stone amongst themselves, like jewelers appraising its value. When they threw the stone back, the man bolted out of the circle just as one of the guards fired an arrow into the hole. The arrow's shaft stuck out of the soil as if it had been planted there long ago.

Salamago was next. He stepped forward and placed the stone cube in the lowered bucket. After raising the rope, the guards examined the stone. In between scrutinizing the stone, the guards peered down at Salamago pensively as if judging his worth. Should he live or die? Then they lowered the bucket again. Salamago reached in and took out half the carcass of a chicken. The savory smell attracted a crowd. Sighs rumbled through the cave. Manuel drew Andrés and me into the circle to protect Salamago from the more intrepid prisoners. Salamago had already pulled the arrow from the ground and was brandishing it threateningly. The crowd parted in deference to Salamago's martial display. Nonetheless, as we walked passed the throng, several prisoners tried to grab the prize. Salamago jabbed them with short, quick thrusts. The victims cried out, then retreated, whimpering, cursing in whatever language they could muster.

After seeing Salamago wield the arrow, the other prisoners scattered. We marched back to our shelter like a victorious army. We sat down on the mosaic and passed around the chicken. A faint, familiar taste of charcoal slid down my chest, summoning the past, an image extinct. Just below my ribs, I could feel a hollow space, gnawing, longing for another place, a different night. Before my brother took the Cross, we held a feast in his honor in the Great Hall. My father chose Sergio to carve the roasted chicken. My brother, a knight in God's army. His soothing smile grew blurred, fading, swallowed by the earth.

After that episode, every group in the prison approached us to trade for the mosaic's stone cubes. We were able to acquire rats, snakes, wood, sharpened sticks, and other precious stones.

The incident piqued interest in our shelter. The other prisoners did not forget the succulent aroma of that chicken. Salamago pointed out scouts from the larger groups studying our position, our habits. Following his instructions, we dug through the mud for a small arsenal of rocks that we kept in a pile in the middle of our group. We never strayed far from each other. At least one of us remained awake to warn the others if an attack seemed imminent.

Perhaps because of their proximity, the Germans could not resist. I was on guard at the time. Their eyes appeared suddenly like crystal stars in the midnight sky. The stars drew closer. I shook the others awake. We gathered the biggest stones in our hands.

"They will try to separate us,' Salamago said, 'to kill us one by one. Stay together. If you find yourself alone, fight your way back to the group.'

The eight Germans divided into two lines of four. They were swinging heavy sticks. One line withdrew as the next attacked. I did not have a second to catch my breath. Intruders charged forward, then retreated before I could strike back. I was waving my rock at phantoms. A stick thumped across my face. My nose cracked. I dropped the rock. I fought on with bare hands. My fists were bloodied, my right hand broken on the hard jaw of one of our attackers.

'Stay together,' Salamago yelled.

The next line fell hard. The point of a stick thrust into my stomach. I bent over, clutching my insides. I raised myself in time to see the rock poised above my head. The blue glimmer of mica. Then I felt nothing, no pain, just floating in a starless sky.

I woke, skidding on my back, across the muddy path between factions. We were travelling away from our shelter, toward the other end of the cave. I tried to grasp the black slime. There was no handle, no catch. Raising my head, I looked forward. Three Germans, racing backward, were dragging me by my legs. Just beyond my attackers, I saw a man standing in the middle of the path. He had a shaggy beard. He held a stone in one hand, an arrow in the other. It was Salamago. I don't know how he got there. Maybe he flew above us to the other side of the cave. Or maybe he knew a secret path to outflank my assailants. The gap between us was closing fast. I lay back down and felt the cool mud on the back of my hands.

Salamago's rock connected with the head of one of the Germans. Sparks dashed, the victim propelled into the shadows. The others let go of my legs. When I rose, Salamago had already plunged the arrow into the chest of another German.

'Come,' Salamago said.

He sprinted back toward our comrades. I followed closely.

Two Germans lay dead in our shelter – facedown on the mosaic. Andrés and Manuel were faring badly, though. The remaining Germans had backed them up against the rock wall.

I approached the fighting on the run. When I reached the combatants, I lowered my shoulder and slammed into one of the Germans. He had not seen my approach. His head snapped back and smacked against the sharp rock face. His body collapsed.

I had lost my footing in the collision. I crawled toward the wounded German. I leaned over him. My hand passed over a large stone. I picked it up and felt its edge. The German was moaning. A bloody gash covered his forehead. I raised the rock and brought it down with all my strength. His face shattered. The moaning ceased.

When I looked up, the remaining Germans had fled. My comrades were standing at the front of our shelter. Salamago and Manuel carried the three bodies in our shelter to the common walkway. I rested against the rock wall. My limbs weary, I slumped to the ground and fell asleep.

I was waked by a rasping noise. It sounded like fabric ripping. I saw Salamago sitting up. He had cleared the mud from the ground and was gazing down at the mosaic. Andrés and Manuel were sleeping. The bodies from the walkway had disappeared.

'Did they bury their dead?' I asked.

'No,' he responded.

The sour scent of blood wafted through our shelter.

'Flesh eaters,' Salamago said. 'Even the Christians are heathen down here.'

Stubborn limbs were torn unhurried, frayed and split. The bones snapped like twigs. The tough meat was chewed methodically. The sound, grating and unholy, reverberated through the cave.

After that perilous escape, we held to the same routine – sleeping in shifts, upgrading our arsenal by digging for bigger and sharper stones. They never attacked us again, though. Not the Germans. Not any group.

The balance of power shifted after the assault.

We had killed five Germans. The three remaining men could not defend the antechamber or their wood supply. Within hours following our battle, the Venetians ventured from their rock fortress and evicted our neighbors. The Germans did not even put up a fight.

Thenceforth, the Venetians rotated their contingent between the two shelters. Salamago liked to say that the Venetians had a castle in the city – the fortress in the middle of the cave – and an estate in the country – the antechamber next to our camp.

Four more Venetians entered the prison some weeks later. With the additional members, the Venetians had sixteen men, more than twice as many as any other group – a superior fighting force with control of the wood supply.

They used their power to improve their situation and the conditions in the prison. Once a month, the Venetians levied a tax on each faction. They divided the responsibility of collecting the fee amongst themselves. The nature of the charge varied from group to group, depending on the current supplies of the Venetians, the group's resources, and the mood of the tax collector.

Salamago befriended our tax collector – an old sailor named Giovanni. He had been the captain of a merchant ship, an old man who claimed to have seen every port in the world. In the cave, he was one of the leaders of the Venetian faction. Salamago and Giovanni spoke Catalán to each

411

other. Giovanni seemed to speak every language invented by man.

Giovanni would usually ask Salamago for one or two stone cubes from the mosaic. The haggling could last the better part of a week – neither man in a rush to return to the dark monotony of our lives in the prison.

'You joke, old man,' Giovanni would say, after perusing our offering. 'Perhaps you mistake us Venetians for Genoans. Our cousins might be fooled by such crap, but not Venetians. We are sophisticated, world travelers. Show me some turquoise from the mosaic's river.'

'Walking between your shelters in this cave,' Salamago would say, 'does not make you a world traveler, Giovanni.'

Their conversations would steer to which one had seen more of the world, or which country produced the finest mariners, or any other vaguely related topic. They would not return to the matter of the tax for several hours or even days. Andrés and I listened to their exchanges. In rare moments, their banter helped us forget our situation. Occasionally, Giovanni would turn to Andrés or me, as if he had just noticed our presence.

'Who are these people, Salamago?' Giovanni would say. 'Your King Jaime sends boys into battle?'

'I am twenty-one years,' I said, more than once.

'And I am twenty-one also,' Andrés would follow.

'Forgive me, then,' Giovanni would say. 'I remember when I was that age.' Then he would launch into some tale from his travels – a whore he fell in love with in Sicily, a battle with a pirate ship off the coast of Cyprus, a gray pearl he found on some beach in North Africa.

After recounting numerous stories and grumbling a couple of hours, Giovanni always ended up accepting Salamago's initial offer.

'The problem,' Giovanni would say, 'is that I am too generous. From now on, I will send Paolo to collect your taxes. You will like him. He bites the heads off live rats. Good luck, Salamago. And you too, Knights of Calatrava.'

Giovanni returned every month, though.

The Venetians gradually asserted control in the cave, imposing an order governing various aspects of prison life. Periodically, Giovanni would stand in the middle of the walkway to proclaim new regulations. He would usually give examples and cite the punishments for various offenses. Then he would repeat himself in at least five different languages.

To improve hygiene, the Venetians supervised the digging of latrines at the edge of the cave.

'Contrary to the perception of the infidels,' Giovanni declared, 'you are not animals. Although you sometimes live like them – walking and sleeping in your own excrement. No more. Henceforth, you will relieve yourselves in latrines – and only latrines.'

413

First-time violators received a fine – a cockroach, a rat, a snake. Second-time violators received ten lashes from a wooden stick.

The Venetians also forbade the eating of human flesh, dead or otherwise. They instructed each group to bury their dead. The Venetians provided a priest – Father Gabrio – to recite a few prayers during the burial.

You did not need to have monastic training to recognize that Father Gabrio was no father. Not in the clerical sense. His brawny forearms seemed more suited for raising a mast than distributing the bread of communion. He walked precariously, unbalanced, as if he was not quite comfortable on land.

The prisoners did not mind, though. Father Gabrio knew a few Latin phrases and the general rhythm of the prayers, even if he butchered most of the liturgy. Giovanni confided in us some months after the establishment of Father Gabrio's ministry that the prison priest had been a servant in a monastery outside of Venice when he was a boy. That's where he had learned to mimic the monks' prayers.

'At sea,' Giovanni said, 'Gabrio used to cry out in his sleep. I once asked him what dark visions had visited him. Gabrio said that every night he dreamed that he was a shepherd, trying to steer his flock back home in a blinding storm.

'A man can sail the world,' Giovanni continued, 'but eventually he must face his destiny.'

Despite his lack of training, Father Gabrio's words lent an air of solemnity to the proceedings, as if the Lord took note of the life and death of each prisoner in the cave. Eventually, almost every prisoner attended the burials, no matter the identity of the deceased, just to hear Father Gabrio's mumbled service.

The Venetians also prohibited fighting between and within the factions. When conflicts arose, the parties were to submit the problem to the prison court, which meant Giovanni. He donned a black robe for the mediations. He would listen to the disputants patiently, then render a decision. There was no appeal. If the losing party resisted the execution of Giovanni's ruling, sixteen Venetians armed with rocks and sticks would soon convince them of the wisdom of Giovanni's judgment.

The Venetians welcomed new arrivals, fed them, tended to any wounds, and explained the prison rules. After a week or two, they would introduce and transfer the new prisoner to the group of his countrymen or religious cohorts.

Giovanni announced the institution of a criminal code for the prison – banning stealing, assault, and murder. Depending on the seriousness of their crimes, the perpetrators were subject to severe punishment, including amputation of fingers or hands, even death.

Only one murder took place after the Venetians asserted their control in the cave. A Turk killed a German in a dispute over food. The trial was held in public view, next to the spring. Each group brought a torch to the proceedings. The accused stood on a stone platform surrounded by guards recruited by the Venetians from different factions.

The Turk stated that his victim had tried to steal a snake he had captured. After the Turk's explanation and its translation into various languages spoken in the cave, the gallery of prisoners turned their attention to Giovanni, who mounted the platform and faced the defendant.

'Death by hanging,' he pronounced.

One of the Venetians immediately began to climb the rock wall. He had a rope coiled around his shoulder. A short distance up, he looped the rope around a rock that jutted out of the wall. He dropped the other end toward the ground. It had already been tied in a noose. One of the guards placed it around the neck of the condemned. Then he pushed him off the platform.

The rope had apparently been twisted. The Turk's body twirled in a circle. He knocked into the rock wall several times. He was kicking frantically, trying to gain a foothold. When the struggle ended, the body swung gently. The flames glistened against the wet stones. The trickle of water was the only sound in the cave.

The rope had been acquired several weeks earlier from the Sultan's guards. After a feeding, Giovanni had lined up behind the other prisoners seeking to exchange a precious stone or chunk of valuable metal for a scrap of food. When Giovanni's turn came, he placed a golden goblet in the bucket. One of his countrymen had discovered the object while digging a latrine. Giovanni had showed it to us the previous day. It bore the Latin inscription 'Citizen of Rome, citizen of the world.'

As the guards perused the strange item, Giovanni shouted up to them in Arabic. He later reported the substance of the negotiations.

'Five blankets,' he said.

At first, the guards laughed at Giovanni's presumption.

'You will receive what we give you,' one of them shouted down, 'if we decide to let you live.'

'We have discovered other treasures,' Giovanni shouted back. 'We will dig for still more. That is, if you wish us to.'

The laughter stopped. The guards studied the goblet, conferring amongst themselves.

Eventually, they gave Giovanni two blankets and the rope that was used to hang the German. Giovanni did not receive exactly what he had asked for, but he had established a new practice, a new commerce for the prison. Soon the Venetians were able to acquire many other useful items – cups, clothes, shoes, small knives, even flint rocks to help start a fire and oil to make a torch.

'For the right price,' Giovanni said, 'I could spend the night with the Sultan's daughter.'

The Venetians would barter many of the items received from the infidels to the other prisoners for gold, silver, and precious stones. Then the process would repeat itself. With the chance to gain access to goods outside the cave, the other groups increased their efforts to mine the old palace for its treasures.

When I wasn't sleeping or hunting for rodents, I spent my time scooping the earth with my hands into a pile of mud next to our shelter. We sifted through the dirt for several weeks before finding anything of value – small pieces of gold and silver. Subsequently, Salamago found a statuette adorned with red rubies – perhaps the Virgin Mary or maybe just a pagan idol.

We did not have the rapport with the infidel guards that Giovanni and the Venetians had established. Nor did any of us speak Arabic. Instead of taking our chances with the guards, we traded our discoveries and the mosaic stones to Giovanni and the Venetians for goods they had received from the infidels. Giovanni's monthly visits became opportunities for bartering, interspersed with the usual stories concerning his past life as a sailor. Soon he stopped collecting a tax altogether.

We had been in the prison for seven months when winter came. Giovanni said it was the coldest few months he had ever experienced in the Levant. No frost covered the earth, no ice on the spring. But the raw dampness seemed to pierce my skin and sow a chill that spread down to the bone. Drinking the frigid water caused my temples to ache.

Despite the suddenness of winter's arrival, we

were well prepared. We had spent the fall months trading for supplies of warmer clothing, blankets, and boots. Most important, we had accumulated enough wood to enable us to maintain a fire through the coldest days. We wrapped ourselves with every piece of clothing we possessed.

Food was scarcer. We had little to trade. We no longer dug for treasures – the earth was too hard. And Salamago insisted on conserving the better part of the mosaic for future use. We continued to hunt, and we learned from the Turks how to set traps for rodents using the smallest morsels of food. Cockroaches seemed to comprise the staple of our diet, though. They entered the cave from every crevice and seemed to feel at home amongst the prisoners – at least until they found themselves between someone's teeth.

Andrés became sick toward the end of winter. Dysentery afflicted each of us, but Andrés' case was more stubborn. For several weeks, whatever he ate or drank would pass through him immediately. He lay immobile on the ground, sweating or shivering, sometimes both. He never complained, though.

Salamago said that Andrés' illness would wane.

'Your cousin,' Salamago said, 'is strong. Have faith, Francisco.'

'Faith in what, old man?' I responded.

Salamago was right, though. Andrés gradually recovered. He lost much of his bulk, but he survived.

We witnessed our first ransom that winter. I

was standing at the falling water, filling a cup to take back to Andrés, when the hatch opened unexpectedly – the guards had fed us only hours before. Normally, the other prisoners would stream toward the light in anticipation of the distribution of food. Not then. Every prisoner froze. Conversations ceased in midsentence.

'Michel Gilbert,' a guard shouted into the cave.

The only movement – one man rising in the French camp, walking cautiously towards the light. He stopped only a few feet away from me.

'Je suis Michel Gilbert,' he said, barely above a whisper.

'Michel,' a man said, looking down from the edge of the opening, 'I am Louis of Toulouse, a loyal vassal to your father. He sent me to Aleppo to pay your ransom.'

The guards lowered a rope. It had a thick knot tied on the end. When it reached the ground, the Frenchman grabbed it and stood on the knot. Tears stained a path down his dirt-covered cheeks.

Several guards helped pull the rope. The attention of every prisoner was riveted on the figure ascending, my own eyes staring jealously at another man's future. Like a full moon gleaming against a black night.

I was watching the two Frenchmen embrace when the hatch shut.

Five other prisoners were ransomed that summer. Three Turks, another Frenchman, and an Englishman.

Oftentimes it seemed as if our existence in the cave spanned one long twilight, interspersed with moments of lucidity when the guards opened the hatch. We could not see the sunrise or sunset. We did not know if it was day or night.

Somehow time moved forward, though. We measured it by the feeding schedule – every other day – as if counting the time would make our sentence a tangible distance, a finite duration.

That duration was mostly consumed with the tasks of survival – hunting, sleeping, digging for gold and silver, trading with the Venetians and other groups.

But there were still many empty hours to fill. Questions that repeated themselves. Questions without answers. Would Andrés and I ever leave that cave? How long could we survive in that prison? Would I ever see you again, Isabel?

The questions resonated against the rock walls, circling back against each other. Sometimes I held my palms against my ears to block out the echo.

Salamago once asked me why I was covering my ears. I told him about the questions.

'Evil spirits,' he said. 'They have visited me too.'

Sometimes conversation could keep the spirits at bay. We would try to prolong Giovanni's visits, his tales of exotic ports and women. When he left, we would exchange our own stories. Never about home, about Aragón. Those intimate details strained painfully against the uncertainty of our predicament. To hear in words what we might never see.

Instead, we talked of battles we had fought in the Levant – repeating anecdotes until we each knew every part by heart. Eventually, we ran out of stories and would tell the same ones over again, changing a fact or two, so that our audience would remain engaged. Two infidel soldiers became three, then four. A straight staircase became steep and winding.

We told Manuel and Salamago about Toron, the execution of infidel soldiers, the massacre of civilians. We told them about the Krak – the castellan Don Lorgne, our successful sortie against the Muslim catapult. About our journey to Aleppo and the procession through the streets of the city.

In turn, Salamago and Manuel described many battles. They had fought in the Levant for five years before their imprisonment. They never spoke of their capture, though.

I was dozing when Andrés asked Salamago how he and Manuel were captured. I opened my eyes and sat up, anxious to hear his response. It did not come. Salamago stood up and walked toward the other end of the cave. Andrés never asked again.

We did learn the circumstances of their capture, though. Salamago was foraging for insects in another part of the cave when Manuel whispered the story, pausing several times when other prisoners ventured near our shelter, continuing only when the intruders were well beyond ear-shot.

'Salamago and I commanded a twelve-man team of Templar knights,' he said. 'We were based at the Order's fortress in Antioch. Princes and sultans had reached agreement to allow for the safe passage of Christian pilgrims to Muslim-occupied Jerusalem. The leaders of both communities had forged an uneasy peace in the region. Our company escorted pilgrims to the Holy City, acting as guides and protectors from the thieves, Christian and Muslim alike, that preyed on civilians.

'I had already accompanied Salamago on seven missions to Jerusalem. On the first six, we had skirmishes with local brigands, but nothing serious. On the seventh mission, a group of bandits ambushed our party. We protected the pilgrims, but lost one of our own – the deputy whom I replaced. Salamago mourned his death. They had been close friends.

'We never had to face an organized Muslim army. Not until our eighth tour. We knew that the Muslims had twice sent delegations to Prince Bohemund of Antioch complaining of Christian knights marauding the countryside. When the Christian Prince failed to put an end to the attacks, one of the Muslim commanders decided to retaliate. Our company was traveling to Jerusalem at the time of the dispute. We had thirty pilgrims in our caravan – mostly women and children.

'On the fifth night of the journey, we camped

423

in a sunken valley shielded from the elements. We woke at dawn to the sight of a Muslim contingent – twenty-four soldiers – surrounding our camp.

'Hysteria spread amongst the civilians. The knights prepared for battle. We were outnumbered two to one – but the Templars had overcome worse odds.

'Salamago hoped to avoid a conflict. He told our company to put our swords in their scabbards. That he would reach a peaceful accommodation with the infidels – to preserve the lives of the pilgrims and his knights.

'With this purpose, Salamago and I rode under a flag of truce to the Muslim lines. The Muslim commander with his own delegation rode out to meet us. Salamago explained the nature of our mission. He referred to the agreements in place between our leaders and the safe-conduct assurances for pilgrims.

'When Salamago finished, the Muslim commander said that he would let our party pass on condition that the Templar knights lay down their weapons – swords, daggers, shields. He said that until Christian attacks on Muslim villages ceased, Christian caravans passing through Muslim territory would be disarmed. He gave his word that no harm would come to any in our company if we obeyed his injunction. Salamago believed him.

'As we rode back to our caravan, I reminded Salamago of the Templar prohibition against surrendering weapons. Better to die a martyr than to

424

put your sword down in the face of the enemy. I told him that if we returned to Acre without our swords, the Grand Master would sanction him severely, that he would probably be expelled from the Order. That, at the very least, his reputation would be forever tarnished.

'"Do you think," Salamago said, "that Jesus Christ would place His reputation above the welfare of His charges?"

'When we rode back to our camp, Salamago explained the bargain we had struck with the Muslim commander. There was distress amongst the civilians, confusion amongst my comrades. We complied, though, stacking our weapons in a pile before the watchful eyes of the Muslim soldiers.

'We mounted our horses and resumed our trek to Jerusalem. We traveled not one mile before the caravan came to a halt. The Muslim soldiers were spread across the plain, swords drawn, preparing to charge.'

Manuel picked up a stone and threw it into the darkness.

'The infidels slaughtered the pilgrims, even the children. The Templars fought with bare fists, determined at least to die with the pilgrims. The Muslim commander denied us that dignity, instructing his men to capture the knights alive. We were to be a gift to the Sultan of Aleppo. Five of my comrades fought with such ferocity the Muslims were forced to kill them. The other seven Templars, bruised, broken, were taken here.

'The Templars sent an envoy to ransom five of my comrades. He left Salamago and me to rot in this godforsaken hole.'

'Manuel,' Andrés said, 'the Templars will send a ransom for you soon. Didn't you say that the envoy had only one hundred coins? If he had brought more gold, you and Salamago would be back in Acre right now.'

'Or maybe Aragón,' I said.

'I lied to Salamago,' Manuel responded. 'With the coins in his purse, the Templar envoy could have ransomed half the prisoners in the cave. His superiors had instructed him not to ransom Salamago or his deputy.'

'Salamago was trying to protect the lives of the pilgrims,' I said. 'They cannot hold you and Salamago responsible for what happened.'

'They can, and they do,' Manuel said. 'I was initially included in the ransomed group. The guards lifted me from the cave and closed the hatch. My freedom was fleeting, though. Since I had been promoted recently by Salamago, the envoy did not know of my appointment. I was standing in the courtyard, shielding my eyes from the bright sun, when he asked the group of us – all six – what positions we held in the company. When I told him I was the deputy, he instructed the infidel guards to return me to the prison. He said that one pilgrim in our caravan had survived. The man had returned to Acre and given an account of the massacre to the Grand Master of the Order.

'"Salamago and you placed your own judgment ahead of the principles of the Order," the envoy said. "For that, you have the blood of children on your hands."

'I pleaded with the envoy to reconsider. I told him that Salamago had made the decision. That I had tried to dissuade him.'

'I do not believe you, Manuel,' Andrés said. 'You would never do that to Salamago.'

'Spend as much time as I have in this cave, Andrés,' Manuel said, 'then tell me what you would and would not do to escape this hell.

'My protestations did not serve me, though,' Manuel continued. 'The Templar representative shook his head and motioned to the infidel guards. As they led me back to the cave, I asked the envoy what would become of me. He said that the Grand Master had yet to decide my fate, mine and Salamago's.'

'Then there is still a chance, Manuel,' I said. 'Your comrades will testify on your behalf.'

'We are beyond their assistance,' Manuel responded. 'Salamago and I will die in this hole.'

Manuel was wrong. He and Salamago did not die in the cave. Several months after Manuel made that prediction, the hatch opened, and one of the guards called the names of both Templars.

Neither Salamago nor Manuel moved. Perhaps they thought they were sleeping, and they were afraid lest they wake and disturb the dream.

'Salamago and Manuel,' the guard shouted again.

Andrés and I roused our comrades.

'You are free,' Andrés said.

We walked with them toward the hatch and stood under the light. Salamago was raised first.

'You will soon be in Acre, Salamago,' I said.

He did not hear me. He was looking toward the hatch. I squinted into the light. I could see several guards. Another man dressed in black, his foot tapping on the edge of the hole, so that fragments of mud tumbled into the cave.

'That's him,' Manuel said. 'The Templar envoy. He has returned. The Grand Master has forgiven us.'

When Salamago reached the surface, the guards dropped the rope again. Manuel rested his feet on the knot. As the rope climbed, Manuel looked down at Andrés and me.

'We will not forget you,' he said. 'As soon as we arrive in Acre, Salamago and I will collect your ransom and return. Your time will come too, Andrés and Francisco.'

When the hatch closed, a different shade of darkness entered the chamber. The blackness spread thin. I could see Andrés' expression clearly – a broad, forgotten smile, all-encompassing.

'I always knew we would leave this prison,' Andrés said. 'I always knew. After we land in Barcelona, we will visit your parents in Montcada for a week before going to Girona.'

'Patience, Andrés,' I said. 'Nothing is settled.'

I did not feel patient, though. I could hear the wind – the soft rustle of the tall grass in the hills of Montcada. For the first time since my arrival in the prison, I could see your face, Isabel.

'You will be with her soon, Francisco,' Andrés said.

My thoughts were exposed. My face flashed red.

'I will see who, cousin?' I asked, feigning disinterest.

'I am naive, Francisco,' Andrés said, 'but I am not blind.'

As Andrés patted my back, light flooded the cave. I could hear a soft thud in the earth. Then another. Two bodies dropped into the hole. Headless.

One of the guards stood above the hatch. His arms crossed, he peered down into the cave and spoke. Giovanni later translated his words.

'Salamago and Manuel, expelled from the Knights of the Temple for cowardice. The Templar envoy paid us a handsome fee to execute them. Precious gold coins he offered. He brings their heads back to Acre to show his Grand Master. The Sultan gives the bodies to you.'

At Andrés' insistence, Salamago and Manuel were buried inside our shelter. He tied two sticks together to make a Cross to place over the graves. Every prisoner in the cave attended the funeral. Father Gabrio conducted the service.

'After several years of captivity,' Father Gabrio said, 'Salamago and Manuel tasted freedom. We thank the Lord for those brief moments when they felt the sun on their face.'

I did not thank the Lord. For what? A moment's illusion. Hopes fostered and then dashed.

We had been in the cave for one year and four months when Manuel and Salamago were killed. After that, we stopped counting the days.

Andrés dug a new trench next to the graves of our comrades. He labored continuously. When he exhausted himself, he lay down in the hole and slept, only to wake and start digging again. He never seemed to find any treasure. I do not think he was looking for it. He was trying to block his view of the cave. That, or bury himself alive.

I hunted occasionally. Mostly, I sat in our shelter, listening to Andrés' exertions, staring into the darkness. Stare long enough, and you can see your own reflection staring back at you.

Giovanni still visited us. He would coax Andrés from his hole with some question about a rock from our dirt pile. We had nothing of value to trade with him. Giovanni always managed to leave us a small supply of food, though, usually in exchange for some worthless stone.

Andrés was scooping dirt from the trench when one of the guards called the name of a German. The light from the hatch emanated all the way to the edge of our shelter. No one answered the call.

He called the name again. Still no response.

Andrés had stopped digging and was peering over the ridge of the trench.

When the guard called the name a third time, Andrés pulled himself out of the hole. He surveyed the other prisoners.

'He's probably dead,' I said.

Andrés nodded, then left our shelter. I yelled to him, but he did not turn around. He was walking slowly, deliberately, toward the light source. When he reached the hatch, he motioned up toward the guards. His face, his blond hair, his naked body, all smeared black with mud. Only his blue eyes remained bare. They shone fierce in the sunlight.

The other prisoners peered over their shelters, scrutinizing Andrés, trying to discern his purpose. I did not know it. Perhaps, I thought, he intended to bring death upon himself. When the guards raised him and learned he was not the ransomed individual, they would kill him on the spot.

I did nothing, though. Instant death might be preferable to slow disintegration in the prison. Andrés, I thought, had made his choice.

Andrés grabbed the rope. One of the guards bent down and took hold of it. As the guard peered into the hole, Andrés reached up with both hands. His body coiled, Andrés let out a savage grunt as he yanked the rope downward. The guard was jerked forward and fell into the hole. He landed in the muck. He raised himself and brushed the dirt off his green tunic. He was chuckling, reaching for the rope. The

431

other guards gathered around the opening, looking down into the cave, laughing at their con-
federate.

The prisoners understood what the guards did
not. They began to shout, to cry for blood. The
fallen guard glanced at Andrés. His smile vanished.
He must have seen a murderous gaze. He let go of
the rope and drew his dagger, like a man who pulls
a handkerchief from his pocket to shield himself
against a storm.

I heard my own voice as if it came from
far away. 'Kill him, Andrés. Gouge his eyes
out.'

As if this man embodied all our oppressors – the
guards, the degradation, the darkness, the Templar
envoy, Don Fernando.

When Andrés leapt toward the Muslim soldier, the guards above loaded their bows hastily and aimed them into the hole. There was
no clear shot, though. Andrés and the guard
were rolling in the slime. The prisoners surrounded the melee, screaming and throwing rocks
up at the guards, who were forced to retreat
from the opening. I made my way through the
crowd and saw Andrés atop his victim, biting
into the man's cheek and spitting out his flesh.
That display enticed the others. They pounced
on the guard, kicking, punching in one swirl-
ing heap.

Eventually, the guards were able to establish a
steady fire into the hole. The prisoners dispersed

toward the dark, unexposed edges of the cave. The bloody corpse of the guard, recognizable only by his torn green tunic, lay on the ground just below the hatch.

'There is your precious gold,' a prisoner screamed in French. 'Come and get it, bastards.'

Even if they could have understood that foreign tongue, the guards had no intention of venturing into the lair. They closed the hatch, leaving behind the body of their comrade.

Andrés came back to our shelter. He was breathing heavily. He walked past me without saying a word. Then he climbed down into the trench and began digging again.

A line of prisoners walked orderly by our shelter, as if they were knights waiting to salute their commander. An act of defiance had expunged a collective shame, transforming captives into rebels. Many of the men carried stones, which they placed on Salamago's grave. They passed by Andrés' trench, trying to catch a glimpse of their leader. He continued to dig, paying no heed to the visitors.

After this tribute, the other prisoners retreated to their shelters. Sleepless, we waited for the Sultan's punishment, listening to the crackle of small fires, whispering memories once forgotten. For a few hours, we felt like soldiers again, on the eve of a great battle.

It was night when the hatch opened. Muslim

guards slid down ropes. They held scarves over their faces so as not to breathe the foul air. They carried swords and whips, marching down the walkway.

A group of Genoans ambushed the intruders, leaping down from the rock walls on both sides of the walkway. The infidel guards dispatched their attackers swiftly. A line of Venetians stood across the path. They were cut down just as quickly. The other prisoners observed the battle, reassessing a resolve, then forsaking it. Stones and sticks were dropped. Heads bowed. The resistance was short-lived.

The Muslim guards fanned out to every point of the cave. Torches illuminated our surroundings, revealing the sloping, uneven walls and the small niches in which each group of prisoners resided. The crack of whips echoed as the soldiers drove the prisoners onto the walkway and under the hatch.

I thought they meant to kill us right there. But the Sultan had other plans. Soldiers looped the rope under the shoulders of a prisoner and raised him to the surface. One by one, we followed. I interposed myself between Andrés and the soldiers, fearing they would recognize him as the killer. They seemed unable to distinguish amongst us, though, or uninterested in doing so. Most of us were covered in mud and blood.

I preceded Andrés. As I was hauled through the air, the rope scraped across my bare chest. My feet dangled. I looked up at the clear sky, yellow stars like bright lanterns.

When I reached the surface, a soldier grasped my hair. He pulled me into a row of other prisoners. Andrés was soon by my side. We breathed the chilled night.

'Strange nectar,' Andrés said.

We stood in a dusty courtyard with sparse patches of grass. We were facing one of the palace buildings. A castle wall rose in back of us. The sides of the courtyard extended indefinite, long enough to accommodate fifty prisoners lined up.

We made a ragged bunch – filthy, shivering in the cold. Many of the prisoners were completely naked. Some held their hands before their genitals, an awkward display of modesty.

A Frenchman was humming a cheerful tune, smiling inanely at the infidel guards. Maybe the idiot thought we had been ransomed.

Giovanni stood about ten men down on the left. He was talking to himself, loud enough so that we could hear. I recognized a few words, about the Lord, about salvation. Hollow words. A blow from a guard's club silenced him.

There must have been four soldiers for every prisoner. They wore handsome green tunics, emerald like a forest. They brandished their swords, as if they faced an army, not a gathering of broken men.

To the right, a small group of soldiers huddled

around a bonfire, warming their hands against the flames.

I scanned the gray stones ahead. Who made their home in that building? The guards? Maybe a family. Cousins of the Sultan. Maybe two brothers, not knowing the forces, good and evil, lurking beneath everything they were and would be.

A large wooden block in the middle of the courtyard arrested my gaze. It was bloodstained, the wood chipped and worn. An arc had been carved in its center.

A soldier stood behind the block, a half-moon axe on his shoulder. The silver blade shimmered against the stars, the fire.

Three men entered the courtyard from the adjacent building. The guards stood at attention. They shouted at the prisoners. Whips snapped. The three walked slowly toward the prisoners. In the center, the commander, a fat man, shuffled forward. A golden breastplate covered his chest – defining muscles that belonged to another.

When he reached the far end of the line, the commander stopped. He inspected the prisoners. Then he pointed to one. Guards grabbed the man and pulled him forward. They marched him toward the wood block.

It was Alberto, one of the Venetians. He did not resist. They walked him around so that he faced us. He kneeled forward of his own accord and placed his head on the block. The brown curls of his hair were the same shade as the blood staining the creases of the wood grain.

The blade cut through his neck and lodged in the soft earth. The head bounced forward, rolling toward the prisoners.

Two guards dragged the headless body toward the bonfire. The second prisoner was already walking toward the block. He broke free from the guards. He ran back toward the hole. He meant to find refuge in that dungeon. The guards intercepted him and carried him toward the wooden stand.

The force of the axe sent the head skidding. Eyes and ears were severed from their roots. Bloody fibers protruded from the fissure, twisting like worms uncovered from the soil beneath a dead log.

A third, a fourth. The heads spread haphazard.

Another. And another.

The executioner's thick forearms were as bloody as a butcher's. His face and cloak, splattered red.

I looked down the row. The commander pointed to the men on either side of Giovanni, passing over our Venetian friend.

'Every other man,' Andrés said.

He was right. The guards were executing half the prisoners. They had no great design. It was merely a matter of placement.

Two, four . . . ten, twelve.

The commander was approaching our position.

The infidels wanted only one of our heads. They bore no preference, no personal grudge.

It was an evil selection, an ugly, ignoble death, half a world from Aragón, not worthy of a knight. The bodies were dragged through the dust, piled on top of other corpses, waiting for the fires. A frozen grimace made public a private moment of foreboding.

If only Andrés and I had died at the Krak. We would have been buried together under the rubble of the castle.

Andrés placed his hand on my shoulder. He pinched my muscle until I turned to face him.

'Francisco, I have seen enough,' he said.

'Enough,' I repeated his last word.

'Do you understand?' He spoke calmly.

He pulled me toward him. A short embrace. The sting of the whip on my back interrupted our goodbye. Andrés pivoted to avoid the lash, then pulled me to the side. A slight rotation. Barely perceptible.

Barely.

The infidel commander walked past me and motioned to Andrés. Two guards seized him by the arms.

He looked back at me on his way to the block. He smiled, a keen smile, intimate, as if we were back at Santes Creus, sharing a secret joke about the Abbot. As if I were his accomplice.

When the last prisoner placed his head on the bloody block, dawn was breaking hard across the courtyard. The severed heads were suffused with a swallow glow. Soldiers yawned. Prisoners yearned for darkness.

The infidels provided two ropes to the cave floor. Most of the prisoners jumped into the soft clay, though, anxious to leave that unhallowed ground.

I returned to our shelter, sitting next to Salamago and Manuel's grave. I never left the enclosure. I would have died, starved to death, if not for Giovanni. He brought me food and water several times a week. I ate and drank only so that he would leave me in peace.

A Venetian trader arrived at the prison some months after the executions. He came to ransom Giovanni and his crew. Half the sailors had been executed. Giovanni chose replacements amongst his countrymen. He also chose me.

I sailed with Giovanni to Italy. When we reached Venice, he booked passage for me aboard a merchant vessel bound for Barcelona.

Unaccustomed to the bright sun, I stayed below in the hold during the day. In the night, I climbed on deck. Just a few mariners manned the sails. I lay naked on the wooden beams of the ship, spread my arms out, listening to the cool breeze across the bow, imagining the metal blade penetrating my neck.

That blade was meant for me. Andrés had switched places. He had seen the pattern. Every other man. So had I.

I think about that moment, our embrace. I imagine a different ending. Sometimes I hate Andrés.

When I left Girona, Isabel, you said to bring your brother home. I did not. But if you look at the reflection off the yellow stone just before dusk, you will see his wan smile. I do.

It was done. Francisco was finished. Thank God. My left leg was numb from sitting in the same position for several hours. The blood in my temples was throbbing.

Indeed, Francisco seemed to have exhausted himself. He leaned against the cell wall. He slid down slowly until his bottom rested on the stone floor. His head slumped forward. He closed his eyes.

'Francisco,' Isabel said, 'the Lord has compassion.'

Her words carried a gentle cadence, her voice fraught with sorrow.

Francisco opened his eyes. He turned toward the girl, his lips skewed unevenly.

'I have seen up close His compassion, Isabel,' he said, 'on the battlefields of the Levant, in the courtyard of the Citadel in Aleppo, on the docks of Barcelona, watching Sergio's ship disappear. Do you think the Lord will have mercy on this sinner?'

'It is you who have tried and condemned yourself,' Isabel said.

Francisco's back tensed. He coiled his fingers into a tight fist.

I thought to intervene, to console Isabel and Francisco, to protect them from each other.

'Francisco,' I said, 'the ways of the world are mysterious. Indeed, it is sometimes impossible to grasp our own intentions.'

'Don't you understand?' he asked.

Isabel did not move. Indeed, her resilient gaze seemed to intensify Francisco's anger.

'He took my place,' Francisco yelled. 'Andrés should have been ransomed instead of me.'

'Francisco,' I said, 'a man can be his own harshest judge. I myself know that well.'

I had more to say. Wise words that might have eased Francisco's burden. But he interrupted me.

'Did you hear what I said, Isabel? I am responsible for the death of your brother.'

Isabel finally looked away from Francisco – out the window, toward the horizon. She reached up and held her hands to her ears.

Francisco stepped forward and seized her wrists. She tried to resist, but he was too strong. He pried her hands from her ears. Their faces were almost touching.

'As much as the axe that severed Andrés' head from his body,' Francisco said, 'I was the instrument of his death.'

Isabel stopped struggling. Francisco released her. She bent down and crossed her arms before her stomach. Then she began to retch on the cold stone.

I tried to support her head. She pushed me away before stepping from the cell and fleeing down the corridor.

CHAPTER 13

A VISITOR

Isabel did not supper that afternoon. She did not breakfast the following morning. By the afternoon, she was running a high fever. We moved her to a bedchamber in the infirmary. I visited after the evening office.

When I entered the chamber, Isabel was lying on the bed. Her head was propped up on a pillow. Her cheeks were flushed pink. Loose strands of hair fell damp across her fevered brow.

I tried to engage the girl in conversation. She did not respond. Indeed, for the next two days, Isabel did not speak or stir from her position.

I consulted Brother Vial concerning the girl's condition. We sat across from each other in the parlor. He inquired as to the substance of Francisco's confession. I told him what had happened to Francisco and Andrés at the Krak. About Andrés' death at the Citadel.

He listened patiently. When I was done, he walked up and down the corridor. Several monks 'praying silently' in the courtyard kept drifting by

443

the parlor, peering at Brother Vial. I shooed them away with sharp words. Brother Vial finally stopped his pacing and sat next to me.

'Most troubling,' he said.

We visited Isabel together. Brother Vial sat at her bedside. He dipped a cloth in a bowl of water and placed it on the girl's forehead. The cool water seemed to revive her. Isabel raised her hand and grasped Brother Vial's wrist.

'Why does he despise me?' she asked. Her first words in two days.

'He does not despise you, Isabel,' Brother Vial said. Then he picked up the cloth and squeezed the excess water on the floor. He dipped it again in the bowl and placed it on her forehead.

'Francisco cannot bear his burden,' he said. 'He seeks to share it.'

That was the extent of their conversation. Before departing the chamber, Brother Vial blessed the girl. Then he bent down and kissed her hand. Sometimes I think Brother Vial forgets himself and the modest manner in which we servants of God must conduct ourselves in relation to the opposite gender.

'Do not fear for her health, Brother Lucas,' Brother Vial said as we walked around the courtyard to the refectory. 'Her grip felt as strong as a soldier's.'

Indeed, the next day, Isabel's fever subsided. In the evening, she drank some wine and ate a piece of bread.

When I visited Isabel the following day, I found her standing in the chamber, glancing out the window. She turned to face me.

'Brother Lucas,' she said, 'I am grateful for your care.'

'I am at your service,' I said.

We proceeded to discuss her accommodations, the weather – pleasant things. She did not mention Francisco or Andrés. I suggested a short walk to exercise her legs. She threaded her arm in mine, and we left the infirmary.

She walked rather slowly, breathing deeply the damp air of the early morning. She had stopped to admire a broad tree just outside the gates of the monastery when we saw one of the novices running toward us as if on urgent business.

I had not seen Francisco for three days – since the end of his confession. In caring for Isabel, I had neglected my friend. It was the first time since his arrival five months earlier that I had gone more than a day without seeing Francisco. I remembered the words of Brother Vial about Francisco's not being able to bear his burden. I immediately imagined the worst. Unfortunately, I let out an audible gasp, which had the effect of alarming Isabel. She gripped my arm tightly.

'Brother Lucas,' the novice said, 'two knights have arrived at the monastery. They fought with Francisco in the Levant. They have come to visit their comrade.'

Recognizing that Knights of Calatrava would

bear the same relationship to Andrés that they did to Francisco, I tried unsuccessfully to dissuade Isabel from greeting our visitors. I did not see what good could come of her presence. Better for Isabel to let the past recede. She rebuffed my entreaties.

We met the two men in the antechamber off the abbey – a cozy room with several chairs and a table carved by the monastery's own monks. The two soldiers were seated when we entered. The man farthest away had his dagger out and seemed to be trying to balance the blade on the oak table. I could not help noticing with regret the indentations made to the table's surface by the point of the knife.

The man closest to our position stood up.

'Brother Lucas, I presume?' he said.

'I am he.'

'Then you are responsible for exorcising Francisco's demons,' he said. 'It is a great honor.' He had leathered skin, a lantern jaw, close-set black eyes that seemed to bore under my skin. The countenance of a warrior, except for a delicate, aquiline nose.

'All thanks goes to the Lord,' I said.

'I have heard that Francisco can recall past events and speaks of battles in the Levant.' The hard edge of his voice rasped against his courteous manner.

'Francisco,' I said, 'speaks with great precision about his experiences on the crusade.'

The other visitor's knife fell to the table. He looked up. Pugnosed, dull-eyed. He glanced at his comrade, then resumed his efforts at balancing his blade on the table.

'You perform miracles, Brother Lucas,' the visitor said, smoothing his purple cape.

'Only the Lord performs miracles. I am His humble servant.'

'Well,' he said, 'I will see that the Crown rewards this humble servant handsomely.'

'The Crown? Knights of Calatrava have such influence in the palaces of Barcelona?'

'I apologize, Brother Lucas, for not introducing myself. I am Prince Fernando, the son of my father, the King of Aragón. This is my faithful deputy Pablo. I am not a member of the Calatrava, but I fought by their side more than once in the Levant.'

Don Fernando. El Conquistador de Toron. Defender of the Faith. Crowned Prince upon his triumphant return to Aragón.

My body strained rigid. My legs fastened to the stone floor like columns.

Prince Fernando did fight by the side of the Calatrava. According to Francisco, he oversaw the massacre of civilians at Toron. Then he betrayed Uncle Ramón at the Krak and delivered Francisco and Andrés to the infidels.

Prince Fernando proffered his hand, a golden ring with the royal seal on his middle finger.

'Will you pay homage to your Prince, Brother Lucas?'

I kneeled and kissed the ring.

447

'Abbot Alfonso,' he said, 'has kept me abreast of Francisco's progress with regular reports. Has he not told you of my interest in this case?'

Abbot Alfonso had mentioned Prince Fernando. That was before Francisco gave his account of the siege at the Krak, an account that portrayed the Prince in a most unfavorable light. Most unfavorable, indeed. Prince Fernando could not have relished the prospect of such a witness as Francisco returning to Barcelona society.

'Brother Lucas, are you well?' the Prince asked. 'You have grown pale.'

'I am a bit tired and somewhat startled to receive such a distinguished visitor. I will call Abbot Alfonso so that we can offer a proper greeting for a Prince of Aragón.'

'No, Brother Lucas. Pablo and I do not want to disturb the Abbot or the other monks. We were passing by Santes Creus and decided to make a stop. I have come only to offer you my gratitude.'

'Then you will not be staying long, Prince Fernando?'

'My duties call me back to Barcelona, Brother Lucas.'

My fingers unclenched. My fears appeared unfounded. Abbot Pedro used to say I had an overactive imagination.

'I will always cherish your visit, Prince Fernando, and your kind words. I will pass your regards and your well wishes to Francisco.'

'You misunderstand me, Brother Lucas. Your

work has finished. I have come to retrieve Francisco and bring him to Barcelona.'

'But Prince Fernando, I cannot . . . Francisco cannot make such a journey. He is still quite ill.'

'Do you have so little faith in the royal clergy, Brother Lucas? I have a practiced exorcist on my staff who can finish your inspiring work.'

'But I know Francisco like no other. I understand his condition, Prince Fernando. I need more time with him.'

'Do not fret about unfinished business, Brother Lucas. You will be fully compensated.'

As I contemplated a suitable response, I heard behind me the slick sound of a dagger sliding from its sheath. I thought perhaps that the Prince's deputy had heard enough of my protestations. I turned around to face my attacker. Pablo's hands were empty, though. Isabel had reached over and grabbed Pablo's dagger. She held it aloft. During my discussions with the Prince, I had forgotten completely her presence. Her face was ashen, her jaw taut, her arm bent at the elbow. Considering her recent illness, the girl moved toward Prince Fernando with surprising agility.

The Prince caught her wrist as she was bringing down the weapon. He twisted her arm until the blade fell, clanging on the stone floor. He smacked the girl with the back of his hand. She managed somehow to remain on her feet and to fasten her teeth onto Prince Fernando's forearm.

'Damn it,' he yelled. Then he pulled free his

own dagger and brought its butt down on Isabel's head. The girl fell with a thud on the floor. She lay motionless.

Prince Fernando was bleeding. He tore a strip of cloth from his purple cape and bound the fabric around his arm.

'Who is the girl, Brother Lucas?' He fixed on me a penetrating gaze that seemed to hold an accusation, as if I had been harboring a fugitive.

'Doña Isabel Correa de Girona,' I answered forthrightly.

Prince Fernando snorted.

'She has the same disposition as her brother,' he said, before nodding to his deputy.

Pablo bent down to reclaim his dagger from the ground. He picked up the blade and grazed his fingers over its edge. He remained squatting next to the girl. He looked down at Isabel's prostrate body. He appeared to be examining the fine strands of her hair. He stroked her head gently. Then he gripped her hair with his free hand and raised her head off the stone, placing the dagger before her neck.

'No.' The scream escaped my mouth unwittingly. A discordant noise amidst the serenity of the monastery. Most uncharacteristic. Indeed, I cannot recall ever raising my voice before that moment.

The vehemence of my tone seemed to irritate Prince Fernando. Scratching the back of his head, he grimaced. Pablo, still holding the girl's head above the ground, looked to his master for direction.

'No, Pablo,' Prince Fernando said. 'Brother Lucas is right. It would be better to deal with the girl later. After Brother Lucas helps us to accomplish our primary mission here. Isn't that so, Brother Lucas?'

'I am not sure what you mean, Prince Fernando.'

'Are you the King's faithful servant, Brother Lucas?'

'I am a loyal subject of the Crown, Prince Fernando.'

'I have heard favorable reports of you, Brother Lucas. Abbot Alfonso gave me his personal assurance of your understanding and respect for the privileges of your superiors. He also volunteered that you nurtured ambitions that might lead you far away from the rustic confines of Santes Crues.'

'Perhaps,' I said, 'Abbot Alfonso misjudged me.' Did I speak those words? To none other than the Prince of Aragón?

His eyes, probing, coal black. That's how Francisco had described them.

'That would be a great tragedy for you, Brother Lucas. The truth is I have come to Santes Creus on important business.'

'What manner of business, Prince Fernando?'

'A delicate manner, Brother Lucas. Your assistance would be rewarded many times over.'

'The Lord's work provides its own reward, Prince Fernando.'

451

'Yes, Brother Lucas, but I have in mind a much more tangible reward. And a tangible penalty if you choose not to perform your duties to the Crown.'

'Penalty, Prince Fernando?'

'A future king cannot very well let his subjects ignore his wishes. My father always tells me his first rule of governance – disobedience means death.'

'Indeed, Prince Fernando, that is tangible.'

'Or you can cooperate and earn my gratitude.'

'A devil's choice, Prince Fernando.'

'Your own doing, Brother Lucas. If you had left Francisco at Poblet with Father Adelmo, this difficult situation would never have arisen.'

'I am a man of God, Prince Fernando.'

'Even a man of God is still a man, Brother Lucas.'

'Indeed he is, Prince Fernando.'

'The most venerated saints had temporal concerns, Brother Lucas.'

'I imagine they did, Prince Fernando.'

'Did not Jesus Himself say to render unto Caesar what is properly his?'

'He did in fact say those words, Prince Fernando.'

'Temporal concerns and temporal desires, Brother Lucas.'

'Desires, Prince Fernando?'

'Aspirations, Brother Lucas. For example, you could live the rest of your days in Santes Creus. But I suspect you would be more comfortable in the palaces of Barcelona, or perhaps in the jeweled parlors of the Vatican.'

'The cost of such accommodations seems exorbitant, Prince Fernando.'

'On the contrary, Brother Lucas, I am not asking you to act in a manner that would conflict with your solemn vows. All you have to do is bring me to Francisco. Then your work is done.'

'I am Francisco's confessor.'

'With you or without you, Brother Lucas, I will fulfill my mission here. Your assistance would merely make the task more convenient and discreet.'

'Discretion seems a rare and valuable quality, Prince Fernando.'

'The more reason I would appreciate and repay your service, Brother Lucas. With the right sponsor, an able monk such as yourself could rise to the highest levels of the clergy in Aragón.'

'How high, Prince Fernando?'

'I have heard that the Bishop of Barcelona is quite ill, Brother Lucas.'

What choice did I have? Prince Fernando stated that they would carry out their mission with or without my assistance. If I refused to cooperate, I would merely be sentencing myself to death. And for what purpose? I would accomplish nothing. At least if I lived, I could do the Lord's work in Barcelona – helping the poor, the downtrodden. And I could try to protect Isabel.

'And Andrés' sister?' I asked.

'Judging by the girl's greeting, I suspect she possesses sensitive information. Information,

453

Brother Lucas, that I would trust only with my closest allies.'

'Isabel was much affected by her brother's death, Prince Fernando. She is a hysterical girl. No one will believe her fanciful stories. Not against the word of Prince Fernando and Brother Lucas, or, dare I say, the Bishop of Barcelona.'

'Perhaps we can let the girl live then.'

'The Lord looks with favor on the merciful, Prince Fernando.'

'Then we understand each other, Brother Lucas.'

'Indeed, Prince Fernando, we do.'

Prince Fernando was anxious not to disturb the monks at prayer. At the Prince's urging, I escorted him and Pablo around the outside gardens. It was a circuitous route to Francisco's cell, avoiding the church and the courtyard. We entered the monastery through a rear window. Pablo climbed the ledge, then helped pull me up. Regrettably, Brother Eduardo had neglected to clean the windowsill, and my white habit was tarnished with grime.

After we had negotiated the window ledge, I led them to the staircase. At the base, Prince Fernando motioned for me to go first. As I ascended, the Prince put his hand on my shoulder. He was close enough so that I could feel his tepid breath on the back of my neck.

When we had almost reached the top, Prince Fernando withdrew his sword. The glint of the blade was blinding. The steps began to meld together, the rock face spinning, twisting toward that same gray vista I had seen in the looking glass. The sky bleeding into the ocean. Right into left. I closed my eyes. Then I lost my footing and fell backward.

Prince Fernando caught me. In the process, he dropped his sword. Pablo tried in vain to intercept it. As it fell, the sword seemed to crash into every step of that winding stairwell. The echo resonated through the corridors.

'Idiot,' Prince Fernando said to me. 'Why don't you just announce our arrival?'

Pablo was already moving down the steps to retrieve his master's weapon. He returned swiftly and gave Prince Fernando his sword.

We stepped into the corridor. My legs were uncooperative, unwieldy. Prince Fernando pushed me forward. My hands were trembling. I felt as if I were walking to my own execution.

We passed seven empty cells before I stopped outside of Francisco's. The door was slightly ajar. Prince Fernando peered inside. Then he gestured to his deputy to push the portal open. Prince Fernando stood back, muscles tensed. The door creaked open. The two men charged into the cell.

Lord, do not desert me.

'Damn it! Goddamn it!' Prince Fernando's curses chafed against the sacred work performed in that chamber.

I stepped into the doorway. The cell was empty.

Prince Fernando stood in the center of the room. Pablo was ransacking Francisco's meager provisions.

Prince Fernando caught my eye. His knuckles had turned white choking the handle of his sword.

'Where is he, Brother Lucas?'

Lord, have mercy on me.

'Where the hell is he?'

'I do not know,' I said.

'I suppose he vanished. Is that what happened, Brother Lucas? For your sake, you should pray that we find your friend soon.

'Pablo, check every cell that we passed – from here to the staircase. If you find Francisco, kill him. Brother Lucas and I will check the other end of the corridor.'

Francisco was not in the section of the corridor that Prince Fernando and I inspected. We searched ten cells, one by one. Actually, the Prince, his sword at the ready, would conceal himself at the side of the entrance and direct me to open the door. Then the Prince would dash into the cell. He returned to the corridor each time, shouting to Francisco.

'You cannot hide, Francisco, you might as well show yourself.'

'Francisco, you are making this much harder on yourself than it has to be.'

'I only want to talk, Francisco, to set the record straight.'

We turned a corner of the corridor, and Prince Fernando searched the last two cells. When he was done, he let loose a torrent of invective. I braced myself, fearing the Prince would direct his ire at me. He did not, though, and we walked back. As we approached Francisco's cell, Prince Fernando called to his deputy.

'Pablo! Stop pilfering from the monastery and get over here.'

As the Prince spoke, I glanced into Francisco's cell. I saw rays of light collecting dust in midair. I heard a bird chirping just outside the window. I saw Pablo. He was facing the blue sky, sitting in Francisco's wicker chair.

'Prince Fernando,' I said, and pointed toward his deputy.

'Taking a rest,' Prince Fernando addressed his deputy, 'when I told you many times the importance of this mission. Francisco de Montcada could bring me down. And where would that leave you?'

Prince Fernando walked into the cell, pulling me along by the collar. Pablo did not respond to his master's chastisement.

Indeed, Pablo was dead. When we walked around to face him, we could see his dagger, the very same with which he had desecrated the table in the reception antechamber. In truth, we could only see its handle. The entire blade was submerged in his chest. His scabbard dangled empty from his belt. His sword was missing.

Pablo's face bore the same glazed look in death as it had in life. His eyes were blank, lusterless, his mouth open wide.

Prince Fernando let his sword drag on the cell floor. As he studied his deputy's expression, his own face became pensive. He squinted his eyes and folded his lower lip into his mouth.

'This affair has become quite a nuisance,' he said.

He grasped the front of my robe and jerked me toward the cell door. When we reached the corridor, he threw me down to the stone. My knees skinned on the rough surface.

Francisco was standing about thirty feet away. In his white cassock, he looked like any other monk. But for the sword at his side.

'You disappoint me, Francisco,' Prince Fernando said.

The Prince held his dagger in one hand, his sword in the other. He advanced on Francisco cautiously.

'I rather like you, Francisco. Your resilience. Your courage.'

Prince Fernando stopped a couple of steps from Francisco. The two men circled.

'It displeases me to kill those who I like. You see, I do not like many people.'

Prince Fernando feinted forward with his sword. Francisco lurched backward.

'The reflexes suffer most when you are away from the battlefield, Francisco.'

The Prince lunged at Francisco, who parried the blow. The two men faced each other again.

'The reflexes, Francisco.'

The Prince crouched as he spoke. He reached his sword forward at Francisco, who deflected the blade with his own. Then the Prince passed by Francisco on the left, holding his dagger backhand.

'You lose a step,' the Prince said, 'but that step is the difference between life and death.'

Francisco's robe was cut open at the thigh. The white threads darkened with blood.

'Tell me, Francisco, how did you kill Pablo? He's a formidable warrior.'

Francisco thrust his sword forward. Prince Fernando blocked the blade. The two weapons grated against each other.

'I suppose you set a trap in one of the empty cells. Pablo always lacked a certain shrewdness. Even so, I am impressed.'

Prince Fernando smiled. The two men circled again.

'And your sense of drama. I never saw that quality in you, Francisco. Carrying Pablo's body back to your cell.'

Francisco swung his sword toward the Prince, who pivoted to the side. Francisco's blade bounced off the stone. Prince Fernando drove his elbow into Francisco's stomach. Francisco grunted.

'I never had any animosity toward you, Francisco. The whole episode with Ramón forced my hand. Your Grand Master was soft.'

Prince Fernando stepped to the left, then changed course and passed Francisco on the right. Francisco blocked his sword, then tried to jump back to elude the Prince's dagger. He was not quick enough. The blade rent Francisco's other thigh.

'Soft and self-righteous, Uncle Ramón. He never understood the Levant. Little girls grow up into women, who give birth to little boys, who grow up into men. The men become soldiers who try to kill us. Why not stop the whole process in the beginning with the little girl?'

Prince Fernando passed his dagger and sword between his hands. He tossed the weapons back and forth with such speed the blades began to blur.

'Do you think the Lord values the life of that little girl more than the soldiers whom you killed in battle, Francisco?'

Francisco feinted, then pulled back. Prince Fernando sprang forward. Francisco sidestepped, then jabbed his sword toward the Prince. The blade penetrated the Prince's shoulder. Blood splashed across his cloak. Prince Fernando flexed his arm. Then he circled again, paying no heed to the wound.

'I will mourn your death, Francisco. You will soon join your cousin Andrés. How did he die?'

The blood from Francisco's wounds ran down his legs and dripped on the stone floor.

'Baibars told me his guards would take you to

the Citadel in Aleppo. I have heard gruesome tales from ransomed prisoners. Is it true that the Christians eat their own dead? Is that what happened to Andrés' body?'

Francisco scraped his sword against the stone floor.

'You do not have the right to utter his name,' Francisco said.

'It's true, then,' Prince Fernando said. 'You can speak. You ask me not to mention the dead. Andrés is dead, yes? It would vex me to have to make another trip like this one.'

Francisco leapt forward, whirling his sword at Prince Fernando. The Prince stepped aside, then rotated his body in a circle, passing his dagger across Francisco's stomach. The robe severed – more blood on the white threads. Francisco slumped down on one knee. He was breathing heavily.

'It won't be long now, Francisco. In a way, I wish you had died in combat with the infidels. A more fitting death for a warrior.'

Prince Fernando feinted. Francisco jerked backward.

'Nothing more to say, Francisco? An epitaph, perhaps? Some words of affection Brother Lucas can relay to your family? He will be joining me in Barcelona. I have promised Brother Lucas a prestigious post in exchange for leading me to you.'

'I had no choice, Francisco,' I screamed. 'He made me. I would never betray you.'

My stomach knotted. Warm tears spilled on my cheeks.

'Come now, Brother Lucas,' the Prince said. 'A man is about to die. This is a time for truth.'

Francisco did not glance in my direction. They were circling again. Francisco stumbled on the uneven stones, but quickly regained his balance.

'Careful, Francisco.'

Prince Fernando feinted with his sword, then thrust his dagger at Francisco's midsection. Francisco twisted his body to avoid the blade.

'At least you and Andrés stained your swords with infidel blood. That's more than one can say about your brother. What was his name? The one who drowned off the coast of Barcelona?'

At the mention of his brother, Francisco groaned. He charged forward, waving his sword back and forth. Prince Fernando trapped Francisco's sword against the floor. Then he brought down the butt end of his dagger on Francisco's hand. I could hear the bones cracking. Francisco let go of his sword.

Francisco's hands were empty. The two men circled around the fallen sword. Francisco reached down for his weapon but pulled his hand back when Prince Fernando raised his sword and shook his head.

Francisco shifted his weight from side to side, then lunged for the sword. Prince Fernando stepped on the blade with one foot, then kicked Francisco in the face with the other. Francisco fell backward. He lay on the stone, looking up at Prince Fernando. The Prince put the point of his blade at Francisco's throat.

'Pablo and I come to visit an old comrade. Possessed by demons, he murders my deputy. I had no choice but to kill him. Pablo's death adds a certain authenticity to the tragic denouement. I expect, Francisco, even your father will sympathize with the cruel task circumstances forced upon me.'

Prince Fernando raised his sword. I was already on my feet, sprinting toward the Prince. I hit him square in the back as he was bringing down his sword. I felt as if I had run straight into a stone wall. I crumpled. Prince Fernando was pushed forward slightly but did not lose his footing. He recovered quickly and attempted to follow through with the flight of his sword. Francisco had used the instant of delay afforded by my intervention to retrieve his weapon. He blocked Prince Fernando's blow. Then he thrust his own sword upward. The blade entered the bowels of Prince Fernando. The Prince dropped his weapon and seemed to be resting on Francisco's sword. His torso was parallel to Francisco's. Then the point of the blade burst free from Prince Fernando's back. The Prince gasped as his body slid slowly down the sword until he was face to face with Francisco.

Prince Fernando's lips were pursed and slightly upturned. He seemed to be smirking, as if he were amused by the circumstances of his death. He dropped his sword and brought his hand up to Francisco's face. He clenched his fingers into a fist, then exhaled one last time before his head slumped forward.

Francisco let go of his weapon and rolled to the side. Prince Fernando's body fell to the stone, impaled on Francisco's sword.

Francisco crawled to the wall and brought himself up into a sitting position.

'He is dead, Francisco,' I said. 'Prince Fernando is dead.'

Francisco gazed down at his open palms. He traced a finger across one of the creases, then back around the other side of his hand. His blood mixed with Prince Fernando's.

The morning sun entered the monastery through the narrow windows and fractured against the gray stone. A shadow bestowed on the dead, a thin light cast over the living.

'Where is Isabel, Lucas?'

'The girl, Francisco?'

Francisco stood up, leaning against the wall.

'Where is she?'

'She is downstairs in the antechamber.'

He ran down the corridor. Actually, it was more of a shuffle, Francisco dripping blood every step.

One might think that an expression of gratitude toward me would have been appropriate, a small acknowledgment of my sacrifices after five grueling months together. Or perhaps Francisco could have simply thanked me for saving his life. Fortunately, the Lord's work provides its own reward.

EPILOGUE

GIRONA

It has been eighteen years since I picked up a quill to write in this manuscript. That's when Francisco and I left Santes Creus. I never returned. I remember those months in Francisco's cell, though. Indeed, I often dream of the monastery. One dream seems to play out almost every night now. I am in Francisco's cell, sitting next to him. He smiles, then he motions to his friend – Andrés, alive, slumbering, his blond hair shimmering in the summer breeze. I sit there for a while. Francisco, Andrés, and I. Then I wake.

Francisco's wounds from his battle with Prince Fernando proved quite serious. It was not clear he would survive the first few days. His condition subsequently improved, but he remained extremely weak. I provided my own chamber for his comfort. I slept in Francisco's cell on his straw mat while Isabel nursed Francisco.

Three entourages arrived in Santes Creus within

466

ten days of the tragic events. King Jaime, Archbishop Sancho of Tarragona, and Francisco's father, Baron Montcada. The most powerful men in the kingdom had assembled at Santes Creus. They came to investigate the death of Prince Fernando. They came to sit in judgment of Francisco and me.

As a result of his condition, Francisco was unable to testify before the respective delegations. In his absence, the burden of providing evidence fell on me. For four days, the delegations held court in the Great Hall. I sat in the middle of the room. Each party took turns interrogating me. The different examiners posed the same questions. The slightest inconsistency in my answers led to a grinding cross-examination.

When they weren't questioning me, the parties engaged in heated debates with each other. The atmosphere was tense. In the tumult, one of the novices spilled a cup of wine on the Archbishop's vestment. His Holiness used his scepter to deliver a severe beating to the boy. Indeed, if not for the intervention of one of the Archbishop's aides, the poor novice might well have faced his own final judgment.

The court's discussions focused on the fate of Francisco and me. The Crown's representative insisted on death for the 'perpetrators.' He opined that any details surrounding the killing of Prince Fernando were extraneous.

467

'The Prince is dead,' the royal representative said. 'That is the only relevant fact. Punishment of the murderer and his accomplice' – the latter reference pertained to me – 'must be swift and brutal.'

Baron Montcada, of course, opposed the execution of Francisco – his one remaining heir.

'Brother Lucas' testimony reveals the circumstances that compelled my son to kill Prince Fernando. Francisco is an innocent man, a veteran of the crusade, whose only crime was to defend himself. If this tribunal executes my son, I will organize an army that will shake the foundations of the monarchy.'

Baron Montcada commanded a formidable force of knights. Indeed, some said that the King ruled Aragón at the pleasure of the Montcadas. That assessment undoubtedly exaggerates the influence of the family. Nevertheless, the Crown could ill afford to ignore the heartfelt concerns of its most powerful vassal.

The Church attempted to interject a note of reason amidst the passions, concentrating on more technical questions. At the outset, the Archbishop sought to clarify whether Francisco's execution would cancel Baron Montcada's bequest of one-third his estate in exchange for the salvation of his son.

'In my opinion,' the Archbishop stated, 'Francisco was saved before the killing of Prince Fernando. Therefore, Baron Montcada's gift has already vested no matter the outcome of these proceedings.'

Several clerical scholars gave lengthy and learned opinions supporting the Archbishop's view.

Baron Montcada cut short these presentations, however. His words on the subject were concise and unambiguous – 'no Francisco, no reward.'

With this technical issue resolved, the Church turned its attention to more spiritual matters.

The Archbishop quoted from the Scriptures: *Vengeance is mine; I will repay, saith the Lord.* 'All men,' the Archbishop said, 'even kings, must strive to forgive those who give offense and leave retribution to the Lord.'

When the testimony finished, the tribunal commenced negotiations. From the courtyard, I could hear the deliberations. Tempers flared, recriminations, accusations.

After two days, the King summoned the suspects – Francisco and me – to receive the court's decision. I sat as before in the middle of the chamber. Francisco sat beside me. Isabel had assisted Francisco into the chamber and did not leave his side.

The King stood to pronounce judgment.

'I have listened to the testimony of Brother Lucas,' the King said. 'It has the ring of truth. I have long known that my son Fernando's path was not a straight one.

'I grieve for my son. My advisers counsel against mercy. But I will not compound my sorrows by imposing the same cruel price upon my friend and vassal Baron Montcada. Francisco de Montcada and Brother Lucas shall live.

'Despite the extenuating circumstances, though, the killers of my son cannot escape without some punishment. Francisco de Montcada and Brother Lucas, for your roles in the killing of Prince Fernando, you will be exiled from Barcelona and its environs, including Montcada, for the remainder of your natural lives. Francisco, you shall live in Girona on the estate of your uncle, the Baron Correa. In deference to my friendship with your father and your family's service to the kingdom, your progeny will inherit the Montcada mantle and may return to Barcelona. Brother Lucas, you are expelled from the monastery at Santes Creus. May God have mercy on both of your souls.'

As the King sat, his representative rose.

'Two more administrative matters,' the representative said. 'First, in accordance with documents signed by Baron Montcada and Archbishop Sancho, and witnessed by King Jaime, Francisco is considered exorcised. His soul saved from the demons that beset him in the Levant.

'Second, to respect the memory of the deceased, the Crown has drafted an official version of the tragic events that took place at Santes Creus, as follows: Prince Fernando discovered that his deputy Pablo was an agent of the King of Navarre. He confronted Pablo. In the ensuing conflict, Prince

470

Fernando killed the traitor, but received a mortal wound. The Crown considers the dissemination of contrary information a capital offense.'

'One more issue remains, King Jaime.' Isabel raised her voice above the commotion in the chamber. 'Three hundred serfs live on the Correa estate in Girona. All in need of spiritual guidance. His Majesty and His Holiness would do a great service to permit Brother Lucas to minister in Girona.'

The Archbishop deferred to the King.

'So be it,' the King said.

The youngest prior ever appointed at Santes Creus moves to the countryside to lead a flock of serfs. My brothers probably shared a long laugh over my change of fortune. I suppose the alternative was worse – wandering the countryside as a mendicant pilgrim.

I never mentioned this manuscript to the delegations. I would have gladly turned it over to the tribunal, but I was afraid to reveal its existence. The trial had ended, and I was relieved to be alive. I did not want to do anything that might reopen the proceedings or perturb the Crown. I decided silence was the safer course. I hid the manuscript in the bottom of my wood chest, which was transported to Girona. The parchment has remained untouched for the last eighteen years.

When Francisco had recovered enough to travel two weeks after the verdict, we set off for Girona. A team of knights from Baron Montcada's entourage escorted us to the Correa estate.

I became a parish priest in Girona. Holy communion, sermons, baptisms, marriages, funerals, mediating family disputes. My days have been busy indeed. One year seems to blur into another.

I kept a frequent correspondence with Brother Vial at Santes Creus until his death six years ago. In his last letter, he wrote: 'After a long journey, Brother Lucas, you have finally stumbled upon a true path of service to the Lord.'

A true path of service to the Lord. Those were his exact words. I keep the letter on my night table.

I have grown close to many of my congregants. None more so than Andrés de Montcada. It is for him that I preserve this manuscript. So that one day, after my death, Andrés may know of the spiritual struggles of his father and the nature of the union in which he was conceived.

Andrés is the only person on the estate who does not address me as Father Lucas. He calls me uncle, ever since he could speak. He is fifteen now. He has the same gray, prescient eyes of his mother and the sinew of a man, the same build as his namesake, his blood uncle, Andrés.

I have been both father and mother to the boy. Francisco died when Andrés was only two. Despite Isabel's attentions, Francisco never really recovered from the injuries inflicted by Prince Fernando. He would have a good week, even a good month, then a bad one. The infection in his stomach proved resilient. Eventually, the old wound killed him. Isabel followed him one year later, when the fevers passed through the province and claimed the lives of one-fourth of my charges.

The Crown appointed me guardian of Andrés in his fifth year, after the death of Baron Correa. I have spent a great deal of time with the boy. I have taught him to read and write. In the last year, we have discussed all manner of philosophical and theological issues. Indeed, the hours I have spent with Andrés have been a welcome respite from the ordinary rigors of my duties. The boy inherited the sharp mind and sensitivity of his parents.

Andrés is heir to two fortunes, the Correa and Montcada estates, albeit minus the one-third share of the Montcada holdings taken by the Church in exchange for Francisco's salvation. Even so, the Montcada landholdings are more extensive than those of any other vassal in the kingdom.

Soon, Andrés will have to decide upon which estate he will live. One might think he would readily choose Montcada. The boy seems immune to material attractions, though, and exceedingly comfortable in Girona.

Baron Montcada writes frequently to Andrés, explaining the benefits of residing in Montcada. Six months ago, the Baron visited his grandson. I was present when the two met in the main parlor. Baron Montcada instructed Andrés to pack his bags and prepare for the journey to Montcada. Regrettably, the Baron misjudged Andrés' temperament. The boy can be rather stubborn, stubborn and independent. Baron Montcada left the estate several hours after his arrival without his grandson.

Time has not dampened Baron Montcada's generosity. Nor his resourcefulness. Indeed, the Baron appreciates the manner in which the Lord's representatives seek to glorify His Name. He has volunteered to endow the construction of a monastery in Pedrables, near the capital city. He has made funding contingent upon Andrés' moving to Montcada.

Since Baron Montcada's visit, Archbishop Sancho of Tarragona and I have resumed our friendship. Indeed, we have exchanged correspondence concerning Andrés' choice of residence.

'I have heard that Andrés places great trust in his guardian,' Archbishop Sancho wrote. 'This trust should give you leverage over the boy.'

'Thank you for your kind words,' I wrote back to Archbishop Sancho. 'Indeed, Andrés seems quite attached to me. I wonder if Andrés' reluctance to leave Girona stems from this affinity.'

Archbishop Sancho responded forthwith.

'To avoid a painful separation between a guardian and his pupil,' the Archbishop wrote, 'perhaps your exile from Barcelona and its environs could be lifted.'

Archbishop Sancho mentioned the possibility of creating a bishopric just outside the city limits of Barcelona, half an hour's ride from the Montcada estate. Evidently the proposed bishopric would encompass over one thousand hectares and possess five hundred serfs. *Bishop Lucas de Santes Creus.*

Girona has provided a nurturing environment in which Andrés could grow up. There comes a time, though, when a man must put away childish things. He must see himself for who he is.

I pray that I will provide wise counsel when the time comes for Andrés to make a decision.

GLOSSARY

Abbot – the superior of a monastery.

Baibars (1223–1277) – Muslim warrior and Sultan of Egypt and Syria. His reign was marked by continuous and largely successful military campaigns against the Mongols and Christian crusaders.

Benedict, Saint (480–546) – Italian monk, called Benedict of Nursia, founder of the Benedictines. He authored the rule of Saint Benedict around 530.

Benedictines – monks of the Roman Catholic Church following the rule of Saint Benedict.

Castellan – the commander of a castle.

Chain mail – flexible armor of interlocking metal rings.

Chapter House – a meeting room in a monastery.

Cistercians – monks of a Roman Catholic religious Order founded in 1098 in Cîteaux, France. While using the rule of Saint Benedict to govern monastery life, the Cistercians sought to recover the original ideals of the Benedictines, including a return to an ascetic life of poverty and manual labor.

Constable – the governor of a town or city.

El Cid – the informal title, meaning 'lord,' of Rodrigo Díaz de Vivar (1043–1099), a soldier who led successful campaigns against the Muslims during the Reconquista of Spain.

Enceinte – a line of fortification enclosing a castle.

Foot soldiers – soldiers who march or fight on foot. Usually with little or no armor, foot soldiers accompanied and supported knights in battle.

Francis, Saint (1182–1226) – founder of the Franciscans, one of the most renowned Christian saints. During his lifetime, Francis gained the Pope's approval to establish a new rule and monastic Order based on his teachings.

Franciscans – members of the several Roman Catholic religious orders following the rule of Saint Francis.

Golgotha – the hill just outside Jerusalem where Christ was crucified.

Grand Master – the head of one of the military orders of knights.

Hauberk – a tunic of chain mail; one of the main components of a knight's armor in the thirteenth century.

Hospitallers – members of the military and religious Order of the Hospital of Saint John, recognized by the Pope in 1113. The object of the Order was to protect and aid Christian pilgrims in the Holy

Land and to fight the Muslims for control of the Holy Land.

Kaffiyeh – an Arab headdress consisting of a square cloth folded to form a triangle.

Knights of Calatrava – the first religious and military Order native to Spain, recognized by the Pope in 1164. The Order focused its attention on the Reconquista of Spain from the Saracens but also sent knights to the Levant.

Krak des Chevaliers – meaning 'castle of the knights,' considered the most formidable fortress ever built by the crusaders. Located in northern Syria, the castle was controlled by the Hospitallers during most of the crusades.

Latin Kingdom of Jerusalem – feudal state created by leaders of the First Crusade in areas they had conquered from the Muslims, including the City of Jerusalem, which fell to the crusaders in 1099.

Levant – the countries of the eastern Mediterranean. The crusaders also referred to the area as Syria.

Liturgy (Roman Catholic) – the series of rites prescribed for public worship, which centers on the Mass. The liturgical hours or prayer offices include matins, lauds, prime, terce, sext, nones, vespers, and compline.

Mail coif – a hood of chain mail worn over the head.

Oblate – a child dedicated for a prescribed period by his parents to the monastic life.

Poblet – a Cistercian monastery in the area of La Conca de Barberà, Spain.

Prior – following the Abbot, the second-ranking member of a monastery.

Reconquista – term used to describe Christian reconquest of Spain and Portugal from the Moors. The Reconquista took almost eight centuries, ending in 1492 with the fall of Granada to the Spanish forces under Ferdinand and Isabel.

Richard the Lion-heart (1157–1199) – King of England and one of the leaders of the Thrid Crusade to the Levant in 1190.

Rule of Saint Benedict – the chief rule of western monasticism, used by Benedictines and Cistercians. Its prologue and seventy-three chapters govern all aspects of communal life, including work, prayer, eating, and sleeping. The rule conceived the monastery as a devout Christian family with the Abbot as the father.

Saladin (1137–1193) – Muslim warrior and Sultan of Egypt. Of Kurdish descent, he united Muslim forces against the crusaders and conquered Jerusalem in 1187.

Sant – meaning saint in Catalán. Santa is the feminine form.

Santes Creus – Cistercian monastery in the area of Alt Camp, Spain.

Sapper – a member of a military engineer unit trained and equipped to dig tunnels under enemy fortifications in order to undermine and destroy them.

Saracens – term commonly used by Christian Europeans in medieval period to refer to the Arabs and Muslims.

Seneschal – a vassal or steward of a great lord responsible for managing the estate.

Squire – one who carries and tends to the armor of a knight and cares for the knight's horses.

Surcoat – a sleeveless, loose-fitting tunic worn over armor and often emblazoned with a symbol or heraldic device.

Take the Cross – to follow the path of Christ. In medieval period, the term referred to going on the crusade against the Saracens.

Templars – members of the military and religious Order called the Knights of the Temple of Solomon, from their house in Jerusalem. Recognized by the Council of Troyes in 1128, the Order's primary function involved protecting pilgrims and fighting the Muslims for control of the Holy Land.

Teutonic Knights – German military and religious Order founded in 1190 during the siege of Acre in the Third Crusade.